The Half-Life of Carson Hood

CHUCK CARTER

PUBLISHED BY
DFH BOOKS

To Deborah

Contents

Note to the Reader

The events driving the three main characters occur in different times and places, thus I initially use these chapter symbols to indicate when the focus shifts. It doesn't happen often, and the changes are discontinued when the conflict accelerates.

Carson Hood

Rafael Quinterro

President Chambers

Beware the fury of a patient man.
—John Dryden

Main Characters

CARSON HOOD is a paradox, a loner who pretends to enjoy a crowded room, and a peaceful man who has killed with his bare hands.

RAFAEL QUINTERRO, wealthy, powerful and well-respected, has secretly turned against America for reasons personal, cultural and political.

ANN CHAMBERS is the president. With the country on the brink of civil war, she chooses a plan no president has ever had the courage to try.

Supporting Characters

CLAIRE MARKHAM—gorgeous, brilliant and knows more than she tells.

SHERIFF RYAN ELLIOTT—Carson Hood's best friend, suddenly in ICU.

MACK MCCALLAN—toughest SOB who ever commanded the Coast Guard.

TAZ—an ebony beauty who can find anything.

BENICIO—so rich he doesn't need a last name.

HECTOR STROM—shy scientist who accidentally kills his cocaine-addict girlfriend.

DR. BRAD WHEELER—world-famous physician with too many secrets.

Prologue

The Present

Glynn County Hospital

Elsie Hood's bright blue eyes never left mine and I wondered if she already knew. I had come to tell her everything, but now I wasn't sure. Someone let me live protected from the truth. Perhaps that's how I should let her die.

So I waited, afraid of what might come if I started to speak. I smiled, and said nothing, and held her cool hand in mine. And I wondered, how could I tell my mother that I now knew the secret hidden from me all these years. I now knew we had not always been alone.

I once had a brother.

A twin.

I knew because I just killed him.

Chapter 1

The Beginning

40 Years Ago

Jake Eastman made few mistakes in his life. In the next 24 hours, however, he would make two. He would never know the first one.

———————————

The ribbon of bone-white concrete lay flat and straight, narrowing in the distance, disappearing in a shimmer.

Scruffy grass bordering the pale pavement ran thirty yards to a tall fence. The fence held back a ragged wall of wilderness. Pines, palms, palmettos and a jungle of lesser plants pressed hard against the metal mesh, straining for sunlight and soil that once was theirs.

In the slanted morning light, a yellow-trimmed box turtle had forced his way under the fence and made the long crawl to a single dandelion at the pavement's edge. He stretched his wrinkled neck, tore away part of the yellow flower and chewed it with his lower jaw. He was reaching for more when a sound in the distance stopped him. When it grew louder, the turtle abandoned the flower, pulled himself up on the pavement and started across. He was halfway when the sound became a roar. Obeying instinct, with a snap he vanished into the safety of his shell and waited.

"Shit!" Jake said, too late to react.

His tires missed the turtle. His afterburners didn't. The jet's fiery blast propelled the hapless reptile backwards down the runway, sliding, spinning, bouncing, pitching off into the grass, rolling to stop upside down. The silver craft screamed into the distance becoming a bright speck down the long runway before launching into the air, banking hard right and disappearing in the bright morning sky.

When the lingering roar subsided, the turtle peeked out from his seared and battered shell. Seeing no evil, he righted himself with his long, muscular neck, pivoted in place, and began the hurried trudge back to the safety of the wilderness.

Beyond the fence Mother Nature still ruled life and death as she had for a million years. Inside, however, Uncle Sam had bulldozed nature under and built a new, gray world bordered by miles of razor wire. The concrete and steel civilization stood in stark contrast to the surrounding wilderness.

But Arnall Air Force Base brought perils of its own—new ways of dying Mother Nature never imagined.

———————

Jake flew again that afternoon. After debriefing and a shower, he drove eastward across Glynn county heading for the four-mile causeway to St. Simons Island. There, on the banks of Village Creek, No-See-Ums Bar and Grill awarded free seafood dinners to Arnall test pilots who set new records. Jake was now the fastest man alive, and hungry.

In the fading light, he aimed his red Mustang's headlights, half-steering, half-wallowing through Harrington Road's deep, sandy ruts until he reached a driveway of oyster shells at the road's end. At the far end of the unpaved parking lot, an old building sat perched on a forest of twelve-foot stilts high above the creek's black mud banks. Beyond the building's soft glow, a green sea of tall spartina grass disappeared into the coming night.

Jake left the top down and took the rickety outside stairs two at a time. Still the Marine, he scanned the room as he pulled the old wooden door closed behind him. No-See-Ums was worn but warm, thick with the aroma of shrimp and beer. For thanks today and luck tomorrow, he winked at the voluptuous brunette lounging on a long green sofa in a painting over the bar.

Jake got coffee from the bar, slid into a booth and opened a small notebook. Nothing was obvious about Jake—brown hair and eyes, medium height and weight. And a face that would be more handsome if he showed more expression. But in a world of everyday people, Jake almost disappeared.

Hidden within this nondescript Marine, however, was the best test pilot the military had ever recruited—and a temper that had twice taken him within a gnat's ass of a Court Martial.

Jake's two flights today had been about speed. Tomorrow's would test the jet's ability to evade surface-to-air Missiles. The SAMs were computer generated, of course, and out-flying make-believe missiles was great fun. It was also dangerous as hell.

Death, the pilots said, was nature's way of telling you to slow down.

It was Elsie Raney's first night, and busy. Jake hadn't noticed her until she appeared at his table after dinner.

"More coffee, sir?" she asked smiling, returning a wispy blond tendril behind her ear.

Even inscrutable Jake found it hard not to smile at someone who was smiling so completely at him. He had just decided no more coffee.

"Yes, thank you."

He watched as the petite girl leaned toward him and carefully filled his cup.

"You're new," Jake said.

"Is it that obvious?" Tiny wince.

"Only because of your smile."

"What does that mean?"

"New waitresses either smile a lot, or look scared. And you don't look scared."

"I'm not," she said, bright blue eyes smiling, walking away.

Jake smiled, thinking about that reply. And the way her button-up blouse fit across her chest. He watched as her shapely legs and cute bottom disappeared behind the bar. He knew he'd done more than meet a new waitress. He'd stumbled upon a serious distraction.

For the next two hours Jake drank coffee, made notes and talked to Elsie when she passed by. The snippets of conversation were awkward but sincere, and each felt strangely at ease with a new friend. After closing, they sat under the stars on No-See-Ums open porch and talked, then went to her apartment for a snack. They talked all night in her kitchen until it seemed they had known each other for years. He kissed her before dawn and they went to her room.

Three hours later, Jake was back in the cockpit, standing on the brakes, easing the throttles forward. The silver jet roared and trembled in place before beginning a slow roll. Seconds later, Jake pushed the throttles all the way and felt the g-forces press him hard against the seatback. Less than halfway down the runway the jet jumped from the concrete as if resenting gravity and streaked skyward like a rocket. Jake watched the earth drop away and nudged the stick forward to remind the experimental aircraft he was in control. When the altimeter read 2500 feet, he banked hard right and headed east for the Atlantic Ocean. The skies were clear, and even with no sleep, he felt relaxed, ready.

Soon he saw the sun reflecting off the tidal rivers and creeks snaking through the emerald salt marsh separating St. Simons Island from the rest of North America. Seconds later as the four-mile-wide estuary slid behind him, he crossed over St. Simons Island, a second narrower estuary, and finally the smaller Sea Island.

As the expensive beachfront homes disappeared behind him, replaced by the blue Atlantic, Jake radioed the control tower, "Feet wet." Four minutes later he reached the offshore test area and eased the stick forward taking the jet down to the starting altitude—*if you can call 200 feet altitude*, he thought.

He radioed "Ready" to the control tower and SAM trailer. When he heard "Begin," he shoved the throttles forward, and the man and plane became one living thing, streaking, screaming across the horizon.

Twenty-three minutes later, Jake had again impressed officials by outflying everything they had thrown at him.

"Almost done, Captain."

"Copy that," Jake replied from the tight cockpit. After debriefing and a quick shower, he'd drive out to see Elsie. He felt a slight twitch in his lap.

Full-velocity, maximum-G turns require total concentration in any airplane. In an experimental aircraft at low altitude, they require more than that.

After successfully evading twelve computer-generated SAMs, in the middle of a crushing left turn, the jet slammed into the water and exploded like a star being born. In an instant, man and machine became one for the last time as both were shredded across a mile-long burning stretch of Atlantic Ocean.

———————————

Twelve miles away, beneath the faded quilt from her grandmother's hands, beneath the warm sheets of an early morning bed, beneath the smooth, flat stomach of a young girl still dreaming, there was another dividing taking place. One as old as life itself.

Jake had left a son.

Chapter 2

Blood on the Playground

Elsie Raney named her son Carson. Jake had said it was his middle name. When Carson was old enough, Elsie told him about his father, how brave and handsome he had been. She said that when most people die, God takes their souls to heaven, but leaves their bodies on Earth.

"But sometimes," she said, "God takes their bodies to Heaven too. And that's what happened with your father. He was flying a new airplane and God reached down and took him straight to heaven, then let the plane fall into the ocean."

Elsie smiled when she told the story and said that Carson should be proud of his father. And he was. But as he grew, he missed the father he would never know.

When young Carson told a third-grade classmate about his father, and the boy laughed, Carson's reaction was swift. The boy went home with a black eye and split lip.

Carson's mother told him he should have walked away. He understood, but inside he knew, if it ever happened again, he would fight again.

But he never told the story to anyone else. It became a dream, and a pain, he kept to himself.

During Carson's senior year in high school, his mom married Ray Hood, son of a local businessman. A few months later when his mom's new husband asked about adopting Carson, she loved the idea, but the boy stubbornly refused.

"I don't have my own father's name," he argued, "why would I want another man's?"

But in the weeks that followed, Carson realized how important it was to his mom. So he agreed. And with the stroke of a pen, he became Carson Hood.

He told himself it didn't change anything. But every time he wrote his name, he felt further removed from the father he had never known, and never would.

————————————

All high schools have bullies. Glynn Academy's was Butch Klett.

Carson's mother said bullies usually have their own problems, and Carson might forgive him if he knew.

But nothing could make Carson forgive the bully for how he preyed on others. He was a monster and the only two things Carson knew about him were fear and hate. So he looked the other way when the bully showed off. There was a fine line between helping others and letting their problem become yours.

Then came March 15th, a day so plain, gray and cold that history could have forgotten it altogether.

Not at Glynn Academy, however. And certainly not Carson Hood.

It was his own fault. He knew Butch was on the field after school, and he should have taken the sidewalk around. Too late now.

As he crossed the sandy field, he thought he saw Butch moving toward his path and hoped he was wrong. He looked for an alternate route that would take him away from the terrible intersect forming on the horizon. But it was obvious Carson was headed toward the only gate at the far end of the field.

As Carson walked on, into the coming storm, he prayed for a miracle, a major distraction. As he got nearer to the beast, he felt the space around him collapsing into a black hole from which there was no escape. Butch's path and his were converging into one horrible point. Carson's books seemed heavier, his breath shallower. He looked away from the bully and tried to make himself smaller, invisible, something with no size, no weight.

When their paths silently crossed, Carson breathed relief.

Until he felt a sickening tug from behind, his coat's zipper tight against his throat.

"Where you goin', Shithead?" Butch said, as he pulled tighter on Carson's hood, stopping him in midstep. Carson waited, petrified, hoping Butch just wanted to make him look stupid, then move on. But he knew it wouldn't end that way. Too scared to turn around, he felt sick for allowing himself to get pulled into the monster's realm. As Butch tightened his grip, Carson winced as the zipper tore a ragged, bleeding line across his throat.

Time stopped, then accelerated to lightning speed. Butch pulled tighter on the coat's hood and leaned hard to one side, dragging Carson sideways in a circle. As Butch swung him around, Carson fought to stay on his feet. The distant ring of onlookers smeared into a streaked watercolor. He made it around three times, stumbling, falling, watching his world turn into a sickening blur. As the spin devolved into a rhythmic centrifugal force, Carson heard his tormentor. "Here . . . comes . . . Shithead . . . !" And with one last heave, the big bully let go.

Carson hit hard and rolled. When he stopped, he waited, and prayed it was over. He slowly pushed up onto his hands and knees, and brushed sand from his face and mouth. One massive book lay on the ground before him, open to a torn map of Brazil.

Blood from Carson's lip dripped onto Rio de Janeiro.

His wrists and knees hurt. His breathing was fast and thin. He leaned sideways, spat dirt and shook sand out of his hair. Laughter trickled out from the crowd.

Carson slowly stood up. He folded the map of Brazil along the tear, wiped blood and sand from the page and closed the heavy book.

A few yards away Butch Klett scanned the crowd, basking in a gladiator's glory.

"Ain't that too bad?" the bully said to the onlookers, "the little asshole tried to fly, but . . . he crashed and burned."

Maybe it was those last words. Maybe it was just time.

When Carson turned toward Butch, the bigger boy still faced the crowd, laughing. Carson stepped toward the monster, tightening his grip on the heavy book until his fingers burned.

When Butch started his turn, Carson lunged, swinging the book with every muscle in his body. Butch's eyes flashed wide as the third edition of McMillan's Earth Sciences slammed into his over-sized Adam's apple, creating a loud, coughing choke from his windpipe as it spasmed and closed. The bigger boy bent over, holding his throat, gasping for air that wouldn't come. He never saw Carson's second swing—a sweeping uppercut that crushed his nose, breaking it like cheap plastic and spraying blood across both boys.

Doubled over again, still gasping for air, blood streaming from his broken nose, Butch tried to speak, but only hissed and choked and drooled blood. When he looked up, tears running down his cheeks, Carson's third swing with the heavy book caught him square across his eyebrows. The final impact stood the bigger boy straight up and over, crashing onto his back. In Carson's hand, the book's broken spine dropped pages that fell to ground and fluttered away on the breeze.

The only sound was the bully gasping for air as he now lay in a fetal curl in the sand. With every coughing exhale, blood shot through his fingers and sprayed red flecks on the ground in front of his face. In the crowd, no one spoke, no one moved.

Carson's head throbbed, but his hands were still, his breaths were slower now and deep. He walked around the body on the ground and dropped into a squat at Butch's head. He grabbed a handful of the bigger boy's hair, wrenched his head upward and said, "If you ever touch me again, one more white shirt'll do you."

The crowd began to move as Carson gathered his books. He walked off the field, and never looked back. And Butch Klett never touched him again.

How do I know so well what happened that day?

Because I am Carson Hood.

Chapter 3

Ryan and *Rivianna*

Ryan Elliott was my best friend in high school. And we couldn't have been less alike. He was six-feet-four and the ultimate sportsman—big, loud, lover of hard-contact competition. I topped out at six feet and could usually be found in the stands with a date. My idea of contact sports was *way* different.

I escaped total shame by running track in the Spring but lost macho points in South Georgia because it wasn't a contact sport. I didn't care. I was good at it, and I liked the solitude.

After high school, I went to Georgia Tech in Atlanta, and Ryan went to the University of Georgia in Athens. We stayed close, visited often and remained best friends, growing even closer as we matured.

In the spring of our senior year, he said he was joining the Marines. I thought he was kidding.

"I want to go into law enforcement," he said, "and the training will be good. What about you, Peckerhead? What are you going to do to grow up?"

I laughed it off, but the question stuck. I had worked my way through college as a photographer's assistant, eventually doing some of the shooting myself, mainly parties, reunions, modest weddings. Sometimes I felt more like a spectator than participant in life. I wanted to change that, but always felt that something was missing, and that I needed to know what that was before committing to anything. Or anyone. Ryan was the only person I ever told about that.

As graduation grew closer Ryan kept daring me. "Come on, Peckerhead," he laughed, "the Marines are looking for a few good men, but they might take you."

I could resist his kidding, but not what he said next. "Wasn't your old man a Marine?" When I didn't reply, he added, "Hell, you don't have a choice . . . it's in your blood."

When I realized during employment interviews that business and industry had not been waiting breathlessly for me, I enlisted.

Nine weeks into boot camp at Parris Island, South Carolina, my Drill Instructor cornered me on the field during war games and screamed at me loud enough to be heard offshore. "*Hood*, you stupid son of a bitch! You *can't watch* the fuckin' battle! What the hell are you doing! Get in there! *Now*, goddammit!"

He was right. I had heard it before. Regardless of the challenge, something held me back. It wasn't as simple as procrastination or as deep as fear. I was just that spectator again.

Until my DI kindly explained that in war, waiting means dying.

So, I learned how to stay alive by killing. Fortunately, the only time I needed it was in Grenada. More about that—and that nasty scar on my neck—later.

After two years in the Marines, I returned to Atlanta, still unsure what to do with my life. Except for how to kill people—*not the best thing to mention in a job interview*—the only thing I really knew was photography. I went to the big paper, showed them my portfolio, and was hired on the spot.

People said I cared about my subjects. I smiled and wished it were true, but it was just work, and I shot deaths as easily as debutantes. I stole split-second slices from other people's lives. My own life was half empty.

One day when a reporter walked out on a breaking story, I wrote the article from his notes, adding what I remembered from shooting it. The next day his editor called me in and said he'd pay me more to write articles than take pictures. I took the job.

Ironically, I was good at writing for the same reason I had been good at photography. My editor called it objectivity. I knew it for what it was— not getting involved.

Years went by and soon I was the paper's youngest business editor, ironically still praised for my caring approach to the work. It's not surprising that both of the great lies of my life began unraveling at once.

Along the way I had married a wonderful girl named Jill. The honeymoon was short-lived, however. The poor girl had waited her whole life for the right guy to come along. And I showed up instead. I had been so sure she would fill the void in my life. And I was so wrong.

While my marriage was disintegrating, work turned into a free-for-all. Management called in humorless suits to reorganize the newspaper into "cost centers." By the time they were through, every copy, coffee cup and paper clip had to be charged to a specific department. At first it seemed like harmless, pain-in-the-ass accounting, but when bonuses started vanishing, morale fell faster than a drunk on an icy sidewalk. Thanks to the starched experts, our new priority was bottom lines, not deadlines. And loyalty and cooperation were things of the past. Overnight we became a news organization of competing departments run by paranoid employees. The fun was gone and I wanted out too.

A headhunter called one morning representing an investor buying an underperforming weekly paper in north Atlanta. He asked if I would consider running it in return for a sizable share of the ownership. Well, *yeah* . . .

A month later, I walked away from the bullshit of cost-center accounting, and with my new business partner's money began converting the little weekly from a society page into a real newspaper. While my former employer continued to chase the big stories—like another airport cost overrun—we covered the local suburban news that actually affected day-to-day lives—zoning changes, small business news, and keeping big-city crime out of the suburbs. Using talented, mobile reporters and economies of scale, we soon expanded into other Atlanta suburbs, and took advertising away from the bigger paper. Our readership, revenue and profits soared.

Although I enjoyed the work, the rest of my life was still empty. Therapists and friends said that I was missing the father I never knew—and might always feel that way. They meant well, but their attempts to help didn't.

It wasn't long before our little newspaper business had grown into a network of nine suburban weeklies throughout Atlanta. We had become a big business, and although the money was great, the fun of building the business was over. I took a few days off to see my mom on St. Simons. While there, my business partner called and asked if I would be interested in selling. I asked how much. He told me. I said maybe.

———————————

One beautiful morning while Mom and I were walking around the Golden Isles Marina, we came upon a vintage motoryacht looking like something out of *The Great Gatsby*. Except for a thin ribbon of blue bottom paint at her waterline, she was as white as angel wings from her broad, straked hull to the top of her deckhouse. Contrasting the white were golden teak decks and varnished mahogany trim. The bright gold of a T scrolled on the bow matched the polished brass of the portholes along each side.

"She's a Trumpy," a big man said, pointing to the gold T. "Seventy-two-footer. Built in '58."

"What?" I said, not sure he was speaking to us.

"Come on," he said smiling, looking like an out-of-work Santa Clause. "I'll give you a tour of *Rivianna*." *Why not?*

As we stepped onboard, he grabbed my hand with skin that felt like old rope. "Captain Jack," he said. "Welcome aboard." I liked him immediately.

"John Trumpy built boats in the early 1900s," he said, driving his thumbs under wide, faded suspenders. "Broad beams, lotta headroom, and full galleys for great meals. Remember the Presidential Yacht *Sequoia* Kennedy used to party on? A Trumpy. Quite a perk for the Oval Office, until Jimmy Carter sold her. Said the Secret Service didn't like boats." He shook his head.

"Come on," he said, "we'll start in the office."

The office was the pilothouse where the helm station had a gorgeous wooden wheel, modern instruments and a magnificent view across the gleaming bow.

The door aft led to the spacious deckhouse with separate living and dining areas, full-size furniture and elegant wooden trim everywhere. "Grain-matched Burmese teak and Philippine mahogany," Captain Jack said.

At the far end of the long room, a pair of wide doors opened onto a magnificent fantail stern that extended several feet out over the waterline.

Below was a bow V-berth cabin, a fully equipped galley, a walk-in engine room, and two spacious staterooms. The larger one had a king-size bed centered on the wide rear bulkhead, surrounded by built-in compartments, desktops and bookshelves. Daylight streamed through prominent portholes on both sides.

Back topside, I said, "She's beautiful."

"She's yours if you want her," Captain Jack said. "Owner in Boston is selling her—new wife can't swim." He leaned forward, adding, "If you ask me, he's getting rid of the wrong girl."

I smiled and said, "Look, I'm not in the market, but just for fun, what's he asking?"

"He's ready to let her go," he said, handing me a brochure. "Here're the specs. Broker's card's inside. Call him. I'll be here a couple of days waiting on a new bilge pump. Come back. We'll go for a ride."

I took the brochure, thanked him, and Mom and I walked up to the marina restaurant for mimosas at the outdoor bar. Years ago I had owned a little Sea Ray that I kept on Lake Lanier outside of Atlanta. I loved being on the water and dreamed of one day owning something big enough to live on. What I had told Captain Jack was only partly true. My head might not have been in the market for a boat, but my heart always was.

"It says here," Mom read from the brochure, "*Rivianna* was custom-built for Mr. Elbert P. Peabody of Boston, and her original name was *Burma.* She's had five owners, five different names, and has been home-ported in Martha's Vineyard, Palm Beach and Seattle, where—then named *Rendezvous*—she barely survived a marina fire. The current owner bought her, replaced everything mechanical, and modernized everything else."

I looked over the deck plans and photos, smiled at Mom, then picked up the broker's card and called him.

After his pitch on Trumpys, he said, "What do you think?"

Instead of all the intelligent questions I might have asked, I said, "I thought it was bad luck to rename a boat."

"That's the rumor," he laughed, "but when people buy a boat like this, they always change the name. If something goes wrong, they blame it on that. But that doesn't stop 'em."

When we hung up, I watched Captain Jack ease *Rivianna* from the fuel dock to one of the transient slips. I thought about *Rivianna* all the next day, spent two days on her with Captain Jack, then called my business partner.

Two weeks later, we sold the business, and I bought *Rivianna*—along with a month of Captain Jack's time, agreeing to fly him home afterward, first class.

I leased a condo at the marina for a legal residence and mail drop but spent every moment I could with Captain Jack on my new boat.

Side by side, he taught me about every instrument, radio, switch, motor, pump and appliance. I learned about fuel tanks, water tanks and holding tanks, and all the lines that lead to each. Next I learned when to relax and when to worry by memorizing every sound, smell and vibration. And just when I thought I knew enough, Captain Jack dragged me to a nearby boatyard to show me sad sights so I would know what kills boats and why.

We practiced up and down the three marsh rivers between St. Simons Island and the mainland, and in and out of the channel to the Atlantic. He made me bring her in from upriver and down, in every combination of daylight, dark, weather and tide.

When Captain Jack's month was over, we went out for a fabulous dinner at one place, then went drinking at another. When I woke up the next morning, he was gone. The harbormaster said he took a cab to the airport. The note he left on the helm said: "Remember, bridges are not your friend. Captain Jack." The message seemed strange. Yes, he had warned me about bridge pilings and tidal currents, but this note seemed to be saying more than that. I'm still not sure I understand it.

But I think about it every time I see a bridge.

———————————

In the following weeks I made day trips up and down the Intracoastal Waterway and couldn't wait to sail off for days.

After dark I drank wine in the sweeping curve of *Rivianna's* fantail stern and watched the amber lights on the Sidney Lanier Bridge five miles away. Shimmering high above river and marsh, they drew a comforting figure in the night sky, a golden constellation that never moved.

Sometimes friends from Atlanta would call and ask if I had thought about moving back. The first person I told about my new life on *Rivianna* sounded so confused that I never explained it again. I lived in a different world now. One they would never understand. After the rise and fall of the tides and *Rivianna's* comforting movements, a house would never seem alive again. And I needed something alive in my life, something connecting me with the world. Maybe even changing me from the spectator I had always been into the participant I wanted to be. To really live. Maybe even love another woman someday.

I treasured *Rivianna's* small, personal spaces, how everything fit exactly where it needed to be, and how every sound had meaning. Mooring lines rubbed. Hinges squeaked. The whole boat moaned as it rocked. Little wavelets slapped the hull and ran its length. These were the sounds that belonged in my life now. They were the rhythm of my day world, and the music of my nights.

I knew that *Rivianna,* and my time with Captain Jack, were gifts from the sea. And I knew that no one else would understand that.

Ever so slowly a gentle peace found its way into my life.

Until last Sunday.

Chapter 4

Cemetery Surprise

Last Sunday Morning

"Coming to the party, Carson?" Mack hailed from the next slip.

"Aye aye, Admiral," I replied, looking up from the paper. "There *will* be adult beverages, right?"

"Absolutely!" the stocky man smiled, coiling a line between his hand and elbow.

"What birthday is this, Admiral, seventy-seven?"

"*Sixty*-seven, you little cretin!" he snapped, straightening up to his full, five-nine height. "And anytime you're feeling froggy, just jump."

I winced in mock pain as he draped the perfectly coiled line over a glistening winch, shook his head and disappeared below deck.

If things ever turned fecal, I'd want Mack on my side. He was absolutely fearless, and never heard of the word quit. Plus he was smart—streetwise, bookwise and otherwise—and I felt fortunate and proud we were friends.

Hearing a guttural *craw* nearby, I lowered the paper just as two scruffy pelicans soared by an inch above the water, never moving a feather.

Above, the sky was clear-morning blue, but a deep tone from the south said fog still menaced the shipping channel where the big RoRo ships carried a million automobiles a year to and from the Port of Brunswick.

In the distance the white diagonal cables of the beautiful Sidney Lanier Bridge made two bright pyramids suspended in the morning sky. Deciding the day was too beautiful to waste, I leaned forward and let my feet drop from the railing.

I forgot about the Bloody Mary.

My heel sent the tumbler spinning, and I watched in dismay as the thick red liquid spun out across the teak deck.

I was rolling off paper towels when the red word "BULLETIN" flashed silently on the bright screen of the muted TV. A handsome reporter stood in the foreground of a smoking building as his close-captioned report crawled across the bottom of the screen. "Three people have been confirmed dead in last night's bombing of the Richard B. Russell Federal Building in Atlanta."

I snatched the towels, hit the volume and heard " . . . radical Hispanic group Militia Americana has claimed responsibility for this second attack on a U.S. federal office building."

The image changed to a file photo of the president as the reporter continued: "In response to last night's attack, President Chambers has invoked the country's two-hundred-year-old Insurrection Act, amended under former President George W. Bush to allow the president to deploy state militias *without* approval from governors. The president has ordered National Guard troops to establish 24-hour protective perimeters around U.S. federal buildings in all 50 states and U.S. territories."

When the story shifted to governors angry at having their authority usurped, I decided not to spoil the morning with news of the country ripping itself apart. Let the president deal with it. *She* started it.

I turned off the TV, hesitating as the bright image faded. From the now dark screen, my reflection stared out at me, holding me in place. I wanted to turn away, not do this now, but it had already started.

What do you want?

I had heard the question a thousand times, but didn't know if I was asking the man in the reflection, or if he was asking me? So I stared, wondering, until I heard the Admiral lock his hatch and step off *Biscayne*. "See you at the party, Paperboy. Hampton Point, three o'clock."

I shook off the reflection and said, "Aye aye, Admiral." But he was already gone.

Still shocked by the explosion in Atlanta and haunted by the reflection in the TV, I knelt at the spilled drink and scrubbed, trying not to think about anything except getting the damn red stain off my boat. Gradually the teak came clean. But the peaceful Sunday morning was gone.

———————————

"Paperboy" was the Admiral's reference to my former career. I may have just sold a newspaper business and bought an antique motoryacht, but it wasn't retirement—I wasn't rich enough or old enough. It was, however, homecoming. I was raised on St. Simons Island.

The Admiral is William Alexander "Mack" McCallan, former Commandant of the United States Coast Guard. That had been his whole life until last year when Washington politicians started telling him how to do his job. Too smart and proud to play their stupid games, he resigned his presidential appointment, retired his five stars, and told one U.S. Senator to kiss his salty ass.

Years ago he had been a visiting instructor here at FLETC, the Federal Law Enforcement Training Center, and fell in love with the area. So after leaving the Coast Guard he bought a house on Sea Island for Bess, and a forty-seven-foot sailboat for himself. His sleek, blue-hulled *Biscayne* gleamed in the slip next to my *Rivianna*.

On sailing days, Mack and I would ride the wind offshore on *Biscayne*, then relax under the canopy on *Rivianna's* rounded stern. With a bottle and chessboard, we would solve the problems of a wayward world, most recently what the media had dubbed "America's Hispanic Civil Rights Crisis."

Despite the strong work ethic of most male and female Hispanic immigrants, two decades of unchecked immigration, plus high birth rates among the new residents, sent the Hispanic population soaring. Then the South American drug cartels tripled their U.S. smuggling and distribution operations, resulting in more of everything bad—school dropouts, unemployment, homelessness, crime, overdose deaths, you name it. Support services couldn't keep up, and the problem rapidly grew from isolated incidents and pockets of protest into a full-blown national disaster. And just when it appeared things couldn't get much worse, a group known as Militia Americana blew up a federal office building. Then another one.

As Mack's whistle faded in the morning breeze, I thought about how dangerous America had become. The Hispanics had made it clear there would be no more compromises. They had been lied to enough.

And unfortunately, America's first female president had chosen this as her way to prove she was as tough as any man who ever sat in the Oval Office. The resulting standoff meant innocent people were being killed. And, as if things weren't bad enough, *The Wall Street Journal* printed a letter to the editor from a former U.S. Senator saying America could be headed toward civil disturbance never before seen at home if a promising solution wasn't found soon.

I thought about how lucky I was to have a friend like Mack who knew what was going on behind the scenes, thanks to contacts way up in the Department of Homeland Security. I knew I could trust Mack with my life.

I just didn't know it would happen so soon.

Mack's birthday party that afternoon was fine, except for there being too many faces and not enough names. And the alcohol that improves my personality does nothing for my memory. *Oh, hello, yes . . . nice to meet you . . . see you . . . see you again . . .* Whatever.

After Mack cut his cake, I slipped out, thankful for the quiet of the empty car. I was driving south on Lawrence Road when I remembered the note on the passenger seat:

Carson, please stop by the cemetery and be sure the gate's closed. I know the old man was a you-know-what, but I promised his sister we'd check it. Thanks. Love you! Mom

I didn't want to do it. Mom was right. The "old man"—her ex-husband's father—had been a real son of a bitch. Besides that, the afternoon had turned cold and rainy, and the old cemetery was so deep in the woods, no one even knew it was out there.

I passed the driveway to Frederica, then pulled off onto the shoulder. I switched off the ignition and waited, hoping for rain, any excuse. I hated everything about that land, and the man who once owned it.

When no rain saved me, I got out, found what was left of the abandoned road, and started walking. Long grass painted my shoes wet as I ducked dripping palm fronds and soaked Spanish moss narrowing the path into a tunnel. Eventually I saw the black points of the wrought iron fence surrounding the small family cemetery, one massive granite marker towering over all the others.

There you are, you dead son of a bitch.

I walked toward the gate, remembering Raymond Hood, Sr., the grand old man with a lie for every occasion. My mother had been briefly married to his son—but he had owned me as much as he had everyone else. I was frequently tempted to change my last name. Hell, it wasn't mine anyway.

I stepped through the iron gate and looked up at the huge monument. Turning up my collar against the cold, I thought, *I hope it's hot as hell where you are today.*

Disgusted, I turned to leave, then remembered, the gate hadn't been closed. I'd do it as I left.

I glanced around, remembering how the old man had built this private cemetery on his own land, planning exactly where he wanted each one of us buried. He even had headstones made for all of us. Had Mom and I known she wouldn't be married to his son forever, we could have saved him the money for our two.

I turned to leave, then stopped. I couldn't remember ever seeing my headstone. How would it feel to see my own name and birthdate carved in granite? I started looking.

Raymond's wife was beside his monument to himself. Other deceased family members were all tucked in, just as Big Raymond had planned.

Bent over, I zigzagged around the old graves, and heard rain on leaves overhead. I hurried, but tall grass, weeds and weathered headstones made it difficult. I decided it wasn't there and turned to go.

That's when I saw it. My name and date of birth, carved on a headstone. It looked a lot stranger than I expected, and even knowing I would never be down there, it gave me the creeps. I shook off the cold and was turning to leave when I noticed something else. The ground in front of the headstone seemed different, a little higher maybe. I walked closer, dropped to one knee and brushed away dead leaves. I touched the raised earth to be sure of what I was seeing, then snatched my hand back and stood up. As the rain turned steady, my skin turned to ice. I wanted to say something, but couldn't. I wanted to run, but couldn't make my feet move. The impossibility of what I saw froze me in place.

Somebody was in my grave.

Chapter 5

I'm not dead, right?

The next thing I remember was a faraway light. *Oh, shit! I'm dead.*

"Sir?" a deep voice said.

Uh-oh. I wanted to explain. "I jus'. . ." I tried to move, but pain wrapped around my head like a steel band.

"Don't move, sir."

I lay still while senses returned. *I'm on the ground, my head's killing me, and who knew God had such a southern accent?*

"I'm not dead, right?"

"No sir, Mr. Hood. You're not dead." *Not sounding glad enough to suit me.*

"Wha' happen'd?" I was having a hard time with words.

"Well, I first thought maybe you drank too much at the Admiral's birthday party and came out here to sleep it off."

I looked at him with one eye, letting him know he wasn't funny.

"Then," he drawled, finally moving his damn flashlight out of my eyes, "I saw the blood on your collar and called EMTs."

I tried for a deep breath, but moving brought out the colored stars of pain, and I said something really foul.

When the pain ebbed enough to talk, I lay perfectly still and asked, "Who ah you?"

"Corporal Clark. Glynn County Police Department." *Automaton.*

He already knew who I was.

"EMTs will be here in a minute," he added.

I lay on the wet ground, listening to night sounds, wondering what the hell happened.

Moments later, more lights and voices appeared. Hands wrapped a foam collar around my neck and strapped me onto a hard stretcher. All I remember after that was a haze of bright lights, sterile smells and the same questions asked over and over by different voices.

I woke to daylight and a blurry uniform at the foot of my hospital bed.

"Any idea who hit you?" Glynn County Police Chief Ryan Elliott asked.

"A meteorite?" I said, reaching for my tender scalp.

"We probably would have found that," he answered, dropping his wide-brimmed hat in a chair. "What were you doing out there after dark, Peckerhead?" He still calls me that, like we're back in high school.

"It wasn't dark when I went out there."

"Not an answer, is it?"

"Excuse me?" I said, "am I a victim or a suspect?"

"I didn't say you were suspected of anything," he said, "I asked what you were doing."

"I was on my way back from Mack's party—which you apparently skipped—and stopped to see if the cemetery gate was closed. Mom asked me to. Do I need a reason?"

"I remember how close you were to the Hoods," he said sarcastically, referring to the family my mom was briefly married into, thus giving me my last name, which wasn't mine. Stroking his short gray mustache, he said, "There'd be icicles in Hell before you got sentimental about them."

"I didn't say I was sentimental. I wanted to be sure the gate was closed. Didn't I just *say* that? And *you* said you'd shave that damn mustache before the election."

"You let me worry about my mustache," he snapped back, then smiled and added, "and oh, we got your keys from the ER and drove your car here to save you a tow. It's out front."

I was saying thanks when there was a knock on the cracked door, and a voice called Ryan out into the hall. When he came back, he grabbed his hat and said, "I got to go, but we'll talk."

"Go."

We would definitely talk. I had never brought it up before, but Ryan Elliott owed me. Bigtime.

———————————

As boys, Ryan and I had been best friends. As Marines, however, we were more than that. The Corps' legendary training had succeeded. We had pledged our lives to each other. It's what kept us alive when our 22nd Marine Amphibious Unit invaded Grenada. I hadn't thought about it much, until a nurse asked where I got that nasty scar on my neck.

Ryan and I and 400 fellow marines boarded helicopters at sea before daylight, and headed toward the island of Grenada, where a bloody coup had isolated the island, and bad guys had issued shoot-to-kill orders enforcing a 24/7 curfew.

There were 600 American students at Grenada's St. Georges School of Medicine, and President Reagan was not about to let our country suffer a Caribbean-style repeat of the 444-day Iranian Hostage Crisis. He told the Pentagon to go get those kids and bring 'em home. Now.

Thanks to the assholes at CBS telling the world we were on the way, our drop-in was not going to be the surprise the Brass had planned.

It had only been a five-day war, but it changed my life. I saved Ryan's life one morning. But I had to shoot a woman in the face and kill a man with my bare hands to do it. The scar on my neck came from his knife.

That next morning, years ago, our positions had been reversed. Ryan had looked up at me from *his* hospital bed.

"You saved my ass," he said groggily, then added, "You know, in some cultures, that means you're responsible for me now."

"I thought it was the other way around."

"Oh, maybe so, I don' know." He was dopey from pain meds.

"OK," I said. "Let's just say we're gonna look out for each other."

"Yeah," he said, through eyes half shut, raising his hand to shake, "I take care of you, and you take care of me."

I was saying, "It's a deal," as his eyes slowly closed and his hand went limp. He was snoring before I got to the door. I stopped, and looked back at him, and didn't know why, but knew what he said was right. I did feel responsible for Ryan now. Strange.

Chapter 6

Claire Markham

After getting knocked on the head Sunday in the old family cemetery, I napped most of Monday in the hospital, thanks to a little white pill from a big blond nurse. Once while awake I called Claire and got her voicemail. The timbre of her beautiful voice made me smile.

I first heard that fabulous voice in the next room at a cocktail party last year. Clean, smart, deep for a woman. "We're making a mistake beating up Hispanic residents, illegal or not," she said. "We may as well be doing it in the streets of Brazil or Venezuela. Everyone in South America hates us for it."

The U.S., tired of being jerked around by OPEC, had agreed to pay Brazil big bucks for its recently discovered offshore oil. And the woman was right—the Hispanic Crisis within our own borders was threatening our critical new friendship with South America.

I stepped closer to look around the corner. The woman was tall, facing away from me. Shapely legs rose out of four-inch heels and disappeared into a narrow black skirt. Above a small waist, her billowy white blouse ended in a low collar showing off a long, sensuous neck. Her dark hair was pulled back into an elegant swirl with a little tail that bobbed when she talked.

I started through the doorway to get a better look when she turned and stepped toward me. I smiled and stepped back as she glided by. All I remember were eyes so brown they looked wet.

I waited in the kitchen for a moment, then casually followed her into the living room. She moved slowly, with an effortless grace, always using the tips of her long, sexy fingers, to pick up a napkin, touch it to her lips or hold her glass of champagne. I saw her meet men and women, and treat them all the same, never flirty, never cool. She had a relaxed, easy charm.

But none of that is what held me. I watched until I realized what it was. She was perfectly self-contained. Independent without being remote. Private without being cold. Whatever her position was in this world, she knew it and was completely comfortable with it. She didn't try to impress. She just did.

When our eyes finally met, I was sure she saw straight through me. I didn't care. She didn't have a wedding ring on, and I was too fascinated to let her slip away. When she went to the patio, I strategically positioned myself by the French doors and waited.

When she reappeared moments later, I almost missed her because someone's banker-uncle was boring me into the doldrums with his views on budget deficits. I wanted to tell him I lived on a wooden boat and was more concerned with barnacles than budgets, but didn't think he'd understand. When I saw her coming, I hastily excused myself from Uncle Banker, gently took her elbow and slipped away from South Georgia's answer to Warren Buffet. I even used the old fart as my excuse, thanking her for rescuing me from something called "substantial penalty for early withdrawal." Thank goodness, she laughed.

After a more appropriate introduction, I eased the empty champagne glass from her long, sensuous fingers, set it on a passing tray and persuaded her to accompany me to the bar. She smiled and said OK in that fabulous voice.

A few moments later we were on a garden swing in a backyard full of flowers. I tried to pay attention when she spoke, but her eyes wore me out. One second, they smiled and pulled me closer. Then she'd look away. Not wanting her to feel uncomfortable, I decided to watch her mouth more than her eyes. Big mistake. I don't even know what I missed, because I couldn't watch her lips and listen at the same time. This woman was gorgeous, smart and charming. And driving me crazy.

Looking back on it, maybe it was the flowers. Or her perfume. Or the smell of champagne on her breath when she leaned close and laughed.

The only thing I knew for sure was that sitting close to Claire Markham that night was almost scary. Like lighting a fuse and not running.

If I hadn't been so infatuated with her, I probably would have paid more attention to the fact that her answer to my question about her work was vague—something about a medical foundation in Atlanta. And her reason for being on St. Simons? Visiting old girlfriends, whose names she never got around to. I'd love to say that I didn't get good answers because I was being a gentleman and not pushing. But later I wondered if she was just politely clever at keeping the conversation where she wanted it.

We met in the village for lunch the next day. She wore jeans and a T-shirt, and had her dark hair pulled back in a long ponytail. I told her she looked like a runaway princess. She liked that.

We strolled the pier and the village, talking until she had to leave for Atlanta. She eventually did tell me a little about her work and how the foundation she works for funds science and medical research, but no real details. She also mentioned the names of the two girlfriends, classmates from Auburn, but said they were also from out of town and drove here for the weekend, so I probably wouldn't know them.

When the conversation turned briefly to personal lives, we learned that we both had survived turmoil in recent years and laughingly agreed we probably needed more of an emotional rest than a new relationship. We would just be friends. Geography even helped. Atlanta was 300 miles away.

I wanted to be mature about the just-friends thing, and ignore the fact that she was the most beautiful, fascinating woman I had ever met. And I faked that pretty well until she put a hand on my shoulder and leaned toward me to adjust the strap on her sandal. The loose neckline of her T-shirt billowed open, briefly revealing smooth, close cleavage of the most beautiful, natural, creamy-white breasts I had ever seen. I had already known I was going to miss this girl. *That* . . . well . . . you know.

Not unexpectedly, after a few weekends together—here and Atlanta— our relationship had progressed remarkably well. Every moment together was special. Was I crazy about her? Definitely. Did I let it show? Not so much. She was fascinating, but still mysterious. There was no framework of family or friends around her to help me see who she really was. When I casually mentioned that once, she smiled and said, "And you think you're different?" And I realized she was right. We were both loners, a little short in the family and friends department.

I wasn't sure about my own heart, much less hers. So we took it slow, had great fun in and out of bed, and always looked forward to being together.

Ironically, however, as our relationship grew more intimate, the time and space between us that once seemed an advantage began to change. Missed phone calls and misunderstood messages are to long-distance relationships what insects are to a good picnic. Throw in a couple of trips canceled at the last minute and you have disappointment that outweighs reason every time.

It was never intentional—just responsibilities, schedules, whatever. But through the lens of distance, innocent actions can look like indifference, and I think we both would have given up several times if there hadn't been something more. Somewhere beneath the tossed surface, there must have been something stronger, something calm and nameless that never stopped pulling on us.

And we were still here trying.

———————————

The hospital released me at ten o'clock Tuesday morning, and instead of waiting for the pink lady—whatever that was—I headed for the elevator, which thankfully was empty. As the doors slid closed, however, the image of another man appeared—my reflection in brushed metal, staring at me, split in half by the crack between the elevator doors. I tried to ignore the divided man, but he moved every time I did, so I half-stepped to the left to make him whole. When I still couldn't see his eyes, I looked away until the elevator stopped and the doors slid open, ending the familiar stranger's intrusion.

I met Ryan for lunch at the marina restaurant. He was sitting in a back booth when I arrived.

As I slid in, he said, "Except for the knock on the head, how the hell are you?"

"OK. A little confused."

"About?"

I hesitated while a gum-chewing waitress brought water and menus and left. "You questioning me at the hospital, as if I had done something wrong."

"That just seemed like a strange place for you to be."

"I was heading home from Mack's party, and Mom had asked me to see if the cemetery gate was closed. That's all. What's the big deal? And, more importantly, any idea who hit me and why?"

"Not yet. I'm sure you noticed your money and credit cards weren't with the other items the hospital returned. A druggie probably slammed you for whatever you had in your pockets. I already cancelled the cards for you. How much cash did you have?"

"Probably two hundred dollars. Not much."

While he wrote that down, I asked, "Why would a druggie be way out there?"

"Who knows? They never have good reasons."

When he didn't say anything else, I said, "I have another question."

"Shoot."

I leaned closer. "I think there's a body buried in the cemetery."

Ryan tilted his head. When I didn't say anything, he leaned forward in mock conspiracy. "No shit. Ain't that what cemeteries are for?"

"No, no, wait—in *my* grave," I whispered.

"What?"

"I'm serious. I think somebody's buried in my grave."

The spearmint-smacking waitress reappeared with pen and pad, looked at me, fake-smiled and waited.

"Yes, I'd like the veggie-burger, please, on a tofu roll, with hot seaweed tea."

She never flinched. "How 'bout a cheeseburger and Coke, wiseguy?"

"Diet."

"Me too," Ryan said, "coffee."

As the waitress left, I asked, "What do you think?"

"*Why* in the world would you think somebody's buried in your grave?" he asked, gently shaking his head as if to escape an annoying thought.

"The ground in front of the headstone is raised, like all the other occupied graves. All the empty ones are flat."

Ryan hesitated, not seeming to like that answer, then said, "I'll drive out and take a look. I have to be careful. There's an election coming, you know, and that smartass lady lawyer on the county commission now wants to be police chief. You read the news. I can't buy the right toilet paper for the jail. It's either too expensive for cops and crooks, or it's not good enough because it doesn't come from our pine trees."

"Maybe what you need is a toilet paper endorsement from Martha Stewart."

"Not funny," he said, "it could be a hard fight. She has an impressive criminal prosecution record, and she's got the mouth and money to run a helluva race. All I need is one screw-up, and she could whip my ass all over Glynn County. I *need* this job. I'm too old to be Ryan Elliott, P.I."

"It's my grave," I said, "can't I give you permission to dig it up?"

"What am I supposed to do, tell the judge I have permission from the occupant to dig up his grave?"

"Not occupant. Owner."

"Do you actually own the grave?" he asked, knowing the answer.

"It has my name on it."

"Oh, you'd be a big help in court. Look, I owe you. You saved my life, and I will never forget it. But why don't we do this after the election. If somebody's down there, he ain't going anywhere."

He was getting riled up, so I changed the subject. In the end, he agreed to look into it.

———————

After meeting with Ryan, I went back to the boat, showered and decided to drive back out to the cemetery—in broad daylight, looking over my shoulder.

Wondering what I would do when I got there became moot. A Glynn County patrol car blocked the way. I pulled up behind it, got out and quickly learned the officer was not happy to have company. Before I could say anything, he was out of his car and snapped, "This area's closed, sir."

"Yes sir," I replied politely, "my name is . . ."

"I said, this area's closed, sir."

We were still walking toward each other. "Thank you, officer. I'm just here to check on my family cemetery, if that's OK?" It was partially true.

"No sir," he said, arms crossed on his chest, "it's closed today."

I tried politely one more time, and he said, "May I see your driver's license, please?"

He took the license, told me to stay there, then walked away pulling a cell phone from his belt.

I listened but couldn't hear anything. He looked agitated.

A minute later, he returned. "OK, sir, here is your license. You are free to go."

I drove off doing all the safe-driving stuff I learned a hundred years ago from coach somebody in Drivers Ed. A mile away my phone chimed and scared hell out of me. Voicemail from Claire.

As I listened to her message, it sounded like she was laughing, and I was not in the mood for one of those guess-what-just-happened stories. But then I realized she wasn't laughing, and a chill ran across my scalp. She was crying, almost out of control. I could only catch pieces . . . "home to check on something . . . door wasn't locked . . . know better . . . shouldn't have gone in . . . I thought he was going to kill me . . . where *are* you?"

Claire's message ended, voice trailing off, still crying. I pulled off the road, slammed to a stop, and punched the shortcut to her number. *Come on, dammit, answer!* Nothing. Voicemail sounded like everything was fine.

Dammit, Claire! Answer the phone!

I hung up, hit redial. Same thing. The world around me swirled as my mind raced. *What the hell just happened?*

Chapter 7

Weak Smile, Strong Hug

Twenty minutes later, back at the boat, I got her. She had been at the police station filing a report, looking at mug shots. She was better. I asked her to tell me what happened.

She'd gone home for a quick lunch, but upon arriving, noticed the door to her condo was ajar.

"I thought maybe the property manager was checking on something," she said, "so I went in and said, 'Hello?' and left the door open behind me." She stopped. I could hear her breathing, then a sniffle.

"Claire, are you OK?" No reply. I waited a few beats and asked again. "Would you rather not talk about it now?"

"Yes. No. I don't know." Silence again. Then, "Can I come down there? I don't want to stay here tonight."

"Of course. Are you sure you feel like driving?" I looked at my watch. It was already after three. "Do you want me to come get you?"

"No, no, I'm fine. I've had so much police coffee, I'll be awake till midnight. I'll throw some things in a bag and come on."

I hated to think about her driving nearly five hours, but she was a big girl, and smart, and I didn't blame her for not wanting to stay there. Plus, she needed someone, and I was glad it was me. I hadn't felt that much in my life.

Claire didn't have many other people she could call. She had been in Atlanta for a couple of years, but working long hours in her new job at the foundation hadn't left much time for new friends.

As I picked up around the boat, my phone rang. Ryan said, "I hear you met one of my officers today."

"Yeah, what was *that* about?"

"I want to look around out there more. It's a crime scene, remember? You going to be around, right?"

"Is that cop talk for don't leave town?"

"No, Peckerhead. I may have questions."

"Claire's driving down from Atlanta. She'll be here around nine."

He hesitated, listening to someone else on his end.

"We'll talk later," he said. "I gotta go. Call me." He hung up.

I couldn't help thinking that Ryan's attitude about the cemetery seemed strange, like a problem he didn't want to deal with.

It was dark when Claire called from the causeway. I walked up to the parking lot to meet her and got a weak smile and a strong hug. Back on-board I poured us wine, sat on the sofa beside her and learned more. She had gone home for lunch, found the door open, went in and was floored by a guy in a big hurry to get out.

She said the cops took fingerprints, and the door and lock showed no signs of forced entry. But one crime scene man said there were tiny scratches on the inner rim of the keyhole, indicating the lock *may* have been picked. Unfortunately, there wasn't any other evidence to indicate what the guy had been looking for. Claire and the cops searched the rest of the condo, but found nothing missing, or out of place. That concerned me, but I didn't say it.

The cops gave her their cards and a case number. Then she added, "Why in the world would somebody break into my condo?"

I turned toward her and said, "He was probably after anything he could sell for cash."

"Maybe you're right." Then changing her expression, she set her wine glass down and said, "You know, the more I think about it, the madder it makes me. That little son of a bitch broke into my condo, and because of that, I'm not sure I'll ever feel safe there again. And, that's after I add more locks and security, which I have to do now." Then with a subtle shake of her head, she said, "I should have had my gun out. I'd have shot that bastard in a heartbeat."

Here was a Claire I hadn't seen before. And my eyebrows showed it.

"What?" she asked.

"You have a gun?"

"Yeah, I told you that months ago. A little Ruger .380 semiautomatic. And I should have had it out. And used it."

"You sound like you know how."

"I keep one in the chamber, and I wouldn't miss at that range."

I nodded and decided to let it go. Talk more about the gun later.

I didn't tell her about getting knocked on the head at the cemetery. We could discuss that later too. I didn't think they were any more than strange coincidences. Although it did seem unusual that they occurred within 48 hours of each other.

It had been a long day for both of us, and it didn't take long for the wine to do us in. I held her all night.

Sometime before morning, I woke with a start. It was a dream. I had been with a group in a hotel lobby, about to board a bus, but couldn't find my nametag. It had my picture on it, and I couldn't go without it. But I had to be on that bus. It was maddening.

I lay there, staring at the ceiling, breathing hard, still seeing the image of my missing nametag. I wanted to go back to the dream. I couldn't let someone else use my face.

Chapter 8

Rafael Quinterro

Ten years ago

The front door of the old Pasadena tailor's shop was locked and the closed sign was out. Giorgio Como's only customer today would be Rafael Quinterro. He was being fitted for handmade suits, and he demanded undivided attention. The exquisite, imported fabrics were expensive, and Como's custom tailoring took time. But it was worth it.

"Ah, Giorgio," the big man said, smiling when he saw the champagne, "you are always surprising me."

"You are too kind, Mr. Quinterro," replied the tailor, "it is an honor to serve you." He smiled nervously as he spoke.

"May I pour you champagne, Mr. Quinterro?"

"Yes, Giorgio, please."

At 51, Rafael Quinterro was six feet, four inches tall, weighed 255 pounds, and had skin like old copper. Underneath his perfectly tailored suit, there was hidden power in strong muscles wrapped tightly around a heavy frame. His face and head were large, like a totem carved from oak. Thick, black hair swept straight back from a prominent forehead above full, dark eyebrows. Despite the angular exaggerations of his features, his deep black eyes and quick smile made Quinterro a handsome man.

As Quinterro sipped the champagne, the tailor thought how delicate the crystal flute looked in the man's strong hands. And although his nails were always manicured, and he secretly used a cream to soften the cracks and scars, there was no hiding the fact that he had not always enjoyed the life of a gentleman. Growing out of the soft, linen coat sleeves and starched white cuffs, Quinterro's gnarled hands looked like thick roots ripped from the earth.

As a young boy working in the hot fields in Mexico, he was

frequently the youngest of the crew. The older boys had tools, but not Rafael. He would use both hands to twist and crumble the lumps of hard dirt. His fingernails stayed shredded, and they had dirt caked underneath that could not be washed out. His hands were constantly scabbed and bleeding.

Rafael had not always been forced to work in the fields. His mother had been the only child of a wealthy Mexican farmer. But she was disowned at 18 for eloping with an American border guard.

Rafael had only vague memories of his parents. Sometimes he remembered them smiling and laughing and holding him between them as they danced. He remembered feeling safe, and loved by two people who were always happy. It was not to last.

When Rafael was five, his parents were killed in a small plane. The accident report said the crash was the result of pilot error. There was no mention of the fact that the sons of a powerful U.S. senator from Texas had been in the area that day with a new hunting rifle. It was just a crash of a small private plane in the middle of nowhere, with no one famous onboard. Far below the threshold of media attention, the incident passed quietly into local history.

When Rafael's parents died in the crash, his only living U.S. relative was his father's brother, a lazy alcoholic who had never married and couldn't keep a job. Through his alcoholic haze, he saw Rafael as a half-breed burden, unfairly thrust upon him and sometimes beat the boy for no reason. Rafael would cry himself to sleep and start each day scared.

One afternoon while he waited on his uncle to come out of a bar, he saw a big farm truck pull into town and stop. When the driver got out, a small group of young boys spilled loudly from the back of the truck, and raced into one of the stores, laughing and pushing. They came out in twos and threes, eating candy and ice cream, and sat on the curb behind the truck.

When Rafael's uncle stumbled out of the bar after dark, he couldn't have cared less that Rafael was gone. When the boys had piled back onto the truck, Rafael had quietly hopped on too. He didn't know where he was going, but it had to be better than this.

For the next few years, Rafael lived and worked with the migrant crew, moving from farm to farm, and state to state. The days were long, and the work was hard, but there was always enough to eat and no one beat him at night. On an Arizona farm one spring, Rafael came down with scarlet fever. Having no resources to care for the now-eleven-year-old boy, the man in charge did the only thing he could think of. He wrapped the fevered Rafael in a heavy blanket and left him in the farmer's barn. By the time Harold Quinton found Rafael in his barn the next morning, the work crew was miles away.

Harold and Gloria Quinton took Rafael in and began nursing him back to health. They had planned to turn him over to the authorities when he regained his strength. But the healing took longer than expected.

The Quintons' only son had been killed in a car accident years before, and they had been reconciled to living out their days alone on the quiet ranch. It wasn't long, however, before Harold Quinton noticed a change in his wife's behavior. Caring for the boy had given her a purpose again, beyond the everyday chores of running a house. Because Spanish was usually spoken on the work crew, most of Rafael's English had been lost. Fortunately, Gloria knew enough Spanish to begin communicating with the boy. She worked hard to revive his little bit of lost English and help make that his language again.

Still afraid he would be returned to his cruel uncle, Rafael pretended not to know his real last name. The Quintons however were well respected in the sparsely populated ranch lands of Arizona, so when Harold and Gloria filed adoption papers, an understanding official at the county courthouse used a legitimate workaround to bypass formalities. Soon the boy legally became Rafael Quinton.

Because the ranch was so remote, and Rafael was far behind other children his age, Gloria decided to home-school him. She had taught before and easily updated her qualifications while obtaining all the required materials.

Rafael learned fast. He also worked hard to change his speech, to sound more like the Quintons than a field worker.

As his health continued to improve, he took on more responsibility, and grew stronger and bigger as the years passed. By the time he was 16, he had grown into an impressive young man. When he said he was ready for public school, Harold and Gloria understood. That fall, Rafael began the 10th grade at the high school in town. Having been home-schooled alone, he was accustomed to rapid and concentrated lessons, so moving to a full classroom where the pace was slower was a big change. In order not to be bored, he would read ahead. And his grades showed it. He excelled in every class.

Although Rafael had never played football, he was eager to try it, and like in the classroom, he learned quickly, with a natural awareness of where the ball was and where it would be in the next instant.

When he graduated three years later, he was at the top of his class and one of the best high school linebackers in the state, earning a full scholarship to Arizona State University.

Further success there—in school and on the football field—brought more opportunities. After graduating from ASU with a degree in economics, he decided against NFL offers and enrolled at Pennsylvania's prestigious Wharton School of Business, where he earned an MBA.

Despite loving his adopted parents, he would look at the name on the awards and diplomas—and he would know—he was not Rafael Quinton. But the memory of losing his real parents, and living with the abusive uncle were too vivid. He would never go back to who he was then. He was someone else now, and he wanted his own name.

One day he saw a photograph of a young boy blowing out five candles on a birthday cake, and the memories came rushing back. *His* fifth birthday. The last birthday with his real parents. He took out his pen and wrote the word quintero on the page, a derivative of the Hispanic word for fifth. He wrote it again, this time with two r's. Quinterro. He stared at the word—the name—and liked what he saw. He liked that the new spelling was reminiscent of the word terra, meaning land. He remembered his hard life as a boy working in the fields, the difficult lessons he learned, and how they made him strong. Yes, he said to himself. That is where I came from. That is who I am. I am Rafael *Quinterro,* a man of the land.

Because the Quintons' friend in the county courthouse had perfected young Rafael's identity years ago, he had no difficulty legally changing his name.

After Wharton, Rafael accepted a position with a Wall Street brokerage firm where his hard work and strong analytical skills served him well, as did the early work he had done on his speaking. Because he was young and handsome in a rough, Latin way, and because he spoke so well and thought fast on his feet, he was soon handling many of his firm's speaking responsibilities, both for institutional investors and the media. It was there that he caught the eye of a wealthy California real estate developer, who hired him away to be the company's new front man, especially for projects in the Hispanic areas of Los Angeles. Rafael was so smooth that hardly anyone noticed how he spoke perfect English in commission meetings and courtrooms, and added a hint of barrio when speaking to neighborhood groups. His success with the company made him wealthy before he was 30.

He met Natalie Marshall, a beautiful and successful real estate attorney in an LA firm when they were on opposing sides in a bitter zoning battle and lawsuit over a new retail center for Rafael's company. Because it would displace smaller local businesses, racial tensions flared, and a riot made national news when an elderly Hispanic man died from injuries suffered in a fall. The fight quickly became one of the most publicly debated real estate conflicts ever fought in California courts.

The chairman of Natalie's law firm had taken the case, opposing the zoning change that would permit the new center. He never anticipated the severity of the backlash.

The bottom line—for Natalie and her firm—was that there was no way to win. The case had become a fiasco, and Natalie felt she would be fired as soon as it was over. The handsome, smooth-talking Rafael Quinterro was causing her downfall. And there was nothing she could do about it.

One day near the height of the trial, when it appeared that, regardless of the outcome, the damage was going to leave everyone bloody, Rafael walked into the courtroom full of cameras and proposed a compromise. He suggested that his company would dedicate a portion of the retail center specifically to Hispanic-owned businesses, and voluntarily reduce the size of the facility in order to make space available for a beautifully landscaped neighborhood park. And the retention basin required for rainwater runoff from the parking lot would be made into a beautiful pond. Rafael further suggested that the park—and the retail center—be named for a well-known local Hispanic World War II hero. Rafael's company would even create a nonprofit fund, paid for by his company and the tenants, to maintain the park for as long as the center existed.

Tensions on both sides had been so high for so long, that it took a moment for everyone to realize the proposal was ingenious. More than a compromise, it was a victory for both sides. Because, Rafael said, he had gotten the idea from something Ms. Natalie Marshall had said in court one day, he suggested the plan be named after her. The judge couldn't have cared less if the proposal had a name or not, but the media loved it. And of course—as Rafael knew they would—the newspapers gave it a slight twist for their headlines. The Marshall Plan, they said, provided a perfect solution to the most divisive California real estate conflict in over 100 years, and set a precedent for solving future land use conflicts throughout the state.

A month after the agreements were signed, Natalie became a partner in her firm.

Two months later, she became Mrs. Rafael Quinterro.

Chapter 9

Q

Natalie Quinterro

Eight Years Ago

With Natalie, Rafael was happier than he had ever been. He was sure she was the answer to a prayer he had never put into words.

The memories of his birth parents, killed when he was a boy, were so long ago, they seemed like a dream. And even though his adoptive parents had been loving and supportive, he still could not have imagined any love like what he now felt. He and Natalie wanted children, but not yet. They loved work, travel and being together. There would be time for children later.

Rafael's work had gone well. His personal wealth had grown rapidly, and so had his position in the community. Soon he was well known all over California and beyond. He was frequently seen in high-profile business meetings and social events in New York and Washington, D.C., and had even become a personal friend of the President of Mexico. The immigration issues continued to be important, and when U.S. senators needed to know the Mexican President's true feelings, they frequently called on Rafael.

On the Quinterros' third anniversary, they were in London having lunch outside at a corner café in Mayfair. The day was bright and beautiful, sweater weather in England. Natalie was reading a neighborhood paper, and Rafael was enjoying the day, the city, and his beautiful wife. *How is it*, he thought, *that so many women can spend so much time and money trying to look sexy, and my wife looks sexier than them all without trying?* He smiled at the thought and looked forward to the afternoon nap they had planned.

Somewhere in the distance, there was a muffled boom, a small,

"

everyday noise, like a delivery truck's rear door rolling closed. Natalie and Rafael didn't even look up.

A moment later, a woman screamed. Rafael turned and saw two men running down the sidewalk in their direction. In the street, a compact car roared in low gear, keeping up with the runners. One of the car doors flew open and the driver was shouting, waving madly at the two men. But this was London, where cars outnumber parking spaces, and there were no easy gaps for the running men between the cars packed tightly along the curb.

Rafael was already moving when the first automatic weapons ripped through the air. He flipped the small table out of the way, grabbed Natalie and fell to the ground, cushioning their fall with his broad shoulders, then immediately rolling over to cover her body with his. More shots were fired, shop windows shattered, and someone screamed, "Get down! Get down!"

Rafael's mind raced. He wanted to help. He hated doing nothing, but nothing was what he must do to protect Natalie. Still covering her with his body, he looked up. The men were closer now, running wildly, knocking people down. One fired an automatic pistol into the air. Rafael bent further over Natalie to protect her as the men got closer. He remembered thinking they would be OK, the running men would keep going.

But the table Rafael had chosen that morning was near the intersection, where the long line of parked cars ended. Rafael saw the men turning and realized what was happening. He pulled Natalie tighter and hoped the men would go past them, hurdle over them if necessary, make it to the car and be gone.

As the men angled toward the intersection, one of their police pursuers fired. The first man's head snapped back, and he went down, hitting Rafael hard in the ribs, and pushing him partially off Natalie. The other man hesitated, dropped to one knee and fired a long burst at the police. He tried to raise his companion, but felt his limp body, and saw the dark red pouring from the man's neck. He dropped him, and still crouching, fired another long burst toward the police.

Rafael shifted to better cover Natalie, but the movement startled the crouched man and he reacted wildly, firing two shots into Rafael's side. Natalie didn't know what had happened but felt Rafael's weight.

When more shouts sounded closer, the man looked around and realized he was being surrounded. A foot away, Rafael tried to move, but couldn't. He could feel his peripheral vision going gray. The last thing he saw was the man jerking Natalie up and holding her in front of him, dragging her toward the street. As his world went black, Rafael heard his wife's scream, and the sound of a car screeching away.

Over the next few days, Rafael Quinterro went through a hell no one should have to endure. The men who took Natalie were Islamic militants robbing an armored car to finance terrorism. When their robbery failed, they panicked, killed a guard and ran. One militant was killed at the scene, and one drove the getaway car. The wounded man survived and was taken prisoner, but the fourth man escaped by using Natalie as a human shield.

That night, the group posted a video online demanding the release of their wounded comrade—and $3 million in cash—in return for Natalie's release. The speaker wore a hood over his face and held a long, curved knife over Natalie's head. He vowed in the name of Allah that if his demands were not met, she would be executed. Beheading was the obvious threat.

Immediately following the attack, Rafael had been rushed to surgery and remained unconscious for several hours. His wounds were serious, but not life threatening. When he regained consciousness in ICU that night, law enforcement officials told him about Natalie's kidnapping and the ransom demand, but left out the part about the threat against Natalie's life. Rafael became enraged, tore tubes and sensors from his body, and tried with all his might to get out of the bed. After he was forcibly subdued, the physicians had no choice but to place him under sedation and restraint.

In New York, Rafael's banker heard the news, rushed to the office and wired Rafael in the hospital, saying that the arrangements had already been made to transfer the $3,000,000 anywhere in the world at a moment's notice. The message said, "Say the word, my friend, and the money will be sent within seconds, any time, 24 hours a day. I will not leave this phone or this office until I hear from you. Get Natalie and come home. All our thoughts and prayers are with you."

The wire from his banker was the only good news Rafael received. The following day officials from Scotland Yard and the U.S. Embassy came to his hospital room, but all they had were excuses. He raged at both of them.

"Here I have Europe's best law enforcement agency and an official from the most powerful government in the world, and my banker is the only one with brains and balls enough to see what needs to be done!"

Regardless of his rantings, the physicians refused to release Rafael from the hospital. They agreed instead, because of his improved condition, to move him to a private room. Moments after pretending to fall asleep in the new room, he called the concierge at his hotel and got a change of clothes delivered to his hospital room. Fifteen minutes later, taking stairs at the end of a corridor, he walked out.

Ten minutes later, he was back in his hotel room, calling his banker in New York to confirm that the money was ready to go. Next, he connected his computer and went to the website where the terrorists' video had been posted, to see where they wanted the money sent. The hospital had refused to let him see the video, afraid of his reaction. He had been told, of course, in general terms, what the video said, but nothing about the threat to his wife.

There, alone in the hotel room, he watched in horror and disbelief. Before the 40-second video was over, he was retching violently into the brass trash can beside the bed.

Moments later, there was a knock on the door. Two men with Interpol badges asked if they could come in. Rafael agreed and began immediately telling them not to waste their time. He was already prepared to wire the money as instructed. The men exchanged a glance and asked Rafael if he would please sit down. He knew something was wrong and refused, but before he could say anything else, one of the agents dropped the bomb they had come to deliver. Under direct orders from U.S. President Ann Roberts Chambers and the British Prime Minister, there would be no negotiations with the terrorists. The man wounded and captured at the scene would not be released.

Chapter 10

President Ann Roberts Chambers

Unlike the soft-sided, smooth-talking lawyers who got to the Oval Office from the U.S. Senate or a comfortable governor's mansion, Ann Chambers was a product of the criminal court system—a tough DA, Assistant Director of the FBI, and finally Secretary of the Department of Homeland Security.

During the previous administration, Islamic terrorists had attacked government facilities as well as soft targets like malls and office buildings. Initially, critics and the media demanded action, but lost interest when the new wore off. There were newer stories to tell.

The people who buried family and friends, however, didn't forget. And when Ann Chambers ratcheted up the Department of Homeland Security into the world's most sophisticated anti-terrorism operation and started paying million-dollar rewards for tips leading to the capture or killing of the terrorists, the nation took notice. Terrorists were killed and captured in record numbers, and the ones who were taken prisoner were tried, convicted and executed with as much media attention as Chambers could encourage. She did it that way, she said, not for her own reputation, but for the results. And because she didn't walk or talk like a politician, the people had no reason not to believe her. When terrorist attacks on U.S. soil virtually ended, but continued around the world, Ann Chambers was practically drafted into campaigning for president. And she was good at it. She leased *The Magellan*, the armored train FDR and Truman had successfully campaigned on, and practically lived on it while she made whistlestops from South Beach to Seattle and Mexico to Maine.

For her running mate, she chose Paul Collins, a well-respected U.S. senator from California, and a perfect insider.

Together they appealed to all minorities who saw hope for their own causes in Chambers' rise to power. Thanks to a brilliant campaign and a divided competition, Ann Roberts Chambers became the first female President of the United States of America.

After the election, although there were no major terrorist attacks, there had been kidnappings in which the Islamic militants demanded money in return for their hostages, usually a wealthy individual or an entertainment celebrity. And before the new credibility was established, there were tragic endings, of course always played out to the fullest by the media. Before the government increased its own security protocols, a U.S. senator from Ohio was kidnapped and executed when Chambers refused to meet the terrorists' demands. In every case, true to her word, Chambers stood firm. Four years later, she was easily reelected.

Soon after her reelection, however, her detractors rose in number and voice, and the honeymoon ended. The public opinion polls of all presidents are divided, but never had it happened so quickly. And never had the gap between the opposing sides been so wide and the conflict so fierce. To the detractors, people were being murdered, and the government was standing by, watching it happen. To Chambers and her supporters, yes, it was terrible, but unless the citizens of the United States wanted to get used to living like this, always wondering who would be next, and paying millions to help arm the militants, this was the only sane option.

The only way to stop negotiating with terrorists, she said, is to stop negotiating with terrorists.

Rafael Quinterro tried everything in his power. For the next three days, he worked nonstop, only leaving the hotel room to meet face-to-face with anyone who might be able to help. He rarely ate and slept only minutes at a time.

He called in every favor from every high-ranking official he knew, made promises that would take him a lifetime to keep, and even sent messages to the terrorists explaining his predicament, begging for more time. At one point, he even considered offering a huge financial reward to any organization—drug lords, organized crime, even mercenaries—who could break the Islamic prisoner out of jail and release him to his own people.

Twice the terrorists extended the deadline by 24 hours, but swore to Allah it would not be extended again. On the last day, when there were only hours remaining, Rafael called the White House from London and asked to speak to the president. Because of Rafael's high-profile reputation and the glaring media coverage of the incident, he made it through the main switchboard. The White House operator, knowing this was way over her head, transferred the call to the Chief of Staff. Unfortunately, neither he nor his secretary was in, and an assistant took the call. She listened to Rafael's story, then placed him on hold while she checked "to see if the president was in." When she returned, she apologized and said the president was unavailable. Rafael knew what that meant. Either the president herself, or someone close to the president, had made the decision not to help. When he hung up the phone, he sank into a place he didn't know existed.

The fear was mind numbing. He sat on the floor at the end of the bed in the hotel room and turned on the TV for the first time since that first day. There, sitting among soiled clothes and towels, stacks of dirty room service trays, scraps of paper and unread newspapers, he stared at the screen, without moving. For the next 20 hours. He was without hope.

Finally, through the veil of fear and shock, he heard the announcer's words. Natalie was dead. Stunned into disbelief, Rafael reached for the remote to turn off the TV. But the announcer was talking fast, and Rafael heard the words that split his brain in two and sent him into another world.

"Mrs. Quinterro's beheaded body was found . . ."

Three months after Natalie's funeral, Quinterro set up an office at home and began quietly liquidating his assets, never disclosing to one party what he was doing with another. He spread his sales of stocks, bonds and real estate over several weeks in order not to draw attention to himself or the transactions. He sold to a wide range of buyers, and often tangled the paper trails by using multiple transactions and unwitting middlemen, as well as attorneys, trusts and shell corporations.

For the direct sales of his equity shares to his wealthy real estate partners, he said he needed to raise capital to buy controlling interest in a new business overseas with foreign investors. His partners never questioned his decision or his story. They trusted Rafael, and knew the value of what he was selling. They also had the cash to buy him out.

When the last deals were closed and the millions safely deposited in numbered accounts, Rafael Quinterro turned off all the computers, phones and TVs in his house and sat there for two days. He drank a lot, ate almost nothing, and cried until his head hurt. On the third day he made one call, to a man known only as Benicio.

In the predawn dark of the following morning, the pilot of a sleek Gulfstream 550 spooled up the plane's two Rolls-Royce BR710 turbofan engines, released the brakes and began the take-off roll. In the luxurious cabin capable of carrying 18 passengers in club chairs, recliners and side-facing sofas, Rafael Quinterro sat alone. As the jet streaked skyward into the night, he watched the twinkling lights of Los Angeles fall away. While the aircraft banked toward South America, Rafael sat like a man-child, his forehead pressed against the cold window. He watched until the last lights disappeared behind him. When nothing was left in the dark window but his own reflection, Rafael looked away. He touched a button and the electric window shade closed. The flat-panel LCD screen on the forward bulkhead showed the aircraft's position as it began to move away from the U.S. Rafael watched how slowly the plane's tiny image moved, and how far it had to go.

Moments later, the jet reached its cruising altitude of 42,000 feet, and an attractive flight attendant in heels and a simple suit walked forward from her seat in the rear to check on her only passenger. As she passed the aft-most club chairs and tables, she stopped. The cabin was empty. He must have gone to the forward restroom, she thought, so she continued walking forward to check on the cockpit crew.

Then she saw him. Two seats ahead on the left. He was bent over, his head almost between his knees. She thought he was ill and stepped forward to help. But then she saw he was not sick. His whole body was shaking, and his face was buried in a white handkerchief in his big hands. She silently stepped backward, turned, and walked back to her seat at the rear of the plane. Sitting there staring at the jet's expensive carpet, she felt shaken. She had never seen anyone cry that hard.

——————————

When the housekeeper arrived at the Quinterro residence Monday morning, she found no one at home and assumed Mr. Quinterro was traveling. He used to do that a lot. But he always left her a note, and always in her native language. It was simply to say hello, and maybe make her smile. She was from Mexico City, and he knew she was homesick. She didn't mind that he forgot the note this morning. She knew how sad he had been. But when she realized all the electronics and phones were unplugged, she thought that odd. Before leaving that afternoon, she grew concerned and found the courage to call a number in New York he had given her several years earlier. Someone here, he said, will always know where to find me.

After a moment on hold, she heard the woman in New York come back on the line and assure her that no one there had heard from Rafael in weeks. With that, the housekeeper grew scared and called her brother. He told her to call the police.

In the weeks that followed, the authorities questioned neighbors, friends, business partners, anyone who may have had any contact with Rafael. But all they learned was that Rafael Quinterro had told no one he was taking a trip. Told no one he was leaving. He left no forwarding address, no phone numbers, and no instructions. He told no one goodbye.

He just disappeared.

——————————

At 11 years old, Benicio Delgado lived on the street selling trinkets to tourists in Porlamar, Venezuela, on the Isle de Margarita. Other vendors sat on their blankets, passively displaying their goods, but when Benicio saw a prospect coming, he sprang to his feet smiling, introduced himself and politely asked their names, and usually for help with the correct pronunciations, whether he needed help or not. When they smiled back, he placed one of his most beautiful pieces in their hands and told his new friends how much skilled work had been required to create such a perfect specimen. He told them about the importance of finding the right materials, and how only a few artisans were skilled enough to create treasures of such lasting beauty.

He worked tirelessly to learn the different languages of the visitors, frequently asking his customers about new words he heard them use.

His competitors were street vendors. Benicio was a salesman. With his enthusiasm, product descriptions, and familiarity with foreign languages, he turned trinkets and souvenirs into exotic jewelry. He learned what an heirloom was, and told his new friends, "Someday your daughter will give this beautiful bracelet to her daughter. And she will tell her it is special—not because it was lovingly made by an artist in a faraway land—but because you chose it for her. Many years from now, when you look down from Heaven, you will see your granddaughter wearing this, and you will smile, knowing she thinks of you."

By the time Benicio was 16, he had his own store. By 18, he had two more. And by the time he was 20, he had stores in every port on the island, all in his name. He was becoming well known and wealthy for a young man, and decided, like other celebrities worldwide—Pele and Madonna—he no longer needed a last name. Benicio became more than his name. It became a personality, a persona, and the symbol of his success.

When Benicio's businesses sold more jewelry than he could obtain locally, he built small factories around the island and hired artisans to create new products. Soon he had his own shipping agent license and became well known in the local import/export business. When he couldn't find enough room on local boats to move his products to and from the profitable locations on the nearby Grenadines and the other Windward Islands, he bought his own boats. On his 25th birthday, he bought his first ship.

By the time the man known only as Benicio was 43, half of all consumer goods made in South America left the continent on his ships. He was a powerful man with powerful friends—on both sides of the law. In dealing with the corruption rampant in third-world countries, he had learned the hard way that success sometimes required more than salesmanship and cash management. It sometimes required absolute ruthlessness. So he maintained certain necessary connections. And few knew Benicio's warm smile hid a cold heart.

Chapter 11

Officer Down

Last Wednesday Morning

Glynn County Police Chief Ryan Elliott closed his office door and snatched the handset off his desk phone. "Goddamn you, Taggart, what the hell kinda stunt was that?"

"No names, dumbass!"

Elliott didn't reply.

"Look," the caller named Taggart continued, "that guy was in the wrong place at the wrong time, and my clients and I got way too much tied up in this. The item has already been moved, but we still can't afford anybody snooping around out there. You're getting paid plenty to be sure we don't have this kind of problem. Now do your damn job." The line went dead.

Ryan didn't like it. It was supposed to be simple. No drugs, cash or weapons. Just a stolen piece of electronic equipment. All they wanted to do is store it somewhere safe in rural Glynn County until it was needed. Hell, it was Taggart who picked the cemetery.

Last Monday night, one of the men told Ryan to meet him at the side door of an old riverfront warehouse on Blythe Island, to get the rest of his money. Ryan had almost forgotten that ancient RoRo warehouse even existed. Inside, the building was dark except for a small area near the door, where the man told him to wait. When the man was gone more than a minute, Ryan quietly walked to another door off to the side, and peeked in. Inside was a huge armored vehicle, the kind used to carry tons of cash between banks, casinos, and the like. When the man came back and saw where Ryan was, he looked displeased but didn't say anything. Making light of the matter, Ryan tilted his head toward the armored car and jokingly said, if he had known they were bringing that much cash, he'd asked for more. The man grinned, handed Ryan an envelope, and said nothing as he escorted him out of the old building.

He hadn't felt right since that night. And now this.

He rubbed the side of his head and put his elbows on the desk. He felt another headache coming on. He took two aspirin, swallowing them without water, when the intercom buzzed. "Traffic complaint, wants the chief. Line one."

Ryan rolled his eyes, picked up the handset. "Chief Elliott."

After couple of polite "yes ma'ams," he winced from the headache pain and reached for the aspirin again. Strangely, he couldn't find the plastic bottle in the drawer where he had put it. He was feeling and looking, and vaguely aware that it was time for another "yes ma'am," when he realized the inside of the desk drawer was darker.

"Are you listening to me?" the caller asked, sounding far away. Ryan tried a "yes ma'am," but couldn't finish it. The pain was getting worse. He couldn't hear the caller anymore and his office seemed darker. His head slowly fell forward onto his left forearm.

By the time the traffic lady called back, the flow of oxygen-rich blood to the Chief's brain had been diverted to a tiny hole in the center of his head, where it leaked into puddles in the folds of his brain doing absolutely no good whatsoever.

Ten minutes later, after the ambulance screamed away from the Police Department, a white van pulled away from the curb across the street.

Eight miles away in the Village on St. Simons Island, Vic Kilgore sat in an old, black BMW, sipping coffee, watching tourists and fishermen on the long concrete pier.

When the flip phone on the seat buzzed, he thumbed it open and heard, "Courier report. Delivery complete."

Kilgore asked, "Verified?"

The answer: "Yes. Recipient left the building."

The coded message was clear. Glynn County Police Chief Ryan Elliott just left the department in an ambulance.

Kilgore closed the phone and broke it at the hinge. He wiped both halves and put the display half into a small sack with his empty coffee cup. The keypad half went in his coat pocket. Flip phones were cheap, untraceable and easy to destroy. They're all he used.

Leaving the car, he dropped the crushed paper sack into a pier trash barrel reeking of yesterday's bait. He then strolled to the far end of the pier, leaned against the weathered rail and watched the outgoing tide swirl hard against the concrete pilings below. He eased the bottom half of the phone from his pocket, held it close to his stomach, then dropped it into the fast-moving water. A gull swooped at the small splash, but flew away disappointed.

———————————

After surviving a home burglary, a long day with Atlanta cops, then a five-hour drive to St. Simons, Claire was sleeping soundly in *Rivianna's* big bed Wednesday morning.

When a nearby sportfisherman's diesel inboards roared to a start, she blurted, "What's that?" head up, eyes wide.

"Sea monster. Run for your life."

She closed her eyes, dropped her head back to the pillow and slid her lips to one side, showing faint appreciation for my early-morning humor.

"Fishing boat," I corrected, sitting beside her, "go back to sleep."

I looked at that beautiful face and wondered how I got so lucky. I knew our relationship grew stronger every time we were together, and yet there was still so much I didn't know about her. She had said last night that sometimes I looked at her as if I didn't know how I felt. How could I tell her it was because I was falling in love with her, but had no idea how she felt? She was the most provocative and irresistible woman I had ever known. And the most mysterious. Every time I thought I knew who she was, something unexpected would happen, and I would realize there were still parts of her I didn't know at all. Sometimes I had to ask myself if I was falling in love with a woman or a mystery.

In this world of no absolutes, however, we had one. We would never lie to each other. Ever. It was a sacred promise, a vow, between a man and a woman, and there was no room for exceptions, excuses or conditions. Our trust was absolute. I didn't know if it was friendship or love or something else entirely. I just knew how good it felt.

That's what I was thinking when I remembered last night Claire had felt the bump on the back of my head, and I hadn't answered her question. It had, after all, come at an inconvenient moment. "Later," I had promised.

And now it was later.

But first I wanted Ryan to talk to Claire's Atlanta detectives—cop-to-cop—and see what they would tell *him* about her break-in. He could mention my incident in the cemetery and see if they thought a connection was possible.

I swung both feet to the deck and called Ryan's office.

"Police Department."

"May I speak with Chief Elliott, please?"

"The Chief is out. Can I help you?" He was abrupt.

"Do you know where I can reach him?" I asked. "It's urgent."

"No sir, I don't. I can take a message."

I asked about reaching him on the radio.

"I can't do that now, sir. Do you want to leave a message?" He sounded stressed.

"I'll call back."

"What is it?" Claire yawned, pushing up on her elbows.

I politely motioned *wait* while I tried Ryan's cell. No answer. Mailbox full, as usual.

Ryan always answered my calls, sometimes just saying, "Not now," and hanging up.

I was cynical before the newspaper business, but dealing with crooks, liars and politicians had given me a graduate degree in suspicion. I looked up the number of the hospital, started dialing, then turned to Claire. "I called Ryan and they refused to try to reach him on the radio. And he doesn't answer his cell."

"Maybe," she said, eyes smiling, "he did the same thing we did last night and he's just too tired to talk?"

"No, not today," I said, still trying to dial the hospital without completely discouraging the babe in my bed. "There's an election coming. If he's not at work, something's not right."

Claire, grinning mischievously, said. "Did you say there's an erection coming?"

"*Election*," I corrected, starting the hospital's number again.

"Oh. Then I'm voting for you!"

"Look, I love it when you talk like that, but can you give me just a minute?"

Claire, still smiling, pulled the sheet over her face as the hospital answered."

"Please connect me right away with the physician in charge of Police Chief Elliott's care. It's urgent."

Claire reappeared without the smile, sat up, ran her fingers through her hair, and mouthed, "What?" as the hospital operator transferred me.

A young, female voice answered, "Second, East." I repeated the request for Chief Elliott's physician.

"I'm sorry, Dr. Dillon is with a patient."

That confirmed it—Ryan was in the hospital. I also recognized the voice.

"Look, I know all about HIPPA, but this is official business. What can you tell me?"

"I can't tell you anything."

"You were working this floor on Monday, right?"

"Yes. Why?"

"My name is Carson Hood. I was in 212 and you brought Chief Elliott to my room, remember?"

"Yes, Mr. Hood, I remember you. Not a very cooperative patient."

"Sorry if I was an impatient patient," I said, trying not to sound impatient. "Listen, you also know the chief came to see me because I was the victim of an attack, and he personally was working on the case. Now something's happened to him, and I worry the two could be related. I need to know what happened to the chief. Now. Others may be in danger."

She hesitated, then said, "I'll tell you what anyone in the hospital could have seen. That's all. The chief was unconscious when the EMTs brought him in. And he went straight from ER to ICU."

"What about his injuries?"

"No visible injuries."

I thanked her and hung up.

Claire stared, "What?"

"Ryan's in the hospital."

"How'd you know that?" she said.

"There's something else I need to tell you."

When I finished telling Claire about the cemetery, my knock on the head, and meeting with Ryan, she stared at me for a moment, then said, "That's not all, is it?"

"Let's just say I hope your break-in in Atlanta and my little cemetery adventure are nothing more than coincidences."

She thought about that, then said, "Wait. Are you involved in something that could have caused both?"

"No," I said emphatically, "are you?"

"No. Of course not."

"I'm sorry. I didn't mean that like it sounded. Look, why don't you relax here for a while. I'm going to the hospital."

She swung her feet to the floor, "Not without me."

Chapter 12

Two Doctors. No Diagnosis.

After two years in downtown Atlanta's Grady Memorial Hospital, and six years at the Mayo Clinic in Jacksonville, Florida, Travis Dillon, MD, thought he'd seen everything. Nothing, however, could have prepared him for the MRIs of Police Chief Ryan Elliott's brain. The unmagnified image looked like a tiny broken blood vessel in his brain. The magnified image, however, showed a perfect, empty sphere.

Dillon's first reaction was that the MRIs had to be wrong. Part of the digital image was missing. He called the technician in the next room, but she was already coming through the door. "I know," she said, staring over his shoulder, "I've already run diagnostics. Everything checks out."

"Come on," Dillon said, "this can't be right."

"I ran the full diagnostic program," she repeated, "it says the machine is operating perfectly."

"Run the diagnostics again. If you get the same thing, call whoever sold us the machine. Call the manufacturer. I want someone to tell us this happened inside the machine, so I don't have to believe it's happening inside a man's head. Go."

Dillon rubbed the side of his face, got up, and headed down the hall. At the nurses station, he interrupted a conversation. "I need two things, both stat. Send Brad Wheeler at Mayo Jax copies of the chief's MRIs. Then get him on the phone."

Claire and I got to the hospital at 10:30. I asked at the information desk about Ryan. A nosey television reporter nearby heard me.

"Excuse me," she said, "Are you related to Chief Elliott?" Her pen and pad were ready. A cameraman waited over her shoulder.

I almost answered her, when Claire took over, "Oh, I'm glad you're here. What can you tell us about the police chief—what was your name again?" I watched Claire. *Amazing.*

"Jane Rivers, Channel 8, Jacksonville," she answered, proudly offering her hand. Claire took her hand but continued the question instead of introducing herself.

"Do you know what happened to Chief Elliott?" Claire asked, "we're friends of his."

I saw Miss Rivers' subtle hand signal to the cameraman. As he waddled up beside us, Claire again rose to the occasion. "Please, no video," she said, still polite, but more direct now. She leaned in and said in a conspiratorial voice, "Look, my job involves government contract work, and I can't have my face on TV." Before the reporter could reply, Claire added, "My boss would call yours and ask that the video not be used. Your boss would agree. Let's just keep this off the record now anyway, OK? You help us now, and maybe I can help you later."

Claire won. The reporter told us about how she was at the Mayo Clinic in Jacksonville waiting to video a pre-surgery interview with Brad Wheeler, the neurosurgeon recently featured in *The Wall Street Journal* for his work on circulation issues in the brain. Right before the interview, Wheeler had taken a call, then bolted out the door in his scrubs. Obeying instinct, the reporter and her cameraman followed him the eighty-something miles from the Jacksonville Mayo Clinic to the Glynn County Hospital, staying back far enough not to be obvious.

"When we got here," she continued, "we heard about the Police Chief and wondered if he was the reason Wheeler is here. Unfortunately, nobody will tell us anything. And my news director is pissed—*excuse me.* The Jacksonville hospitals have a spokesperson who will say something we can use for a sound bite. Here, they just ignore us."

Thankfully, Miss River's cell phone rang and she and her cameraman left for the parking lot.

When I turned back to Claire, she was distracted.

"What?"

"I know who she's talking about. Wheeler."

"How?"

"His name has come up at the foundation. He was involved with some government research a few years ago."

"What does that have to do with Ryan?"

"I don't know. But Ryan showed up unconscious this morning, and before lunch Wheeler's here. Maybe a coincidence, maybe not."

I was thinking about that when Claire said, "I'm going to ask Taz at my office to find everything she can about Wheeler—clinical studies, research, grant work, everything."

"Can she do that?"

"Oh, yeah. Taz can find anything. Her work plays a big part in how we evaluate proposals."

While she called Taz, I tried to find out more about Ryan, but only confirmed he was still in ICU. And stable, whatever that means.

———

Travis Dillon, MD, set his coffee down and turned the monitor toward Brad Wheeler, who, at Dillon's request, had just driven in from the Mayo Clinic in Jacksonville, Florida. Wheeler just stared as if he were confused by the images, but he knew exactly what he was looking at. A chill ran down his spine and he tried to hide the shock from his friend.

"What do you think?" Dillon asked.

Wheeler didn't answer. He needed to calm his nerves before speaking. *My God*, he thought, *this can't be happening*. The project was canceled. No one knew how to make the device work. But somebody *had* made it work. That was the only explanation.

The images showed that Chief Ryan Elliott had a small, perfectly spherical, empty hole in the center of his brain. It was slowly leaking blood, and there were no signs whatsoever of what the hole was or where it came from.

"Maybe," Wheeler said, "the shape is an anomaly." He hoped that sounded good.

Dillon didn't reply, and Wheeler knew his answer hadn't been good enough. He had to buy time.

Wheeler looked up at his friend who was now standing beside him, looking over his shoulder. Before he spoke a nurse knocked on the cracked door, stuck her head in. "Excuse me, Dr. Wheeler? Did you know there is a TV reporter from Jacksonville in the lobby asking for you?

Wheeler felt the cold knot in his gut tighten.

"Actually," the nurse added, "the reporter was *asking* earlier. Now she is demanding to see you."

Wheeler felt light-headed, glad he was seated.

The nurse waited a couple of beats, then asked, "What would you like me to tell her?"

Wheeler's head was reeling, and before he could say anything, the nurse added, "She also has a cameraman."

Brad Wheeler swallowed and tried to appear relaxed. He looked from the nurse back to his friend. "She must be the one I was supposed to see this morning. When you called, I completely forgot."

"Her card says Channel 8, Jacksonville," the nurse confirmed.

Dillon turned to his friend. "What's this all about?"

Still struggling inside, Wheeler said, "I was supposed to do a short interview this morning before surgery, and when you called, my partner took the surgery, and I forgot about the interview. Maybe I was the only thing on the reporter's schedule, so she followed me here."

Dillon said, "What do you want to do?"

The nurse at the door spoke to someone else in the hall, then said, "Actually, Dr. Dillon, what Dr. Wheeler wants to do may be only part of it now."

"What do you mean?" Dillon asked.

"It seems the reporter is mad because we don't have a *spokesperson* to answer her questions. She's demanding to speak to the hospital administrator, or *the CEO*, as she says. She says she's not leaving until she does."

Wheeler turned to Dillon, still trying to buy time. "This is your hospital. I think you should talk to her."

"And tell her what . . . we have a patient we can't diagnose?" Dillon said. "No way. Besides, she probably just wants the interview with you."

"I'm not sure." Wheeler said. "She saw me leave Mayo and followed me here. She thinks something's up . . . and probably wants it for the six o'clock news."

When no one said anything, Wheeler added as calmly as he could, "Travis, I don't think we should let anyone know about the chief's condition, not yet."

The nurse was still waiting at the door when someone called her back out into the hall. She held the door, and reappeared. "Well, the reporter got to the administrator. His secretary says he's not happy."

Still struggling to appear calm, Wheeler asked, "How much of a problem is this going to be?"

"I don't know," Dillon said, "you stay here, and I'll go try to placate the reporter." Then turning back to the nurse, Dillon said, "Tell her *I*— not Dr. Wheeler—will be out in a minute. But no cameras. This is not a news conference."

The nurse left and Wheeler said to Dillon again, "Travis, remember, nothing specific about the chief's condition."

When Dillon left the room, Wheeler walked to the door, closed it tight and pulled out his phone. He took a deep breath and entered a long distance number he hoped he would never need.

Chapter 13

I Love Claire. I Wonder Who She Is.

After being stonewalled about Ryan's condition, and waiting to see what Taz found on Wheeler, Claire and I grabbed drive-through sandwiches and drove to a small marshfront park with picnic tables. We wondered if our imaginations were being overactive, or if our peaceful little world was really changing.

Claire was telling me more about her work at the foundation and why Wheeler's name was familiar when her phone vibrated on the wooden table. She said, "Taz," to me, then answered, saying, "Hang on, I'm going to speakerphone."

"After you called this morning," Taz began, "I found abstracts and articles on brain circulation in which Wheeler was either involved, or his work was referenced." Her continued keyboarding sounded like a toy machine gun through the phone's speaker.

She continued, "A lot of it's medical jargon, over my head. But something bothered me. So I compiled what I had, put it into one of our programs. I found two things, neither of which seemed significant alone, but the combination was interesting. The first was a gap in Wheeler's published works, about two years' worth. That's not unusual for researchers—sabbaticals, contract work, whatever. Next however, I found several databases where some of Wheeler's publications had been listed and then removed. Not rotated out because of age, but removed soon after being published."

Claire looked at me, and asked Taz, "Why would that happen? Conflicts of interest, or inconsistent protocols?"

"Nothing. He's squeaky clean. The listings just disappeared. So," Taz continued, "I backdoored one of the databases—and don't worry, no one will ever know I was there—and found the change logs." Claire glanced at me again while Taz continued. "Normally the logs just tell who changed the database, when, why, etc. And usually, it's just out-with-the-old, in-with-the-new, on-what-date, period. And change logs are usually sacred to IT types. They are the only records of what happened and when online. Without them, the past in cyberspace would just disappear."

"Why do I have a feeling I know where this is going?" Claire said.

"Right. The logs were there, but there was no mention of any of Wheeler's stuff going in or coming out. Nothing." She hesitated, then, "Pretty stupid if you ask me. Surely, whoever pulled the files and doctored the logs knows that other computers have snapshots of their database. That's how our search found the aberrations in the first place. Once something's posted online, you can't pretend it was never there."

I understood enough not to like it, and I was about to ask a question when Claire replied to Taz. "OK, now what?"

"Well, whoever doctored the logs is probably an IT wonk who maintains change logs as part of his routine responsibilities. And he was probably ordered to do the dirty deed by someone higher up. It may be hard for us to understand, but to an IT specialist who earns his income— and self-respect—by keeping his world in perfect order, being ordered to delete files and doctor change logs would have gone totally against his nature. It would have been like a local politician telling the town librarian to burn some of the great, old books because it was too expensive to keep 'em anymore. Well, like the librarian would have hidden those old books somewhere, I guarantee you the IT guy kept copies of those publications and change logs. Besides being the right thing to do, it would be a small but appropriate act of defiance, like telling the boss to shove it without actually telling him."

I understood that part and nodded. Always had a warm place in my heart for little acts of defiance. Rage against the machine, but don't get caught.

Claire ignored my smug look, and Taz continued. "The copies are probably still on the organization's computer, hidden with a new file name, so the IT guy could get to it quickly if he ever needed it. If I'm right, I may be able to get in, find the backup and see what was pulled and when. Getting in and doing a quick look isn't difficult. It's staying in and searching. That's when I could get caught. I've lived with striped sunshine before, and I don't want to go back. Sorry. I probably shouldn't have said that on the phone."

My smug look disappeared and I mouthed, "What?" Claire waved me off.

"Forget those change logs," she told Taz. "If somebody pulled Wheeler's publications, one, there has to be a reason, and two, there must be other clues somewhere. Keep searching and call me back when you find something."

Claire hung up and before I could say anything, she said, "I know, I know, I should have told you about that."

"Striped sunshine?" I asked. "*And* you never told me Taz's real name. Is there a reason?

No. It's Theodora. And she hates it. Her mom nicknamed her Taz because she learns everything so fast.

"And yes, Taz did a little time awhile back. She was a kid. Her older brother asked her to temporarily turn off a repair shop's security system so he could get his *unrepaired* TV back without paying a service charge. Unfortunately the detective on the case found out Taz helped.

"Anyway, it was a low-security women's prison, and she was only there a few months. She was a model prisoner, earned college credits, and got out early. The judge who sent her up was so impressed, he personally called the foundation to see if we could use her on a work-release plan. We said OK and it's worked out perfectly.

"And you'd love her. Million-dollar smile, the most beautiful ebony complexion you ever saw, and she's probably the smartest person at the foundation. I'd be lost without her."

"Suits me," I said. "Besides, I'm a lot more interested in what happened to those missing publications. And, now that we know Wheeler has skeletons in his closet, it's no wonder he's hiding from that TV reporter. She may not be able to get to him, but I bet I can."

"What? How?" Claire said staring at me.

"Come on. Let's go."

"Wait," Claire said. "*Wait!*"

I was a rolling boulder ready to get to Wheeler any way I could when Claire stopped me.

"Look," she said, now dead serious, "we—and *Ryan*—are caught up in something we don't understand, right?"

"Right."

"Carson, that guy in the cemetery could have *killed* you. The burglar could have killed me. And we don't even know what's happened to Ryan, right?"

"Right."

"And, if we keep blindly poking at whatever this is, things could get worse, *fast*."

I nodded. *Sometimes I think I'm not as smart as I think I am.*

"Carson, you once told me that to know the whole story about anything, you have to find the answers to the W words—who, what, when, where, why—*right?*"

When I didn't respond, she said, "How much do we know about those now?"

I didn't say anything.

"Nothing."

She let that sink in, then added, "I think we should talk to somebody we know, and trust, somebody with experience dealing with serious stuff."

I said, "The Admiral."

"Exactly."

She was right, of course, and had given me another reminder that being in love with a really smart woman could be quite rewarding. And a little humbling.

I called Mack and said Claire and I wanted to take him and Bess to dinner tonight, on us.

He asked, "What are you selling, boy?"

"You know me better than that." I said, "I'd never subject your charming wife to something so crassly commercial."

"Good," he replied. "She can't come anyway. This is her bridge night. *However*, as long as you're buying dinner—and *not* selling anything—I would love to spend time with that brilliant, gorgeous woman you should be marrying instead of dating. Say when and where."

———————————

We met Mack at the best restaurant on the island. I didn't even know Claire had brought a little black dress with her from Atlanta. More about that later. Mack barely acknowledged my presence. He handed me the wine list, saying he wanted something big, red and expensive, then turned to Claire and gushed about how fabulous she looked. He was right. Did I mention the little black dress?

I was about halfway through the cabernets on the wine list, when a group came in and settled at a long table nearby. The environment quickly became too loud for the conversation we'd planned. Claire got it too, and barely moved an eyebrow. So, I chose a Sparkman cab, and we had a fabulous, relaxing meal, telling stories, laughing and making plans.

For me the real treat was watching two of the smartest people I have ever known—and my two favorite people in the world—having fun getting to know each other better. The real bonus for me, however, was just watching Claire.

I loved how she imbued every moment with a sense of casual importance, whether reaching for her wine glass or asking Mack what it was really like being commandant of the United States Coast Guard. She turned prose into poetry and brought grace to every motion, and charm to every spoken word. And it wasn't only her attention to detail. It was her deeper, more considered view of the world. When I thought about having spent most of my deadline life running so fast, missing so much, I admired her slower, truer appreciation of little things. I wondered sometimes if we were living side by side in different universes. She saw me thinking and gave me a wink, causing a twitch in my lap. That damn little black dress.

And Mack either saw her wink, knew something was up, or both. "OK, you two, this has been great, but you didn't invite me here for this. So, what's up?"

When I hesitated, wondering where to start, Mack turned toward Claire.

"Admiral." Then, "*Mack*," she corrected, "we need a little more of your time. And a quiet place."

Mack glanced at me, then immediately back at Claire. He nodded OK, and said to us both, "Until I know more, I'd like to leave Bess out of this. Let's take both cars and go to the marina."

The night had turned windy and cool. As Claire and Mack settled in *Rivianna's* main salon, I closed the windows and turned the music on low, outside speakers only. Mack watched me and raised an eyebrow.

Five minutes later Claire's recounting brought us from Sunday afternoon to now. Mack's memory got it all, and he said it back to us almost verbatim:

"Sunday afternoon. Carson gets hit on the head in the old family cemetery, after seeing what appears to be somebody buried in his grave.

"Next. Tuesday. Carson has lunch with Ryan, who seems more curious about why Carson was at the cemetery than what happened there. Later, same day, Carson goes back to the cemetery, but a county policeman says it's closed. Meanwhile, 300 miles away in Atlanta, Claire runs into a burglar in her condo. Nothing seems to be missing, and the lock may have been picked.

"Next day. Wednesday morning, Ryan is rushed to ER, then ICU, with no visible injuries. Soon after that, a Dr. Wheeler from the Jacksonville Mayo Clinic shows up, followed by a TV reporter. And, from Claire's work at the foundation, she recognizes Wheeler's name. Right?"

Claire nodded.

"Same day, Wednesday afternoon. Claire's assistant in Atlanta finds that some of Wheeler's online publications have disappeared, along with records proving they ever existed.

"What am I missing?" Mack asked.

"I think you got it," I said. Claire nodded.

Mack said, "The first thing that bothers me is this has been going on for four days and I'm just now hearing about it." He stared at me.

I said it all happened kinda fast. He said, no shit, then apologized to Claire for the S word.

He glanced back and forth between Claire and me, and leaned forward. "OK, pay attention, because this is important. One thing I've learned from danger at sea is you can usually survive almost any *single* problem." He waited a beat, then added, "It's when they show up in bunches, you're in trouble."

Claire and I didn't speak or move. The word "bunches" hit home.

"And," Mack continued, "when they *do* show up in bunches, you better find out fast how they're connected. Because, that may be the only way to survive."

I felt a chill on the back of my neck. My mind raced through the last four days, but it all seemed so separate, random. Claire stared ahead, thinking.

When we didn't say anything, Mack added, "If the connections aren't obvious, treat it like a jigsaw puzzle. The first piece is what happened first. Next try to find a piece that fits into that one."

"The cemetery was first, right?" Claire said.

Mack nodded and said, "And piece two. Both Carson and Ryan had just been to the cemetery.

Three," Claire said, "Ryan's behavior about what happened there seemed odd, right?"

"Right," Mack replied.

"OK," I started, "I'd love to think this one's unrelated, but, what about Claire's burglary?"

Mack faced me and said, "Well, it might be unrelated, but that could be a dangerous assumption. It's possible that whoever clobbered you in the cemetery knows about your relationship with Claire and wanted to know more about her."

"That could be," Claire said, "I never did find anything missing."

"Let's assume for now it's related," Mack said. "We just don't know how."

Claire again. "I don't know how this fits in, but Ryan's in ICU, not CCU, so it probably wasn't a heart attack. And if Wheeler's here because of Ryan, that means it's something to do with his brain, right?"

"Right," Mack confirmed, "which also means Ryan's problem must be unusual, because Wheeler's not a guy you call about a simple stroke. And TV reporters don't follow unimportant people from one state to another."

"Right," I said, then added, "so, Ryan can't tell us anything; the TV reporter doesn't know anything; and the burglar has disappeared. So that leaves Wheeler."

"Can you get to him?" Mack asked.

When Claire and I hesitated, Mack's admiral voice said, "Do it."

Chapter 14

One Word

At nine the next morning, Claire and I strode across the hospital lobby. I told the petite retiree at the information desk, "I need Dr. Dillon. It's an emergency."

A moment later, phone at her ear, she said, "Dr. Dillon's nurse wants to know who you are, and why you want to see Dr. Dillon."

I smiled, reached for the phone, got it, and said to the nurse, "I am Carson Hood, and I have critical information for Dr. Dillon regarding a patient of his."

She started with how busy he was. I cut her off. "It's about Chief Elliott."

A pause, then, "Wait there."

Seconds later an unmarked door opened, and a woman in blue scrubs motioned me over. "Mr. Hood?" Then, "Who's this?" indicating Claire.

"We're here to help." I answered. "Where is Dr. Dillon?"

She thought a second, then said, "Follow me." Leading us through the unmarked door and down the hallway beyond, she said over her shoulder, "This better be good," then stopped, and pushed a door halfway open.

A man in green scrubs didn't stand, didn't introduce himself, and didn't seem amused with the interruption.

"Dr. Dillon?" I asked.

"Yes. Can I help you?" he said, looking at me, Claire, me again.

"My name is Hood, and Sheriff Elliott is a close friend of mine. We met on Tuesday and discussed something in private. The fact that he's now here, in ICU unconscious, and somebody called—" The door opened and another man in green scrubs walked in. I gambled. "Dr. Wheeler?"

He answered yes before Dillon could stop him. But Dillon cut me off again. "The chief is my patient, and I'll address any concerns about his condition."

"I know who Dr. Wheeler is," I said, "a TV reporter from Jacksonville followed him here."

"What's your point, Hood?" snapped Dillon.

"I know about Dr. Wheeler's research on brain . . ." I stopped when I saw Wheeler staring at Claire.

Claire calmly stared back. And said one word. "Janus."

When I looked back at Wheeler, he was white as a ghost.

Punching a button on the room phone, Dillon said, "Security to Room 110."

Claire said to me, "Let's go. Now."

The morning was not turning out at all like I expected.

––––––––––––––––––

On the way to the car, I said, "Who the hell is Janis?"

Setting a brisk pace, Claire said, "Not Janis. Janus with a *u*." And not who. What."

I was waiting to hear what a *Janus* was when we reached the car and climbed in. Claire continued. "Taz found a reference online to something called Janus, and whatever it is, Wheeler's involved—or was."

"Wait a minute. When did this happen?"

"Taz called this morning. You were in the shower."

"And?"

"I didn't say anything because it's something we're not supposed to know."

"You know it," I said.

"Yes, but right now, we need to concentrate on what Taz just said.

"OK," I said, agreeing, not understanding.

"Taz said whatever Janus is apparently started as a research project at the National Institutes of Health. Then it was moved to another agency, and apparently became classified. Taz might have lost it, but the transfer record included a reference code linking the old project number to a new one. After that, nothing. All the leads died. *Except*, for a later reference to something called Janus. And that's all we know. Except, that Janus was *not* something Wheeler wanted to hear."

"I don't get it," I said.

"Taz is looking. She'll come up with something. She always does."

"What do you mean, 'She always does?' You just said it was a classified government project?"

"You don't know Taz."

I was thinking about that as we pulled into the marina, and Claire's phone rang. She said, "Taz" to me, then answered. Silence. I tried to stay calm while Claire listened, but it wasn't easy. Her poker face let her down.

You know that feeling you get in the ocean when something brushes your leg?

Chapter 15

NIH and CIA

I pulled into a marina parking space, and was turning the car off when Claire said, "No." She had just hung up with Taz and looked like she didn't want to tell me something.

"Let's go," she said, refastening her seatbelt. "Taz says we need to keep moving."

"What does that mean?"

"I'll tell you while you drive."

"Drive where?"

"Anywhere. Let's go."

I backed out, and we left the parking lot heading back toward the mainland. "OK, talk to me."

Claire hesitated, looked at me, then back at the causeway, and said, "Taz thinks we may be in danger, and shouldn't go to *Rivianna*. We should get a room somewhere, not in our names. I think she's right." Her voice trailed off, but it was obvious there was more.

I took her hand and said, "Look at me. I'm here, and I'm going to take care of you. Got it? Now tell me exactly what Taz said."

Claire breathed deep, waited a long pause, then said, "Some of this she said earlier this morning. Some just now. OK?

I nodded, and checked the rearview mirror, not sure what I was looking for.

Claire began. "While Taz was searching for those missing reports of Wheeler's, she found a research assistant who once worked with him, and talking with her, Taz learned a lot more."

"And . . . ?

"Wheeler once headed up a privately funded research grant involving radiation beam treatment for deep-tissue tumors. When the National

Institutes of Health learned about it, they took an interest and began sending NIH observers. Apparently pleased with what it saw, the NIH offered to assume funding responsibility. No one saw anything wrong with taking the government's money, so everyone agreed.

"When the new fiscal year began, the NIH funded everything. With that, of course, came oversight, and soon the NIH began showing interest specifically in proton beam therapy, at the expense of the other radiation therapies. No big surprise. The proton models were promising the best outcomes.

"According to Taz's source," Claire continued, "months later two NIH guys walked in and said the project was canceled. All personnel would be paid through the end of the quarter, but, effective immediately, the project was over. Before anyone could ask any questions, all employees were politely asked to leave the building. Women were allowed to take their handbags—after they were searched—but nothing else. And all employees were told their mobile phones and other personal items would be delivered to them at home within 24 hours. Then they were all politely ushered to the front door. Their IDs and entry cards were taken, and they were bid good day.

"Wheeler hadn't been present that morning, but as project director, he was frequently away at meetings. Later, a team member tried to reach him, but his phone numbers had been reassigned, and neither the main switchboard nor the lab had any forwarding information. The team members assumed that, as project director, he might have been privately informed of the cancellation, and maybe transferred to another NIH project at a different lab. Regardless, Wheeler had disappeared.

"Using the Janus name, however, Taz was secretly able to track the proton beam project to—get this—a research division of the CIA."

"What?" I asked incredulously.

"Yes. There's more."

Claire continued. "When Taz learned enough to talk intelligently about it, she used an untraceable Internet phone line to call an unsecured phone at a CIA HR department. Using real budget acronyms, she said she was calling from the office of a CIA contractor and needed to locate an employee to verify project cost data. She couldn't get any classified information over the phone, of course. But she did pick up more abbreviations and references, and using those, was able to dig deeper. Using her expertise with codes and hidden meanings, she was able to learn what had happened to an innocent NIH proton beam medical project. And why the Janus name was appropriate.

She said, "You still with me?"

I said yep as we reached the end of the causeway and turned left heading downtown.

"I did some of my own research too, "Claire said. "When Taz first told me about the name Janus, I looked it up. Some of what I found didn't mean much then, but it does now.

"Janus, it turned out, was the Roman god for whom January is named. He presided over beginnings, or more literally, over doorways. Romans who prayed to the gods, prayed to Janus first. And when Rome went to war, the Arch of Janus was opened, and it stayed open until the troops came home.

"But," she continued, "there was another reason this god of beginnings and doorways was valuable. Janus was a god with two faces. He could look forward and backward at the same time, giving him a remarkable advantage in combat, and earning the envy of Roman warriors. With two faces, Janus could also simultaneously look into the future as well as into the past, giving him a perspective humans don't have.

"Or," she continued, "more importantly, Janus could show you one face, while hiding his true intentions in the other."

Several minutes later, when Claire finished, we didn't know who had named the project, but we now knew why it bore the name Janus. The project represented both a new beginning—and a two-face dealing—as well as anything one could imagine. The new beginning reflected the rebirth of a controversial U.S. foreign policy discontinued years before. And the two-faces reflected the perfect deception of using an innocent cancer treatment for something not taught in medical school.

This new Janus was more than a god of beginnings and two faces. This Janus was a god of death.

Somebody in the federal government wanted the perfect assassination weapon. And the Janus Project was created to provide exactly that.

By then we had looped through downtown Brunswick's waterfront and were turning back onto the causeway to St. Simons. I drove silently for a few minutes, trying to digest what I had just learned. And trying to figure out how finding somebody in my grave in a remote country cemetery had led us to something as bizarre as our country's secret plans for carrying out political assassinations. I was still mulling that over when the shit hit the fan. Bigtime.

The human brain is an amazing thing. It runs quietly in the background, never revealing its true powers. However, show the brain life is ending *now*, and that wet, convoluted computer between our ears can go absolutely berserk. Survivors of near-death experiences usually say they saw images of three things—Family, Friends and Flashbacks. It's the three Fs, and the brain flashes through 'em like a screensaver on steroids—no words, just pictures.

I had always suspected my brain was wired differently, but it took a brush with death to prove it. My first two Fs weren't Family or Friends. They were Fred Flintstone.

Claire and I were about a hundred yards from the tall, fixed bridge over the Intracoastal Waterway when the traffic unexpectedly slowed. I eased off the gas and touched the brake. Nothing. I screamed "shit." Claire screamed, "What?"

"No brakes! Hold on!" I stomped on the parking brake. Nothing.

The world in front of me was a thousand taillights. And all I could see was a cartoon caveman dragging his feet to stop the Flintstone mobile.

Oh, yeah. My third F wasn't a picture. It was definitely a *word*.

Right before the tall bridge, there was a turnoff on the right where the original roadway led to the old drawbridge. I jerked the wheel to the right, crossed the narrow bike path, and plowed into a low forest of scrub oaks. A limb shattered the windshield into a web of a million pieces as Claire grabbed my arm and reminded me that Jesus' middle initial was H.

We were still flying along when we broke out of the heavy brush and bounced hard on the abandoned roadbed that led to where the old drawbridge had been. The hard bounce jarred some of the shattered glass out of the windshield frame and I could see that, unless we found a way to stop, we'd run out of land before we ran out of speed and make a nasty splash in a deep tidal river. I knew the tide was going out, and this was not a good time to go swimming, especially in an automobile.

As the dead-end loomed ahead, I tried everything again, fast—brakes, parking brake, downshifting. Nothing. My ass was chewing a hole in the seat and Claire was helping by screaming, "Do something!"

To our left, there was nothing but rows of massive concrete pilings supporting the tall, fixed bridge, so I aimed right, into more heavy brush.

"Hold on!" The thick brush was slowing us down, but also blocking my view. Any second, we'd burst into the open and plummet into deep, fast-moving water.

When the brush abruptly ended, we had less than fifty feet before the sea wall. I cut to the right toward a row of palms, aimed for a gap, hoping we'd slip through and spin out in the soft sand beyond, hopefully without flipping over.

I realized too late the gap wasn't wide enough. We slammed to a stop as the front fenders jammed between the two palms.

I forgot about the airbags.

Seconds later, Claire and I were pushing the hot fabric out of our faces, when I saw flashing emergency lights in my outside rear view. Still woozy from the adrenaline and impact, I remembered wondering where they came from. I was reaching for Claire with my right hand and pulling on the door handle with my left when a paramedic appeared. He pulled the door open, and slapped an oxygen mask on my face, hard.

Except, it was definitely not oxygen.

Chapter 16

Kidnapped

Side-to-side rocking. Droning motor. Strange ceiling.

Senses slowly returned and the world around me gradually came into focus. I was lying on one half of a V-berth in the forward cabin of a small motor cruiser. The distinctive rocking said we were cutting diagonally across a low chop somewhere offshore. I eased up into a sitting position and saw Claire on her back on the other berth. Seeing her jarred back the memory of the brake failure on the causeway. I quickly checked my pocket for the nine-millimeter Glock, knowing it wouldn't be there.

I held on and slowly stood up, remembering my car jammed between two palm trees, and the EMTs from nowhere, apparently responsible for our current accommodations. Still holding on, I stepped gingerly toward the cabin door, knowing it was locked before trying it.

I was gently checking Claire when the engines throttled back. As the boat lost plane and settled into the rolling water, I pulled close to one of the small portholes above Claire and saw off the starboard bow a much larger boat.

A radio call blared on the other side of the door, and someone answered with a short string of words and numbers. A code.

As we turned and eased closer to the bow of the big boat, I saw a man with an assault rifle on an upper deck. Claire was stirring and I was wondering how to tell her that I didn't have answers to all the questions she was going to have.

We were proceeding just above idle, but too fast to be this close. I held on and put my other hand on Claire's shoulder. There was another engine cutback, further slowing, and then the world went dark. I pulled close to the small porthole and saw us passing through huge sea doors in the larger boat's bow. As my eyes grew accustomed to the dark surroundings, I saw that we had eased into a sea-level compartment inside the bowels of the bigger boat. Boat, hell. We were inside a small ship. I was impressed, curious. And worried.

The growl of our engines reverberated in the metal enclosure like artillery, and I saw armed men along the metal decking on our starboard side. Claire was stirring more.

With the echoing roar of our idling engines still deafening, we drifted forward until I felt our driver pull his throttle levers into reverse, then quickly back to neutral. Dead stop. He killed the power to both engines and the echoing roar disappeared, replaced with soft sloshing.

Claire slowly rolled over, pushed herself up into a sitting position and was about to say something when a key rammed into the locked door, and it swung open. A man in black shirt and pants holding a pistol jumped back and called over his shoulder when he saw us both awake. When other men with rifles moved closer, he motioned us out of the cabin. We were ushered up a step and onto the metal decking beside the boat, where we were both patted down.

While we were being searched, a man at a control panel threw a switch and the big sea doors started pulling closed. The guy threw another switch, as men pulled the mooring lines of the smaller boat tight, centering it in the slip. It rocked once, then rose out of the water on two padded rails. The sea doors pulled tight with a loud lock. Daylight disappeared, replaced with bright overhead halogens.

As if things weren't strange enough, at the far end of the compartment sat an enormous, gleaming armored vehicle with double wheels on both rear axles. A shield-shaped logo on the side said International Security Services. Directly in front of the armored car, swung up and secured to the wall, was a massive, hinged floor grate that could be lowered for moving the vehicle in and out.

Still under the lingering effects of whatever the EMTs used on us, I was having a hard time figuring out what was stranger . . . our boat being swallowed by a ship, or being in an ocean-going garage with an armored car the size of an RV.

The guards walked us through a waterproof door into a corridor, and locked Claire in a small room. They marched me upstairs, through wood-paneled doors into an impressive office with a far wall of solid glass. I saw blue water stretching to the horizon, before I realized a thin man was standing in front of a big desk to my right. He wore a pretend-navy white shirt with black, gold-striped, epaulets on his shoulders, and had a white goatee way too big for his narrow face. It made him look like a fool, but I didn't see anything to gain by mentioning that.

So, no one spoke.

I learned from lawyer friends, when things look bad, fools speak first.

The silence dragged on until Captain Whiskers said, "Mr. Hood, tell me who you have spoken to about your recent discovery."

Even with a hangover from being drugged and kidnapped, it wasn't hard to guess he was asking about the occupied grave under my headstone.

I didn't answer.

"We don't have time to play games," he said more forcefully.

I didn't answer.

"Very well." He turned to one of the guards, saying, "Bring the girl up here," and got a "Yes, Captain," in reply.

When the guard returned with Claire a moment later, I assumed the captain was going to question her. Instead he looked at me. "Mr. Hood, I suggest you talk."

Claire didn't say anything, but her eyes asked me, *what?*

"Mr. Hood . . . ? he said.

"What do you want?" I answered.

The captain told the guards to get the chairs ready, and they placed two metal armchairs side-by-side a foot apart. They pushed Claire down in one of the chairs and I thought they'd put me in the other one. Instead, one of the guards changed position and pointed his rifle at my chest, while a guard behind Claire pressed down hard on her shoulders, holding her in place in the chair. Another used both hands to pull Claire's right arm across the divide between the two chairs and hold her wrist hard on the arm of the empty chair. The fact that the captain hadn't given any specific orders meant the guards had done this before. I was already worrying when a third, larger guard in back stepped forward, and raised his right knee above Claire's slender arm. The only reason I hadn't completely panicked yet was because I was convinced this was a practiced bluff.

"Continue," the captain said. I thought he was talking to me, but the big guard started to rock forward onto Claire's arm.

I screamed "No!" The guard holding the rifle on me jumped closer, and Claire shrieked my name. While all this was happening, an intercom buzzed loudly and the captain's arm shot up as he shouted, "Wait." In that next second, a voice through the intercom said, "Incoming chopper. It's him."

"Get her below," the man said, and they jerked Claire up and pushed her through the door before I could see her face. Her scream and the guard's knee above her arm felt like a knife in my brain.

And outside, the roar of an approaching helicopter said things were about to change.

Chapter 17

No Lifeboats

The deck shuddered beneath our feet as the helicopter landed somewhere above us. We felt more than heard the pilot cut the power, and seconds later footsteps in the corridor said a visitor was approaching. The goateed captain moved away from the desk as the newcomer entered. He was short, stocky, with a dark tan and a narrow black mustache.

"What did he tell you, Captain?" he asked.

"Nothing. He's playing stupid," the whiskered man said as he left the room.

The newcomer stared at me. I waited.

"Mr. Hood," he said, "you understand why you're here, right?"

"No, I don't."

"There is a reason, Mr. Hood, why I don't want Miss Markham in this room." He hesitated and my stomach knotted. "I have seen her photographs. I know she is quite beautiful, and that you are a lucky man."

"She is not my wife," I said, hoping to distance Claire from whatever trouble I was in. "And more importantly, she has nothing to do with this. Hell, I don't even know what *this* is."

The man replied, "It is important that you understand what I say." He looked down briefly, then back at me. "Under other circumstances, I would love to meet Miss Markham, to see her soft, dark hair, beautiful brown eyes and lovely figure."

He stopped again. I was getting worried.

I waited, afraid to think what he would say next.

My mind raced. *What in hell does this have to do with us?*

"Miss Markham is not here now because I do not want her to be real to me."

Before I could think, he dropped the bomb that cramped my chest so tight I couldn't breathe.

"If you do not tell me what I want to know," he continued, "I will send these men to hurt Miss Markham." Before I could recover, he continued. "This is not what I want to do. But, if you leave me no choice . . ." He let that hang in the air.

Real fear is a gut-busting reaction that changes everything. Control becomes an illusion. Body temperatures and heart rates rise. And sweat and shallow breathing reveal our helplessness.

A moment ago I had thought a man arriving by private helicopter was intelligent, willing to listen to reason. I was wrong. Without warning he had turned into a monster. My gut turned to ice. Sweat ran down my sides.

I felt the beginnings of panic and fought for control, knowing I couldn't do anything if I couldn't think. Then—from nowhere—I remembered what the Marines taught us to do if taken prisoner: above all, stay calm, use your head. I forced slower breaths, and concentrated on relaxing neck and shoulder muscles during those few seconds of silence. Then, in that slower, deep breathing, a strange thing happened. I decided what happens to me doesn't matter. The only thing that matters is Claire . . . getting her out of here safely. I was still worried, but the debilitating fear I had felt a moment ago was turning into something I could use. And I knew I would do whatever it takes to get Claire out of there—lie, cheat, steal. Kill.

I breathed again. An idea was taking shape.

The bright sunlight streaming through the floor-to-ceiling windows dimmed unexpectedly. Like a shade slowly being pulled, low dark clouds slid across the sky, turning the blue water black. The man turned away from me toward the darkening scene outside and stared.

In those few seconds of quiet, I had a plan. It was pure bluff. A huge lie. And one hell of a dead-end. But the long term wasn't my problem right now. The short term was killing me. I needed time. And I needed to buy it any way I could.

"OK," I said. "I'll tell you what you want to know."

"Talk."

"I'll talk when I see that the woman has been safely released onshore, and she calls to confirm she's safe."

He didn't like that.

"I lied to the captain. I know more about what's going on than you think," I said, lying about lying.

He didn't like that either, but I had him wondering.

"Think about it," I continued. "That silly accident you staged to get us kidnapped? And the fake EMTs who never delivered us to the ER? You think nobody saw that? Right now, cops are crawling all over Glynn County looking for us. I don't know how you got us from the ambulance to the boat, but somebody saw that, and they are telling cops right now."

He was about to speak again when the deep throb of the engine room increased, and the ship moved. He steadied himself with a hand on the desk and looked confused. Before he spoke, there was a low rumble in the bowels of the ship, the unmistakable sound of a windlass and chain pulling a massive anchor from the sea floor.

He stabbed a button on the intercom phone and loudly demanded, "What the hell is going on?"

The captain's voice replied, "Storm is coming, Benicio. We have to move."

"This is my ship," the man named Benicio snapped back, "I'll say when we move."

The captain continued more politely, "Yes sir. But you specifically told me we must not do anything that could, in any way, risk the cargo."

Benicio? I filed that name away, and wondered if the cargo was that big armored car below. Meanwhile, this Benicio became furious at his name being used and told the captain.

"Tell me," Benicio said into the phone, "that this circus I am hearing about how you got the man and woman onboard is not true."

There was a pause before a reply. "I am sorry sir. I am a ship captain, not a gangster. The message I got was to get them onboard, without fail, and that's what I did."

Benicio slammed the intercom handset down. Veins stood out on his neck and forehead, and his chest rose and fell with each breath.

As the anchor windlass droned on, a blast of hard-driven rain splatted against the huge window, turning the view into a gray blur. When the big boat listed to port from the strong wind, I saw a different look on Benicio's face. It was only there an instant, and before I had time to process it, his old face was back, staring me down.

"*Great*," came a sarcastic whisper from one guard to another.

Benicio turned toward the guard and demanded, "What?"

The guard turned back to Benicio, "Excuse me, sir," he said, "I was just saying we had to leave the lifeboats behind."

"Why?" Benicio demanded. "Who gave those orders?"

"The captain did, sir," the guard replied. "He said the armored car was too heavy."

Benicio thought about that and said to the guard, "What about the boat that brought him and the woman?"

"It did not stay," the guard replied.

Then Benicio got that look again. Only this time, I knew what it was.

The son of a bitch couldn't swim.

Chapter 18

Stormy Seas

The man named Benicio was still thinking about no lifeboats when I repeated, "I'll tell you what you want to know, but the woman has to be freed first. And I have to know she's safe. Otherwise, no deal."

He turned to the guards. "Take him below."

Locked alone in a small room with no porthole, I couldn't see the weather, but I could feel it. If Hell is anything like seasickness, I'm going back to church.

Sometime later, two guards came for me. In the hallway, we met up with Claire and her two guards. She looked almost as bad as I felt, but damn if I was going to mention that.

The ship was rocking so hard, the six of us looked like drunks in a carnival funhouse, bouncing back and forth and side to side in the narrow hallway.

After several challenging sets of stairs, we reached the upper decks where large windows showed the stormy afternoon had become a stormy night. I heard serious arguing up ahead. Benicio and the captain were at it bigtime. The goateed captain said the storm was getting worse, and the big chopper was too heavy.

"It's changed our center of gravity, and we are rolling too hard. We could lose the whole ship. I'll have my men cut it loose and push it over the side."

Benicio's face was suppressed terror. He turned to the helicopter pilot. "Let's go."

The pilot's eyes went wide. "I can't take off in this weather. It would be suicide."

While Benicio hesitated, the ship rolled hard again, catching everyone by surprise. The captain said to one of his men, "Go to full speed and cut the bird loose. Push it off the stern."

"No!" Benicio shouted. He pulled a black handgun, put it under the pilot's chin. "You are going to fly us off now, or you're going to die."

The pilot said nothing. Benicio thumbed back the hammer. The pilot said, "OK, OK." Then looking like he'd prefer the bullet, he said, "I need five minutes to spin up. And Captain," the pilot said as he turned to leave, "I need eight of your strongest men to hold the lines."

Still in the haze of seasickness, I had assumed Claire and I were only spectators in the unfolding drama. I nearly shat when Benicio turned to us and demanded, "Let's go."

What?

Claire pulled up tight against my side.

The guards tightened their grip, spun us around and slapped life vests on us. Claire looked at me wide-eyed. I tried for the, *I got this* look, but her eyes said, *not buying it.*

I shook off the pukin' haze. The good news was limited. Claire and I were good swimmers.

The bad news was more complicated. I had no idea how far we were from shore. I never swam in a typhoon. And I never escaped underwater from a sinking helicopter. Except for that, I felt pretty good about our chances. I decided to go over all this with Claire later. I gave her a subtle thumbs up, Her expression said, *I'm gonna kill you.*

I was thinking about that when we were push-pulled through a waterproof door into the storm. The roar of the wind was deafening. Driving rain stung our faces. More guards formed a moving huddle around us to shepherd us toward the big helicopter lashed high above. In the bright lights illuminating the helipad, I saw the big blades slowly starting to turn as the men forced us up the steep steps. Gradually the whine of the chopper's big turbines and the whup whup whup of the long blades could be heard over the wind. On the helipad, the men shoved us into the chopper's wide door, and strapped each of us in with a combination seat and shoulder harness with a big release knob on our chest. The fresh air felt good, but the thought of trying to get out of this bird while it was sinking made me miss my little windowless stateroom with a trashcan full of vomit. A guard slammed the wide door closed, which stopped the wind, but not the roar of the turbines overhead. I don't pray much, but did then.

In one seat, the pilot was making hurried adjustments on a huge, red-glowing instrument panel. In the other seat, Benicio just stared. The pilot looked out his window and shouted into his helmet microphone. On the deck below, a man gave a thumbs up. On the bench seat behind us, three guards were seriously tightening seat and shoulder harnesses.

The pilot glanced over his right shoulder and said loudly, "If we go in, she can float for a few seconds—*if* a blade doesn't hit the water first. It if does, we'll flip over." He showed us with his hand, *as if we needed that.*

"If things turn to shit," he continued, "remember—up is down! Got it?" He didn't wait for replies.

Claire's dainty hand had my wrist like a blacksmith shoeing a wild horse.

The vibrations intensified as the whup whup whup of the blades increased to a roar. The ship heaved mightily beneath us, and I realized the pilot's first challenge would be split-second timing—riding an upward swell to the top and then blasting off. Too soon, and the fast-rising deck could catch up with the chopper, sending us into an uncontrolled slide into the drink.

With the way the ship had been pitching and rolling for the last few hours, the only thing that kept the helicopter from falling overboard were the eight lines tied tight to the thick, metal rim surrounding the helipad. Those lines were still wrapped once around the chopper's skids, but one end of all eight had been untied and were now being held by a gaggle of wide-eyed guards scared shitless by the whirring guillotine a few feet above their heads. If this whole thing was going to happen like clockwork, they would all have to let go at the same instant.

Sitting there, waiting, tossed by the heaving ship and shaken by the vibrations of the twin turbines screaming above us, I thought about all that had to happen exactly right for us to be alive two minutes from now. Claire says sometimes I think too much. This is a good example.

As the ship dropped into a deep trough and started back up, I looked again at the handle on the door beside me and tried to imagine what it would feel like in the dark. Under water. Upside down. The helicopter shook more violently, and I felt Claire's fingernails go through the skin on my wrist.

The roar of the turbine engines above our heads was so loud I could feel it in my chest. And every pitch and roll of the ship threw us around like crash-test dummies. I couldn't see the ocean, but I could feel the ship dropping into deep troughs, riding swells to the top, then dropping again.

One wave sent so much water across the ship that two of the line-holding guards on my side had been washed off the helipad to the deck below. The loose ends of their two lines blew free and writhed on the pad like long snakes straining to get away from the mechanical monster.

As we hit the crest of the next swell, the pilot went for it. We were barely off the pad when I looked down and saw the ship's stern coming up fast. The pilot saw it too. The chopper lurched hard right, and out of Claire's window, I looked straight down into white caps and black ocean. When the chopper rocked hard back to vertical, I turned and saw the ship off to the left, pitching like a toy in a tub. I remember thinking the ship might not make it—the big ocean would swallow her like an hors d'oeuvre. And for a moment, I felt safer in the helicopter . . . until I saw the pilot wrestling with the controls like he was riding a wild bull with a butt full of bees. Benicio was pale with fear.

Gradually, I felt us accelerating forward and realized we were finally actually flying instead of just fighting for our lives. The pilot turned a dial on the instrument panel, looking for a heading, and then screamed over his shoulder, "Hold on. It's going to get worse before it gets better."

Worse? No way.

I was wrong. Our forward motion introduced a new variable and subjected the craft to sudden storm blasts from all directions. The earlier pitching and buffeting had been uncomfortable. This was violent.

I tried several times to hold Claire's hand but couldn't. We both needed two hands to hold on to the seat. I gave her a quick reassuring smile just as a sudden gust crashed my head against the door. As it did, I saw over my shoulder two miserable faces in the dark behind us. The third guard had his head between his knees, and I prayed he wasn't puking. We'd know soon.

I was still thinking about that when the pilot motioned to Benicio and pointed to something ahead. When the nose dropped, I saw blurry lights low on the horizon. *Land. Thank God.*

Benicio shook his head at the pilot, pointed to the left, and said above the roar, "That way. And below radar."

The pilot looked at him briefly and shouted back, "The turbulence must have damaged a fuel line." He tapped his finger on one of the gauges. "We have to go straight in."

Benicio shook his head no.

The pilot fingered the gauge again and shouted, "We don't have enough fuel!"

Benicio shouted. "Do whatever you have to. Fly faster, fly slower, I don't care. But get us below the radar and take us south."

Benicio and the pilot were both upset. I glanced past them when the blurred streak of lights on the horizon showed up again, now realizing the pilot was giving up altitude. I couldn't tell how high we were, but I knew it wasn't much. He also seemed to slow down some to conserve fuel. Lower and slower were good. We were still being tossed around, but the intensity had eased. I had an idea.

I turned to Claire, put my mouth against her ear and said, "No matter what I do next, don't react. Got it?"

She nodded but looked unsure.

"Trust me," I mouthed.

No reply.

I leaned way over putting my head between my legs and started heaving like I was about to puke. While bent over with my hands hidden, I unfastened the metal knob at the center of my chest, freeing myself from the combination seat belt and shoulder harness. When mine was loose, I reached over and pulled Claire down like I wanted to tell her something, and while we were huddled close, I undid her harness. For what I had in mind, I only needed a couple of seconds with no one looking. Betting that no one in his right mind wants to watch someone puke, I faked a heave as hard and loud as I could. Out of the corner of my eye, I saw the pilot and Benicio both turn to see what the noise was, and as I hoped, both immediately looked away. I couldn't see the guards, but I prayed their reactions had been similar.

No time to worry about that now. The seat Claire and I were on had no armrests and was little more than a bench with a low back. In the split second that Benicio and the pilot looked away, I grabbed as much of Claire's life vest as I could in my right hand, and pulled the lever on the door beside me with my left. In the same instant, I lunged left with every muscle in my body, crashing into the door, dragging Claire with me.

I was vaguely aware of the door slamming against my head, Claire screaming like a banshee, and rain that felt like bullets as we fell deeper and deeper into a black hole.

Chapter 19

Eye for an Eye

Seven Years Ago

After Natalie's death, Rafael Quinterro spent the next few weeks traveling under an assumed name and ID in Europe. One morning eating breakfast outside a cafe in Lyon, he heard someone behind him softly say his name as a question. He turned and saw Laurel Candler, an anesthesiologist from LA who had been a tenant and equity partner in a medical building.

"It *is* you," she said smiling. He rose and she gave him a big, comforting hug, then leaned back, with her hands on his arms. "How are you, Rafael? I have thought about you so much. I called, several times, months ago, but no one knew where to find you. I have been so worried about you."

"I am fine. Really," he said, with a little nod. "I just needed to get away. But what about you?" he asked, changing the subject. "How have you been? And what brings you to Lyon?"

"You won't believe it," she said coyly, offering her left hand. "I got married last week, and my husband Roger and I are on our honeymoon. We started in Paris and are now driving through the rest of the country. I want you to meet him."

Roger was shorter than Laurel, quite handsome, and he introduced himself with a big smile and a firm handshake. As Laurel was giving him a quick rundown on how she and Rafael knew each other, Rafael noticed the subtle recognition in Roger's face. He knew who Rafael was. Everyone in America knew who Rafael Quinterro was. He was that wealthy man whose wife was kidnapped and beheaded by terrorists. Rafael could tell Roger was now at a loss for what to say, but before Rafael could say something to fill the silence, Roger started. "I am so sorry about what happened." Rafael saw Laurel's fingers tighten around Roger's arm, but it was too late. "I can't imagine what you have been through. And I wouldn't blame you for what you felt toward that sorry bitch, Ann Chambers." By now, Laurel's nails were almost through the fabric of Roger's shirt, and he went quiet.

Rafael smiled at them both, acknowledging the awkwardness. "Laurel, it's OK. And Roger, thank you for your concern. It is still hard. But I get up every day and get dressed, and get by. Maybe someday it will get easier."

After a moment more of small talk and well wishes, they were off. Rafael returned to his meal, but only stared at it. He paid and left and went for a walk, hoping fresh air would help make him feel better. But it didn't. Roger's words kept coming back to him, over and over. "That sorry bitch, Ann Chambers."

Later that night, lying on his back in the dark, Rafael cried until tears ran down both sides of his face. He said to himself, *I thought I was better, but I'm not . . . maybe I never will be.* He lay there, hearing Roger's words again . . . "That sorry bitch, Ann Chambers." All she had to do was negotiate the release of one terrorist. But no. Politics were more important. And national security was the catchphrase excuse. Chambers could have done whatever she wanted. What did she care? She could say how sorry she was—that this is the only way to win the war against terrorism—sacrifices on the altar of freedom. Easy to say when it's not your loved one being sacrificed. *That sorry, political bitch.* A real leader would have done something. Ann Chambers was a pathetic, backslapping, backstabbing bureaucrat, and it was her fault Natalie was gone.

She's the one who should be dead.

Chapter 20

Crash of a Small Plane

At first, Rafael's anger came in small doses. Sadness channeled into blame didn't hurt any less, but it gave the terrible feelings a direction. Then slowly, something else began to change. Rafael had always been proud to be an American, but now he began to notice more criticism overseas aimed at the U.S., specifically at the president.

As *The Times* of London pointed out: "While the U.S. is obsessed with Islamic terrorists—and the fear that they'd stop the flow at the gas pump—America is rapidly losing its influence closer to home."

For years the Monroe Doctrine forbade European meddling in the Western Hemisphere, and countries in Latin and South America appreciated having the U.S. as their big brother. Many were small, uncivilized, and benefited by growing slowly, preserving their culture.

But the world's rapid growth, in communication, transportation, and especially its appetite for oil, changed everything. Many of the countries soon outgrew their Third World status.

At home, ironically, the relaxing of U.S. immigration policies began the Western Hemisphere's problem. Less stringent rules and relaxed enforcement brought millions of lower income Hispanics into the U.S. over a short period of time. Because Texas and Florida—states that had always had significant Hispanic populations—were affected the most, the initial increase went largely unnoticed. Even when the migration spread to other states, it caused no alarm. Migrant Hispanic workers had long been a part of the national landscape. They blended in well, took lower-income work, worked hard, paid rent, bought groceries, and stayed out of trouble. Any conflicts that made the news usually arose, not from the workers, but from unscrupulous employers and landlords who took advantage of the circumstances.

The situation didn't become serious until the Hispanics grew into a significant minority on America's demographic landscape. Without warning, there were too many immigrants, not enough jobs, and not enough money. Gradually the ubiquitous poverty that plagues suppressed minorities everywhere overtook the quiet, hardworking Hispanics, first showing up in their youth. Rebellion against authority, loud music, and a disdain for education all raised their ugly heads. The gangs, drugs and crime came next, and soon the conflict began to look like the '60s all over again.

The blacks had paved the way to civil rights, so the Hispanics would never have it that hard. They would not have to reinvent the wheel. They would, however, have to make it work for them.

Unrelated problems abroad created further resentment, both against and within the U.S. The wars in Iraq and Afghanistan had turned into more Vietnam quagmires, endless debacles with questionable causes and weak justifications. The most powerful nation on earth was caught up in civil wars in lands it didn't understand. Simple roadside bombs detonated with mobile phones killed Americans every week. Other nations withdrew their support and pulled further away from the United States. Several painted the U.S. as a bully that couldn't be trusted.

Closer to home, both Bolivia and Chile elected new anti-populist presidents. Peru followed with a far-left leader, and Mexico with another anti-American. All paled by comparison, however, to the new Venezuelan president who openly called the U.S. president a fascist on the order of Adolph Hitler.

As more of South America leaned left, U.S drug forces were sent home in droves, and major multinational corporations were pressured to sell their Latin and South American facilities to competitors headquartered in the southern continents—or risk losing them under less favorable means.

Rafael watched all of this going on. Soon he realized that he wished to go home, not to the land, but to his culture, his roots. Back to his people. Late in April, he made a phone call to the only man he knew he could trust with anything—even his own life.

"Yes," Benicio agreed with Rafael, "the situation in America is unforgivable. Why has not the United Farm Workers been more effective? They used to do good things for our people in America. What has happened to the great spirit of Cesar Chavez?"

"Unfortunately," Rafael replied, "Cesar Chavez had Robert Kennedy on his side. The UFW today has no powerful friends. The U.S. government has declared political war on virtually all Hispanic organizations, especially the UFW. The president tells America it is not a legal association of agricultural workers, but a mob of uneducated, illegal immigrants who demand what's not theirs. I'm afraid, my friend, we are past that. Past any political solution."

"I suspected that," Benicio replied, "I was only waiting to hear you say it."

The two old friends talked at length, discussing what, if anything, could be done. Both agreed that nothing was off the table.

"The difficulty," Benicio said, "is that the problem is a multi-headed monster. There will be no simple solutions. Any course of action will require the help of others."

When Benicio ended the call, he vowed to keep their conversation private, and to quietly look for others who may be willing to help.

Rafael Quinterro and his friend talked every week for a month. One day, Benicio said, "I have found several individuals who I think we should meet with. I'm sending my jet for you. Can you be ready by 10 a.m., your time, tomorrow? Good. I'll see you soon, my friend."

Twenty-four hours later, Rafael was standing in Benicio's private office high over the Rio de Janeiro harbor.

"Our meeting is scheduled two days from now—for privacy reasons—at my mountain house. I wanted you to have time to rest."

"I do not need rest, Benicio," Rafael replied smiling, but confused. "Our people need us. We should be meeting now."

"Yes, I agree, Rafael." Benicio's countenance turned more serious. "But there is another reason I wanted to see you, alone, first."

Rafael said nothing. He didn't like the change in his friend.

"I have someone," Benicio began, "that you should meet."

"Of course, Benicio, that's why I am here."

"No. This is not someone we will be meeting with later. This is different."

"What is it? Why are you talking like this?"

"I have someone here who has knowledge of something you need to hear."

"Is he here, now?" Rafael asked impatiently.

"Yes, my friend, he is right outside that door."

"Bring him in, please. And let me hear his story."

"Very well."

After Benicio's private secretary showed the little man in and left the room, Benicio looked at Rafael and said, "This is Elorri Munio." The man was old, and thin. He nervously nodded silently, first toward his host, then toward Rafael.

"Let's all sit down," Benicio said kindly, pointing the timid man toward the black leather sofa. The old man moved to the sofa and waited for Rafael and Benicio to take the two chairs across the low coffee table.

"Go ahead, Elorri," Benicio said calmly. "Don't be afraid. Tell Mr. Quinterro what you told me."

Rafael watched the old man shift nervously.

After a long moment, staring at the floor, Elorri began. "Years ago, when I was much younger, I worked in America, in Texas, on a big ranch, near the Rio Grande. The ranch was owned by a rich man. While I was working for him, he went to Washington and became a senator of your country." Elorri was now looking at Rafael.

When no one said anything, the old man continued. "The man had two sons. They were wild boys. Always in trouble. The man, he was always gone. To Washington, I think. And the mother, she drank a lot. She could do nothing with the boys. One day, I tell the man, his boys are much trouble. They doing drugs and going crazy. They going to hurt somebody someday. He tells me to work and mind my own business. So I do."

The old man quit again and stared at Benicio.

"Go ahead, Elorri," Benicio said, "it's OK."

The old man stared at Benicio, then Rafael, and continued. "The man had many rifles in his house. I never saw him shoot one, but he loved to show them to his friends, and tell them how he hunted all the time. One day when the man was gone to Washington, the boys take one of his fancy rifles. I see them getting in the truck. They have wild eyes and talking stupid. They drive fast away from the house, down toward the river."

The man stopped again, pained, as if he could never go on. This time, Benicio waited for him.

"Later that afternoon," Elorri said, "a little plane fell from the sky. Crashed, down near the river. There were three people inside. All three died. I hear someone say it was an American plane returning from Mexico."

He continued, "I was there. There was much confusion. But something else. There was much loud fighting. The deputies and others who came did much screaming and arguing with each other. They don't think I understand. But I do."

The old man stopped, stared at the floor, then looked up at Rafael. "I hear one man say there is bullet hole in the plane that caused the crash. The others say, *No!* There is no bullet hole! When some leave, I look when no one is seeing me. Yes. There is a small hole. In a side window. And much blood."

When the old man stopped again, Rafael turned to his friend and said, "I don't understand, Benicio. What does this have to do with us?"

"I'm afraid it's not us, my friend. It's you." Then turning back to the old man, "Show him, Elorri."

Elorri reached inside his shirt pocket and pulled out a yellowed, folded newspaper clipping. "I save this. I don't know why." He handed it toward Rafael.

Rafael took the folded paper, still confused. He unfolded it carefully and saw the faded photograph first. A small broken plane lay upside down on the hard ground. The caption said the plane crashed on land owned by U.S. Senator Grant Willoughby, Chairman of the Senate Committee on

Armed Services. The first line of the story stated that the crash had been determined to be the result of pilot error. The next paragraph identified the three people killed.

Rafael never made it to the pilot's name. The two passengers were his parents.

Two days later, Rafael and Benicio met with the men Benicio had assembled. They were all wealthy, powerful and motivated to bring an end to the American President's mistreatment of Hispanics. After heated discussions of possible solutions—most political in nature—the group agreed that more drastic measures were called for.

Rafael stood before them and said, "It is our responsibility to show the whole world that no country—not even the strongest country in the world—will be allowed to get away with the personal, cultural and political abuse of honest, hard-working Hispanic men and women. We must prove our commitment to our people everywhere by punishing America in the most extreme and convincing way possible. We must remove the evil president from power, through whatever means necessary . . ."

He left that last sentence hanging. They knew what he meant.

By the end of the meeting, the group had decided that Rafael, by the nature of his personal involvement and clandestine existence, would pursue the needed resources; Benicio would provide ships and private aircraft for transportation, and be Quinterro's number two; and others present would provide the funding.

After the others left, Benicio said to Rafael. "This is serious business, my friend. If something goes wrong, the others in our group will be invisible. But you, Rafael, will be on the front line, recruiting the people and obtaining equipment. You will have nowhere to hide. Are you sure about this?"

Quinterro looked at his friend. "Benicio, U.S. President Ann Chambers was directly responsible for my wife's murder. She could have saved her, but . . ." He could not go on.

"I know, my friend," Benicio whispered, remembering the horror of Quinterro's wife's beheading.

"And two days ago, standing here in your office," Rafael said, "I learned that the drunken sons of another high-ranking American politician were responsible for my parents' death. And *he*—their father, the senator—was responsible for the cover-up. Do you know how many times I have wondered about the crash? Did my parents have time to suffer, to cry, to hold each other, to worry about me, their five-year-old son?

"And now, I learn that it was worse than I ever imagined.

"I hear their cries, Benicio," he continued, "like I still hear Natalie crying out for me. And you ask me if I am sure about going through with this? What do you think?"

Benicio replied, "I understand, and I am with you one hundred percent."

Chapter 21

The President's Problem

Last October

President Ann Roberts Chambers pitched the report across the French writing table she used for a desk. Her Chief of Staff Richard Culligan reached for it but missed, and it cascaded over the edge onto the Oval Office carpet. Culligan hesitated, stooped and retrieved the stapled sheets, hiding his expression. He half-heartedly straightened the pages as White House Press Secretary Maria Esperanza stood beside him, silently waiting.

As usual, White House employees had wished everyone they met a good morning. But it was not. The president's poll numbers had tanked again.

"Dammit, Dick, why didn't any of you people see this coming?" she said. "It didn't start yesterday." She turned toward the thick windows behind her and stood up, rolling her chair away with the back of her knee.

Her three-inch heels made her seem taller than she was, and the dark Armani suit made her appear more confident than she felt.

With the president facing away, Culligan stole a glance at Esperanza, but said nothing. They had been here before. The White House Chief of Staff knew there was nothing he could say. He pretended the question was rhetorical and waited. The first female President of the United States of America stared across the Washington skyline beyond the bullet-proof windows.

To break the silence, Press Secretary Maria Esperanza said, "Madame President, if I may . . ."

"Oh what, Maria?" said the president, spinning back around, "you of all people should be able to help. It's your people who want me hanged from the portico."

Esperanza lowered her head. She should have expected that. She nodded and said nothing.

It was true, Esperanza thought. *I should be more help to the president.*

White House Press Secretary Maria Esperanza desperately wanted to make the president—and her own people—proud of her. More than that, she wanted her people to be proud of themselves again.

But instead, Maria Esperanza felt trapped in the worst no-win situation of her life. Her boss, the President of the United States, who had so deftly handled the nation's battle against Islamic terrorists, was failing miserably dealing with the issue of illegal immigrants flooding into the country from the south.

The problem that began under the previous administration had grown worse, and the melting pot that was America had finally boiled over. The rapidly spreading illegal Hispanic population had outgrown America's support systems, court systems and patience. And civil rights unrest worse than that of the '60s overflowed the barrios and ran into the streets of Middle America. Violence became the norm on the nightly news.

The country's leaders were worried. The Hispanics in America were demanding more of everything, and they wanted it now. Privileges that were once considered temporary political concessions had become permanent, God-given rights. The Hispanics considered themselves Americans now. And there was no going back. Not figuratively, not literally. The Hispanic multitudes were here to stay. And they demanded—for themselves and their descendants—the same rights and privileges enjoyed by every other generation of Americans.

But the white majority resented it. The swelling, illegal ranks of the Hispanics were too much.

The demands of the quiet ones sent the cost of social services spiraling out of control. And gang violence erupting in cities across America brought curfews where the word had never been heard before.

Even the African Americans stood up against the Hispanic masses. Instead of showing support for brothers and sisters of a fellow minority, they feared losing their hard-fought ground to a larger, better-organized group.

Vice President Paul Collins told Chambers months ago, "I have been in Washington long enough to know that the office of vice president is nothing. I have only one job, and that is to make you—the president—look good. I know that," he said, "and I'm onboard with it."

The two met every morning, and true to his word, Collins minimized his role in the administration, concentrating instead on helping the president at every turn. As a long-term Washington insider, he had crucial insight into the workings of the complex machinery of the federal government, and he never failed to provide valuable advice. His help enhanced her standing with congress and the public, and as he promised, with no obvious benefits to himself. She soon learned to trust his judgment, even when his recommendations contradicted others. He always kept his promise and made her look good.

Collins walked into one of their morning meetings and said, "I've been mulling over this Hispanic mess. Here's what I think."

For the next hour, he explained his proposal. "The only good president is a strong president," he said. "Look at recent history. Jimmy Carter failed by trying to be a nice guy. Before him, Lyndon Johnson tried splitting the difference—coddling the public with his Great Society and manhandling the military in Vietnam. *He* failed so miserably, he didn't even run for a second term.

"Compare those two," Collins continued, "with Harry Truman or Ronald Reagan. Truman was bold enough to drop atomic bombs on Japan, ending World War II, *and* keeping the Russians at bay for years.

"Under Reagan, when the nation's air traffic controllers threatened to strike—endangering thousands of lives and crippling the country's air transportation—he called their bluff and fired them the moment they walked off the job, without a hitch.

"And don't forget," Collins continued, "Reagan was bold enough to use a pure fabrication to bluff the Soviet Union into competing with our nonexistent Star Wars Missile Defense System. The result was a bankrupt USSR and the end of the Cold War.

"The only way, Madame President, to attack this Hispanic Crisis," Collins said, "is head-on. Not only does the situation demand it, but as America's first female president, it is your duty to set an example—a precedent—and prove to your country, and the world, that you are as strong as any man who ever held this office."

The president liked what she heard. Bold presidents were heroes. If Truman can drop atomic bombs, and Reagan can end the Cold War, she thought, I can handle this.

Later that week, President Ann Roberts Chambers made the announcement that sent shockwaves rippling through the White House Press Room, the Capital, and the United States of America.

"This administration—and this country," she said, "will not be pushed around anymore by illegal aliens. American citizens, their finances, and their wellbeing have suffered enough. And now, this administration is going to fight back."

And thus, at her vice president's urging, President Ann Roberts Chambers proudly announced she was choosing the Hispanic Crisis for her proving ground.

Faster than a soundbite, the compassion she promised in her campaign was gone. Even politics-as-usual were gone. It was now all about one thing. Power. She had it and intended to use it, to put an end to this "Hispanic Uprising."

Not surprisingly, the initial reaction—from the media and the Hispanic community—was a disaster. Demands, protests and riots erupted nationwide.

"Don't worry," Collins said, "after your bold announcement, it has to get worse before it gets better. Stay the course. You are doing the right thing."

Over the next several days, following her vice president's suggestions, she issued Executive Orders specifically crafted to give the White House authority over federal, state and local law enforcement. She declared

Martial Law in Florida, Texas, Arizona and California, and mobilized National Guard troops to take action—as aggressive as necessary—to maintain order, protect the peace, and stand guard over critical infrastructure.

In spite of the initial negative reactions, the new president liked the way it felt to take bold steps. She could weather the criticism and continue the fight, she told herself, because she knew she was doing the right thing.

And once her aggressive attitude was unleashed, subsequent decisions became easier. In her continued bidding for a prominent place in American history, Chambers went on to study the powers of her office. Slowly at first, then more aggressively, she pushed at the boundaries, demanding her staff to find Executive Actions she could take without approval from the Legislative or Judicial Branches.

When well-meaning advisors questioned some of her chosen battles, she grew impatient. When relationships with the other branches of the government started deteriorating, instead of remembering the D.C. adage that to get along, you have to go along, she turned insensitive and arrogant, and refused to negotiate, regardless of importance or ramifications. Behind closed doors, her most loyal and respected advisors were worried. How long could they keep this ill-driven administration from derailing?

Unfortunately, the president's plan to rule by aggression ruptured faster than a botched Formula One start. Soon Washington, D.C. was littered with casualties: failed presidential appointments who either withdrew or were defeated in the Senate; resignations of key cabinet members and top aides; and formal condemnations from the United Nations and the leaders of nearly every Spanish-speaking nation in the world.

Except for a few right-leaning outlets, the worldwide media crucified the new president. The editorial cartoonists blasted President Ann Roberts Chambers with her initials—ARC. In papers, magazines and websites around the world, she was caricatured as the new Joan of Arc, burning at the stake of the Washington Monument.

Her Oval Office had become a cold castle keep where the president of the most powerful nation on Earth hid from the dangerous world outside.

And her own vice president was nowhere to be found, always out of the country on urgent business.

The President plopped into her leather chair. She needed a way out of this disaster. But no white knight was going to charge across the White House lawn and rescue her from her troubles. She was going to have to do this by herself. *Think, dammit,* she told herself.

But nothing came to her. The more she dwelled on the problem, the worse it seemed. Giving in now would make her look like a coward and the biggest loser to ever sit in the Oval Office. No. Giving in was not an option.

She turned and looked across the Washington skyline. I'll figure this out, she told herself. Even if it kills me.

Chapter 22

Sink or Swim

Last Friday

I let go of my death grip on Claire's lifevest as we cleared the helicopter door. Through black rain and howling wind, I heard her screaming all the way down. I hit water with a wrenching jolt, plunging deep into the silence before my auto-inflate lifevest jerked me back to the storm on the surface.

"Claire!" I screamed before breathing.

She coughed behind me and I called again, spinning, grasping in the dark.

The chopper's turbine was fading in the distance when I heard her again. I reached and pulled her to me.

"You son of a bitch!" she screamed, swinging at me with both hands, "you could have killed me!"

I tried to calm her, with no luck, and finally grabbed a strap on her lifevest and jerked her close. "Shut up, dammit! We're OK."

A couple more coughs, then she said, "Where are we? Won't they come back?"

"No, they're low on gas. They're headed for land. And we are too."

At the top of the next swell, I pointed and said, "There."

"What?"

"Land. Let's go."

"What land?"

"Who cares, dammit. Do you want to stay out here?"

"Can we make it?"

"Not if we stay here and keep talking." I couldn't see her expression, but the silence said she didn't like that answer. "Come on," I added, trying to sound kinder, "I'll help you."

We rode a wave up and found the lights again and started in that direction. I hoped we wouldn't be swimming against the current. We'd know soon enough and have to change plans if we were. I didn't know what the new plan would be and didn't like thinking about it. "Come on," I said again, encouragingly, "we can make it."

We struggled along for several minutes before Claire stopped and said, "Wait! I hear 'em. They are coming back!"

"No, wait, listen." I said, "that's a boat." From nowhere a spotlight beam swept the sea, passing overhead twice before locking on.

I remember thinking this is either the best or the worst luck I've ever had.

"Who is it?" Claire asked.

Before I could answer, an amplified voice tore through the roar of the storm. "United States Coast Guard. Raise your hands out of the water, now."

Seconds later the boat was on us. In the shadows behind the spotlight I saw men with automatic weapons, their barrels following us in the swells. Over the gurgle of idling engines, I heard two splashes. Seconds later, divers surfaced behind us, holding us still with one hand and frisking us with the other. One of the divers shouted to the boat that we were clean, then told us, "Do exactly as you are told. Understand?"

Moments later Claire and I were hoisted onboard, frisked again more thoroughly, then ushered through a waterproof door. Inside, men in uniforms tossed us towels, said sit, and then stared at us. The boat turned in the water and got underway.

When another officer entered, one of the men told him that we had carried no weapons, no IDs, no money, no jewelry, nothing, and that we were found near where their radar had shown something dropped from the helicopter. The new officer turned to us and said, "Talk fast, folks, starting with who you are."

Claire and I looked at each other, and then gave him our names, addresses and a couple of other details answering his questions.

Before he continued, I asked, "Where are you taking us?"

"To the marina," he answered curtly. "After that, you're somebody else's problem."

An hour later we were in a Coast Guard office at the Golden Isles Marina, warm, dry and wearing new blue Coast Guard jumpsuits.

I asked to use a phone and was told no.

"I thought we could make a phone call . . ."

"Yes sir," one of the Coast Guard men replied. "If you are arrested. You haven't been arrested yet."

Claire stood up and said to the ranking Coast Guard officer, "Sir. We . . ." She glanced at me, then back to him, correcting herself, "*I* work for a company that does contract work—frequently highly classified—for the federal government. You can verify my clearance. I have information regarding an urgent Homeland Security issue."

Every head in the room spun toward her.

"Let me make a call now and I can help. If you refuse, the results could be catastrophic, and I'll have no choice but to let officials know I offered help and you refused."

All the heads spun back toward the Coast Guard officer. Except mine. I was still staring at Claire. She glanced at me expressionless, then looked back at our host.

He stared at Claire and said, "What do you want?"

"A phone call. You can listen. No one else."

The Coast Guard officer waited a long second, then said, "Come with me."

I stood up too, but sat down slowly when two M-16s turned my way.

Claire and the Coast Guard officer left the room. Claire never looked back.

Ten minutes later she and the Coast Guard officer returned. He said to one of his men, "Take them to FLETC. Someone will meet you there." I knew exactly what FLETC was. Claire hadn't looked at me yet, but I could tell she didn't need me to explain FLETC to her. She knew about Brunswick's Federal Law Enforcement Training Center.

I was beginning to get the idea that my girlfriend was not exactly who I thought she was.

Chapter 23

Federal Bureau of Investigation

The 20-minute drive to the Brunswick FLETC campus took ten. The Coast Guard sedan had blue lights on top and the driver used them.

On the way, I asked my sweet, increasingly mysterious girlfriend what the hell was going on. She smiled, apologized and said she would tell me soon. She patted my leg, and I tried not to take it like it felt.

A guard at FLETC's front gate was expecting us, and the gate arm was on the way up as we passed the brick guardhouse and a stop sign three times the normal size.

We wound our way around what looked like a dull college campus until stopping in front of a nondescript building. Two rifle-toting guards from the front door walked out to greet us. "This way, please."

Inside, we turned down several bland government corridors before entering a conference room much too big for the occasion. Three men in suits were standing behind a long wooden conference table waiting on us. One of them dismissed the two guards who ushered us in, then said to us, "Thanks for your call, Ms. Markham. It's been a while. And Mr. Hood, I presume," he added glancing my way.

The fact that he knew Claire was another surprise.

"I'm Jack Blake, Special Agent with the FBI, and these two gentlemen are with me," he said to me. Then, back to Claire, "We need to talk, but first, I have no information about Mr. Hood's security clearance."

Claire said, "I'll take responsibility."

Blake didn't like that much, but before he spoke, Claire added, "He's the reason we know everything we do. And we need his help."

"Very well, for now," Blake said. "First, I want everything he knows. Then I'll decide what, if anything, we can share with him."

For the next few minutes, Blake recorded the meeting while Claire recounted the story of the last few days in the order of events. The incident in the cemetery; the break-in at her Atlanta home; Police Chief Ryan Elliott's apparent stroke; Doctor Brad Wheeler's involvement; then our wreck on the causeway and subsequent kidnapping. She was answering their questions about the big boat and its captain, when the door behind us opened and we were joined by a guard accompanying another guest. Claire kept talking to Blake as I turned to look.

Blake interrupted Claire. "Ms. Markham, I think you know Doctor Wheeler." She turned and nodded, and said, "Yes, we've met."

Wheeler nodded without smiling, glanced my way, and sat down.

Before Blake let Claire continue, he asked Wheeler if there had been any luck finding Strom.

Whoever that was.

When Wheeler said no, Claire's lips tightened ever so slightly.

Who the hell's Strom?

Agent Blake then turned to one of the other men and told him to check with Washington for any word on Strom, then added to us, "If we can get our hands on him, I'll feel a lot better."

For the next twenty minutes, I heard more about the Janus Project, including what Taz had found. It apparently began as a secret defensive study requested by the Secret Service to better protect the president. Somewhere along the way, it went deep underground and became a top-secret CIA operation to evaluate assassination options that could be carried out against terrorist leaders, or other serious enemies of the good old U.S. of A. I never heard what happened to the Secret Service part of the study, but the CIA's Janus Project was apparently killed when a senate subcommittee got too nosey. A couple of years—and several terrorists crises later—the Janus Project was resurrected, behind tightly closed doors. And with one slight change. All the original participants were located, except one. Doctor Hector Strom.

The good doctor had vanished. Police and security agencies in all fifty states and several countries around the world were looking for him but couldn't find a trace.

"If we can't find him," Blake said to Wheeler, "what do you think that means?"

"Well," Wheeler said, "I am assuming the FBI cleared him originally, so there must have been no problems then. And he apparently passed the interim security checks the agency did, so maybe he's not hiding. Maybe you just can't find him."

When no one said anything, he continued, "On the other hand, if he's still alive, and disappeared on purpose—if that's the case, then—" Wheeler stopped, thinking.

"Then what?" Blake asked pointedly.

"Well—if I follow your line of thinking—if Strom's hiding somewhere, and, for some unknown reason, working on the same things we were working on during the original Janus Project—then, I guess what you need to know is that he was extraordinarily brilliant, and involved in every aspect of the work. In fact, besides me, he was the only one who knew everything we were working on.

"Of course," Wheeler continued, "all the possibilities we considered back then had significant obstacles. The old saying is, 'Particle beam weapons are weapons of the future, and always will be.' Those weapons we were evaluating didn't exist. And still don't.

"I mean," Wheeler added, "as far as we know."

I sat there impatiently for another ten minutes, while the Feds grilled Wheeler on Janus, how far the project had progressed, and what he thought Strom might be capable of.

No matter how they asked the question, Wheeler's replies were the same. Even if Strom had been working on the same ideas, if he was alone, with no funding, there's no way he'd produce a new technology capable of long-distance assassination. There were too many major obstacles. All the options they looked at were, in Wheeler's terms, Star Wars dreams.

That seemed to make everyone in the room feel better. I asked Blake why he was so concerned.

"Because," Blake said, as if he was answering a fool, "The President of the United States of America will be here tomorrow."

"What?" Claire and I said simultaneously. "Where?"

"That's our concern, not yours. The trip is Top Secret because the president wants it that way."

Blake seemed to relax some, apparently because of Wheeler saying Strom's disappearance was nothing to worry about. I could tell, however, by the way Claire was fidgeting, she wasn't happy. She nudged my foot with hers and said to Blake, "I need to make a call."

Blake nodded an OK and handed her an extra cell phone from his case.

"It's a little warm in here," Claire said casually. "OK if I step outside?"

Claire was already pressing numbers on the phone, and I said, "Good idea. I'll go with you."

Blake told one of his agents to stay with us . . . "in case they need anything," he said. *Right.*

Claire pressed numbers while we walked and shushed me twice on the way to the door. By the time we were outside, she had Taz, and for the next few minutes I listened to her tell Taz everything I heard inside. The FBI guy was watching, but not close enough to hear. Hell, it was an FBI phone. I knew damn well somebody was listening.

I paced, feeling better in the cool, night air while Claire told Taz that Wheeler said there was nothing to worry about. Then Claire abruptly stopped talking. The look on her face said *uh-oh.*

When she ended the call, she stared at the phone, then looked at me. "Wheeler's lying."

"What?" I asked.

"Taz says Wheeler's lying. She's sure of it."

"Oh, come on. There's no way she can know more about the Janus Project than Wheeler."

"That's not what I said!" she snapped back at me in a whisper. "She said, he's lying!"

"Why would he do that?"

"I don't know, but she's sure of it. She has proof. Maybe they'll let us go to *Rivianna* and get cleaned up."

I agreed we needed to get out of there, but I had a different destination in mind.

"Come on," I said.

Seeing as how Blake knew Claire and understood her involvement, he was OK letting us take a FLETC car, supposedly back to *Riviana* to get cleaned up and change clothes.

A few minutes later we were sharing the vinyl of a government sedan's front bench seat. I drove. Claire talked.

She said Taz had been frantic since we disappeared on Wednesday. Then added, "Gosh, was it two days ago?"

I nodded, and said, yes, adding that I, too, had been a little worried since I disappeared two days ago. "Now will you please tell me what's going on? And how the hell do you know Blake?"

"OK," she replied calmly, "I'll tell you everything. But first, I want to tell you what Taz said about Wheeler, because we need to know why he's lying."

"Go ahead," I said, making a left turn onto the F.J. Torras Causeway through a yellow light turning red. It was still dark, but a thin glow was visible ahead on the eastern horizon.

"When Taz couldn't reach us," Claire began, "she didn't know what else to do. She hasn't left the office since Wednesday morning. She's been living on coffee and vending machine food and sleeping on the floor in my office after hours. All she could think to do was to keep digging into Wheeler and the Janus Project. Not surprisingly, she hit brick walls everywhere. She expected to. That meant she had to forget regular channels and try backdoors, passwords, hidden networks, etc."

"Hacking," I clarified.

"*Anyway*," she continued, with a sideways glance, "she eventually got into Wheeler's stuff, and found a copy of a report saying, in science-speak, that none of the trials turned up anything positive enough to pursue."

"That's what Wheeler just said!" I replied, more irritably than intended.

"Let me finish," she snapped.

"Sorry." We were both tired.

"Taz could tell that the copy of the report she was looking at, was just that. A *copy*. No, I don't know how she could tell, but she could. So, she kept searching to see if she could find the original, digital version Wheeler wrote. When she eventually did find it, it said something else."

"What?"

"The original document on his hard drive said that the proton beam device looked like the best possible avenue to pursue—that there were still obstacles to overcome, but it was his opinion that a proton beam weapon for assassinations was feasible. But, after he wrote that, he made another copy of the document, deleted the part that said a proton beam weapon was possible, and said instead, that the Janus Project had not come up with anything promising."

While I was thinking about that, she said, "There's more. Then Taz scoured every bit of Wheeler's computer, and the entire lab network, but couldn't find anything except where other stuff had recently been moved or erased or both. She was at a dead-end, and she still couldn't find us, and she was going crazy. So, like they say, when you've tried everything that's possible, time to try the impossible. She figured somewhere in the lab Wheeler had a laptop computer. Probably one with wireless capabilities, whether or not he used them. Sometimes, for security reasons, people don't use wireless networks, even if they're available, because of the slight chance that someone on the outside could pick up a signal and latch on."

"OK. . ." I said, more listening than understanding.

"So Taz figured if the laptop was there, and had wireless capabilities, she'd find it."

"Suppose it was turned off?" I said. *And I used to be the optimist.*

"It *was* turned off," she shot back, "but it was plugged in and charging, and Taz knew how to ping its wireless antenna, wake up its internal network, and then turn on the laptop itself."

"No way."

"Yes. Don't ask me how."

"I don't want to know."

"Anyway, once she was in the laptop, she found more. A lot more. She found actual plans and specifications for a proposed proton beam weapon. The footnotes disclaimed the actual probability of the weapon's ability to be produced and used, but did outline a few of the obstacles that would need to be addressed. And more importantly, it gave an estimate for the time it would require to overcome those obstacles."

"Well?"

"Three years. Almost exactly the time since Strom disappeared when the original Janus Project was disbanded."

Chapter 24

The Plan

Daylight pierced Sea Island's oak canopy as we turned into the Admiral's driveway. I had called from the causeway and he was waiting at the door.

I climbed out of the FLETC car and half-saluted. Mack shook his head. "You look like shit," he said. "Oops, sorry Miss Claire."

"Forget it, Admiral," she said, "I do too."

"What are you two birds doing in a FLETC vehicle and Coast Guard jumpsuits?"

"Mack, we need to talk."

"I figured *that*," he said. "Come in. Bess is fixing breakfast."

As Claire and I followed Mack down the hall to the kitchen, he said over his shoulder, "I assume this has to do with our talk about problems in bunches."

Bess interrupted from the kitchen: "Mack, I think you better see this."

He walked faster. Claire and I froze, then dropped into the dark living room and fast-crawled to a curtained window facing the front yard. A swarm of unmarked vehicles with no lights quietly roll to a stop. "What the . . ." I never got the rest out. Car doors flew open and men with black vests and guns swarmed toward the FLETC car and house.

"Get down!" Mack shouted from the kitchen. We already were.

Claire faced the hallway and said loud and fast, "Admiral, you can't let them take us!"

A pause, then, "OK. Stay down."

Seconds later, the hall light went off and Mack was at the living room entrance. "You two come with me."

We followed him across the hall and into a dark study with a corner fireplace and high windows. "Stay low and near the fireplace wall." We did. The doorbell rang.

Mack cast a wary eye at us, then walked to the front door.

We heard him unbolt and open the door, and say, "I am Admiral Mack McCallan, former Commandant of the United States Coast Guard. You better have a damn good reason for storming my home!"

I heard somebody ask about me, and Mack said, "Yeah, he's a friend of mine. Dropped the car here—with my permission—he'll be back later. Why?"

Next came the voice of FBI Special Agent Blake. He and Mack spoke quietly, the conversation ended, and the front door closed and locked.

When Mack came back to the den, he left the lights off and reached into a drawer. In one slick motion, he chambered a round into a black pistol and pointed it at the floor directly in front of us.

"What I just did," he began, "goes against everything I have done in my career." Then added, "This better be good."

"Why did you do it?" I asked.

"Because I don't know him. And I do know you. Now, talk fast before I change my mind."

Claire was saying, "We'll tell you everything . . ." when I interrupted.

"What did Blake say?"

"Blake said you're both wanted by the FBI in connection with a plot to assassinate the president."

"That's ridiculous," I said, turning to see an expressionless Claire.

Mack wanted an answer. "Why does the FBI want you?"

I was wondering where to start when Claire began.

"Admiral. Remember the other night, during our talk about problems in bunches, when I said my assistant at the foundation, Taz—*at my request*—was looking online for Wheeler's missing publications?"

Mack said, "I do."

"Well, Taz is very good at finding things that some people don't want found. And the deeper she dug, the stranger the things she found. The bottom line is that the clues eventually led to something called the Janus Project, a Top Secret CIA program to develop silent weapons of assassination. And when the Feds realized someone was hacking into their files, and the evidence pointed to Taz, they connected the dots and found me."

Mack said, "Blake's accusation is a lot worse than that."

"That's because a man named Hector Strom mysteriously disappeared three years ago."

"What does he have to do with this?" Mack was getting impatient.

"Strom was one of the principal scientists working on the secret weapon, and although the device wasn't perfected when the Janus Project was abruptly canceled, the team was making progress. And Strom was a big part of that.

"What does that have to do with you?"

"I hired Hector Strom."

When Mack didn't say anything, Claire explained, "*Not* for the Janus Project. For some unclassified work before that. But *when* I hired him may be a moot point to the FBI now.

"So," she summed up, "I hired Strom. I'm responsible for hacking Janus Project files. I'm on St. Simons. And the president will be here soon. With all of that, I guess Blake doesn't want me—or Carson—running around loose this weekend."

Mack stared at Claire.

After a moment, Mack said, "I need to know more."

For the next hour, we told Mack everything, including what we hadn't told Blake at FLETC—that Wheeler was lying about the Janus Project never developing any weapons of assassination.

He thought about everything we told him, then nodded and said, "Got it. And I think you're right. Blake's just covering his ass.

"Now," Mack said, changing the subject, "if the president's in danger, she's going to need help. And so are you. Wait here."

Claire stood up with her phone, half-smiled at me and said, "I've got to get Taz," and went back into the hall.

Mack reappeared, handed me two mobile phones, and said, "The smaller one is a conventional cell phone, but no ID or GPS. The larger one works the same, plus it scrambles the conversation between that phone and mine."

I looked up from the two phones, and he added, "I'm retired, but I still have brains and balls. There's a small group of us here, and that's all you need to know."

He said he knew through back channels about the president's visit but couldn't say anything. Obviously he had no clue about our involvement. And like us, he was concerned that the FBI and Secret Service weren't taking Strom's disappearance seriously. And now that *he* knew Wheeler lied about the Janus Project's success, he was worried.

"I'll be on *Biscayne*," he said. "I still have all my Coast Guard radios, and my comm account and password are still good—retirement favors from the Joint Chiefs. If something happens, I'll hear it. And if you learn anything, you tell me at once. Got it?"

"Got it."

"Mack," I said, stopping him before he continued, "Claire and I can't stay here. They'll be back with a warrant. You know that. And we sure as hell can't go to *Rivianna*. If we're going to do any good, we need a place to hide, and time to see what else Taz can come up with."

Mack knew what I meant and didn't like it much. He left the room. When he came back, he handed me a floating key chain. "I was hoping you had forgotten my son's boat is here. I'm supposed to put a new radio in it, not get it shot up."

"You know this is the right thing to do."

He nodded without actually agreeing, then said, "It's at a friend's dock on Jones Creek. He's going to install the new radio for me. The boat is ugly as hell, an embarrassing, bright-red, go-fast that I wouldn't be caught dead in. My son bought it at a government auction," he said, then added as an unpleasant afterthought, "it was probably a damn drug runner.

"But," he continued, "it's a jet-drive and sits low in the water, only drawing about a foot sitting still, and half that planed off. And in addition to being able to go where most prop boats can't, the hideous son of a bitch has three 400-horsepower waterjet engines. On a short course, it can outrun and outmaneuver just about anything. The straightaways are where big outboards with highspeed props can catch you. Remember that."

"Thanks, Mack. I'll try to return it in one piece." I had no idea how hard that was going to be.

Claire walked back into the room, heard the tail end of the conversation and said, "What?"

Mack went back to the kitchen, and I explained to Claire. "We're borrowing his son's boat. These islands have a lot more water than roads, and with all the backwater tributaries, we'll have good places to hide, especially at night. Plus, with marine radios and the secure phones Mack just gave me, we should be able to hear most of what's going on. And if Taz finds out more, we'll be able to tell Mack and the Feds immediately."

Her slow nod said, *I understand*—not, *I like this idea a lot*.

When Mack returned, he explained that he'd drive us to his son's boat on Jones Creek in his new two-seat Mercedes. More specifically, in the *trunk* of his new two-seat Mercedes. "I'll take that silly-ass, little spare out," he said, "and anything else I can, but it will still be tight as hell. But the drive up Frederica Road won't take long, and with the Feds looking for you, I don't know any other way."

I thought about claustrophobia, and wanted to say, *What about Bess's minivan?* but didn't.

"Here's what we're going to do," Mack continued, "First, you two stay here, keep out of sight, and keep trying to reach Taz to see what else you can learn. Get cleaned up—you'll feel better—and then get some shut-eye if you can. You gotta be tired.

"I've called my buddy on Jones Creek and told him we're going to take the boat out. He doesn't ask questions. While you two are getting cleaned up and resting, I'm going to take *Biscayne* up there so I can use her later to tow the speedboat out of Jones Creek. That thing's so loud, if we crank her up at his dock, a nosey neighbor might call the law. And we don't need that.

"One more thing," Mack said. "My buddy Fish Williams drives that big, blue, ugly-ass, double-hull, gambling boat, the *Lady Luck*. He was my number two in the Coast Guard, and he'll do whatever I ask. He's bringing his boat back from a private party up at Savannah, and the Secret Service is going to let him cruise back to just outside the three-mile radius around the president, right offshore at Gould's Inlet. He'll have to wait there until they say he can proceed to his dock. I'll tell Fish you may be calling. Here are his numbers." He handed me a folded note, and added, "Don't lose this."

I thought I heard the Mission Impossible theme song in the background, but damn if I was going to mention that.

Chapter 25

Claire's Secret

After getting our instructions, Claire and I went to one of Mack's back bedrooms where Bess had already pulled the curtains. Claire tried Taz again. No luck. And I wanted to know how Ryan was, but knew that wouldn't happen until this was over.

I turned to Claire. "In the Coast Guard car to FLETC, you said you'd tell me later what's going on."

No reply.

"There are bad guys after me, and good guys after me, and I don't know why. But I think you do."

Claire barely smiled, let out a where-do-I-begin sigh, and pulled her dark hair behind one ear. Finally, "OK." Another hesitation. She sat back against the upholstered headboard and began. "You remember my first job after college was with the State Department, right?"

I nodded.

"They recruited at Auburn, so no big deal. I started as an intern, worked with smart people, and living in D.C. was cool."

I waited.

"Soon I got promoted and worked on bigger projects. I liked the work, and life was good. Then one day my boss, whom I seldom saw, came into my office and closed the door. After one second of small talk, he told me I had scored high on aptitude tests during my employment interviews. Nobody ever said anything about those, so I just assumed I had done OK."

Claire shifted around, put a pillow behind her and continued. "Anyway, he said I had done well in two areas where they don't usually see much correlation—science and finance. He said those test scores—and my first few months of work—indicated that I was ready to assume more responsibility. And . . . in areas involving higher security. I remember he stressed that part, as if to see my reaction. I had no idea what that meant. I guess I was flattered, and hoped I would get a raise. But I wasn't prepared for what he said next."

Claire was hesitant about continuing. I reached out, rubbed her leg, and waited.

"Then, what he said really confused me." She hesitated again. "He wanted me to resign. For personal reasons, he said. And go find a job in the private sector. Preferably away from D.C. Anything, he said. Anywhere. Just nothing involving the government. Well, I guess I was about as confused then as you are now."

I agreed with a nod.

"He said not to worry if my new job didn't pay well because, from time to time, I would receive money to help with expenses. It would be cash, so I would be expected to use it like cash, meaning not report it or deposit it.

"Then," she continued, "he said after a few months someone would contact me and tell me where I could apply for a new job. It would be a good position in a respected part of the private sector, and one where I could use my specific skills and interests, and make good money. When I asked about the legality of taking the cash, he said the interim job was the important thing—inserting a gap between the State Department and the employment that would come later—and the cash was an unspoken, but approved, expense to facilitate the interim job."

"And?" I asked, when it appeared she had stopped again.

"Well, it didn't sound like I had much choice, so I quit. I used to think I wanted to be a chef, so I got an intern job at a classy cooking school I knew about in Auburn. The money wasn't great, but, as promised, about every forty-five days, I got one of those big credit card application envelopes in the mail. Only mine had twenty hundred-dollar bills inside."

"Nice," I said.

"Yes," she agreed. "Then one day in the parking lot at work, a lady drove up and handed me a small envelope, saying I had dropped it. I took it before realizing it wasn't familiar, but she drove off before I could stop her. So I opened it and the only thing inside was the name and address of the Grace Foundation in Atlanta."

I nodded, showing I knew where she worked. She hesitated, tightening her lips. "OK, what I have told you so far is lower-level stuff. I would probably just be fired for saying it. What I have to say next is deeper. Much worse results if somebody finds out. Prosecution. Incarceration." She hesitated to be sure I was with her. "Got it?"

I nodded. Agreeing, definitely not understanding.

"First, you need to know my work at the foundation required me to have a security clearance. That was one reason for the interim job. It took the FBI six months to process it. Apparently, that's not unusual."

I didn't see that coming. "So, I've been sleeping with a spy?"

"No. Let me finish."

"What kind of security clearance?"

"It doesn't matter."

"What level?" I asked, showing I knew something about security.

She exhaled. "Top Secret."

"Holy shit."

"Yeah."

"So, the Grace Foundation is a bunch of spies?"

"No! If you'll let me finish . . ."

I said, "OK," secretly thinking how sexy it was to be sleeping with a spy.

She continued, "Now, something has gone wrong. And, *one*—I don't understand how, but I may have been involved."

"Holy shit again."

"Yes. And, *two*—I need your help. And you can never tell anyone I have shared this with you. Deal?"

"Deal."

She waited.

"I *promise*."

She pushed herself up against the pillow behind her, and continued, "OK. I researched the Grace Foundation and saw that it funded a lot of sophisticated research. That seemed to fit well with the finance and science test scores my State Department boss mentioned. So, I figured, the foundation must be the right place."

She shrugged, and added, "And after taking somebody's cash for months, I didn't think I had much choice. So I submitted preliminary bio information online to express my interest in employment, and they invited me to Atlanta for interviews, tests, etc. Three trips total. The whole time, nobody said anything about something going on beneath the surface. I didn't mention it.

"Finally they made me an offer—a good job with a nice title and a decent salary. I took it and moved to Atlanta. Weeks passed. Then one day, I realized the 100-dollar bills in the mail had stopped. That's when I knew I was where somebody wanted me."

"Makes sense," I said.

"A few weeks later, my department head at the foundation asked me to meet her in the boardroom. She said my work was great and she wanted to talk to me about taking on more responsibility. When I said I'd love it, she said she had several more things to tell me. She explained that the foundation had deep pockets of its own and funded a lot of research with its own money. But because the foundation had a good reputation for funding successful projects, it also was frequently employed by other foundations—and sometimes wealthy individuals—to help them direct their funds into promising research. You with me?"

"Yep."

"A few years ago, Uncle Sam noticed how successful the foundation was, especially in recruiting good researchers. And although the federal government has unlimited funds, a lot of top researchers would rather work somewhere else, without the red tape. And politics."

She hesitated, then added, "So, sometimes the government comes to the foundation for help."

"You mean like funneling federal money into certain projects, sometimes with specific researchers, *without* burdening the researchers with government red tape?

"Yes. *And* without the politics."

"Like Congressional oversight?" I asked.

"Yes."

"Is that what happened with the Janus Project?"

"Not exactly. Remember that research on radiation beam treatment for deep-tissue tumors Taz found . . . the one the NIH took an interest in and started funding?"

"Yeah."

"And remember it got abruptly canceled, and Wheeler disappeared?"

"Yeah."

"And the next thing Taz found was the name Janus and a link to the CIA?"

"Right."

"Well, there's a gap in there, before the CIA, that no one is supposed to know about."

"I don't understand."

"The reason the NIH project got canceled was because its research started crossing over into an area that involved classified information another government entity was interested in. So, the research was basically transferred into another new project, where everything became classified. The new project was named Strong Shield and was requested by the Secret Service."

"What?"

"Yes," Claire continued, "And it was a good thing, at least initially. The Secret Service knows someone always wants to kill the president, and it's their job to stop it, right?

"Right."

"Which means they need to be prepared for anything . . . which means they need to know what's possible.

"Makes sense."

"The question now," she added, "is not about that. It's about the project when it was resurrected. And renamed Janus."

"So, *you* worked on the Janus Project?

"No," she said emphatically. "I never had any connection with the Janus Project. I helped recruit Wheeler—and the scientist named Strom everybody's looking for. I recruited them both, for the original Secret Service project, Strong Shield. I didn't have anything to do with it when it was restarted as the Janus Project. I don't think anyone at the foundation did."

"So you know Wheeler?"

"Yes, kinda, from several years ago. But I don't think he recognized me at the hospital until I said the word Janus."

I nodded.

"One more thing," she added, "and then I'm through with all my secrets."

"I just *love* stories like that."

"It concerns the night we met."

My eyebrows said *keep going*.

"The girls I was staying with *were* friends of mine from Auburn, but that wasn't the reason I was here."

"And . . . ?

"I'm getting there," she snapped. "It's just hard to admit now that I have been keeping something from you."

"You're married and have a family in Wichita?"

"Will you be serious a minute?"

"Yes."

She rolled her eyes. "That weekend was months after Strom disappeared. And export records showed some sophisticated cancer treatment equipment being shipped to Brunswick. But there were never any other records. The stuff just disappeared. And, because I had done the research on hiring Strom, and recruited him for Project Strong Shield, the FBI wanted me to see if I could find any connection to his disappearance and the missing equipment. I never did. No one ever did. If there was a connection, whoever covered their tracks did a good job.

"And now," she continued, "I am confused about several things. One, and most importantly, why is Wheeler lying about the possibility of a proton beam weapon? Two, why did Strom disappear?" And three, what, if anything, do those guys on that boat offshore have to do with any of this? Are they just smugglers who hid something and think you know about it?

"Or," she said, now looking at me sideways, "Are you sure *you* don't have anything to tell me?"

"I'm married and have a family in Wichita?"

She hit me.

After I convinced Claire that I had nothing to hide, she apologized for how cynical she had become, and tried to reach Taz again. Still no luck.

By then we were both pooped. We'd been up for 24 hours, wrecked my car, been kidnapped and jumped out of a helicopter in a monsoon. We shed our blue Coast Guard jumpsuits, showered, and crawled in bed around noon. I was sure we'd both would be out in two minutes, but Uncle Wiggly had another idea. I tried to ignore him. Then Claire tried to ignore him. Finally Claire thumped me on the head. Then we all went to sleep.

The first time I woke up, she was draped all over me. The next time, I was holding her. Both were wonderful. I loved this girl. I just wish I knew who she was.

We slept off and on during that day, tried Taz again, ate again, and slept again when the sun went down.

The Admiral rapped on the door, waking us up at three a.m., Sunday morning. *Oh-three-hundred*, he said. Minutes later we were back in our Coast Guard jumpsuits, and Mrs. Mack came in with breakfast, plus sandwiches, soft drinks and a thermos of coffee to go. "Be careful," she said sweetly. "And please don't let anything happen to Mack. I've been waiting for that man to come home from the sea for 35 years."

"We'll take care of the Admiral," I said, wondering how in hell we were going to do that.

Soon we were walking down a dark hallway toward the garage and the Admiral's too-small two-seater. The single passenger seat and the narrow slit behind the two seats were piled high with stuff for the Admiral's boat, reminding me that Claire and I would not be traveling First Class on this leg of the trip. When Mack opened the trunk and I saw the tiny compartment where Claire and I would ride, my puckering butt was the only thing that kept my stomach from hitting the floor.

The Admiral said, "I turned the trunk light off, so it wouldn't come on when you two climb out. It wouldn't be on while you're in there anyway."

I was thinking about being locked in that tiny, dark place when he added, "Bess spread that blanket in there to provide a little cushion."

"Is this a good time," I asked, "to mention that sometimes I get a little claustrophobic?"

The Admiral looked at me, not smiling. Claire was still staring at the tiny trunk. Not smiling either. "Oh, come on," she finally said, "it'll only be a few minutes."

The Admiral said, "Carson, you get in first."

"That's what I was thinking," I lied.

"Come on, time's wasting," the Admiral said, "hop in."

In slow motion I crawled in like one of those sluggish lizards with pebbly skin and socket-ball eyes. I shrunk, twisted and folded, and realized my knees bent the wrong way for this. I was about to say this ain't working, when my two helpers decided all I needed was a little push here and tuck there. *Thanks guys.*

Once I was all the way in and down, I could feel my heart rate start to climb. Then Claire jammed herself in and pushed me back farther in every direction, and I wondered how I was going to breathe.

The Admiral eased the trunk lid closed, and it caught with a loud click. The word "dark" does not do justice to our surroundings, and I wondered if Mrs. Mack's blanket was dry clean only.

As the Admiral got behind the wheel, we heard the garage door go up and felt the car come to life. I wanted to say something but couldn't think of anything nice. Claire sensed my anxiety. She found my leg and patted it, whispering, "It's OK. Think about something else."

"I only have enough air to think about dying in here."

She patted me again as Mack backed out of the garage, turned and headed down the driveway. As we bounced gently onto the road, I started sweating.

There were a couple of light raps on the wall behind my back and we heard the Admiral's muffled voice say, "There was a car watching the house, so don't be surprised if he radios ahead and we get stopped."

While that was sinking in, he added, "I'll keep 'em out of the trunk."

Good, there's no room in here for 'em.

"What do we do if they open the trunk?" Claire asked.

"Don't worry," I said, trying not to worry. "The Admiral won't let that happen."

Trying to get my mind off the near panic I felt, I said, "I like the way your hair smells."

"*God*," Claire replied, "now I know you don't have enough oxygen."

I think I actually smiled about that when we rolled to a stop much too soon. We both quit breathing when we heard two muffled voices. *Oh shit.*

But the Admiral was good. He called the officer by name, and politely reminded him that he was *Admiral* McCallan, and that they had played on the same team in the FLETC golf tournament last year.

"Oh, yeah, Admiral." the other man replied, "How are you?" Then, "Kinda early. Where you headed?"

"I'm going fishing offshore with a friend later today, after the Secret Service gives us back our island, and have some things to deliver to his boat ahead of time. Hey, you know your invitation for an offshore adventure is still open. Wanna come?"

Nice touch.

"Thanks," the man said, "some other time. We'll be busy with debriefings for a while."

"Yeah, I guess so. Well, let me know." We were pulling away while the other man was saying so long.

Smooth, Admiral. Very smooth.

We breathed again, as the car accelerated. After another few seconds, there were another two knocks. "You OK back there?"

"Peachy." Me.

While we rolled along like sardines in shipment, I tried to distract myself by keeping up with where we were, which stops were which intersections. I was doing pretty well until, "Uh-oh."

"What?" Claire whispered anxiously.

"Can claustrophobia cause nausea?"

"If you blow beets in my hair," she said, "I swear, I'll turn you over to the Feds myself."

I didn't reply.

Another few minutes bumping along, and finally I had to say, "Is this your elbow?"

"Yes," she said, then shifted and apologized. Then I felt like a jerk and apologized.

"It's OK," she said, "surely we're almost there." It was a question.

I was trying to think how to say I'd lost track of the turns when the road noise changed. Frederica Road had ended and we were now on Hampton Point Drive.

"Yes," I answered confidently, "almost there."

A minute later we slowed and turned right into a driveway. When the Admiral finally stopped and turned off the engine, I reached over Claire and gave the inside trunk release a good tug. The lid popped up an inch, I raised my head and sucked in a lungful of cool night air. "Wait," she said, as I started to squirm.

"I got to get out of here. Now. Move."

She was hesitant, but the driveway and yard were dark. I pushed again, and she pushed back, until finally the Admiral stood over us, shushed us and raised the trunk lid. "Hop out. Stay here and keep down."

Claire will tell you I pushed her out. I was just trying to help.

We sat in the dark on the driveway by the car, breathing beautiful, cool air, waiting for the Admiral's OK. Soon the three of us were on a dark, downhill tabby path toward Jones Creek and a speedboat that probably smelled like illegal drugs. *Great*, I thought, *in addition to the FBI and Secret Service, we can add DEA to the list of Feds who'd love to put us away.*

On reaching the dock, the first thing we saw was the Admiral's beautiful *Biscayne*. In the dark, starry night her polished teak and brightwork glistened like a boat-shaped constellation.

And then, we saw it—the long, low profile of the red speedboat. On the hull, foot-tall, white letters screamed *Jock's Trap*. The Admiral's son played college football. Over his shoulder, Mack said, "Asinine."

We boarded *Biscayne* and the Admiral showed us below, where the lights were dimmed to pretty much nothing. "Stay here," he said, "and away from the portholes. I'll tie the speedboat to the stern, then we'll shove off. Tide's coming in, so that'll keep the red boat behind us until we're well underway."

Minutes later he was back. "Got it," he said. "Stay down here until I say so."

A moment later we heard the start-up and gentle rumble of *Biscayne's* gasoline engine. We waited, listening to the soft idle of the engine and the Admiral moving around on the deck over us, freeing us from the dock. Then there was another, softer hum and I felt us moving gently sideways. I looked at Claire and grinned. "Got to love bow thrusters."

"What?"

I thought for a second and realized I love the way this girl looks at me when I know something she doesn't. Doesn't happen often. "I'll tell you later."

As our direction of travel eased from sideways to forward, we felt the whisper of cool night air find its way into the galley and salon. After a delicious moment of that, Claire asked, "What's going to happen tonight?"

I put on my best don't-you-worry smile and said, "Everything will be fine."

She was too smart to be put off that easily, and I knew it, so I kept talking, hoping something good would come out. "Look, something is wrong right now. We know that. But you and I haven't done anything wrong, and as soon as everyone knows that, we'll be fine. You'll see."

I was bluffing.

Well, kinda. I was pretty sure the long run would be OK, but I thought the next 24 hours might be a little dangerous.

I had no idea.

Chapter 26

MD, PhD, Murderer

Four Years Ago

Hector Strom splashed his face with cold water, then unfolded one brown paper towel, and patted it dry. He leaned on the small bathroom lavatory, staring at the man in the mirror. How in the name of God did he end up here? Genius. Physicist. Physician.

Murderer.

No, he thought to himself, don't think like that now. There is no time. Quinterro will be here tomorrow. I must be ready.

But he was so tired, and felt tears were moments away. He walked back to his office, dropped into his chair, opened a desk drawer, then couldn't remember why. He closed the drawer and let his head ease down onto his folded arms. A few minutes, he thought, I must close my eyes.

As a boy, Hector was tall, thin, not one of the handsome boys in school. He would have liked to date, but the girls went for the better-looking guys and the athletes. Hector, finding it too painful to be turned down, quit trying.

Though he was not handsome, or an athlete, Hector was the smartest student in school. Genius, they said. He liked that. So, instead of dances and backseats, he spent his time in libraries and laboratories, and was rewarded for his efforts with a full scholarship to MIT. Three years later, a year early, he walked out with a BS in Physics. Summa.

When Harvard heard of his interest in the biological sciences, they offered him a custom work-study position. Four years later, he had a Harvard degree. He did brief intern and residency work but grew bored with patients. One of his MIT professors who moved to Caltech told Strom that's the place to be. He looked into it and agreed. Within three years he added a PhD in Biochemistry to his CV and accepted a promising research position at Fermilab in Batavia, Illinois, specializing in biological applications of accelerator physics.

Barely a year later, he was recruited by the Grace Foundation in Atlanta to work on a classified research project undertaken at the request of the U.S. Secret Service. The goal was look into the near future and evaluate new technologies that could possibly be used as methods of assassination. The project leaders stressed that it was the highest priority in order to provide maximum protection for the president. Homeland Security had turned up rumors of terrorist plans for assassination attempts, and the Secret Service was not taking any chances. The secret project was code named Strong Shield.

The work was heady stuff that appealed to his ego and his sense of patriotism. And the pay was good. Also, he admired the other team members, all of whom were brilliant and dedicated scientists. He particularly grew to respect Project Manager Brad Wheeler.

Over the next few months, the scientists approached their tasks with minds wide open, and looked into the near future, evaluating new technologies that could possibly be used for assassination. They created a list of possibilities and set about finding the best way to protect against each.

As work progressed, however, the research began to focus more on—not just proposing—but perfecting a couple of the possible new weapons. Plus, new faces began to show up at their product demonstrations. The new faces were introduced as Secret Service, but Strom had doubts.

One day during a weekly meeting, Project Manager Brad Wheeler announced an administrative change. "It's paperwork," he said. "I'll take care of it."

When he was pressed for details, he told them that new mid-year funding had been approved, and Operation Strong Shield was now to be known as the Janus Project.

Soon, however, more new faces appeared at the team's demonstrations, and it became apparent that something else had changed. When the scientists refused to do more until they learned the truth, Wheeler finally told them: Strom and his team no longer worked for the Secret Service. The Janus Project now belonged to the U.S. Central Intelligence Agency.

———————————

Strom and his team were incensed. But the announcement that they were now working for the CIA took place shortly after a new senate sub-committee was created, and before Strom and his team could decide on a course of action, Wheeler made another, more drastic announcement. The Janus Project was being canceled immediately. No reason was given. Everyone on the team was given 90 days severance pay, valid-sounding filler for their CVs and told good luck.

They were all well-respected professionals, and none had problems finding good jobs. Wheeler returned to medicine and joined the staff at the Mayo Clinic in Jacksonville, Florida.

Strom returned to Caltech in Pasadena and continued his work on biological applications in accelerator physics. Life went on.

One sunny day at a sidewalk café in Pasadena, Strom met Giorgio Como, an Italian tailor, who like Strom, was shy and soft-spoken. They started having lunch together and soon became good friends. They laughed often and told each other about their work and their dreams. Como was fascinated by the way Strom talked about subatomic particles traveling at the speed of light. And Strom loved to hear Como tell about his wealthy clients and the stories they told during their long fitting sessions.

One morning at work, Strom met a cute administrative assistant at the Caltech particle physics lab who shamelessly flirted with him, something he had never experienced. When she invited him to lunch the next day, he eagerly accepted, and they became friends, and were soon meeting for drinks after work. It wasn't long before she invited him to her apartment for dinner, and more. Strom was ecstatic about his new girlfriend and was sure he was in love. When he shared his secret with Como, the Italian tailor seemed cautiously happy for his friend, but reminded Strom that affairs of the heart can bring pain as intense as the pleasure.

The tailor's advice to the scientist was well founded. The new girlfriend had been borrowing money from Strom supposedly to pay off old medical bills. When he learned that she was using the money instead to finance her cocaine addiction, *and* that he was the latest in a string of men she had been using, he was heartbroken and confronted her in her home. When she laughed in his face, he lost all control and brutally backhanded her across the room. The blow sent her reeling, and she fell, hitting her head on a heavy end table, breaking her neck. Strom's new love was dead.

The brutal rage he felt turned to shock, then fear. He had killed a human being. He was a murderer. People at Caltech and nearby neighbors would quickly identify him. He would be arrested, charged with murder, found guilty and sentenced to life in prison, or worse. No, he thought, that must not happen. This was not his fault. She and her filthy drugs were to blame. And he won't pay the price for this corrupt woman's sins.

He carefully stepped over her body, not looking down, and grabbed a dish towel from the kitchen. As quickly and thoroughly as he could, he wiped down everything in the apartment that could hold a fingerprint, careful not to skip even the tips of light switches or the edges of the cheap furniture. It took much longer than he wanted, but this was not the time to cut corners. He looked everywhere, every drawer, under the bed, in the closet, behind the furniture, everywhere for anything that could be traced back to him. When he was sure, he glanced one last time toward the living room. All he could see was the woman's feet. He wanted to feel more. But the fear blocked out everything. He turned and walked to the door without looking back. He locked the door behind him and walked to the only place he knew to go.

Chapter 27

Q

Quinterro Buys a Scientist

In his Pasadena tailor shop Giorgio Como slowly sank into a chair upon hearing his friend's horror. Surrounded by rolls of expensive suiting fabrics in a thousand shades of black, blue and gray, the two men sat across from each other, neither saying a word. Finally, Como stood, told Strom to wait, and disappeared into his office at the rear of the shop.

Fingers trembling with doubt, he made one phone call—to the only man he knew who may be able to help. Rafael Quinterro had been in the shop the day before and would still be in town.

Quinterro, now living in South America, periodically returned to California under a false identity to meet secretly with Hispanic leaders—political and underground—to discuss ideas for improving their people's plight. While in Pasadena, he sometimes saw his tailor to be fitted for new clothes.

Quinterro knew the tailor would never ask for a favor unless it was important. He told Como to wait, he would be there soon.

When Quinterro arrived, Como did the talking, telling Quinterro everything he knew about what had happened. Strom, helpless, sat quietly, listening to his own tragedy unfold. Quinterro listened, showing no reaction.

When Como saw that Quinterro was unmoved, he turned to Strom and said, "Tell him, my friend. Tell Mr. Quinterro what a smart man you are, a medical doctor, and a brilliant scientist. Perhaps there is something you can do for Mr. Quinterro."

Strom hesitated, then with no enthusiasm, briefly recounted his various degrees and achievements. He ended with, "Yes, Mr. Quinterro, I am . . . was . . . a smart man. But I'm sure you must be thinking, how does such a smart man ruin his life so quickly, and so completely."

Still no reaction from Quinterro.

When Como and Strom sensed that the one man who might be able to help was not moved, Como turned to his friend and said, "Hector, forgive me for saying this now, but you told me you once worked on a special project for the American government. You said the work was secret, something you must never tell anyone. Maybe that's true, my friend. Or . . . maybe now, you should tell Mr. Quinterro. You and I are asking a great deal of him. Perhaps there is something you can offer him in return."

No one spoke.

Strom felt like his head would explode. As the completeness of despair closed in, he knew he had no choice.

When Quinterro shifted in his seat, Strom thought he was rising to leave.

"Yes. OK," Strom said to Quinterro. "I will tell you everything."

Como stood. "I will get us coffee."

For the next hour, Strom told Quinterro how he was first recruited by the Grace Foundation, then found himself working for the United States Secret Service, and then the CIA. He explained how the Janus Project looked for possible weapons of assassination. "But I am afraid that I do not have much to offer you from that work. The project was canceled when a new senate sub-committee found out about it, and we were all dismissed. We made good progress, but more work was needed."

When Strom finished, no one spoke for a long time. Quinterro watched the scared little man man fidgeting in the hard wooden chair, staring at his clasped hands in his lap. Como sat quietly beside his friend. After a moment, Quinterro said, "Tell me about the woman."

Strom and Como looked up, confused.

Quinterro spoke again. "The woman," he said, "did you love her?"

When Strom realized what Quinterro was asking, all he knew to say was the truth. "Yes. I loved her. More than my own life. More than anything." Strom took a deep breath and continued, "She gave me the greatest joy I have ever known. Then, suddenly, anger, like something straight from Hell. And now, finally, the deepest sadness. All of it will be with me forever."

Quinterro saw the man's pain and remembered his own despair at losing his wife Natalie. He pushed the memories away and forced himself to think about now, not then.

He knew there were times his South American friends could have used a good doctor. One who could be trusted not to tell a soul whom he treated or why. A doctor who never asked questions. Quinterro was intrigued by the idea. He also liked the thought of having his own scientist and inventor. Perhaps this Doctor Strom could be useful.

Quinterro had friends who could take care of Strom's problem if they acted immediately. It wouldn't be cheap, but money was not an issue.

If Strom accepted his offer, Quinterro's friends would take care of the murder scene, provide an alibi for Strom, and do whatever else was necessary to guarantee that there would never be a connection between the woman's death and the scientist. In return, Strom would quit his CalTech job and move to South America, where he would be given a new identity, further protecting him from his recent past. He would be paid a handsome salary, would become and remain fully current in practicing medicine, and be on call 24 hours a day, 365 days a year, to be available to travel anywhere, anytime, for any reason. No questions asked.

He would also be furnished with a modern lab for his continuing research and would undertake any projects Quinterro directed.

To Strom, the only thing more terrifying than taking Quinterro's offer was not taking it. Soon his face would be on television, and he would be identified. For Strom, America meant prison. Or worse.

He had no choice.

Three Years Ago
Rio de Janeiro

In time, the California woman's murder went down as an unsolved, drug-related killing. There was never a hint of a link to Strom. Had there been, Quinterro's friends had arranged witnesses who would vouch for

Strom's whereabouts that afternoon, as well as many afternoons during the past year. He was clean and free.

And now owned by Quinterro.

Strom quit his job and he told his coworkers he was moving to Europe to work with a fellow inventor. He did fly to Europe, but only long enough to disappear, and re-emerge with a different name and past. When that was done, he flew to South America.

As Quinterro promised, Strom's new responsibilities required him to travel throughout South America, Europe, even the Middle East. Sometimes, the calls came late at night, requiring him to leave at once. "You are needed in Geneva," the caller might say. "The jet will be waiting for you at the airport."

He was always met by a different driver who knew him on sight. He was taken to richly appointed offices, luxurious penthouses and lavish estates. Other times it was a tent in a jungle, or a falling-down, dirt-floor shack high in the hills. He proved to be a valuable asset to Quinterro and his friends.

When not traveling, he spent his time researching cancer beam treatment alternatives. He was hamstrung by limited resources and working alone, and discouraged because he knew, even if he made a significant discovery, the credit would go to someone else. So he stayed current on emergency medicine and studied new oncology protocols when time allowed.

One day he was summoned to meet with Quinterro in an elegant hotel suite. Two other Hispanic men he had never seen before were there. The strangers were well educated, and in a meeting that lasted for hours, they questioned Strom in detail about his work on radiation therapy. He was asked what he needed that he didn't already have at his disposal. He said he would need a few hours to make a list. Strom had always been hopeful he could do something to improve radiation therapy and was excited about the possibility of advancing his research, even if it meant he would never be able to take credit in his own name.

Before the meeting ended, one of the men whispered to Quinterro, who paused, then turned to Strom. "Tell me about Wheeler."

Strom, confused by the question, hesitated. "You mean Brad Wheeler?" he asked Quinterro.

"You know who I mean, Doctor."

Strom had no choice and knew it. "Dr. Brad Wheeler was the Project Manager."

"The weapons project?"

"Yes."

"And . . . ?"

"Wheeler was a smart researcher, and excellent project manager."

Strom expected more questions, but Quinterro was through. He dismissed the two visitors.

When they had gone, Quinterro asked Strom, "Do you remember your answer many months ago when I asked if you loved the woman?"

Strom, caught by surprise, hesitantly answered, "Yes."

Quinterro added, "You said, you loved her, yes?"

Strom nodded, still confused.

"More than life, more than anything. Correct?"

Strom nodded again.

"And," Quinterro continued, "do you blame yourself for her death?"

"No," Strom said, more definitively than he felt.

"Who, then?" Quinterro asked.

Strom, increasingly confused, did not answer.

"Tell me," Quinterro said, "who is to blame for her death?"

"The drugs," Strom answered, uncertainly.

"I said *who*, Doctor. Who is responsible?"

"Then," Strom said, "the man who gave her the drugs."

"Yes, Doctor. And what would you wish for that man?"

"I would hope he would die. And never again be able to hurt anyone."

"Yes, Doctor, that is correct," Quinterro said. "Now, listen carefully. Your doctoring days are over."

Strom started, "I don't understand . . ." but Quinterro's raised hand cut him off.

"Men like the one responsible for your love's death must be stopped."

Strom remembered the love of his life, crazy on cocaine the day she died. Yes, Strom thought, he would like to see somebody punished. But he had no idea what this had to do with him.

"Governments have failed. So it's time for us to act. We are going to amputate the head of the monster. And every new head the monster grows. And that's where you come in, Doctor. You are a genius, and the right man for the job."

As Strom heard and felt the compliment, Quinterro dropped the bomb. "I want you to build a weapon that will kill a man without a sound, a flash or a trace of any kind. The longer the range the better."

"But, Mr. Quinterro," he said, "As I told you before, the Janus Project was canceled before we found a way to make such a weapon."

Quinterro smiled at Strom. "We both know, Doctor, how far science is progressing every day. Physicians can now save lives with miracle machines undreamed of a few years ago."

Strom waited, terrified.

"What I want you to do," Quinterro continued, "is use science to help bring an end to the evil that took the life of the woman you loved."

Strom was speechless, light-headed.

"Give me my weapon, Doctor," Quinterro said, standing, showing the meeting was over. "You can do it. I am certain."

Stunned, still seated, Strom looked up at the big man and asked, "But, what if it's not possible? What if I try, and I can't do it . . . ?

Perturbed at the mention of failure, Quinterro dropped the smile he wore a second earlier and told Strom he would soon be joined by others who would assist with the project. When Strom asked who, Quinterro told him simply, "You concentrate on the science. And let the others know what you need. They are good, you will see. And you will have access to anything you need.

"You see, Doctor," Quinterro added, "I'm doing you a great favor. I am taking away all your excuses for failure. So you must succeed."

There was a long pause before Quinterro added, "You don't want to go back to Pasadena in handcuffs, do you?"

Visibly shaken, Strom couldn't speak.

"We'll meet again in a month," Quinterro said. "I'll expect a detailed progress report then, and every 30 days after that. Good day, Doctor."

When he was dismissed, Strom was petrified. So far all he had done for Quinterro is provide medical care for mysterious friends. Now—to save his own life—he must create an impossible weapon. He was not opposed to seeing people in the illegal drug business die, but the idea that he, a physician trained to save lives, must create a machine to kill, was too much. He looked for a way out, but knew there was none.

He was a prisoner in a world he created.

———————————

Strom returned to his lab and spent days recreating his notes from the Janus Project, barely stopping to eat or sleep. Out of all the options the Janus team had studied, only one had shown any real promise—the proton beam currently used in hospital settings to treat some cancers. Strom threw all his energy and time into it. When he succeeded, even he found it hard to believe.

Within a few months, using every miniaturization technology available, he and his new team had created a portable cyclotron accelerator. And using a rapidly alternating, microwave-frequency electrical field, he accelerated protons in a vacuum up to 62 percent of the speed of light—115,320 miles per second. Once the particles reach the desired speed, a beam extractor coupled with a fast-acting magnet redirected the protons out of the accelerator, and through a narrow array of room-temperature, superconducting electromagnets where the beam was stabilized and then fed into a firing tube.

There—except for additional, precise aiming and shaping—was where a conventional hospital-based proton beam did its job destroying cancer cells. In the hospital, the therapy beam would be further directed through additional focusing magnets and lenses before entering the patient, perfectly aimed and shaped to conform to the exact position, depth, size and 3-D shape of the tumor.

For safety reasons hospitals also required an emergency shut-off and a beam dump to dispose of excess protons. Strom didn't. Patient protection was not a concern.

Meanwhile, deep behind closed doors in Washington, DC, the CIA had received approval and funding to resurrect the Janus Project, and the old team members were being brought back in.

All except one.

Hector Strom had disappeared.

Old records proved Strom and Brad Wheeler had worked closely together. Wheeler, now at the Mayo Clinic in Jacksonville, Florida, was rounded up to rejoin the team and questioned extensively about Strom and their relationship. But he knew nothing about Strom since the project was disbanded.

One day as the team was being reassembled, Wheeler answered his home doorbell and was met by a well-dressed man who introduced himself as Will Bannock, an attorney with Coussins-Hale, representing the Mayo Clinic. Once inside and seated, Bannock confirmed that his firm does indeed represent Mayo—that's how he obtained Wheeler's home address—but he was there today representing another of his firm's clients and had an offer for Wheeler. During the next few minutes, Bannock explained that his client, who would remain anonymous, was a wealthy investor who had learned through a confidential congressional source about the government's secret plans to create a weapon for assassinations. When Wheeler shifted uncomfortably, Bannock told him to relax—he was *not* going to ask him any questions about his work.

Bannock went on to explain that his client was an honorable man, a decorated military veteran who believed it would be a serious mistake for the United States to resort to assassination for any reason, and he was confident the next administration would put a stop to it. In the meantime, however, he was willing to make an investment to delay whatever ongoing progress he could. That's all. And all he was asking Wheeler to do was downplay the possibility that the weapon could be developed within the existing timeframe and funding. As Bannock rose to leave, he handed Wheeler a thick, sealed envelope, saying it contains a 10 percent deposit as proof of his client's commitment, and said the remaining 90 percent would be wired to a foreign bank account as soon as his client received proof of Wheeler's successful actions to slow the weapon's development.

When Bannock left, Wheeler opened the envelope and found $100,000 cash. He searched online for the Coussins-Hale law firm and the attorney Will Bannock, but found no trace of either.

When the man named Bannock returned to the airport and boarded the waiting Gulfstream, he sent an anonymous coded message to a mailbox with a fictitious corporate name, telling Rafael Quinterro the message and envelope had been delivered.

Chapter 28

Crash of the Phoenix

Last December

President Ann Chambers buzzed her appointment secretary. "Cancel the rest of the morning." The secretary was reminding her of visitors waiting in the Roosevelt Room when Chambers cut her off. "Just do it!"

Chambers pushed a button on a console and large wooden panels across the Oval Office slid open, revealing a row of seven television screens, all on, all muted. It only took a moment to see that Venezuela's National Assembly had given the country's president authority to rule by presidential decree, a move similar to how Fidel Castro took control of Cuba. Venezuela was becoming a dictatorship. Which meant there was no more denying it—America's Hispanic Crisis was spreading beyond its borders, and democracy was no longer the world's shining example of successful government.

My God, Chambers thought, *this can't continue. I must do something. Regardless of whether the vice president set me up to fail—or he was just wrong about his advice—I can't do anything about that now. I'm the president and I must fix what I can as soon as I can.*

The realization was troubling. *I am the President of the United States,* she said to herself, *and I have made a huge mistake. And now I am paying for it.*

And, I'm the only one who can fix it.

She spun around in her chair, thinking, and saw the small wooden plaque, in the room since Harry Truman. "The Buck Stops Here."

Yes, it does, she acknowledged quietly. *There is no one else to blame. And no one else to run to. This is my problem, and I will solve it.* Her face brightened at the next thought.

And I will start by showing the world that I am not only as strong as any

*man who ever held this office. I am stronger. Strong enough to do something
no male president has ever done. Strong enough to admit when I am wrong.*

She turned back to the muted television screens. *And all you
pretty-boy and semi-sexy reporters who were doing the weather in Wabash not
long ago—are going to help me. Whether you want to or not. You may not
respect me, or this office—but the people you work for do.*

She punched the intercom.

"Yes, Madame President?"

"Tell Dick Culligan and Maria I'd like to see them right away."

Moments later, her Chief of Staff and Press Secretary knocked
and entered.

"Sit down," the president said.

"I owe both of you—and millions of people in this country—
an apology."

Before they could process that, the president half-smiled and added,
"*And,* we have a lot of work to do, and not a lot of time."

———————————

Except for the beautifully renovated old hotel and a few of the
surrounding cottages now part of the resort, it is hard to tell that Jekyll
Island was once a playground for the richest men in America. Rockefeller,
Vanderbilt, Morgan and Pulitzer, to name a few. At the beginning of the
last century, America's super-rich escaped the northern winters, gathering
at their elegant Jekyll Island homes. Cottages, they called them.

Located a mile south of St. Simons Island, across the channel where
strong tides change direction approximately every six and a half hours,
Jekyll Island is a sleepy beach community, where growth has been restricted by the fact that the State of Georgia now owns the whole island.
And most people—except for a few eager developers—like it that way.

According to local lore, in 1907 Mr. Rockefeller's guest, a Mr. E. M.
Patterson of New York mining money, was horseback riding on Jekyll's
north end, and asked about the land across the mile-wide channel. The
next day he borrowed one of his host's small, crewed yachts and sailed

across the channel to the southern end of St. Simons Island, where he spent hours walking. Upon returning to Jekyll, he went straight to Rockefeller's private telegraph office and wired his attorney in Buffalo: *Found perfect place for new golf course, men's club. Please join me here immediately to acquire same. EMP.*

Within thirty days Patterson knew what parcels he wanted, negotiated prices, and had his New York architect and a famous Scottish golf course designer working on the project. He bought a house on St. Simons and divided his time between New York and the island. During design and construction, at every turn, he chose the high road. When his bankers politely questioned the lavish spending, Patterson smiled and said, "This is not spending. This is investing."

When the magnificent golf course and clubhouse were completed, Patterson christened the new facility The Barrier Island Golf Club.

During the first few years, the club added members slowly and quietly, and according to rumor, only by unanimous approval of current members. There were never announcements of new members, guests, or club activities. Outside the entrance, the only thing known for sure was that no one knew anything for sure. Only that it was a club for very rich, very private men.

Ironically, the club's success at remaining private, coupled with the rumors of its excellent golf course and clubhouse, made it all the more mysterious to the outside world, including professional golfers. And soon club members began inviting well-known pros as their guests.

Hero worship is not new, nor limited to those of lesser means. The rich and successful men of the Barrier Island Club thoroughly enjoyed having real champions in their midst. By 1927 these visits had become such a regular occurrence that the inevitable happened. Several champions ended up at the club during the same week. Put a bunch of competitive, grown men in a room with a lot of brandy and fine wine, and it doesn't take a genius to know what happened next. As fast as a man can say, "I bet he can," polite challenges were made, pairings were offered, and tee times were scheduled for the following morning. Anyone planning to leave the club the next day wired his office, saying he had been detained. No one left for the next four days. And though few realized it that week, they had witnessed the birth of what would become one of the most prestigious golf tournaments in the world.

Even for an organization as private as the Barrier Island Club, it was impossible to keep secret what happened that week. There were just too many great moments of golf, too much alcohol and camaraderie, and too many guests, and a few members, who couldn't resist telling friends about the most amazing golf week of their life.

It also didn't take long before the story was leaked to a Chicago sportswriter, and once that happened, news and rumors flew like balls on a crowded driving range. The club members had inadvertently started something that everyone found irresistible—players, guests, press and public. The story of the tournament's accidental beginning amid late night drinks, dares and bets became one of the great legends of the game and would be told and retold by golfers for as long as the sport was played.

Immediately, the press bombarded the club with questions about next year's match, and it was obvious The Barrier Island Golf Club had an annual tournament on its hands. The next order of business for the club members was to give the tournament a name befitting its already legendary status. After great debate, they decided on Golf's Game of Champions, and were proud of the choice. But they needn't have worried much about the official name. The sportswriter who broke the story had already given the new tournament a name the public, and the press, found irresistible. The official "Golf's Game of Champions" name would appear in all the proper places, but the name given to the tournament by the Chicago sportswriter, taken from the club's own initials, would be in every headline and what every player and fan called it. It was, then and forever, simply, the BIG Game.

Chapter 29

United States Secret Service

Last January

The president stared across her desk at White House Chief of Staff Dick Culligan and Press Secretary Maria Esperanza. "Dick," she started, "what was the name of that mens-only golf club on the Georgia coast you guys talked me out of going to during the campaign?"

Culligan hesitated, wondering where this was headed.

"Lew Arnold at *The Wall Street Journal* is a member and invited me," Chambers added.

"You mean the Barrier Island Club on St. Simons?" Esperanza asked.

The president nodded. "Yes, one of the most private clubs in America. And I have an idea."

Over the next ten minutes, President Chambers outlined her plan. Her two closest advisors were shocked. And loved the idea. They would be the only two who would know about the plans for the president's historic apology to the nation—and her administration's reversal on the Hispanic Civil Rights Crisis.

When Dick Culligan returned to his office, he called Lew Arnold, Chairman of the Board of *The Wall Street Journal*. When Arnold came on the line, Culligan explained the president's invitation, *without* revealing that the president was planning on personally apologizing to her guests that weekend—and to everyone in America the day afterwards. Chief of Staff Culligan said it was going to be a great opportunity for media executives worldwide to meet face to face with the president, to exchange ideas about how best to address the current U.S. Hispanic Civil Rights Crisis. It would be a long weekend—on neutral turf—with formal and informal gatherings, golf and fine dining. And one-on-one meetings with the President of the United States of America.

Culligan told Lew Arnold the president wanted a fresh start, a two-day opportunity to reach beyond the reporters, and talk personally with the media owners, to explain her plan for getting the country back on track. She needed their help.

When Arnold asked why the president didn't just invite everyone to 1600 Pennsylvania Avenue, Culligan said she knew that would look heavy handed, like the President of the United States was trying to manipulate the media. And it was crucial for her guests to understand that the requested meeting was her way of asking for help from equals. Plus, the remote, private location would enable the plan to get off to a running start before millions of Americans heard of it.

After Culligan hung up with Lew Arnold, he made the same phone call to 23 other major media players around the world. As expected, a few expressed concern that their frontline employees would not feel comfortable with the idea. Without revealing the planned groundbreaking presidential apology, Culligan replied that the president was also inviting a small, representative press contingent of reporters and cameramen to attend portions of the weekend to prove there was nothing unethical in the works. That appeased the ones who were hesitant, and within 24 hours, all had accepted the invitation. As requested, Lew Arnold secured exclusive use of The Barrier Island Golf Club for the first weekend in May.

Last February

One out of every eleven U.S. Presidents has been assassinated. And attempts have been made on one out of every four, including every president since Lyndon Johnson. And although the public soon forgets failed attempts—and never learns of others—history does not forget.

Given the obvious need for presidential protection, and the strong presence of today's agents, it's hard to imagine a U.S. President without a Secret Service. But for many years—even after Presidents Lincoln and Garfield had been assassinated—Congress refused to provide funding for presidential protection. Bodyguards, they said, were for royalty and had no place in a democracy.

After an assassin killed McKinley in 1901, Congress finally authorized the Secret Service to protect the president—temporarily. Funding had to be re-approved annually.

Fifty years later, after President Truman narrowly escaped an assassination attempt that looked like a shootout out from the wild west, Congress finally authorized the Secret Service to provide full-time presidential protection.

The mission is simple: Protect the president. No excuses. And the men and women who do that are extraordinary—intelligent, self-disciplined, well organized, and highly focused. When the shooting starts and human nature screams *take cover,* Secret Service agents do the opposite, rushing into the line of fire with a fierce counterattack. Training ensures their response is Pavlovian.

In addition to the plain clothes agents always near the president, another crucial part of the protective shield is provided by the agency's black-clad Counter-Sniper and Counter-Assault Teams, whose members are sometimes visible on the periphery or nearby rooftops.

For the Secret Service, every day is Super Bowl Sunday. There are no practice days, no regular-season games, and no way to make up in the play-offs for a loss today. The Super Bowl of protecting the president must be won every day, on different fields, in different cities, even different countries. And most importantly, against opponents about whom the Secret Service probably knows nothing.

———————

U.S. Secret Service Agent Jeb Howton fastened his top shirt button and pulled his tie tight.

"Somebody will try to kill the president today," he said. "I have to stop it."

He began every morning with that mantra. Other agents may not have said the same words, but they thought them. In the Secret Service, obsession is not an occupational hazard. It is the job. *Somebody always wants to kill the president.*

Jeb spent the last four years on the Presidential Protective Detail, the PPD, and was scheduled to rotate off later this year. Five years was the max on PPD. Agents were transferred before stress, exhaustion or routine could lead to a mistake.

The PPD are the men and women nearest the president. Walking when he walks, stopping when he stops. They walk the ropelines, staring into crowds, looking for the one face that doesn't belong, searching for the one person doing something different. Agents are trained to spot fake smiles on faces they've never seen and begin moving toward the problem before the threat materializes. Healthy paranoia and the ability to strike like a coiled rattlesnake are job requirements.

The men and women of the PPD are also trained to be among the fastest, most accurate marksmen in the world. Agents must be able to hit a moving target, fire accurately from a speeding automobile, or surgically take out a firing gunman standing next to a pregnant woman in a crowd.

As a recent Secret Service Director put it: Our mission is simple—three P's—Preparation, Prevention and Protection. We start with an enormous amount of *preparation*. When that's done right, we've created *prevention* by removing opportunities for an attempted assassination. And when opportunities for attempts never occur, the result is *protection*.

Our job is not to *be* bodyguards, but to make sure the president doesn't *need* bodyguards.

In addition to watching the crowd, PPD agents are also trained to watch each other, to look for any signs of stress or fatigue. With his natural instincts and years of experience, Jeb Howton was at the top of his game. He was also good at hiding the fact that he was exhausted.

On a rare morning in his cramped office on the ground floor of the Executive Office Building, Jeb tucked the telephone in the bend of his neck and pulled up his calendar on the computer screen. He scrolled forward, found the May weekend the caller asked about, and said, "Yes sir, no problem."

The weekend was marked Disney World.

A few "yes sirs" later, Jeb hung up. *How in the hell am I going to break this to Jimmy and Cole?* he thought. The Orlando trip was for his twins' fifth birthday.

Never mind that now, he told himself, *I'll deal with that tonight.*

He deleted the Orlando trip from his onscreen calendar and entered a new password. A second later, he was looking at a map of the United States overlaid on a high-definition satellite image of North America.

"Now," he said with a sigh, "where in the hell is St. Simons Island?"

Four Weeks Before the President Arrives

The White House is the ultimate fortress. Inside the president is safe. Outside, however, that same president—now visible and exposed—immediately becomes the most tempting target in the world. And whether the president is crossing the street or an ocean, the Secret Service is responsible for creating an impenetrable shield of absolute safety.

A month before the president's visit to St. Simons Island, Lead Advance Agent Jeb Howton and two other agents arrived to meet with the Resident Agents from the Atlanta, Savannah and Jacksonville Field Offices.

On the following day, two additional agents arrived. Unlike Howton and his associates in coats and ties, these two were casually dressed. One posed as a professional photographer for a national wildlife magazine. The other, as an investment banker planning to relocate to the area. Both agents had perfect covers. They would have no public contact with each other, nor with the first group, and would move freely around the island, taking pictures, making notes and asking innocent questions. Each night, in a rented marsh-front home invisible from the street, the group would meet privately, make decisions and forward the team's findings and recommendations to Washington. There the information would constitute the earliest beginnings of what would become the comprehensive Security Plan for the president's trip. It would address every aspect of the operation, and involve hundreds of people, thousands of man-hours, and millions of dollars. A design that didn't exist a few days ago would eventually amount to a step-by-step plan the size of a King James Bible.

A visit by the President of the United States also requires a tremendous amount of manpower provided by local law enforcement. And because State Patrols and local Police and Sheriff Departments are all heavily involved, coordinating who does what, when and how is a massive undertaking. Fortunately, because many agents began their careers in local law enforcement, the agents and officers speak the same language. Plus, the local officers are a wealth of information, especially regarding the terrain and possible vulnerabilities, like a storm sewer drain concealed by undergrowth, or a hidden access to a storage room in an auditorium.

If there are known "unfriendlies" in the area, perhaps people who had written nasty letters recently to any federal employees, they would have to be politely questioned, and sometimes secretly watched until the president departs.

Also all recent gun sales within 100 miles would be analyzed, and every person who bought a gun between now and the president's visit would be interviewed in person.

The Secret Service was also concerned about the supplies of local law enforcement uniforms. Had any recently gone missing? For the next month, there would be no uniforms sent to commercial laundries and dry cleaners without an officer present to account for every article of clothing. The Secret Service already monitored all worldwide sales of law enforcement uniforms, and would pay special attention to any shipments to the southeastern United States.

Local law enforcement personnel were also reminded that bad guys may try something nearby—either as a distraction to weaken the president's protection—or maybe just to take advantage of the fact that local law enforcement is spread thin. An example: During the 2004 campaign when President George W. Bush and candidate John Kerry were in Davenport, Iowa, on the same day, bad guys robbed three banks and got away.

There was a lot of responsibility to go around, and it all began with Howton. It was up to him to make recommendations for inner and outer security perimeters, secure motorcade routes, including alternates and "backdoor" emergency routes, and helicopter landing sites for Marine One. He would also identify the nearest hospitals and other emergency health care facilities, and would suggest locations for Safe Houses along any possible motorcade routes.

And there can be no excuses, no delays with any of the prep work. The president's schedule is "carved in stone."

Air Force One would land at the larger Brunswick Golden Isles Airport on the mainland. From there it would be a five-minute helicopter flight on Marine One to the smaller airport on the island, whose main runway ended directly across the street from the president's ultimate destination, the Barrier Island Golf Club.

Last April

Daniel Taggart answered on the second ring. "Yes?" Caller ID was blocked. Most calls he got were.

"Early next month," the caller said. Taggart recognized the emotionless voice of Vic Kilgore.

"Where?" Taggart asked.

"That'll come later."

Taggart hated Kilgore and his condescending attitude. He'd be glad when this job was over and he wouldn't have to deal with him anymore. "Not good enough," Taggart said, hoping he pissed off Kilgore. "Too much has to be done. I have to know."

"You'll know when it's time for you to know."

"Right." Both men ended the call.

Kilgore sat there for a moment. He hated phones. You never knew who was listening. Especially now. The government was paranoid about everything.

He removed the battery from the phone, broke the phone at the hinge, and tossed each piece into a separate, fast-food paper sack. The sacks would then be casually dropped into separate trashcans outside. He pulled a new phone from a box containing twenty more, each bought in a different place, registered to a different user. He pictured the man he just spoke with doing the same.

He slid his laptop closer, pulled up his brokerage account, and saw that the market was down again, taking his pathetic few investments down with it. Who cares, he thought, about losing a few hundred bucks. Soon I'll be pissing away more than that on margaritas on a beach in the Caribbean.

Chapter 30

Q

Fireworks

One Year Ago
Rio de Janeiro

Rafael Quinterro stared at the machine. Instead of the compact, sophisticated device he expected, it looked like a homemade collection of components cabled, bolted and piped together in a twisted array that had no beginning or end. The only recognizable feature was a digital counter flickering so fast that most of the display was a shimmering red blur.

A door opened behind him, and Hector Strom walked in wearing a white lab coat, looking older, tired. A younger assistant followed, carrying a laptop computer.

"Good evening, Mr. Quinterro."

Quinterro didn't answer, and when Strom saw the expression on his face, he spoke fast, "Mr. Quintero, please remember this is only a working prototype. The final product will be smaller and look very different. The important thing is, this works. You will see."

No response.

While the younger man connected the laptop to the machine, Strom turned to Quinterro. "Only a moment now."

Again, Quinterro didn't reply, and the silence grew awkward until the assistant said, "Ready, sir."

Strom nodded and directed him to the far end of the room where he slid open a wide door Rafael hadn't noticed. Beyond the door, in a small room, a young black and white goat tied to a metal ring on a post ate out of a shiny pale. The animal looked up briefly, then returned to the food.

Half of the laptop's display now showed a target sight overlaid on the goat's head. Strom said to Quinterro. "Ready?"

When Quinterro nodded, Strom tapped once on the keyboard,

the device made a barely audible click and whir. The goat mindlessly chewed on.

Strom turned to Quinterro. "Except for the soft sound you heard, there was no flash or noise. And there will be no sign of anything wrong with the animal for hours."

No reply.

"We will come back tomorrow," Strom said, "and see the results."

Quinterro said, "I have questions."

Strom hesitated, then said, "Certainly, sir. What would you like to know?"

"How my new device works."

Strom, momentarily taken back hearing Quinterro call the device his, said, "Very well." He excused his assistant, and he and Quinterro sat down.

"I'll start with an accurate but abbreviated summary," Strom said. "Please stop me if you want more details."

Quinterro nodded and Strom began. "As you know, we use low-power x-rays to look inside the body. Or we can focus those x-rays into a beam so narrow it will actually damage tissue, like a cancer. However, because x-rays act like light, they scatter, like a flashlight beam spreads out. Thus healthy tissue is damaged too.

"And," Strom continued, "because the x-ray beam continues through the cancer, it damages healthy tissue beyond. So, the question becomes, how to kill the cancer, without killing the patient? The answer is, use protons instead of x-rays. Because protons are particles, they are heavier and pass through tissue better. This means they scatter less and remain in a tighter beam. Plus, their speed *and* their depth of penetration can be controlled, allowing us to direct where they release the greatest amount of energy. This means more damage to the cancer, and less to healthy tissue."

When Quinterro remained quiet, Strom added, "Think of fireworks. They are launched from the ground, but nothing happens until they reach a preset point, where they burst and release all their energy.

"So," Strom continued, "like sub-atomic fireworks, protons travel harmlessly through healthy tissue, release a burst of energy within the cancer, then go no farther, thus sparing the healthy tissue beyond."

Before Strom could continue, there was a knock on the door. "Yes?" Strom said. His assistant had a message for Mr. Quinterro.

Quinterro stared at the note, then asked, "Doctor, how long before this device can kill a man a few miles away?"

"Soon," Strom answered proudly. "Work is progressing well. Please remember, however, only short-range shots like today are possible until the long-range targeting and stabilization components are added."

"I know," Quinterro said, "I am shipping the finished weapon in the armored car to the states. The targeting components will be added there."

"The states?" Strom asked, confused. "I thought it would be used here, in South America."

"Doctor," Quinterro replied, "Remember, my targets are the leaders of the illegal drug trade. And the United States is their biggest market. You," Quinterro said, pointing at Strom, "build the weapon. I'll decide where to use it."

"Yes, Mr. Quinterro," Strom replied, "but why not install and test the targeting components here?"

"Doctor, I already have the state-of-the-art targeting and stabilization system, thanks to the United States military. Obtaining it was difficult and expensive, and I am not going to risk it by moving it between continents. It's safely hidden, where no one would ever think to look.

Chapter 31

The Goat

Quinterro returned the following morning with an immediate question.

"Doctor. If the protons are that successful at damaging tissue, why isn't their effect on the target visible sooner?"

"Please remember," Strom began, "the fireworks analogy is a metaphorical image to describe the results, not the process. Proton beams are not about tiny explosions, and the damage is not physical. The fast-moving protons strip away electrons from nearby atoms, thus damaging strands of DNA, and destroying a cell's ability to survive, reproduce and live.

"And with the state-of-the-art electromagnets and focusing lenses, the proton beam can be configured so it literally ends in a three-dimensional shape conforming to the exact size, shape and depth of the tumor. There the protons will release virtually all their destructive energy, thus sparing surrounding tissue."

When Quinterro didn't respond, Strom nodded to the assistant who opened the sliding door at the end of the room. The goat was lying on the ground, untied from the post, but struggling unsuccessfully to stand. Strom walked toward the goat, motioning to Quinterro, "Come, see."

When they reached the struggling animal, Strom squatted and grasped its horns. He rolled the animal's head in his hands. "See? Strom said, "not a trace or a mark anywhere. The only damage is inside the animal's brain. Death will be soon now. Maybe an hour or two. And there is no way to change that."

Quinterro dropped to one knee and took the goat's head away from Strom and held it in his huge hands. Using his thumb, he pushed the fur away in several locations and directions, verifying there were no marks on the underlying skin.

"Very well," Quinterro said, standing up, still staring at the goat. Strom waited, but Quinterro said nothing more. He was lost in a memory from years ago. A young boy, a pet goat, a home and family. The boy and the little goat played for hours in the yard, until they grew tired and lay down together. Quinterro had named the goat Julio. When his parents were killed in the plane crash, and he was sent to live with his uncle, he had to leave the little goat behind. Over the years, the loss of little Julio had been overshadowed by the greater loss of his parents. But now, the image of little Julio came back. The hard lines around Quinterro's eyes softened, but only briefly. The goat on the ground before him tried to rise again, fell against Quinterro's leg and let out a cry.

"OK," Quinterro said, "now, please put this animal out of its misery."

"What?" Strom asked, rising.

"You heard me," Quinterro replied. "There is no reason for this suffering to go on. End it now."

Strom looked at him, confused. "The goat is not in any pain."

Quinterro glared at him.

Strom tried again. "I have no drugs for that. The animal will be dead soon, maybe an hour. It's only a lab animal."

"Dammit, Strom, do as I say. Now!"

Strom, scared but helpless, looked back and forth from Quinterro to the goat. "Mr. Quinterro, please, understand, I don't have anything to put the goat down. It's not in any pain."

Quinterro stared at the doctor, then closed his eyes for a second. Strom saw his fists clinch, and took a step backward.

When Quinterro opened his eyes, he looked at the animal, hesitated a second, then dropped to one knee. He took the goat's horns in his left hand and the animal's neck in his right hand. Strom was about to say something when Quinterro abruptly raised the animal up and brought it down hard across his knee. The snap of breaking neck bones sounded like a muffled shot, and Strom jumped backward in horror.

Quinterro gently lowered the limp animal back to the ground and stood up. Still staring at the goat, he said, "I want to kill evil men, not hurt innocent animals." And he walked away.

Strom, still trying to breathe, watched him go. Quinterro scared him. He had all along. This whole business scared him. *How*, he thought, *did I end up here?*

The irony of the answer only made it worse. He, who had promised, *First do no harm,* had killed. And he was about to kill again.

Quinterro returned to the states the next day. In the weeks that followed, Strom and his coworkers in Brazil worked feverishly to develop the device from a moderately accurate, short-range prototype into a sophisticated device capable of delivering a tightly focused proton beam to a target miles away. It was a task scientists the world over would have said was impossible. But those scientists didn't work for Rafael Quinterro.

Chapter 32

Phoenix and Candlestick

Two Weeks Before the President Arrives

The Secret Service uses code names for anyone they protect. They are normally two syllables, easy to say and understand, and usually politely reflective of the individual. Subject to those parameters, presidents can usually pick their own. And although no one will officially confirm or deny these, the media will tell you Ronald Reagan was Rawhide; Barack Obama, Renegade; and Donald Trump, Mogul.

Ann Roberts Chambers christened herself Phoenix and was fiercely proud of what the name represented. Like the famous bird in mythology, she had risen from the ashes of obscurity and now soared high above.

If the media learns a president's code name—as it sometimes does—and tells the world—as it often does—the Secret Service may suggest a new one be created. When a reporter overheard the president referred to as Phoenix, and it made the nightly news, the director of the Secret Service politely asked the president if she would consider a new code name. She refused. And that was only the beginning.

The relationship between a president and the Secret Service is delicate. Some presidents take direction graciously. Some don't.

Chambers was courteous at first, but it didn't last. Soon she was ordering her agents out of the room, even in less secure locations away from the White House. At a fundraiser in Houston, cameras caught the president berating a Secret Service agent for standing too close to her while she spoke to a key supporter. America had never seen one of its presidents act in such an undignified manner. The incident was a major embarrassment, and the president's poll numbers dropped sharply. Even supporters in Congress began distancing themselves from the Oval Office.

One Week Before the President Arrives

The Boeing C-17 Globemaster III is smaller than its predecessor C-5A Galaxy, but it has exactly what the Secret Service needs—more flexible cargo configurations, and better safety and maneuverability features. It can, for example, land on shorter runways, *and* back up and turn around by itself.

A week before the president was scheduled to arrive at the Brunswick Golden Isles Airport, two Air Force-gray Globemaster IIIs landed moments apart. They taxied to a wide concrete pad far from the commercial terminal, and while their massive jet engines were still winding down, rear cargo ramps were lowered and locked, and the metal machines began disgorging their valuable cargo—agents, automobiles, technicians and equipment sent ahead to prepare for the arrival of the most powerful person on earth.

Over the next several days, the two large airlifters would make several more roundtrips between the nation's capital and the Brunswick Golden Isles Airport, each time delivering more manpower, vehicles and specialized security and communications equipment.

In a week, the president would land at this larger mainland airport, then take a five-minute helicopter ride on Marine One to the smaller airport on St. Simons Island. From there, the Barrier Island Club was literally across the street.

Ever since Dallas, November 1963, the Secret Service doesn't discuss motorcade routes. They pick several options—primary, backup, alternates, etc.—but don't discuss any.

For Jeb Howton, the fact that the entrance to the Barrier Island Club was across the street from the south end of the small island airport's main runway was a mixed blessing. He liked the proximity. But . . .

"What are our options?" Jeb asked the Transportation Agent.

"Only one makes sense." He traced the route on the wall map as he spoke. "We turn left out of the airport on Demere. Go 450 yards to this traffic circle at Frederica Road. We head south out of the traffic circle, and it's a mile straight down Frederica . . . which ends right at the club entrance. Only two turns—airport exit and traffic circle. A mile and a quarter total. Four minutes, five max. We'd secure a few businesses on Demere, some around the traffic circle, and a few in this larger Retreat Village shopping center, but only for a few minutes. And we'd hold up a few golfers where the Retreat course is close to Federica Road. All easy to do. Especially because once we're on Frederica, the *only* thing on our left is the airport's main runway running parallel to the road.

"Right," Jeb replied, "We know that, and so does everyone else. What else you got?"

The Transportation Agent knew the other two options were disasters. "This island does not have enough roads," he began. "*Both* of the only other options head *away* from the Barrier Island Club, not toward it. Might be OK if they were safer, but they're much more dangerous, a*nd* three times longer."

"Show me," Jeb said.

"The first," the agent said, pointing back to the map, "is over three miles long. Like the shortest route I just showed you, it leaves the airport heading north on Demere, but goes straight through the Frederica Road traffic circle, past several small businesses on both sides of the road. Then, because there's no road through this 400-home Island Club community and Retreat Golf Course, the route takes the motorcade almost to the causeway leaving the island. When it finally turns south on Kings Way, heading back toward the Barrier Island Club, there's a mile and a quarter of two-lane road with mixed-use property on both sides to secure— marsh, homes, two golf courses, and thick natural buffers along both sides. We'd have to close parts of two golf courses, clear out some of the natural buffers that contribute to property values, and still maybe search some private homes."

"The second option," the agent continued, turning back to the map, "takes Demere Road *south*, in the opposite direction, all the way down through the village, then northwest on Kings Way back up to the club driveway. It's three miles on narrow, two-lane roads through tight residential areas with modest front yards. It'd be point-blank range for an RPG or stinger missile fired from any one of a thousand windows. We'd have to secure every living floor, crawlspace, attic and window in a hundred homes. A logistical and PR nightmare."

Jeb stared at the map. The Transportation Agent was right.

"What if we didn't use any of those?" Jeb asked. "Let's install a locking gate in the fence down here at the southern end of the main runway. The airport's temporarily closed, and we can take the motorcade straight down the runway, through the gate, and right into the club entrance."

"No deal. White House said cutting a hole in the fence to add a gate would look like the president was scared."

"I see their point," Jeb said. "Let's assume for now that the short route will be the primary. Let me know later today what you'll need to secure it. And what we need to prepare the other two as backups."

"Got it."

Jeb already knew most of what would be needed, but he would let the Transportation Agent suggest the details. He had other responsibilities. Like constant coordination meetings with everyone involved—Glynn County Police, Brunswick Police and State Patrol managing traffic; Georgia National Guard enforcing an outer perimeter; and Coast Guard patrolling the waterways and providing helicopter support.

Plus, the Navy would have two antimissile ships offshore beyond the horizon, and the Air Force would have an AWACS all-weather surveillance, command and communications aircraft, and a squadron of F-22 Raptors, circling out of sight and sound overhead.

Howton had a highly skilled team, but the weight of details was staggering. There were manholes to be welded shut, sniper and counter-sniper positions to be evaluated, outer and inner perimeters to be established and manned, and back-up motorcade routes from the mainland airport to the Barrier Island Club in case bad weather grounded the presidential helicopters.

There were also meetings with the FAA for establishing a temporary restricted air space; the FCC for scrambling certain radio frequencies the Secret Service would use; FEMA in case of a local emergency of any kind;

local and state DOTs for closing roads; even the Postal Service and all courier services. From now until the president leaves, nothing would be delivered directly to the Barrier Island Club. All mail and packages would be routed to an off-site location for screening and/or opening before being delivered to the club.

By the time Jeb hit the bed that night, he had twice remembered and forgotten he hadn't bought anything yet for his twins' birthday next week.

———

At Howton's recommendation, the Secret Service set up its Command Center in four connecting second-floor suites of the Barrier Island Club. All house telephones, beds and furniture were removed, and every inch of every floor, ceiling and wall was swept for electronic listening devices. Bomb-sniffing dogs would sweep the entire facility numerous times during the next several days, starting with these four suites. Once the rooms were cleared, agents and technicians brought in heavy tables and unmarked cases of every size and shape containing the state-of-the-art security, communications and back-up power equipment that would fill the four-room Command Center wall to wall for the next week. The hallway doors to three of the four suites would be locked and blocked off, and at least two agents would occupy the Command Center 24 hours a day. No housekeeping or room service would be allowed for the duration. And all food, drinks, plates, glasses, cups and flatware entering the room would be from secure Secret Service stock on hand. No one, except specially cleared agents, would enter.

The code name for this Command Center was Candlestick, and the life of the president could depend on split-second decisions made here.

———

On a cold morning in November 1989, Alfred Herrhausen, a key board member of Deutsche Bank, climbed into the rear seat of his custom Mercedes and sat back to read the newspaper. The automobile was heavily armored, chauffeured by an anti-terrorism-trained professional driver, and closely led and followed by two other cars full of armed bodyguards.

It wasn't enough.

A book bag hanging on a bicycle exploded as the Mercedes flew by. The 44-pound shaped-charge TNT detonated at exactly the right milli-second, expending its maximum blast force directly to the target—the weakest part of the rear door on the side where Herrhausen was sitting.

Herrhausen's plan was good. The assassins' plan was better.

This is the kind of scenario that haunts every Secret Service agent, day and night. Have I done enough? Have *we* done enough? Is it *possible* to do enough?

More than any other drills they perform, Secret Service agents practice AOPs—Attacks On Protectees. And most of the AOPs practiced are done in and around automobiles, for good reason. History worldwide has shown that's where assassins most often succeed.

Understandably, when questioned about the presidential limousine, the Secret Service answer is always the same: "We don't talk about that."

Needless to say, it has run-flat tires and is armored to the max, reportedly with five inches of ballistic armor capable of protecting occupants from anything up to and including rocket-propelled grenades. The fully functional transparent-armor windows are as thick as dictionaries and block out so much outside light, the interior has to be illuminated artificially so people inside can see each other. And the doors weigh several hundred pounds each, and have trick outside handles that can be opened only by someone trained to do so.

The car is also sealed against chemical or biological weapons and has the most sophisticated communications equipment in any rolling vehicle in the world. Agents admit it can't float or fly. Other than that, all they'll say is, "It's very durable."

Inside the agency, the presidential limo is respectfully referred to as "The Beast."

Two days before the president arrived, two Air Force Globemaster IIIs returned to the Brunswick Golden Isles Airport with more men and equipment, and four identical presidential limousines. That's right—four. Two of the four limos were secured in a hangar at the large airport in Brunswick and would be guarded 24 hours a day. One would be used to carry the president from the Air Force One's parking position where she would meet briefly with local dignitaries, to the Marine One Helicopter waiting two hundred yards away. The second limo at the Brunswick airport was backup.

The other two presidential limousines were driven to the smaller airport on the island where Marine One would deliver the president. There, they would be part of the 26-car motorcade that would take the president to the Barrier Island Club.

Chapter 33

Teracapacitor

Nine Months Ago
Rio de Janeiro

Because of the urgency, Strom decided to divide his coworkers into two teams. One, led by Strom himself, would focus on the device. The other would concentrate on providing the portable power.

For the device, Strom had to find a way to push the proton beam farther than a few yards. Much farther. And without the atmosphere wrecking the beam's concentration and aim. What he needed was a long, invisible barrel. Which meant, what he needed was a laser.

Lasers using ultra-short bursts had already shown they could produce micro-thin plasma channels through the atmosphere. Some even created a self-focusing reaction within the beam that further enhanced the quality. Strom knew a self-focusing plasma channel was the barrel he needed. With that, a target several miles away would be point-blank range.

Plus, he knew the targeting equipment already used a low-power laser for rangefinder and target-lock. If the two could be combined, the smaller laser would establish the exact aim and range a millisecond before the larger laser created the plasma channel and the protons were fired. And because of the enormous power required to produce the proton beam itself, there was more than enough power to add the second laser. Powering the proton generator and the second laser would only be a matter of timing. Strom had the plan for his invisible barrel.

Meanwhile, the power team considered every combination of generating, storing and delivering electricity to create the powerful millisecond bursts the weapon would need. After considering scores of unsuccessful options, success arrived when they realized the answer was to combine two technologies—one 60 years old and one brand new.

The old technology was the simple capacitor, around since the 1950s. Unlike batteries based on chemical reactions, capacitors store energy in electric fields between finely spaced conductors. They are much better at releasing quick bursts of energy, and can be recharged much faster. Plus, because the technology was simple, improvements came fast. GE patented its first ultracapacitor in 1957.

Despite their many advantages, however, capacitors suffered one major drawback. Size. Because the underlying technology was simple, the only known way to create more powerful capacitors was to create bigger capacitors. Scientists tried to work around the size problem by connecting capacitors together in a series of closely spaced partitions. It helped, but not enough.

After weeks of trying to design a small capacitor powerful enough for the job, one of the team leaders walked in one day, and held up a capped test tube. "Gentlemen," he said, "in a world where bigger is always better, I have proof that tiny is infinitely more fascinating."

The speck in the bottom of the test tube was a clump of carbon nano-tubes, molecules of pure carbon 50,000 times thinner than a human hair. They were 100 times stronger than steel and only one-sixth its weight. And of consummate importance to the power team, they were extremely efficient electrical conductors, *and* could provide an exponential increase in surface area.

"For example," he said, "a solid, one-centimeter cube of carbon has a surface area of about one square inch. Fill the same one-centimeter cube with carbon nanotubes, and the surface area jumps to the size of a football field. And with that kind of exponential increase in surface area we can build our capacitor."

To prevent the microscopic particles from clumping together ran-domly, the team developed dispersants that prevented the clumping *and* preserved electrical conductivity. Next, to arrange the nanotubes in circuit-producing arrays suspended in a nonconducting gel, they used a new form of room-temperature liquid glass. And finally, they used a sophisticated magnetic field to control the positive and negative positions of every one of the billions of tiny carbon particles.

When their work was done, the group had created a portable capacitor capable of storing the tremendous amount of electrical power Dr. Strom would need to accelerate his protons to almost the speed of light, and fire them at a target several miles away.

Now they needed a way to charge their new capacitor.

Sandwiched beneath the armored vehicle's steel-plate floors and the bombproof skid-plate below was the vehicle's massive transmission. The power team replaced it with a new custom-made transmission capable of turning, not one, but two drive shafts. One connected conventionally with the rear axle to drive the vehicle's rear wheels. The other drive shaft angled up, passing through sealed gaskets in the bombproof skid-plate and steel floor, into the cargo compartment. There it connected with a custom-designed generator that would charge the capacitor. And because the two drive shafts could be controlled separately, the one leading into the cargo compartment could be turning anytime the engine was running, whether the vehicle was moving or not.

As Strom perfected his proton laser, and the power team created its teracapacitor, several thousand miles north, a third team was retrieving a stolen military targeting device from its hiding place on rural Saint Simons Island.

Chapter 34

RoRo and Iris

Today Brunswick, Georgia, is the second busiest RoRo port in the country . . . RoRo being industry speak for roll-on/roll-off, meaning cargo you can drive. In plain language, that means nearly a million vehicles a year pass through the busy Brunswick port.

The current, modern RoRo facilities are located on Colonel's Island, south of Brunswick, near the southern end of Blythe Island. Entrances to the huge port are on U.S. Highway 17 about halfway between the Sidney Lanier Bridge to the east, and Interstate 95 to the west. Years ago, however, when a Brunswick RoRo port was only an idea, the powers-that-be built a small test facility three miles farther upriver on Blythe Island, with just one RoRo ramp, dock and warehouse.

When the test facility showed promise, the Georgia Ports Authority chose the larger Colonels Island location for the home of its new RoRo port, and the test facility upriver was almost forgotten. Occasionally, however, someone would ask to use the old facility, short-term, and usually for on- or off-loading a few pieces of heavy equipment. So, as long as rental income exceeded maintenance costs, the Ports Authority kept it, which was good for business, good for the short-term users, and good for Rafael Quinterro, whose name, of course, never appeared on any of the rental documents.

Under an obscure corporate identity, Quinterro leased the old, secluded RoRo test facility months ago, to—as the documents were worded—"ship and/or receive heavy-duty transportation equipment to/from South America."

The ship Quinterro used was provided by his good friend, the shipping magnate known only as Benicio, secretly a firm believer in Quinterro's desire to punish the U.S. for its abhorrent treatment of Hispanic immigrants. Benicio's unique vessel had a water-level compartment hidden in the bow behind large sea doors. Inside was a functioning slip for smaller boats, but more importantly, a strong parking pad for a large vehicle, and a heavily reinforced, fold-down ramp to move the vehicle into or out of the ship.

After the weapon and power systems created by Strom's South America teams were installed in the vehicle, Benicio's ship brought it back to Brunswick's remote RoRo test facility where it was off-loaded and moved into the adjacent warehouse for the installation of the targeting system and final testing.

In this warehouse the targeting team worked with computers with no wireless connections among themselves, and no outside connection to the Internet or any other network beyond the always-locked doors. Because their targeting components required so little power compared to the weapon, and because the connection to the weapon would be software controlled, the targeting team was free to work alone in the U.S., far from Strom and the power team in South America. There was another reason for this. The targeting components were stolen U.S. military property and obviously could not get past import/export inspectors. Therefore, the stolen targeting components had been hidden in a secret location in rural Glynn County for months, and only recently moved to the Brunswick warehouse where they would be linked with the weapon already in the armored car.

One month ago

The team was nearing completion when a vehicle arrived one morning unannounced. The driveway monitor sounded, sending men rushing to designated positions on both floors, all chambering rounds in their weapons along the way. When the driver flashed his lights with the correct signal for that day, the gate to the old Brunswick warehouse was opened remotely, and the men relaxed, but not completely. That wouldn't happen until their visitor was positively identified, inside, and the big doors closed and locked behind him. Even then, two men with binoculars and weapons would stay out of sight at second-floor windows to be sure no other vehicles followed.

Their visitor that morning was Rafael Quinterro, and he was interested in only one thing—the guarantee of a perfect outcome.

The team leader was Colonel Alardo. Not his real name, of course. None of the team members had *real* names. Each arrived with a designated name for this mission, and that name would disappear, just as the man would when the job was over. He would be a much wealthier man then. And only Quinterro would know how to find him.

"Good morning," Colonel Alardo greeted Quinterro, without using his name. Then, turning to a younger man, he snapped, "Luis. Coffee."

Alardo then quickly summoned two others.

Moments later, Quinterro was seated at a metal lab table, sipping hot, black coffee, as the two summoned team members appeared.

Alardo began, "To confirm, we will be provided with accurate lat/long numbers and GPS coordinates to within, say, a meter or so. Yes?"

"Correct," Quinterro replied.

"And," Alardo continued, "the distance to the target will be approximately five miles. Yes?"

Quinterro nodded, "A little less," and sipped his coffee.

"Then, if it pleases you, I will let each of these two team members explain their part of verifying the identity of the target."

Another nod.

"The first speaker," Alardo continued, "will address the first two stages of identity verification—Facial Recognition and Heat Signature. The second speaker will explain the third and final stage."

Alardo had already stressed to the two team members that their visitor does not want to hear about procedures and efforts. He wants proof.

Alardo signaled to the first speaker, who spoke purposefully, using a full-scale model of the targeting device coupled to a video screen showing exactly what the operator would see. While he spoke, he watched for any signs of confusion from his audience of one.

He began. "Using the provided lat/long and GPS, we zero in with the targeting device's satellite-quality zoom lens. Its digital imager processes both true-color for Facial Recognition, and infrared for Heat Signature.

"I will address each function separately, but they occur simultaneously.

"As a quick verification of the lat/long and GPS data, the targeting operator does a fast visual check of the true color image on the monitor. Meanwhile a copy of that image is digitally compared to the known head and facial metrics of the target. When a perfect match is confirmed, the Facial Recognition software releases its hold on target lock.

"Simultaneously, the Heat Signature software projects the infrared image onto a thermal sensor where it is instantly compared to the known heat signature of the target. When a perfect match is confirmed, the Heat Signature software releases its hold on target lock.

"At this point, with the target's identity confirmed by both Facial Recognition and Heat Signature, and their target-lock holds released, the control software switches to the third-level verification, which the next speaker will address."

The first speaker stopped and waited, indicating he considered his report complete. Before Alardo spoke, Quinterro asked, "How accurate is the Heat Signature verification?"

"They are just like fingerprints," the man replied, "every person's is unique. Especially in the head and neck area. You just need the digital sensitivity to prove it. And our thermography software does it as accurately as the FBI does fingerprints, sometimes better. And," he added, "because we are verifying a known heat signature here, not searching for one in a crowd, the process will be almost instantaneous. Time from initial target acquisition to target lock—a few millionths of a second."

As Quinterro nodded, Alardo gestured to the second speaker—a woman, short, blond, stocky and all business.

She began politely but confidently. "It is my understanding that there can be absolutely no possibility of error in target verification. Correct?"

Quinterro nodded.

"Then there is only one way to do that—because all other methods of identifying people have *some* possibility of error. DNA testing is the exception, but that's obviously not possible here, nor necessary, as you will see.

"To be one hundred percent sure, the only way is to use Iris ID.

"The iris is the only internal organ visible from outside the body. It is in front of the lens, but behind the cornea and the aqueous humour. Thus, it is virtually impossible to disguise or alter. Glasses, sunglasses, contacts, and colored contacts have no effect. Our camera sees through them looking in just like the wearer does looking out."

Then, turning to a large, close-up photograph of a brown eye, she pointed and continued, "The purpose of the iris's connective tissue is to adjust the pupil size, thus controlling the amount of light entering the eye. This flexible tissue's pattern is amazingly complex and ridiculously random. And that means every iris is unique. Not even your two are the same. Genetically they're identical. But look in a mirror. They're different, usually markedly so."

Quinterro waited.

"And when it comes to accuracy," she said, "in the best-known Iris ID experiment—over 200 billion samples—there was never a false match."

When there was no response, in a slightly changed tone she added, "There are two ways an iris could be disguised.

"The first is cosmetic eye surgery to change eye color by adding an artificial iris over the real one. But no reputable physician would do the surgery, and nobody in their right mind would have it done because the long-term effects are completely unknown.

The second, known as iridoplasty, can change the contour pattern of the iris, but it's only done to surgically correct an existing eye problem.

"Our research shows neither of these exceptions are relevant here."

Alardo looked at Quinterro for a reaction but saw nothing and turned back to the speaker, saying, "Tell us where Iris ID is being used."

The woman smiled, almost a smirk. "Almost everywhere. Many international organizations and foreign countries—too numerous to name—use it every day. Every year more nations adopt it. Strangely, however, the United States lags behind. The usual privacy and civil rights organizations are more worried about Big Brother than national security."

Quinterro nodded an OK, and the woman returned to stand beside the first speaker.

Alardo then turned to Quinterro and added, "As you've seen, Sir, the three-stage identity verification process—Facial Recognition, Heat Signature, and Iris ID—is incredibly fast. And verifying a match instead of searching for one means we can achieve one hundred percent positive ID in less than half a second. Once that happens, the device's overall target-lock is established, and the stabilization software takes over. The eye-safe laser rangefinder measures the exact distance to the target, tells the weapon's computer, and the weapon is ready to fire. Those steps take about a tenth of a second."

Quinterro thought about that, and said, "Good." He rose, but was interrupted by the buzzing of his driver's mobile phone. The driver handed it to Quinterro.

"Yes?" There was a pause while he listened. He asked a couple of questions and got short answers. Nothing Quinterro heard or said would have revealed the true nature of the conversation. No one listening could have imagined that the two men were discussing killing the President of the United States.

When he ended the call, he returned the phone to the driver, who removed the battery and broke the phone in half at the hinge. As he pulled another phone from a pocket in his sleeveless vest, Alardo held out his hand for the old one, saying "We have an industrial shredder and acid bath."

The driver looked to Quinterro, who nodded an OK. Quinterro then turned back to Alardo and said, "Good news. You will all be home soon. And rich."

Chapter 35

The President Arrives

President Chambers scheduled her flight to St. Simons Island for Friday afternoon. All the invited guests had been asked to do the same. She wanted them to have all day Saturday to relax, play golf, and enjoy fine wine and food. And most importantly, have private meetings with her.

She planned an extravagant dinner party for Saturday night, persuading several of her Hollywood celebrity supporters to join them for the weekend and participate in a brief variety show emceed by the top late-night talk-show host. The celebrities would also be available to mingle with the media executives for chats, autographs and photos.

She wanted the whole group at ease and receptive to her plans. If she was going to save her presidency, she needed their help.

The big meeting was scheduled for 9:00 Sunday morning, supposedly so the media moguls could be home by Sunday evening. Most, of course, would use the time Sunday afternoon, not for traveling, but for more golf at the Barrier Island Club.

Friday

As Air Force One's cockpit crew spun up the jet's four, huge engines, preparing for take-off from Andrews Air Force Base, Ann Chambers sat alone in the aircraft's Presidential Suite thinking about the coming weekend. The roar of the engines grew louder until gradually their mighty whine drowned out all other sounds as the massive plane began a slow roll down runway number one. Over a mile later, the heavy plane's nose gear rose from the pavement as the aircraft gently rotated upward, beginning the steep climb toward the day's 43,500-foot cruising altitude. Below, the Washington skyline fell away and was soon lost beneath a gray overcast.

Several minutes later, the whine of the jet engines lessened, and the heavily modified Boeing 747 gracefully leveled off. Like clockwork, a handsome young Air Force lieutenant politely knocked and entered the executive compartment with the president's ritual Bloody Mary. As she lifted the short crystal glass from the lieutenant's tray, a second of unexpected turbulence sent a shudder through the huge plane. The delicate linen napkin around the base of the glass caught most of jiggled cocktail, but not all. Two small red dots appeared on the president's white silk blouse. The young lieutenant immediately handed the president the small towel he carried for such an occasion. She took it and touched it to the spots, but it was too late.

———————

Hours before Air Force One arrived, a team of Secret Service agents walked the larger airport's runway and taxiways picking up any foreign objects that could get sucked into an engine or damage the plane. Two plain-clothes Air Force officers followed, laying down neatly taped arrows to guide Air Force One to the designated parking place.

Above, Coast Guard helicopters made repeat passes, paying close attention to the ground below the approach Air Force One would follow. The chopper pilots had done this for several days to become familiar with the area. Anything they saw now that looked unusual—especially vans or other large vehicles parked where they hadn't been before—would get immediate attention from Secret Service agents on the ground.

When Air Force One was still 50 miles out, the tightening of the full security plan began. The restricted airspace that moves with the president settled over all of eastern Glynn County, where it would remain until the president's departure on Sunday. While the president's plane was airborne, all local airports were temporarily closed, as were all roads and waterways within five miles of the airport.

Throughout the area beneath Air Force One's approach to the Brunswick airport, undercover agents ratcheted their attention levels up to max. At the airport, black-clad members of the Counter Sniper Team were visible on the roofs of the concourse and hangars. And waiting inside the huge hangar doors, in black SUVs with blacked-out windows and engines running, members of the Counter Assault team waited, weapons locked and loaded.

Air Force One touched down at 3:55 p.m., taxied to its pre-assigned position, and rolled to a stop exactly at 4:00. Air Force One pilots always roll to a stop on schedule. They may taxi at six miles per hour or 26, but unless WWIII has started, they make "block time" every time.

Contrary to appearances on television, the president is not the first one off Air Force One. Secret Service agents, senior White House Staff and members of the press exit the rear stairs, while the red carpet is laid out and local dignitaries are positioned at the foot of the front stairway. The presidential limousines also pull up at this time, accompanied by other motorcade vehicles. Meanwhile black SUVs circle the big blue and white 747, and agents—plain clothes and SWAT—take positions surrounding the temporary arena.

From the moment the Commander-in-Chief walks into the light, every step she takes would be anticipated, coordinated, monitored, tracked, recorded and shadowed. Every move would be timed to the minute, and every agent in the area—ten feet away or ten miles away—was connected by secure, scrambled radio, and would know exactly where the president was at every moment.

At 4:05, Air Force One's front door opened. Thirty seconds later President Ann Roberts Chambers stepped into the bright sun and waved to the small but enthusiastic crowd of invited guests.

At the bottom of the stairway, she was greeted by the Governor of Georgia, along with a small contingent of local government and law enforcement officials.

Notably absent was Glynn County Police Chief Ryan Elliott, still in ICU following an apparent stroke.

After brief formalities with officials at the bottom of the stairway, the president moved toward the compact crowd gathered behind the ropeline 50 yards away. There, with several agents within arm's reach, she shook hands and spoke to a few people near the front of the crowd. Two minutes later, even though the crowd was modest and well-behaved—and everyone there had been through a metal detector—her Lead Agent suggested perhaps that was enough time in the open. She smiled, nodded, waved to the crowd again, then turned and walked with the agents to one of the two identical presidential limousines. It was a short drive to the three identical white-top presidential helicopters 200 yards away, but that was 200 yards the Secret Service did not want the president walking in the open.

The president boarded the first helicopter while Secret Service agents and White House staff boarded the other two. Moments later all three rose in unison and turned east, beginning the five-minute flight to the smaller airport on St. Simons Island.

As soon as the helicopters were airborne, undercover agents around the island airport got the message. A "fisherman" on the pier leaned his pole against the wooden rail and pulled a long "rod and reel" case closer, opening the clasps as he did. In a nearby front yard, a "lawn care employee" moved toward the open rear door of his equipment trailer, his hand inside tight on the stock of an automatic weapon. And a "caddie" on the Barrier Island Club golf course, took a long look around, keeping his hand on the rifle barrel hidden under a fuzzy golf club head cover. All waterways, roads, bike and jogging trails within five miles were closed and would stay that way until the president was inside the front door of the Barrier Island Club.

The three identical helicopters changed positions twice during the short ride to the island airport and landed on an airport taxiway far from the crowd gathered in the shopping center parking lot across Frederica Road. There were no invited guests at this stop.

Before any of the helicopters opened their doors, the president's long black motorcade appeared. The passengers from the two outside helicopters exited first, moving to their assigned vehicles. When that was done, the door of the middle helicopter opened and the president, flanked by Secret Service agents, walked briskly to the nearby open door of one of the two identical presidential limousines at this airport.

Four minutes later, the lead motorcycles of the 26-car presidential motorcade passed safely through the front gates of the Barrier Island Club. All the president's invited guests were already on property.

Saturday

On Saturday, as planned, most of the president's guests played golf on the club's world-famous ocean-front golf course. A few opted for a half-day offshore fishing trip on the club's 86-foot Hatteras. And those who preferred to relax around the main clubhouse enjoyed an open house in the club's magnificent kitchen and wine cellar, complete with personal tours and tastings by the world-renown head chef and the master sommelier.

To round out the allure of the weekend, the president's A-list Hollywood celebrity guests would be available two hours Saturday afternoon for chats, autographs and photos, followed, of course, by their variety show after dinner Saturday night.

All of this was part of the allure the president had used to encourage her guests to join her this weekend at the exclusive and beautiful Barrier Island Golf Club.

Regardless of how her guests chose to relax on Saturday, the highlight of the day would be when each had a private meeting with the President of the United States.

When she explained the idea to her Chief-of-Staff months ago, he said, "What a great plan. You can appeal to each one personally."

"No," she said. "They'd see through that in a second, and resent it. I want each one of them to talk about anything he or she wants to talk about—the Hispanic Crisis, business, politics, grandkids, anything. I need their help. I'll be the best listener they've ever had."

While the Chief-of-Staff thought about that, the president said, "After the one-on-one meetings on Saturday, and that night's five-star banquet and live Hollywood show, I hope they'll be in good spirits, and eager to hear what I have to say Sunday morning.

"I want them to hear my apology," she added, "and know it's true. And be ready to accept the challenge when I appeal for their personal help to begin the healing of America."

Chapter 36

Jock's Trap

Sunday 4:00 a.m.

Ten minutes after *Biscayne* quietly motored away from the Jones Creek dock, Mack called down to us. "Come on up."

After our ride in the trunk of Mack's little two-seater Mercedes, his sailboat's salon felt like a five-star luxury suite. Topside was even better—cool, fresh air, and the soft sound of the sailboat's hull sliding through star-spangled black water. As Claire and I eased into the recessed cockpit, she squeezed my hand and whispered that the sea and sky looked like shiny diamonds on black silk. She liked that, but the Admiral was already giving instructions.

"From here it's about a mile and a half to the Hampton River, where we'll turn right, heading downstream, toward the coast. We'll be going against an incoming tide, so it will look and feel like upstream. It's *not*." He looked at me.

"I got it," I replied to the unspoken question.

"Soon after the turn, the Hampton River will curve to the right, heading south. That'll put the large undeveloped Cannon's Point peninsula between us and the homes back on Hampton Point, blocking a lot of the speedboat's sound. That's also where we'll part ways. I'll take *Biscayne* farther south, down near the mouth of the Hampton River. Probably drop anchor right off Ocean Forest.

"You two," he continued, "in *Jock's Trap,* can go wherever you think is best. And hopefully, *safe*. Keep trying to reach Taz. We're running out of time."

Ten minutes later, we made the right turn from the 40-yard-wide Jones Creek into the 400-yard-wide Hampton River. Twenty minutes after that, with the wilderness of the Cannon's Point

Preserve now on our right and primitive Little St. Simons Island on our left, we were pretty much isolated from civilization.

Mack cut *Biscayne's* speed, and said, "Carson, you come with me. Claire, honey, take the wheel, and just keep us in the middle of the river. I've cut the rpms down to where they should just offset the incoming tide, so she probably won't be moving at all. Just keep her in the middle of the river as it flows under you. Make sense?"

"Yes, sir," she said. When Mack turned, Claire gave me a quick *can-I-do-this?* look. I nodded, *of course.*

With Claire at *Biscayne's* helm, Mack and I stepped up and out of the sailboat's cockpit and onto the short stern deck where the speedboat was tied. Mack grabbed the tow line, pulled *Jock's Trap* close and said, "You first."

He followed me as we made our way across the long bow. I eased over the low windshield and down into the cockpit. It was much deeper than I expected, and I saw why. The two forward positions weren't exactly seats. Each was a shallow, upholstered butt-rest protruding from a thick seatback bolster. The whole setup was mounted to an oversized, shock-absorbing, stainless-steel post. You didn't really sit on it, you leaned against it and strapped yourself to it. I would soon learn why.

Mack said, "I turned the instrument panel lights on for you."

I said, "Got it." Then saw it and said, "Whoa . . ." In front of me was a matrix of dials, switches and buttons in night-vision-red that looked like the cockpit of a fighter jet. *What the hell?*

The Admiral saw me hesitate. "I'm coming."

He eased over the short windshield and dropped into the cockpit like a man half his age, then reached past me and flipped on the three bilge blower switches.

"To clear any gas fumes from the engine compartment," he said. "One stray spark could turn this boat into a hole in the water. Wasn't necessary on your *out*board, but it is here."

"Got it," I said. "*Rivianna's* got 'em, you know."

"I know," he replied, with a sideways glance, "but they're easier to forget on small boats. So *don't*."

I nodded as he continued. "The steering and throttles are similar to your outboard. Mainly, the boat's longer and faster. A *lot* faster. Don't let her get away from you."

"Got it," I said, thinking I understood.

Mack hurriedly walked me through the other dials and switches. I nodded a lot and hoped for the best. By then the bilge blowers had done their job, and he reached up and turned the master ignition switch to ON. After waiting a beat, he pressed each of the three red start buttons one at a time, pausing to be sure each engine was running smoothly before starting the next. One by one, the powerful engines came alive, growling, gurgling and sloshing behind us. Vibrations throbbed through my feet and legs.

I was still staring at the instrument panel when he handed me a cold, black handgun. "Nine-millimeter Glock, 13-rounds, one in the chamber, the safety is the first trigger click. I hope you don't need it, and you didn't get it from me."

"Thanks," I said. "I had one kinda like it two days ago."

He smiled, slapped my arm and climbed over the windshield saying, "You'll do fine," then adding as he stepped back onto his sailboat, "Remember, I'll be monitoring radios and phones. Let me know what's happening. I'll do the same."

"Aye aye," I said before I thought.

"Oh," he said, "one more thing. I just learned the Coast Guard has the cutter *Sullivan* here, from Charleston. Don't mess with her. She's big and fast, and her sonar can hear a flounder fart."

"Yes sir."

He waited. When I didn't say anything else, he continued, now sounding like a teacher. "The *thing* to remember is her *see-wiz* gun."

"Oh, yeah. I know you told me what that was . . ."

"Close In Weapon System. C-WIZ. A big, radar-guided, six-barrel gatling gun that fires 75 armor-piercing rounds a *second*. Can shred missiles, planes and other boats in a heartbeat. I saw one in a demo cut an abandoned tuna boat in half."

My eyebrows went one way. My stomach the other. "What do you suggest?"

"I *suggest* you stay as far away as possible."

"Right."

"OK. I'll set my helm on auto and bring Claire back."

As he turned to go, lightning turned night into day. I ducked and said something I'll probably go to hell for, just as thunder nearly knocked me off my feet. As night returned and the sonic boom rolled away, Mack turned and said, "That's good. The storm will help you hide, and disperse your wake."

"Yep," I replied, like I had already thought of that.

A moment later he was helping Claire onto the speedboat's bow. She sat down fast and fanny-slid toward me like it was a race. I helped her over the low windshield and down into the deep cockpit. In the rush, my hands kinda accidentally got around her tits, which felt pretty good.

"Hey!" Girl talk for *stop it!*

"It was an accident!"

Mack's voice saved me. "Ready?"

I nodded and took the wheel. Mack pulled some slack in the line, untied it and pushed our bow away with his foot. I waited as the incoming tide slowly carried us away from *Biscayne's* stern. Ten yards out, I put us in idle-forward and steered hard to port. Mack secured his tow line and stepped back into *Biscayne's* cockpit. He glanced our way to verify our position, then angled to starboard, setting a course downriver.

Claire and I were alone in a red rocketship with a tacky name.

Over the speedboat's gurgling and sloshing, Claire leaned so close to me, I could smell her hair. She asked, "What about the rain?"

After the accidental fondle, my mind flashed a picture of her in a wet T-shirt. "Rain's good," I said.

She looked at me suspiciously.

I added, "It'll help us hide."

No reply, just that look.

I kept our speed at idle-forward and turned my attention back to the helm, and hesitated.

Claire asked, "What's wrong?"

"Nothing."

"Right."

"OK. I just learned that if we get too close to something called the *Sullivan,* we'll be aquarium food in two seconds."

"I don't understand."

"I'll explain later."

"What do we do now?"

"Try Taz again on the smaller phone Mack gave us, and pray she's found Strom."

I maintained idle-forward while Claire dug out the Admiral's phone with no GPS or ID. A minute later, she was listening to Taz, and turned to me. "She found something about Strom but got kicked offline. Even tried different computers. It keeps happening. She thinks it's a keyboard tracking program that recognizes typing style and kills the connection."

"The damn Feds. Tell her she has to find Strom."

Claire reminded her and ended the call. Then looking forward, she said, "Don't you need to turn on a light?"

"I'll turn on our puny bow light when we really need it. No sense in advertising where we are.

She nodded, and I said, "We need to get going."

I should have been more specific.

Claire was standing in the aisle between the two bolster seats, staring at the confusing array of red dials and switches. "Can you drive this thing?"

"Yeah, no worries." We were already in idle-forward, so I gave the triple throttles a little push. The boat lurched forward so hard, I fell back against my bolster, and Claire disappeared in a flailing blur toward the stern.

The time it took me to lean forward and pull the throttles back to neutral gave Claire time to regain her feet. When the boat almost stopped from the sudden loss of power, Claire came flying back up the aisle, crashed into the padded bulkhead and collapsed in a heap. From that tangled pile of woman in the dark beside me came a feminine, two-syllable f-bomb for the record books.

After helping Claire to her feet, with grovel and apology, and swearing to you-know-who I didn't do that on purpose, we were back on the same team. As soon as we both were strapped in, I tried the throttles again. More respect this time for the unknown. We slowly moved forward, gently eased onto plane, and headed south at 20 miles an hour, purring across the glassy black water.

More thunder and lightning. Like we needed more drama.

From nowhere, a brisk wind picked up, and the smooth water turned into a river full of short whitecaps coming right at us. Low storm clouds rapidly obscured all of what Claire had called "shiny diamonds on black silk." But the same low clouds reflected enough night light to give us decent visibility.

And speaking of visibility, when you see a small light in the distance, and you can tell it's heading straight for you, one of two things is happening. It's either a *lot* closer than you thought, or it's coming a *lot* faster.

I looked behind us to be sure we were alone. We weren't.

A single flashing blue light reminded me that Claire and I were wanted by the FBI, and by now probably every other local law enforcement agency. When Claire saw the blue light too, she said something she didn't learn in Sunday school.

"Hold on!" I said, shoving the throttles forward. We were already planed off, so the boat stayed flat and accelerated like a missile, pressing us hard against the seatbacks. The acceleration was not only more than I *expected*, it was more than I imagined. I was impressed, grateful, and a little worried. I suddenly had a 1,200-horsepower tiger by the tail, and as my brain replayed Mack's warning, "Don't let her get away from you," I tightened my grip on the wheel.

Then the rain started.

Being unfamiliar with the huge instrument panel, and now with a face full of rain, it took me an agonizing three or four glances down to find the damn speedometer. It said eighty, and the wet blast coming over the tiny windshield made focusing on anything ridiculous. Meanwhile, just in case I wasn't distracted enough, the loose ends of the multi-strap seatbelt harness were beating hell out of my legs. Out of the corner of my eye, I saw Claire with the same problem, doing a strange dance, trying to grab and stomp her belts into submission.

"Where is he?" I screamed.

Pausing her bizarre boogey long enough to glance over her shoulder, she screamed back, "Close. Do something!"

Just then, the chase boat's high-power spotlight came on, lighting us up, and I wondered if he was that much faster than us or just had a better head start. Either way, Claire was right. Something needed to be done.

Thanks to the glow from the other guy's spotlight, I saw ahead on the left, at the mouth of a wide creek, a sign saying "Little St. Simons Island." I faked a gradual turn to starboard to lure the lawman to the right, then quickly turned hard to port just in time to shoot through the mouth of Mosquito Creek. The little fake did the trick. Our pursuer was too far right to make a quick turn and would have to do a 180. That gave us a head start up the creek. Plus, because the intakes of our speedboat's three waterjet engines were built into the bottom of the hull, and the three nozzles that propelled and steered the boat didn't require much depth, we had the advantage of a shallower draft. So even though our butt-ugly red speedboat was 35 feet long, it could fly better through shallow water than a Glynn County Marine Patrol boat with big outboards. They would keep him closer to the middle of the creek while we could cut the corners.

I had one more advantage. Years ago, before Little St. Simons was open to the public as a nature preserve, Ryan and I and a bunch of other boys spent many weekends in that wild, beautiful place hunting, fishing, camping and just hanging out. I knew it well.

Now, with my shallower draft, head start in the creek, and familiarity with the watery terrain, I was pretty sure we'd lose the chase boat.

I turned on our excuse for a bow spotlight and shouted to Claire, "I got this!"

Head down, she tightened her grip on the bulkhead grab bar.

Seconds later, I wondered if I had spoken too soon. The high tide meant Mosquito Creek was deep and wide, giving the chase boat plenty of room to fly full speed after us. His spotlight was a hell of lot brighter than ours, and was already visible again and getting closer.

Ahead on the left I saw the lights of the Little St. Simons lodge, cottages and docks coming up, and felt bad screaming by the NO WAKE sign at 60 miles an hour. I'd come back some day and apologize. Maybe not.

Just past the docks, I had to slow down entering the creek's hairpin curve to the right. The speedboat's radio blared, "This is Glynn County Marine Patrol hailing the vessel running high speed in Mosquito Creek. Come in."

Claire stared at me. The call repeated.

"What do we do?" Claire asked.

"Nothing."

The radio blared again. Not as polite this time.

The creek was still too wide for me to take full advantage of our boat's ability to cut corners and pull away. His huge outboards and fast props were driving him closer and closer.

As we flew by a huge oak near the left bank with a limb out over the creek, I remembered from years ago that, around the next bend, there was a hidden secret. Back when the lodge was being built, some big cypress trees were cut down, sawed into long logs and dragged off. And apparently some unenlightened skidder driver piled them up not far ahead, close to the left side of the creek. Later the pile collapsed and some of the trees rolled into the water where they became saturated and sank, and remain today, about a foot below the surface on a good high tide.

I told Claire to hold on and eased the throttles forward.

As we came out of the next bend I aimed left. With our shallow draft, we flew over the hidden logs unscathed, and I hoped the bend in the creek and our wake would lure our pursuer the same way. I shouted to Claire as we sped away, "Watch for him."

After a moment, Claire said, "I don't see him anymore."

"Good."

"What did you do?"

"An old Indian trick—I'll tell you later—gotta keep moving. Patrol boats have good radios."

I maintained our speed, twisting and turning through Mosquito Creek while it got narrower and narrower. Claire went quiet on me.

I glanced her way and said, "It's OK."

No reply.

We spun around a few more curves and moments later we were back in the Hampton River. Claire sorta smiled and I was feeling kinda proud . . . until she answered the Admiral's scramble phone and handed it to me.

"I don't know where you kids are," he said, "but I just heard there's a chopper with a heat-sensing scope on the way."

"Thanks, Admiral," *for bursting my bubble*, "I'll call you back."

I altered course to starboard, hit the throttles and aimed for the entrance to Village Creek, home to the only place we might be safe from a heat-sensing scope. Unfortunately the surrounding area was named for a bunch of dead men.

Bloody Marsh

The inward curve of America's southeast coast is so pronounced, if you travel due north from St. Simons Island, you'll end up in Cleveland, Ohio. Really.

Plus, Georgia's shallow offshore continental shelf extends a surprising 80 miles out into the Atlantic Ocean.

The combined funneling effect of these two geographic features creates extreme tides along the Georgia coast. For example, while North Carolina above and south Florida below have tides that average three feet, the difference between low and high tides on St. Simons Island is seven or eight, sometimes nine feet. That's up and down. *And* we have two highs and two lows every day. Do the math—roughly six hours from one extreme to the other, four times a day, every day.

In the 1700s these tides, not surprisingly, played all kinds of hell with early sailors. If that wasn't enough, Mother Nature also lined our coast with large, ragged barrier islands and their constantly shifting shoals and sandbars. Bottom Line: sailing to the Georgia coast was not for wussies.

The world's two strongest sea powers, however, were strongly motivated, and not deterred.

In the north, the British—already with substantial New England settlements—had recently established new colonies in Charleston and Savannah. British General James Oglethorpe came farther south and built two forts on St. Simons, one being Fort Frederica, currently managed by the National Park Service.

To the south, Spain, the other world sea power, had Florida and most of the Caribbean, all extraordinarily rich with trading goods. To keep it all for themselves, Spain used the Treaty of Seville, which demanded that the Brits keep out, and even allowed Spaniards to search British ships for prohibited cargo.

In 1731 during a particularly combative boarding of the British ship *Rebecca*, Ship's Captain Robert Jenkins found himself separated from one of his ears. Not pleased, Jenkins saved the ear in a jar, sailed for home and personally addressed the House of Commons. Regardless of his physical appearance, his timing was perfect. England had been wanting some of that profitable trading in the south. So, when Captain Jenkins told his government about the Spaniards' bad manners—and displayed his ear-in-a-jar—the British declared a war on Spain that became known as the War of Jenkins' Ear. Honest.

During the war's initial year, the British forts on St. Simons were unmolested. Then one day 3,000 Spaniards arrived on the beach. When General Oglethorpe learned the new visitors weren't unloading coolers and beach umbrellas, he called his outnumbered men together. In typical British, stiff-upper-lip style, he reminded his small militia of England's rich military history. *And*, their current homefield advantage.

At some point during the ensuing combat, the Spaniards on the beach decided to take a shortcut across the wide salt marsh that separates the East Beach peninsula from St. Simons Island proper. Big mistake. The Spaniards were good soldiers, but in the open marsh they became good targets. And the Brits claimed credit for one of the first good-ole, South Georgia ass-whuppins.

Sources said, "The marsh ran red with the blood of the invaders!" Nobody today knows how many Spaniards actually died. History, however, is written by the victors, so the skirmish earned a seriously dramatic name that lives on. The Battle of Bloody Marsh.

Not far north of Bloody Marsh today, where a tidal creek that goes nowhere meets a dead-end road, No-See-Ums Bar and Grill is famous for great food and drinks. And for remaining stubbornly casual. It sits high on a forest of skinny poles, straddling a Village Creek tributary, and is bordered on one side by an oyster-shell parking lot and on the other by a rough-as-a-cob boat ramp.

Inside this unassuming old building, however, is a virtual history of the United States Air Force's presence in Coastal Georgia. The walls are covered with framed black-and-white photographs of airplanes and the test pilots who flew them—men who lived and died while training at Arnall Air Force Base.

And, yes, I have studied those photographs, searching for my father's name or face. And I have had to conclude, that, for a reason I'll never know, he is missing from those walls, just as he was from my life.

———————————

Because of the president's visit, all the surrounding waterways were now officially closed. So, as Claire and I raced up Village Creek after midnight in rain that felt like bullets, not only were we wanted by the FBI, we were screaming along in a red rocketship in a restricted waterway just asking for trouble.

"Where are we going?" Claire asked over the engines' roar.

"Kitchen. You hungry?"

Her eyes said, *just drive the damn boat.*

Chapter 38

No-See-Ums

Sunday 4:30 a.m.

Through curtains of rain, we flew deeper up the tidal creek leading to
No-See-Ums Bar and Grill. When lightning revealed the old stilt building ahead, I reduced the throttles and let our momentum carry us into
the narrowing water. As we eased around the last bend, between walls of
swaying grass I saw the absence I hoped for. No boats, cars, or lights.

"Where are we?" Claire asked.

"Shh! Listen . . ."

Tires on gravel? Wait . . . no. A helicopter, low and close!

"Hold on." I pushed the throttles hard and *Jock's Trap* lunged for the
dark beneath the building. I made one hard S turn to line us up and cut
the power as we disappeared into the black forest of tall creosote posts.
Claire dropped to the deck, and I braced myself with one hand and
full-reversed the engines with the other.

We slammed into the sloped bank and rocked to a sudden stop as I
killed the engines. *Jock's Trap* was up at the bow and listing to port, but
the ugly red boat was hidden deep in the dark beneath the old building.
Behind us, wind and rain erased our wake. *Thank you, Jesus*, as they say.

I checked on Claire, then the scanner volume, hoping the chopper
would be using a channel we received. At first, nothing. Just the scary
sound of the chopper getting closer.

Then, the scanner caught a signal and locked on. "This is Coast
Guard chopper Bravo-Two, calling Glynn Marine Patrol."

The reply was immediate. "Go ahead, Coast Guard Bravo-Two."

"We're registering two heat signatures in the area. Give us a quick
blue-light so we'll know which is you."

"Roger"

A second later, "Gotcha, Glynn. We're turning and closing on the other one. Will let you know."

A moment later, the chopper was directly overhead, drawn to us by the invisible infrared heat radiating from *Jock's Trap's* big engines. Claire gasped and hugged my side as the world around us lit up. The chopper's million-candle-power spotlight turned night to day, sweeping back and forth. Our big red boat glowed from the reflected light, but the chopper couldn't see us. I couldn't tell if Claire's shivering was from fear or the cold rain. The chopper roared. Time stopped.

Finally, the radio again. "Glynn Marine Patrol, this is Coast Guard Chopper Bravo-Two, come in."

"Go ahead, Bravo-Two."

"We got a negative on the second heat signature."

"Say again, Bravo-Two."

"I say, we have a negative on the second heat signature. It's not a boat."

"Coast Guard Bravo-Two, I don't understand your last."

"It's an old restaurant at a boat ramp. Got to be nothing but a hot kitchen. There *is* no other boat. No cars. Nothing."

"Are you sure, Bravo-Two?"

"Affirmative, Glynn, I'm right on top of it. It's nothing but a crummy old fish camp. Stoves and ovens probably been going all day and night. Still hot."

"Roger, Bravo-Two. Got it."

"We'll make another wide sweep and let you know if we see anything. My guess is, if it's a go-fast, it's long gone."

"Roger, Bravo-Two. Glynn Out."

"Bravo-Two out."

As the chopper's spotlight went dark and the sound diminished in the distance, Claire eased away from my side, looked up and softly said, "Pretty smart, Hood."

"Yeah," I sighed proudly.

"Pretty stuck too, uh?" she smiled, with a nod toward our raised bow.

"Yeah," I sighed less proudly.

In my rush to get us under the building, I had driven *Jock's Trap's* long bow deep up on the mud bank.

"I was little late hitting reverse. And I expected more long grass," I said. "easy to push out of."

"Right," Claire said, "long green grass in permanent shade."

"Do *you* want to drive?"

"No way, Rambo. You're doing fine."

I glanced around. I wasn't sure about the tide and couldn't take a chance getting stuck here for hours. I wanted us floating again, now.

I climbed over the side, into the reeds and black mud, slogged to the bow and pushed. Hard. Nothing. Harder. Once. Twice. Three times. Still nothing. I looked around for something to use as a lever. Nothing.

"Give me that scramble phone."

Mack said, "What the hell are you doing stuck under No-See-Ums?"

"Hiding from a chopper with an infrared heat sensor."

"Pretty smart," he said. "Except for getting stuck."

"Yeah, Claire's already mentioned that. Hey," I said, changing the subject, "if you're not too busy, maybe you could do a little something for me?"

"Like?"

"Anything to draw attention away from us so we can get out of here."

"You know, son, grounding a boat can be a career killer for a sailor."

"Yeah, I think I have heard that. But right now, sir, I'm a little more worried about my ass than my career. What do you think?"

"Keep listening to your scanner."

"Thanks, Mack. I owe you one."

"You owe me more than that. And tide just turned. Better hurry."

"Aye aye, sir."

A minute later the scanner crackled. Without identifying himself, Mack hailed the Glynn Marine Patrol, sounding more mullet fisherman than admiral. He said he heard the recent exchange between the Patrol boat and a Coast Guard helicopter, and a few minutes ago he heard what sounded like a go-fast heading north about a mile offshore.

Next, I heard the Marine Patrol boat say thanks, then advise his dispatcher he was leaving Village Creek via the Hampton River and returning to the open water.

We waited an interminable three minutes until the scramble phone rang. Back in his admiral voice, Mack said, "The Marine Patrol boat just turned north out of Hampton River."

"Thanks."

"And I just talked with Fish Williams," he continued. "He's offshore about 15 miles north of here, heading back from Savannah. It doesn't sound like you're having much luck hiding. Plus, it'll be light soon."

"I was just thinking that."

"Call Fish. He has an idea."

"Thanks."

"What did he say?" Claire asked.

"I'll explain later. Right now, we don't have a second to spare getting out of here."

Claire took the helm and followed my instructions. Putting the boat in reverse, we used the high-pressure stream blasting forward from the water jet engines to free the hull and slide *Jock's Trap* backward until she was floating again. No better feeling for a grounded boater.

I backed her into the narrow creek and slowly turned her around.

"Now what?" Claire asked.

"We have a date with *Lady Luck*.

"Hell, I hope so."

I put us in idle-forward and we began to slowly meander out of the smaller tributaries. Soon we were back in Village Creek, easing north toward the Hampton River. I kept us in idle-forward and told Claire to take the wheel while I called *Lady Luck*. She didn't like it, but there was just enough light to see the bank of the creek on our port side. I told her she'd be fine.

I got Fish Williams and he verified his position, and his offer to help.

Claire complained about not being able to see and wanted to turn on the bow spotlight. I said no and went back to Fish. I heard Claire mumbling in my other ear. *Women.*

Fish said, "Can you talk now?"

I replied, "Yeah, go ahead."

I never dreamed Claire would think I was talking to her.

Fish was telling me the approximate dimensions of his boat when Claire found the bow spotlight switch and sent a cone of light across the water in front of us. That was a real surprise.

It was nothing, however, compared to what it showed forty yards away.

Chapter 39

Hunting for Fish

Sunday 5:00 a.m.

Dead ahead, sitting sideways in Village Creek, was the longest Marine Patrol boat I had ever seen. In the pouring rain our spotlight lit up the craft's aluminum canopy frame, glistening bright against the black sky.

Shit! What's he doing here?

In the instant before his big spotlight came on and blinded us, I saw the thin, young face of the driver.

I knocked Claire hard against the cushioned cockpit wall getting to the helm, and shoved the throttles to the stops with one hand, spinning the wheel to the right with the other. The bow went up and to the right, and the crazy tilt pulled the port engine's intake above the surface. A giant sucking noise shrieked as the engine screamed for water, and the boat's twisting angle and acceleration pinned Claire and me against the seatback. I remembered the face I had seen from a newspaper photo days before. The Glynn County Marine Patrol had a new pursuit vessel with bigger outboards and faster props, and the first officer trained to pilot the new craft was a boyish recruit. From Kansas, no less.

In our spinning, bow-high boat, all I could see was dark sky and rain. Above our own engines' growl, however, I distinctly heard the throaty roar of the Patrol boat's huge outboards coming to life.

When our spin-from-hell ended, and we rocked halfway back to level, the waterjet engines caught, and *Jock's Trap* took off like a bottle rocket. I wanted to think our ugly speedboat was leaving our surprise visitor far behind, but the white glare from his spotlight and the flashing blue light reflecting all around us said it wasn't so. The newboy was fast.

We flew through the watery curves of Village Creek faster than I thought possible, but the Kansas farm boy stayed right behind us. My shallower draft took the turns tighter, but it wasn't enough to lose him.

It was a hell of a race, but it couldn't go on forever. The tall grass had already begun to move closer, and our twisty corridor was beginning to fracture into smaller branches that all looked alike. At this speed, I was going to need great instincts and a shitload of luck to keep choosing the right one. Only one of these sorry little waterways went where I needed to go.

I was pretty sure I knew the area better than the Kansas boy behind us, but that wouldn't help much if I couldn't get him off my tail. There was only one more thing I could try.

I pulled Claire close and shouted above the roar of the engines. "Listen! Do exactly what I say. No questions. Got it?"

Scared, she nodded.

"Get the box of food the Admiral's wife gave us and be ready to start throwing everything at the guy behind us."

She didn't say it, but I could see her wondering how ham sandwiches were going to help.

"Just get ready, dammit," I said. "You stand here and, when I say 'go,' you start throwing stuff at him as hard and as fast as you can. Everything. Even the box and the thermos. Got it?"

She nodded, wide-eyed.

"And, when I say 'Down!' you drop to the deck as fast as you can, all the way down flat, close your eyes and cover your head. Got it?"

She nodded again. "What are you going to do?"

"I'm gonna let him get closer."

"*What?*" she screamed.

"Can't talk now!"

The turns were coming faster and the water was getting narrower. I felt like I was trapped in a video game from hell, and I wanted out.

Above the tall grass on our left, I saw the faint glimmer of resort lights. I hoped our pursuer was so new to the area and focused on us that he didn't realize what that meant.

I pulled the throttles back a hair to let the newboy close the gap. I wanted him right on our butt, partially blinded by our reflection in his spotlight.

We were still doing about 50 when we passed where Village Creek converges with the Blackbank River. Because the watery junction looks like all the other branches, I was counting on the newboy not realizing where we were . . . and being too distracted by the chase to remember the Sea Island Causeway's low fixed bridge dead ahead.

I dropped a little more speed and let the Patrol boat's pointed bow close to within a few feet of our stern. He was good, but I knew that kind of driving was the bravado of youth, not what he learned in Boating Safety 101.

It was exactly what I wanted.

We cleared one more turn and were passing some Sea Island docks on our left when I shouted, "Go!" Claire stood up and started throwing everything she had at the chase boat. Out of the corner of my eye, I saw sandwiches, potato chips, bottled water and cola cans flying over our stern. The newboy slowed briefly, confused by the grocery store projectiles, but quickly accelerated again. The distraction was also designed to keep his attention more on us and the groceries and less on those Sea Island docks and what would be coming up in about three seconds, two, one . . .

I checked ahead as Claire was hurling the thermos and empty box over the stern.

"Down!" I screamed and shoved her to the deck.

As fast as I could move, I checked our direction one last time, then ducked below the instrument panel, still holding the bottom of the wheel with one hand.

The concrete bottom of the Sea Island Causeway bridge sheared off our short windshield in a shattering blast that sent metal and glass flying.

Behind us, the new kid on the block was fast enough to duck and save his own skin, but couldn't protect the shiny aluminum frame over his head. The bridge caught it about halfway up and ripped it from its bolts, taking most of the helm with it. It rang like a tuning fork before falling into the water behind the boat.

I was back at the wheel, slowing us down when Claire realized we weren't actually dead. She looked up, brushed crumbles of safety glass out of her hair and said something that would have amazed Miss Manners.

"Sorry. There wasn't time to explain."

She looked up at me. "Is he dead?" she asked incredulously.

"Hell no. He ducked right before the canopy frame hit the bridge."

She looked at me disbelievingly.

"I promise, his light lit up the bridge before he hit it, and I saw him duck. I didn't want to kill him. I just wanted him to go away."

I learned later that the newboy got a few fiberglass splinters, lost his job and was now selling tractors in Topeka.

After Claire calmed down, I said, "Find that damn scramble phone. I've had enough of Bloody Marsh."

We continued south on the Blackbank River, behind the sparsely developed south end of Sea Island. We had enough ambient light, so didn't need our bow light. I kept our speed at idle-forward, got Fish on the scramble phone and apologized for hanging up on him a few minutes ago. He was about 10 miles north, a mile offshore, and heading this way. I told him where we were, and he suggested we stay dark, come out through Gould's Inlet into the Atlantic, and head north to meet him. He said he had an idea.

I said I didn't and was open to suggestions.

I opted for a slow but steady speed that would help us maneuver safely through the crosscurrents of Goulds Inlet. Once we reached open water, past the wide shoals, I turned north, heading for the *Lady Luck* somewhere in the distant dark. I wondered what the hell I was going to do when I found her. I pushed the throttles forward and we accelerated across black water. The wind and rain continued to oscillate between bad and worse.

The Admiral had said the president would be staying at the Barrier Island Club on the south end, and even though all surrounding waterways were closed, the hard-security radius was only three miles. Because that was about the straight-line distance from Gould's Inlet to the club property, I hoped we were far enough away—and heading farther away—not to attract attention. To be safe, I set a moderate speed. And kept looking over my shoulder.

Ten minutes later, through the monsoon we could see a thin glow on the eastern horizon saying sun-up was soon. Then, just to be sure we weren't getting bored, the storm ratcheted up into an offshore version of one of those things on weather TV with bouncing traffic lights and twisting stop signs.

When the scramble phone rang again, Claire got it. The look on her face said it wasn't the Admiral.

"Are you expecting a call from a *Fish*?" she yelled, handing me the phone.

I took it, shaking my head.

"This is Carson," I fairly screamed.

"Carson, Fish Williams. Can you hear me?

"Barely."

"You can't see me, but I see you on radar."

Claire demanded, "Who is it?"

I waved her off.

Fish continued, "Admiral says you need help. Keep coming. I'll call you back when we're closer—*Shit*!"

"What?"

"My radio man just heard a chopper's lifting off from McKinnon Field. Better hurry."

"On the way." I dropped the phone into Claire's hands, said, "Hold on," then shoved the throttles forward. *Jock's Trap* leapt into hyperdrive.

Moments later, the phone rang just as I saw the lights and the big twin-hull silhouette of *Lady Luck* two miles north of us. Claire held the phone out to me.

"You talk," I shouted back over the noise.

She listened, then said, "The chopper's starting his sweep this way. He says hurry!"

The horizon was growing brighter. I hit the throttles hard to max.

"He says swing around and come in from his stern."

Moments later, we passed by *Lady Luck* on her starboard side. I spun us in a tight 180 and started closing on the turbulent wake behind her huge twin hulls.

"He said throw fenders out," Claire shouted. "What does that mean?"

I pointed toward the white, cylindrical fenders rolling around in the back and shouted, "They're tied on. Toss 'em over the side."

At thirty yards, the colliding wakes of her twin hulls churned the surface into white water rapids that tossed us side to side so furiously I couldn't hold course. I started easing the throttles back. "No!" Claire shouted, "He says the chopper's coming. Hurry!"

I gave the throttles a good push and we powered through the man-made rapids and shot into the smooth water in the cavern between *Lady Luck's* two hulls. I eased off the power so we wouldn't pop out in front, and before I could say *what now*, a man hanging in mid-air, standing on the bottom wooden step of a rope ladder, waved me forward. When the bow was right under him, he stepped down, and in one smooth motion, looped a perfect figure eight around the large center cleat. I pulled the throttles back to neutral. A second later he climbed over what was left of the windshield and was standing beside me, hand out. "Fish is at the helm. He said come on up," then added, nodding aft, "I think the storm ate your wake."

He reached over, cut off the three engine switches and the master ignition, and added, "I can't wait to hear your story."

"Thanks for the help," I said, meaning it.

"Fish needs to be on the bridge," he said. "If anyone has to lie to the Coast Guard, Fish wants it to be him, not one of the crew." He smiled, climbed back onto the bow and disappeared up the rope ladder.

In spite of the raging storm a few feet away, we were well protected by

Lady Luck's big hulls on each side. Even the sound of her powerful twin diesels was behind us.

Unexpectedly our new friend's head popped out of the hatch above and shouted down, "Captain says chopper's coming!"

"What do we do?" I shouted back.

"Just nothing stupid."

I knew what he meant and checked our position to be sure we were as far away as possible from both ends of the big boat. I should have known he had tied us in the perfect place.

"What do we do?" Claire asked.

"Like the man said. Just nothing, stupid."

"That's *not* how he said it," she said, pinching hell out of my side.

Thirty seconds later we heard the rapid whup-whup-whup of a helicopter overhead. Huddling in the speedboat, we instinctively recoiled, but there was nowhere to go. As the sound of the chopper got louder, we looked back and forth from the bow to the stern, waiting for the chopper to get low enough to see us.

"Carson, they'll see us! What do we do?"

I didn't answer. I didn't know.

Chapter 40

Lady Luck

Sunday 6:00 a.m.

I was sure the Coast Guard chopper would drop low enough to see us between *Lady Luck's* big hulls. But the pilot had no intention of risking his bird in high winds and huge waves. Besides, what did he expect to see? What fool would drive his boat under another boat in a monsoon?

Our marine radio crackled. "This is Captain Francis Williams of the recreational vessel *Lady Luck*, calling the Coast Guard chopper above my vessel. I am inbound from Savannah, with Coast Guard navigation permission number Echo, X-ray, Dash One, allowing me to return to a point at the three-mile radius around the Barrier Island Club, which is exactly what I am doing. Over."

When there was no reply, Fish let him have it.

"This is the Captain of the *Lady Luck* to the Coast Guard chopper over my vessel. You're scaring my passengers to death! I have permission from your superiors to be on this course. Now get away from my boat, or my U.S. Senator brother will have you busted so low, you'll be driving a trash barge tomorrow. Get lost, now dammit!"

For a second, nothing changed. Then the chopper went away. We breathed.

A few moments later, Fish came down the rope ladder, and climbed into the speedboat's cockpit. "That was close. I don't mind helping friends of Mack's, but, hell, I don't even know what I'd go to jail for yet. I hope this is over before anybody finds out my brother sells cars, not votes."

Claire changed the subject. "I didn't think you had any passengers."

"I don't, but the chopper don't know that. Look, whatever you guys are up to, be careful. Mack told you about the *Sullivan*, right?"

"Yeah. Apparently, that C-WIZ thing can ruin your whole day."

He nodded agreement, then looked at us, both soaked, and me still filthy from trying to get *Jock's Trap* unstuck beneath No-See-Ums. "Why don't y'all come up top for a while, get cleaned up, have some coffee and biscuits?"

"Love to," I said, as Claire stared at the rope ladder swinging freely in the breeze. "It'll be fine," I said, as I put a life jacket on her. Then Fish and I anchored the bottom of the ladder while she slowly climbed, one step at a time, right foot first, all the way.

Fish let us clean up in his private quarters and gave us dry clothes from spares his crew had. The last little while had seen the storm move out just as fast as it had moved in last night. The sky was clearing and bright, and the sea was calm with a few leftover swells. I was drinking water while Claire sipped coffee and called Taz on one of the secure phones. She got her, and listened for a long time, then started saying, "OK. Yeah. I got it. I'll call you back."

"What?" I asked.

"Wait a minute," she said while she punched in another number. "I'm calling Blake, FBI. Listen to this."

He answered and she began, "Blake, this is Claire, don't interrupt me, where is Wheeler? Do you still have him? OK, get him and tell him you know he's lying about the Janus Project—never mind how I know it—he is. Tell him—listen to me, dammit—tell him you know about the Cayman money. Tell him he's about to spend the next 20 years in federal prison if he doesn't tell you the truth right now." She ended the call and stared at the table.

"What?"

"Taz's amazing."

What, dammit?"

"Taz always says the three main reasons people lie are sex, drugs and money, right?

"I've heard that."

"And," Claire continued, "Because Wheeler didn't seem like the sex or drugs type, she figured it was money. So she hacked into recent records of foreign financial transfers, then searched for any between half a million and 10 million containing some of the same alphanumerics Wheeler has used in usernames or passwords."

"And?"

"Bingo. It turns out a Mr. Creighton Groves has a new account at the Bank of the Caymans, with an opening balance right under a cool mill. And all three of Taz's analytical programs identified the account password as containing enough alphanumerics Wheeler has used before to suggest it has a 70 percent probability of being created by him."

"I don't get it. Who would pay Wheeler a million dollars to lie?"

"I don't know. Maybe the FBI can figure that out."

I shook my head. "I don't get it."

"What?" she said defensively. "You heard it all. You know everything I do."

"It's been a long time since I thought that was so."

She gave me one of *those* looks and sipped more coffee. As she set the cup down, she looked straight at me.

"What?" I said.

"I don't know. Something is wrong. Taz sounded different then."

"How?"

"I don't know. She sounded sure about what she was telling me, but there was something else in her voice."

"We've been depending on her a lot. Are you sure about Taz?"

"Yes, absolutely."

A quiet moment passed before she said, "I'm calling her back."

Taz answered immediately.

"Hey, you OK?" Claire asked.

I waited, watching Claire. Everything seemed OK. Then her expression changed. She asked Taz, "What do you mean?"

Another long pause.

"I don't understand."

"What?" I mouthed.

She shook her head at me and said back into the phone, "Taz, where are you now?"

Something was wrong.

"Taz!" Claire was adamant. "You quit, right now. Forget about Wheeler. Stop. Do you hear me? Get offline, now. Leave, go home. No, not home. Go to a friend's house. Don't call anyone, don't go online, just leave . . ."

Claire stopped talking before she was through. She looked confused. She turned to me and explained. "While she was looking for more info on Wheeler, a notice popped up on her screen about illegal searching, violating FBI restrictions. Well, she knew damn well everything she does online is invisible and anonymous. If something triggered that warning, it meant someone was tracking her. That scared her so she left the office and went to a 24-hour Internet cafe to try another computer. As soon as she got online there, the same warning popped up, so she logged out, left and drove back to the office.

She said someone might have followed her. She saw a car behind her make the same turns, but she's inside now and doesn't see the other car."

Claire said, "Taz," but got no answer.

I waited while Claire tried to compose herself.

A long pause, then, "She's whispering, thinks someone's in the building."

I felt a chill on the back of my neck. "Tell her to get out of there!"

"What?" she said, going back to Taz. She listened again and shook her head. Her eyes looked pained. "No, no, no, Taz, please! Do as I say! Go out the front door. I'll call 911 from here. Go! Now!"

Claire looked up at me and winced helplessly. She was still waiting on Taz. I touched her shoulder, and she started to speak to Taz again, but it didn't sound like Taz was listening.

I leaned forward. Claire turned on speakerphone. It sounded like someone was walking. There was a muffled voice. Then the walking turned to running.

"Taz!" Claire's breathing had gone short and shallow. Mine was no better.

On the other end, Taz's voice came through, breathing hard. She was running. "Claire, listen if you can still hear me." She was breathing so hard, she could barely talk. "They want to know where you are. I didn't tell them anything, I promise."

"Taz, who is it?" Claire was almost screaming.

"I don't know . . ."

She was running hard and sounded panicked. I could hear doors opening and slamming.

"Taz, get out of there!" Claire was screaming into the phone.

A scream and three rapid shots came through the phone's speaker so loudly, Claire and I both jumped. Immediately, Claire screamed, "Taz! Taz!" Over and over again. "Taz!"

Nothing.

Claire dropped the phone into her lap and I grabbed it before it slid to the floor. She hid her face in her hands and cried. The sounds were gunshots. We both knew that.

I wrapped my arm around Claire and put the phone back to my ear with my other hand. At first, there was nothing. But the connection was still alive. Then I heard somebody breathing hard, trying to be quiet. They were listening too. I waited. A muffled voice on the other end said, "Don't hang up."

I ended the call and stared at the phone.

Claire was bent over, sobbing uncontrollably. My pulse ran wild, and my breaths came fast and thin. I felt something else, however, stronger than fear. My heart was breaking, watching Claire in such pain.

I rubbed Claire's back with my left hand but realized that my right hand was closing into a fist and opening again, over and over. I watched it, and wanted to stop it, but couldn't. I reached for the Admiral's nine-millimeter Glock.

Holding the weighty automatic gave me a reassurance—and a clarity—I hadn't felt before that moment. The last few days played again in my mind. But instead of a streaming of loose snapshots, I began to see a continuous unreeling of events, a progressively escalating evil that had brought us to this point—the cemetery—Claire's burglary—Ryan in ICU—and now, Taz shot while we listened helplessly. I didn't know how they were all tied together, but now I was sure they were. And I was determined to find the son of a bitch who tied the knots and strangle him with his own rope. I had been confused, scared and angry. And I still was.

But now, I was something else. I was mad.

Through the years, I heard that Parris Island Drill Instructor: *What the hell are you waiting for?*

He was right then. And now. It was time to move.

I tried to console Claire—to cast doubt on what we heard, but it didn't help. We both knew what had happened. That, and the accumulation of what we had been through since last Sunday had finally caught up with her. She had done all she could. It was now up to me to finish it.

Fish appeared and helped me get her to the bed in his cabin. She was still sobbing when we left her. We walked upstairs to the bridge.

The white morning sun streamed through the large windows, bouncing off rows of dials and instruments, sending crazy reflections all over the gray ceiling. Fish Williams stared silently at me while I brought him up to date. When I told him what we had heard, he looked away. After a moment, he looked back at me and said, "I knew when Mack called something was wrong. If he's worried, I'm worried. What do you want to do?"

"Why don't you call Mack and bring him up to date, see if he has any ideas. I'm going to call the FBI guy, Blake, and see if he's had any luck with Wheeler or Strom.

When I got Blake on the phone, he wanted Claire. I told him I was speaking for her. He didn't like that, and I said I didn't give a rat's ass what he liked.

He snapped back, "You don't have the authority to speak for anyone. I demand to speak to Claire Markham now."

"To hell with you, Blake. And what is this shit about Claire and I being wanted by the FBI? What are you up to?"

"Everything about the president's visit was Top Secret. And whenever anyone raises the kind of issues you have, you damn right, the FBI wants you secured."

"Secured?" I said, "is that anything like arrested?"

"Where are you?" he asked.

"None of your damn business."

"Dammit, Hood, I'm trying to help you!"

"Do me a favor. Don't. Your help just got somebody shot."

"What are you talking about?" he asked.

I took a deep breath. "Claire and I just heard her assistant get shot, probably because she was trying to do your damn job."

"What?" he snapped back.

"We were on the phone a few minutes ago with Claire's assistant in Atlanta. She said someone followed her to the foundation office and got inside. We heard her talking to someone, then running, slamming doors. She was trying to tell us something when we heard gunshots. Then nothing."

For a moment Blake didn't say anything. I heard him cover the phone and ask someone a question. When he came back, he said, "Look, someone was hacking into high-level networks. I don't know if it was her or not. But we did what we are supposed to do. We sent a team out to find whoever was doing it and bring 'em in. I don't know anything about anybody being shot."

I didn't know if he was lying or not. Talking to him pissed me off. I changed the subject. "What did Wheeler say when you told him you knew he was lying about the findings of the Janus Project?"

"I'm not at liberty to discuss that with you."

I ignored that, and said, "*And*, that we knew about the money in the Caymans?"

He repeated his silly-ass answer.

"Blake, you prick. We're the ones who told you he was lying! And about the Cayman money! If you want to help, now would be a good time to start."

"Wheeler admitted the money was his, but he refused to admit he'd done anything wrong."

"So, somebody just gave him a million dollars because they liked him. And he thought another country might be a convenient place to open a savings account?"

"It's an ongoing investigation. I can't discuss it."

"Great! Sounds to me like Wheeler just outsmarted everybody and made a million dollars, tax free.

"Look, we do this every day," he replied, "we know what we are doing."

"Blake, I suggest you call the Secret Service and tell them what you know."

"It's already been done."

Chapter 41

Sidney Lanier Bridge II

The original Sidney Lanier Bridge—named for the poet who penned *The Marshes of Glynn*—was opened in June 1956. It was a drawbridge with a center span that elevatored straight up between the thick iron scaffolding of two green, H-shaped towers. Local nostalgics still say it was beautiful, but to the bureaucrats who paid for its expensive maintenance, any beauty it had was in its utility. Like a school crossing guard on a busy highway, the old drawbridge stayed down to let vehicles go north and south, and went up to let cargo ships go east and west. It all worked well. Until a night in November 1972.

The captain of the *African Neptune* made the mistake of trying to shoot the narrow gauntlet between the two bridge towers in a storm and tide that made the maneuver impossible. The ship struck the bridge, sending several sections of the roadway into the dark, rushing water below. Several cars went too. Ten deaths were attributed to the accident. There may have been more. The tidal currents under the bridge are merciless. If the Atlantic Ocean is rushing in, the Brunswick River flows uphill until the water level rises almost nine feet. If the tide is going out, brackish water streams to sea in an unstoppable torrent. A car on the bottom of the channel would be rolled with the prevailing current, and deposited with its lifeless occupants anywhere the tidal river wanted it. There was no way to know only ten people died.

Funeral and memorial services were held, hearings were held, lawsuits were filed, and lawyers made money. The bridge was repaired.

Fifteen years later it happened again. In May 1987, the Polish freighter *Ziemia Bialostocka* struck one of the towers. The damage was less this time, but it was obvious the people of Georgia needed a new bridge. More and larger ships needed access to the growing Port of Brunswick.

The Georgia Department of Transportation and the United States Coast Guard agreed the old drawbridge needed to be replaced with a tall, fixed bridge. One with more room between the supporting towers. A lot more.

In Georgia all replacement bridges must keep the name of the original bridge. Thus the new Sidney Lanier Bridge was begun in July 1995, and completed 10 years—and $65 million—later. It is a high, fixed, cable-stayed bridge, with a roadbed that, at its highest point, is an ear-popping 203 feet above sea level. The two massive concrete towers that anchor the 176 cables supporting the roadbed reach another 277 feet straight up, topping out at an altitude of 480 feet. The true height and magnitude of the massive structure is masked by its mile-and-a-half length, and the gradual slope of its roadbed. It is a lot bigger than it looks. It is, in fact, the biggest bridge in the state.

Unlike the *suspension* Golden Gate Bridge, the new Sidney Lanier is *cable-stayed*. Its roadbed does not hang suspended from a curtain of vertical cables. Each of the Sidney Lanier's 176 large stay-cables rises, not straight up, but diagonally, from the roadbed to where it ties into one of the massive concrete towers. Because these cables pull their loads diagonally—not vertically—there is a compressive horizontal force applied to the roadbed, which adds both strength and stability. The added stability is good for bridges.

And for Rafael Quinterro.

From the roadway's highest point, in the outside, northbound lane, there is a narrow, unobstructed view to the rear patio of the Barrier Island Golf Club, almost five miles in the distance. Exactly where—according to Hispanic maitre'd Plinio Thomás—the President of the United States will be standing at 9:00 Sunday morning as she addresses her media-mogul guests. The exact distance is 4.7823 miles. Almost two miles beyond the three-mile protective radius established by the Secret Service.

Chapter 42

Coast Guard and Close Calls

Sunday 8:00 a.m.

Captain William Tyler and his crew of 167 were on high alert. Every man aboard the United States Coast Guard Cutter *Sullivan*—regardless of other responsibilities—was combat ready.

Twice in the last two years, Coast Guard Port Security crews had been in the news. The first incident involved the arrest of an intoxicated weekend boater who ignored posted buoys and raced deep into a restricted area in the San Francisco Harbor where weapons were being loaded onto a supply ship destined for the Persian Gulf. The Coast Guard later publicly apologized and said the boat's captain should not have been treated like a criminal. Privately, however, Coast Guard Port Security crews around the nation said the drunk probably should have been blown out of the water before he got as far as he did.

The second incident was no false alarm. The Nimitz-class supercarrier *Franklin D. Roosevelt* was leaving New York Harbor following a week-long tribute to the late president for whom she was named. Offshore, southeast of New York harbor, a speedboat sat dead in the water, slowly drifting in the current. The large engine hatch was open on the stern, and two men could be seen moving back and forth between the engine compartment and the helm. When it appeared the disabled speedboat would drift close to the course of the nuclear-powered carrier, the captain of the USCG Cutter *Hensler,* escorting the *Roosevelt* out of the harbor, dispatched a 25-foot, high-speed Defender-class craft to check out the speedboat and tow it away from the *Roosevelt's* course.

The *Hensler's* captain was concerned, in spite of the fact the NYPD's Harbor Patrol had radioed that the disabled speedboat appeared to be a local craft frequently seen in the harbor.

Everything seemed under control until the 25-foot Defender craft pulled alongside the disabled speedboat. Abruptly automatic weapons fire from the speedboat riddled the Coast Guard boat, and the speedboat leapt out of the water like something alive. The open engine hatch snapped off the stern as the go-fast planed off heading directly for the carrier.

The *Hensler's* captain ordered C-WIZ to open fire, and the water surrounding the racing speedboat erupted into a thousand white geysers as the lethal rain of 75 armor-piercing rounds a second found their target. Long shards of fiberglass rose out of the white spray a split second before the speedboat disappeared in a fiery explosion with a world-shaking concussive blast that knocked the Coast Guard captain off his feet and broke over 1,000 windows in buildings ringing the harbor.

The speedboat was loaded with shaped high-explosive charges configured to blast a massive waterline hole in the steel hull of the *Roosevelt*. The men onboard were believed to be Iraqi nationals who had been deep undercover in the U.S. for years.

The *Roosevelt* was undamaged, and the Coast Guard was publicly praised for saving the supercarrier. The Monday morning quarterbacks in the media, however, questioned the Coast Guard's decision not to react sooner to the potential threat posed by the speedboat.

Onboard the *Sullivan* on this bright Sunday morning, Captain William Tyler was not about to let a close call like that happen on his watch.

8:15 a.m.

Secret Service Lead Agent Jeb Howton, noticeably preoccupied, was halfway up the stairs of the Barrier Island Club.

Years ago when President Reagan visited the Demilitarized Zone separating North and South Korea, the Secret Service asked the military to string miles of camouflage netting along the DMZ where the president would be walking. North Korean soldiers with loaded rifles were not about to get a clear view of the President of the United States. Howton had mentioned a similar idea to President Chambers weeks ago, knowing she'd shoot it down.

"Thank you, Jeb," she had said, condescendingly," but I didn't invite the world's wealthiest media owners and executives to beautiful St. Simons to desecrate the gorgeous view—and make myself look scared—by hanging ugly-ass camo like dirty laundry along the waterfront."

Actually, Howton wasn't worried about a threat from the water. The Navy and Coast Guard had secured the channel for miles in either direction with underwater monitors and touch-sensitive nets.

Neither was he worried about Jekyll Island a mile away across the channel. A small army with metal detectors and K-9 patrols had cordoned off the northern end of the island, and spent the last week patrolling, searching and re-searching every tree, bush and sand dune.

What am I worried about then? he asked himself. We have a three-mile perimeter, which is standard for this type of outdoor exposure. And there are no sniper rifles accurate anywhere near that distance. Still, he didn't like all the wide-open space.

As he reached the door to The Champions Suite, Press Secretary Maria Esperanza was leaving.

"Yes," the president said, "what is it, Jeb?" Her tone said she didn't want to be bothered.

"Madame President," he started, "I want to say again that the agency is still concerned about the outdoor location . . ."

"And . . ." she cut him off, "you wish that I had moved the meeting indoors." She stood and walked over to the large window looking out over the green manicured grounds and the wide saltwater channel beyond. "But," she continued, "I chose not to, and that's that."

Howton hadn't expected much better, but as Lead Agent, it was his duty to repeat one last time that the United States Secret Service did not feel comfortable with this outdoor location.

"As always," she said, "I appreciate your concern. And I know I haven't been easy to work with lately, but we must move forward."

Howton nodded, "Yes ma'am."

"Jeb," she said more calmly, "I am about to address the most powerful media executives in the world, in the midst of the most dangerous civil right crisis America has faced since the Civil War, and I am not going to hide inside because the FBI can't find one absent-minded professor who worked for the government years ago."

"Madam President . . ." he tried to say, but she interrupted him again.

"Your own Office of Threat Assessment says they see absolutely nothing to this. Right?"

"Yes, Madame President."

"Not even a good rumor. Right?"

"Yes, Madame President."

"Then, thank you for your concern, but I have less than 45 minutes before addressing my guests, and I need to work on my speech."

"Yes, Madame President," Howton said, nodding slightly and turning to go.

Two stories below, on the rear patio of the Barrier Island Club, maitre'd Plinio Thomás walked by the presidential podium one last time to verify it was exactly where he had told a man it would be. When he saw a Secret Service agent watching, he quickly stepped in front of the podium to be in plain sight and thus not raise suspicion. He pretended to wipe something off the podium, where President Chambers would soon be standing. The agent who watched him walk away checked the podium for himself, but found nothing wrong.

8:30 a.m.

We were still several miles out when FBI Agent Blake called back.

"I have passed your concerns along to the Secret Service," Blake said, "and they have decided not to make any changes in the president's plans."

"I don't guess I should be surprised," I answered sarcastically. "What is her schedule today?"

"I'm not at liberty to say."

"Of course not," I said. "If nothing else, you government guys are consistent."

He didn't reply.

"I just hope you guys aren't protecting the president right into an early grave at Arlington."

He hung up.

I called the Admiral. "I bombed out with the Feds. Is there any way to find out the president's schedule?"

"Usually, no, but let me try. I'll call you right back."

Two minutes later, the phone rang. "She's addressing a group of media bigwigs at nine o'clock—25 minutes from now. And Carson, she's doing it outside, on the rear patio."

"Shit," I said, as that sank in.

"Exactly."

"Admiral, I have a bad feeling about this."

"I know, son. I don't blame you. But I think you've done everything you can."

I didn't reply.

"Look," he continued, "it's my understanding that they have a three-mile hard radius around the president, and no one knows of anything smaller than a missile that exceeds that range with any accuracy. And there's no way anything like that is going to get within 10 miles of here, much less three."

"I know but I can't sit here and do nothing when I think there may be an attempted assassination in a few minutes."

"I don't think there's anything any of us can do now," the Admiral replied.

Chapter 43

Evil on the Move

8:40 a.m.

The 900-horsepower diesel engine roared as Vic Kilgore steered the huge, 80,000-pound armored vehicle out of the RoRo test facility warehouse. He drove down the long driveway, turned south on Blythe Island Highway, then east on U.S. 17. From there he was eleven minutes from the crest of the Sidney Lanier Bridge—and an unobstructed view to the rear patio of the Barrier Island Club, where the President of the United States would soon be standing.

Syd Lomax riding shotgun reread his checklist while Kilgore shifted through the ten-wheel vehicle's powerful transmission. The instrument panel between the seats held the secure radio console and the intercom Kilgore would use to communicate with anyone standing outside. The massive single-body vehicle also had a closed ventilation system, internal power generators, multiple locking mechanisms and air-tight gun ports.

Both men were wearing blue ISS uniforms with logos matching the outside of the vehicle—International Security Services.

Their weapons were loaded, but there was little chance they would be needed. Rule number one for cash-in-transit armored cars was simple. Between destinations, no one opens any door, for anybody, for any reason. Period.

Rule number two said, if rule number one needs to be broken, read rule number one again.

And any law enforcement personnel who didn't already know that could confirm it with a quick radio check with a superior officer.

Kilgore and Lomax weren't worried about needing their guns. They were safe inside behind military-grade, glass-clad polycarbonate windows stronger than bulletproof glass. And every inch of the vehicle's exterior surface was Abrams-grade, anti-tank armor consisting of layered ballistic steel, Kevlar and depleted-uranium. In U.S. military tests, rocket-propelled grenades exploded and bounced off like spitballs.

Back at the warehouse, Rafael Quinterro may have been concerned about the two men doing everything exactly right, but he was not worried they would open a door.

Kilgore drove the speed limit in the outside lane while Lomax watched the road ahead through ten-power, image-stabilized binoculars. The Georgia State Patrol's Jekyll Island office was nearby, and Lomax was praying he wouldn't see one of the GSP vehicles.

Behind the cab, in the modified cargo compartment of the massive vehicle, Hector Strom and Daniel Taggart were strapped in pedestal seats, going over their final checklists. Between them, an insulated housing covered the added drive shaft connecting the vehicle's transmission to the powerful generator for the weapon. Even sitting still, this second drive shaft would be charging the teracapacitor, as it had been for the last two hours.

Strom shook his head, trying to read his checklist as the heavy vehicle lumbered down the road. The device and all its components were testing perfectly, but there were still things he did not understand. If Quinterro wanted to assassinate drug lords, why had they targeted a county police chief?

As far as Strom knew, Quinterro had told no one the identity of the next victim. If Taggart and the two men up front knew, they weren't saying. Strom passed it off. He had other things to be concerned with. Besides, all he had to do was verify the operation of the power supply and prepare the proton laser for firing. Taggart would initiate the aiming and stabilization. He had been well trained for it, and that's all. The computer was programmed to fire when all three levels of target verification were complete. It would all happen very fast. The target's identity was not Strom's concern.

Ahead in the cab, Kilgore checked his oversized, outside mirrors as the armored car approached the crest of the bridge. In the passenger seat, Lomax was head-down, watching rapidly changing GPS numbers on a laptop. Kilgore eased off the gas and checked his mirrors again. A white minivan approaching from behind hadn't noticed the huge vehicle slowing down. Kilgore gently tapped the brake pedal. "Come on shit-for-brains. We ain't got time for this."

Kilgore's destination was the exact crest of the roadway—not an inch farther. He tapped the brakes again, slowing the massive blue and gray vehicle, then flipped on the emergency flashers. As he began easing onto the right shoulder, the minivan moved into the left lane to go around.

Kilgore breathed a sigh of relief and inched forward. The armored car was barely rolling, the huge vehicle's tires just brushing against the thick base of the bridge's low concrete sidewall. Perfect positioning was critical. Adjacent to the Barrier Island Club cottage putting green, there were several large oaks. Stopping too soon could put them in the way. Even an inch too far could put the thick metal of the club's large flagpole in the way. Quinterro had made it abundantly clear. Backing up would be inconsistent with the mechanical trouble Kilgore would report in a few moments. They could not take a chance that moving the truck in reverse would go unnoticed.

Kilgore waited on the signal from Lomax, who counted out loud the changing GPS numbers on the laptop. When the memorized number finally appeared, and Lomax shouted, "Stop," Kilgore hammered the brake, ending forward motion.

Kilgore pressed the emergency brake pedal hard with his left foot so the vehicle wouldn't roll any when he shifted into park and took his right foot off the brake. He left the engine running and looked over his right shoulder through the small window into the rear compartment. Taggart looked up from his computer screen and nodded an OK on the position.

Outside, the right tires of the vehicle were firm against base of the bridge's low sidewall, leaving no room for anyone to walk on the right side of the vehicle, where the one-inch-diameter firing port faced the rear patio of the Barrier Island Club.

The time was 8:50 a.m.

Kilgore reached for the radio handset and his notes, hesitated thinking about his rehearsed message, then keyed the mic.

"ISS dispatch, this is ISS Four-Two. Come in."

He waited. Two seconds later, a woman's voice replied, "ISS Four-Two, this is ISS dispatch. Today's passcode please?"

Kilgore spoke slowly and clearly. "Bravo, seven, sierra, four, tango, two." To anyone listening—and plenty of law enforcement would be today—it would sound like a simple identity-verification code.

To Quinterro, however, listening beside the woman in the old RoRo warehouse, it said the armored car was in position. The vehicle's GPS had already told Quinterro's computer the same thing. The conversation was designed to sound like a valid message between a cash-in-transit armored vehicle and its Miami dispatcher. In the next minute, the woman beside Quinterro would again be the Miami ISS dispatcher, this time calling the Glynn County 911 operator, requesting traffic assistance for the disabled armored car. It was important for anyone already listening to think they just heard the truck and its dispatcher talking about the breakdown.

"Confirmed, ISS Four-Two, go ahead," said the woman.

"ISS Four-Two reporting a Secure Delta-One—repeat, a Secure Delta-One." Kilgore gave what he and Quinterro had agreed would be the ISS code for a non-threatening, but transit-stopping, mechanical problem. One that would require local law enforcement to provide traffic assistance.

"Roger, ISS Four-Two, I see your GPS on my screen," the woman replied, "I will notify local 911 and request traffic assistance to your position."

"Roger, ISS," Kilgore said. He then added, "ISS, Four-Two also requires approved transport to secure site." That was an ISS driver's way of saying the problem could not be repaired onsite, and he was requesting the dispatcher to contact a company-approved, extreme-duty wrecker to tow the vehicle to a secure location.

As rehearsed, the woman hesitated as if thinking about the driver's latest remark. After a pause, she continued for the benefit of any law enforcement listening. "Roger, ISS Four-Two. Contacting local 911 and nearest approved transport. Maintain maximum secure posture and wait for confirmation. Notify ISS immediately of any changes in situation."

"Roger, ISS. Four-Two Out."

The woman turned to Quinterro, who nodded approval. Next, she picked up a mobile phone programmed to appear to be a landline in Miami. Using her notes, she called the Glynn County 911 operator. "Glynn County 911, this is the International Safety Services dispatcher calling from Miami, Florida. We have a disabled ISS cash-in-transit vehicle in your area and need to request traffic assistance."

The Glynn County 911 operator had never heard of ISS, but it wasn't her job to question requests for help. She did as she was told. "Yes, ISS, can you give me the exact location?"

"Driver states northbound shoulder, U.S. Highway 17, a little south of city limits. My GPS indicates on or near Sidney Lanier Bridge." The woman hesitated for effect, then added, "Our drivers are not allowed to radio-broadcast exact location. Can you please contact local law enforcement and request immediate, non-emergency traffic assistance at the site?"

"Yes. Thank you, ISS. Calling Glynn County Police Department now. Please remain on the line."

Through the still-open line, the woman and Quinterro could hear the 911 operator radio the Glynn County Police Department and request immediate, non-emergency assistance for a disabled, armored, cash-in-transit vehicle northbound on Highway 17 on or near the Sidney Lanier Bridge.

When the 911 operator came back on the line, she said two patrol cars were on the way, and asked if other assistance was needed.

"Thank you, 911. Negative on further assistance. We are contacting nearest ISS-approved extreme-duty wrecker." Then adding, in a more relaxed tone, "If your folks can take care of traffic until the wrecker arrives and gets our vehicle secured, we'd appreciate it."

"Will do, ISS. Good luck, and let us know if we can do anything else."

"Thanks. Will do."

The woman ended the call and looked at Quinterro. He ignored her and looked at his watch. It was 8:53.

On the bridge, in the compartment behind Kilgore and Lomax, Daniel Taggart and Hector Strom prepared to assassinate the first female President of the United States without a sound or a trace.

Chapter 44

Sunday Morning Armored Car

8:53 a.m.

I had just finished bringing Fish up to date with everything Claire and I had learned. Somewhere behind him a radio scanner picked up a call from the Glynn County dispatcher, something about a minor accident in downtown Brunswick.

Fish smiled, "Somebody late for Sunday School."

"I thought you only had a marine band."

"Nah, I got more radios than slot machines. Habit leftover from Coast Guard days."

I nodded. "I'm going to check on Claire."

"Carson, let me know if you need anything."

I left the bridge and made it down the first few steps when I heard the scanner again. Different message this time. Something about an armored car broken down on Highway 17. I stopped and listened. The next message clarified the location. On or near the Sidney Lanier Bridge. I turned and retraced my steps back up to where Fish was writing numbers on a clipboard pad.

"You hear that?" I asked.

"Yeah. Probably nothing. The armored car already called 911 for traffic help."

"You have a chart showing the bridge *and* the Barrier Island Club?"

He looked at me funny. "Yeah, over here."

We met at the rear bulkhead where large overlapping charts hung from wooden rods suspended between two big metal rings. I smiled at the homemade beauty of it, and Fish grinned, saying, "Old school. No damn login, usernames or passwords."

"Love it," I agreed.

Then, "Here," he said, standing on the left side of the chart and pointing, "is the bridge." He moved to the right side of the chart, pointed to the southern end of St. Simons, and added, "and here is the club."

The map showed them separated by a lot of green land and blue water.

"How far apart are they?"

He grabbed a marked cord I hadn't noticed hanging on one side of the charts and pulled the loose end to the center of the bridge. He then stretched the cord to the southern tip of the island, checked it and said, "Five miles. Little less."

"Hmm, farther than I thought. But it's all pretty much sea level, right?"

"Yeah," he said, starting at the bridge, "first you got a little over three miles of tidal marsh, then about a mile and a quarter over the sound, then a few hundred yards of low, dry land leading up to the clubhouse. There are a few big oaks between the water and the clubhouse, but it's mostly open golf course."

He looked at me, anticipated my question and added, "The road-way at the center is about 200 feet above sea level. High enough for a long-distance view of the Barrier Island Club, *if* you have a good tele-scope. If that's what you're thinking."

"So, a vehicle stopped on the bridge could have a straight-line view to the club building?"

"Sure, depending on exactly where the vehicle is on the bridge, and what part of the club he's looking for. Big oaks down here might block part of the view." He hesitated, then said, "Anyone who needed a per-fect line-of-sight from the bridge to a specific place on the club property would have to do good homework ahead of time. They would have to know exactly where a target would be, and then determine if anywhere on the bridge would give a straight-line view to that point."

He waited for me again, then added, "But they would need a rifle with the range and accuracy to kill a person five miles away. That kind of gun don't exist."

He looked at me as if anyone should have known that, then added, "Mack used to sit-in on high-level Homeland Security meetings. He never said anything about a rifle that could kill at a range of five miles. It's impossible."

I waited, hoping he would say something to make me feel better.

"Hell, that's way too far to even aim accurately, even for the best high-power rifle scope. The cumulative distortion created by the heat and humidity would blur the whole Barrier Island Club into a shimmering mirage. To see anything, you'd have to have a powerful infrared scope. And even if the scope had the optics—and the infrared—to focus that far, there's no way to align—and stabilize—a rifle barrel for that kind of shot. You'd need the kind of computer-assisted micro-controls astronomers use to look at stars.

"*And*," he added, "even if you could overcome all of that to find the target, and aim at it accurately, it would be impossible to compensate for the winds. Across that distance, a whisper of a breeze could push a bullet yards off trajectory. Figure in the sea breezes we get here—especially on the roadbed 200 feet above water—and even a professional shooter could miss the whole building. And *that's* if he had a rifle with a five-mile range, which doesn't exist."

He was right, of course, but, "What's an armored vehicle doing on the road Sunday morning?"

"I don't know," he said "maybe the safest time to move cash. Less traffic?" He waited for me again and when I still didn't say anything, he said, "Or, maybe he's coming from Miami, and has to be in New York tomorrow morning."

"Yeah," I said, "maybe you're right."

I still didn't like it. "On the other hand, what are the odds of that thing breaking down right there?" I pointed to the bridge, "While the president is right here?"

"Yeah, that's weird. But they asked for the cops to help with traffic. I don't think someone would plan an assassination and then invite the cops. And," he continued, "you're still back to your five-mile range problem."

He was right again. But I couldn't let it go. I looked at the wall clock. It was getting closer to 9:00. "Where are we, how far out?"

He glanced at the shore in the distance, then at his instrument panel and said, "We're two miles offshore from the Hampton River—say, seven miles from the channel. Technically we're already in restricted water, but I've got an authorization allowing me to go a little farther. Why?'

"I'm going for a ride."

He looked at me, raised his eyebrows, and pointed to his radar screen. "You see this blip? That's the *Sullivan*, the big Coast Guard cutter with the C-WIZ gun. It's off the channel about two miles out. Technically, the Secret Service hard radius is three miles, so I don't think anyone will care much if you head away from that three-mile line. They'll probably chase you off, arrest you.

"If, however," he continued, "you do something foolish, like head toward that invisible three-mile radius, the *Sullivan's* C-WIZ will crank up and, in about three seconds, there'll be nothing left of you and that ugly boat but a bloody slick and a few chewed-up seat cushions."

"Fish," I said, getting frustrated, "I can't sit here and do nothing."

"What else can you do? You told the FBI, and they told the Secret Service. It's their problem now."

"Yeah, but they don't know the whole story. I think I do."

"Mack said you needed help. He didn't say you were crazy."

While Fish's warning sank in, my mind went back to the DI stopping me on the field after Boot Camp graduation. *I don't know what you are going to be—senator, bookkeeper, or bouncer in a whore house—whatever it is, you'll always be a Marine.*

Standing on the bridge of that gambling boat in the bright morning sun, I blinked away the memory, but not the message.

"Do me a favor, Fish. Tell the Admiral there's something I have to do."

He nodded, unsure.

"Take care of Claire for me. I'll be back."

———————————

Jeb Howton was standing in the Secret Service Command Center on the second floor of the Barrier Island Club listening to the final radio checks and position reports from the field. Any minute, the president would leave her suite, ride the elevator down to the lobby, and walk outside to address the largest gathering of media executives the world had ever seen.

Howton heard the Secret Service Transportation Agent with the two identical presidential limousines confirm his status and location. As they had been since their arrival, the two limos were parked unblocked, aimed at and near the clubhouse front door under the wide porte-cochere, and their engines had recently been warmed up and all systems checked. Backup SUVs were similarly positioned and prepared near other club-house doors. No other vehicles were parked anywhere near the paths the limos, SUVs and other motorcade vehicles might need to make a high-speed exit from the club property.

A second later one of the Command Center scanners picked up radio traffic between a commercial armored vehicle and an individual identifying herself as an ISS dispatcher. Howton moved to the aerial photograph covering one wall, and quickly found where the Sidney Lanier Bridge crossed the Brunswick River. He breathed easier. The big bridge was far beyond the red three-mile perimeter drawn around the Barrier Island Club.

He reached for the measuring tape pinned to the clubhouse position in the huge photograph, and pulled it out west-southwest, to the center of the bridge. He was reading the distance—a little short of five miles—when a different scanner picked up the ISS dispatcher's telephone call to Glynn County's 911 operator. The men in the room listened carefully as the ISS dispatcher requested Glynn County Police vehicles to the site to help direct traffic around the disabled armored vehicle.

The Command Center Duty Agent seated at the large communica-tions console turned to Howton and asked, "What do you want to do?"

"Send Bouncer One," he answered, using the code name for one of the agency's unmarked SUVs patrolling just beyond the perimeter.

While the Duty Agent was dispatching Bouncer One to the bridge, Howton grabbed a pair of binoculars, left the room, and ran down the stairs, through the lobby and out onto the rear patio. He ran to the podium, jerked the binoculars to his face and found the Sidney Lanier Bridge far in the distance. Blue flashing lights were barely visible approaching from both directions. The cops were already there. Good, he thought to himself as he spoke into his cuff mic to the Command Center. "Candlestick, let me know when Bouncer One is on the scene."

Chapter 45

Leaving *Lady Luck* Behind

8:58 a.m.
Underneath *Lady Luck*, Fish Williams said, "Run the bilge blowers a minute, then crank her up and put her in idle-forward so you'll have steerage. I'll untie you and step off. Whenever you're ready, add some power and pull away."

"Got it," I answered.

"I can't go much farther," he added.

"I know. Thanks."

I ran the bilge blowers, then turned on the master switch providing power to each of the three starters for the powerful waterjet engines. Wondering what I was about to get myself into, I pushed the start button for engine number one. The engine roared to life, sloshing, reverberating between the steel hulls on either side.

The Coast Guard Cutter *Sullivan's* sonar operator's head snapped and he pressed his headphones tighter.

"Bridge," he shouted into his mic, "Surface contact! New engine noise from *Lady Luck*." His right hand rolled the console's track ball while he stared at the scope, trying to isolate and identify the new sound.

Captain William Tyler's response was immediate. "What is it, Sonar? What's her position?"

"Still a mile beyond the hard circle—I'm not sure, sir, I'm picking up a new internal combustion engine."

"Was she running on one engine and started another one?"

"Negative, Captain, she's running two diesels. This is a smaller IC."

"What is it, dammit? I have to know now!"

"I've got zero separation between the sources."

"A thruster maybe?"

"Negative, Captain, it's definitely internal combustion, not electric."

"Get the chopper over that son of a bitch now," the captain said to an officer beside him. "He may be towing a boat close astern that our radar can't see."

"Negative," came another officer's voice, "I'm talking to the chopper now. He just overflew *Lady Luck* and only saw one boat."

"Talk to me, Sonar!" the captain demanded.

"No prop noise, sir," Sonar shot back, "just a running engine."

The captain had had enough. "C-WIZ, target *Lady Luck*."

"Aye aye, sir," the C-WIZ operator replied, "On target and tracking."

"Wait for my command!"

"Aye aye, sir, waiting on your command."

As the number one engine growled and sloshed between *Lady Luck's* huge hulls, Fish was leaning to untie his vessel's line to *Jock's Trap's* bow when there was a shriek from above. "Wait!"

Before he could move out of the way, Claire half-climbed, half-slid down the rope ladder, pushed past him, ran toward the cockpit and climbed in.

"Whoa!" I said, "Where do you think you're going?"

Her eyes were still swollen and red, but her jaw was tight. "You're not leaving me!"

Before I replied, she turned to Fish and shouted, "Untie us, we're running out of time! CNN said the president is speaking outside any minute!"

Fish looked at me, "What do you want to do?"

She cut me off again, "If we don't go now, Taz may have died for nothing!"

I looked at her eyes and knew she was right. I threw a life vest on her, pulled the straps tight, hard, then told Fish, "Cut us loose!"

Like the big guy he was, he pulled slack out of the line with one hand while untying us with the other. Before I could say thanks, he was scrambling up the rope ladder like a man half his size. As soon as he disappeared, the rope ladder flew up through the hatch in two quick jerks and the hatch slammed closed with a loud bam.

I put us in idle-forward to keep us centered between the huge hulls, and my finger was on the number two start button when the scramble phone rang.

"Wait!" Mack said, "Don't do anything until I talk to the *Sullivan*! I just learned you got their panties in a serious wad by cranking up *Jock's Trap*. Sit tight until I call back." He hung up.

———————

"Sonar!" Captain Tyler shouted impatiently.

The sonar officer had just heard the captain put C-WIZ on alert, and he was running out of time. Staring at the screen, watching the vibrating image of the sounds he heard in his headphones, he whispered, "Come on, what the hell are you, you son of a bitch?"

"Get *Lady Luck* on the radio and find out what's going on!" the captain shouted. "Tell him he has two seconds to explain, before he's in deep shit."

The Communications Officer tuned to the emergency channel and broadcast in the open for all to hear. "*Lady Luck*, this is Coast Guard Cutter *Sullivan*, come in . . ."

After an interminable silence, a ridiculously relaxed, southern drawl answered as if finishing the short reply was going to take all day. "*This is Lady Luck. Go ahead.*"

The *Sullivan's* Comm Officer spoke fast. "*Lady Luck*, we're picking up multiple engine noises coming from your vessel. Explain immediately."

A long pause before the drawl answered. "Sir . . . ?"

"Are you the captain of the vessel?"

"No, sir, he's below. I can get him . . ."

The fast questions and slow answers were maddening.

"We are picking up multiple engine noises coming from your vessel. Please explain immediately."

The *Lady Luck*'s man on the bridge was scared. "I better get the captain."

"To hell with this!" said the *Sullivan* captain, "C-WIZ! Stand by to fire."

"Captain," another urgent voice called out, "I have a radio call for you from Admiral McCallan, says it's about *Lady Luck*.

Captain Tyler spun around to the Communications Officer and said, "Put him on."

When the speaker clicked on, every man on the bridge recognized the unmistakable, authoritative voice of the former Commandant of the United States Coast Guard, Admiral Charles Alexander McCallan.

"Good morning, Captain," Mack said.

"Good morning to you, Admiral," Tyler replied, trying to remain calm. "We've got a situation here, sir, can I call you back?"

"That's why I'm calling, Captain. I heard you call the *Lady Luck*. That's Fish Williams' boat. There's nothing wrong there."

"Admiral, I appreciate the info, but something's going on and I need an answer right now! C-WIZ is on-target and tracking."

"Captain, that's Fish Williams! You know him! And you know he wouldn't do anything wrong."

"Fish ain't on the horn," Tyler snapped back, instantly regretting the disrespectful sound of it. "Somebody else could have his boat. Where are you, sir?"

"I'm anchored just inside the mouth of the Hampton River, about five miles north of your position. I talked to Fish three minutes ago. Everything's fine."

"Three minutes is a long time, Admiral. I think we got a problem."

"This is crazy!" Claire said, "we can't just sit here doing nothing."

"Mack said wait until he talks to the *Sullivan*."

"We don't have time to wait! The president will be outside any min-ute. We're sitting here like fools, she may be assassinated, and Taz will have died for nothing. We have to go, now!"

In that instant, I saw the truth in her eyes. She was right. And more importantly, I was wrong. I was doing it again—waiting instead of acting. Exactly what the Marines taught me *never* to do.

I reached around her and pushed the start buttons for engines two and three.

"Two! shouted the cutter's Sonar operator. Then, "Three! Shit! We got *three* new IC engines at the *Lady Luck*.

With all three engines roaring and sloshing, I added power and we pulled away from *Lady Luck*. Suddenly the loud reverberation of our engine noise was gone, but so was our hiding place. I shaded my eyes, got my bearings and wondered if we were causing a stir on somebody's radar.

I had no idea.

"Shit!" The calls came from Sonar and Radar simultaneously.

Radar: "We got two boats, repeat, two boats! Another boat just showed up in front of *Lady Luck*!"

Sonar: "I got definition and jet-drive noise, it's a go-fast!"

The Communications Officer was getting the same alert from a chop-per in the distance.

"Wait, Captain!" Mack said, "I know about the second boat. It's OK!"

"If our positions were reversed, would it be OK with you?" Captain Tyler replied loudly. Then, "C-WIZ. Lock on the second boat and wait for my command."

"Captain, listen to me!"

"Go-fast is pulling away from *Lady Luck*," Radar said. "heading south toward the hard circle."

With the go-fast heading toward the three-mile radius, Captain Tyler prepared to give the order to Fire. When he did, the C-WIZ would rain death on the speedboat. "Talk fast, Admiral."

"You know Fish. And I know the guy in the go-fast. Please Captain. Stand down C-WIZ before something happens we can't undo. They're on our side. They think something's wrong, and they're trying to help."

"By hiding from the Coast Guard in restricted waters?"

"They are trying to warn the Secret Service that there's somebody else out here that *is* dangerous."

"That's what phones are for, Admiral! And, we don't have any other unknown blips out here."

"Captain, the guys in the go-fast talked to the FBI this morning. Nobody will listen to them. They are doing the only thing they can now to warn the Feds something really is wrong. The real threat may be from land."

Tyler sighed, hesitated, then reluctantly gave the order to stand down C-WIZ. "Admiral, they haven't crossed the hard circle yet . . ." He left that hanging. "If they do, I won't have any choice."

Jock's Trap

We were doing about twenty, testing the waters to see what kind of reaction we'd get.

"What are we doing?" Claire asked.

The scramble phone rang before I could reply. She held it to my ear.

"What?" I said to Mack, but he was already talking.

"Wait, dammit!" Mack shouted. "The *Sullivan's* two seconds away from firing C-WIZ!"

I cut the power, spun the wheel to make it obvious we were stopping, and took the phone from Claire. "Mack, we gotta keep going. The president's due outside any minute. Have you told the *Sullivan* we're not the problem?"

"Hell yeah, but you're not making this easy."

"Keep trying! I'll slow down some." Mack was saying something when I hung up.

In the distance I saw the long white cutter with the broad, red diagonal stripe. I had been shot at before and didn't like it, but at least I had a chance. Might not be one today. I remembered Mack's comment about a C-WIZ cutting an old tuna boat in half. *Well, at least we don't have to worry about feeling anything. At 75 bullets a second, we'll be dead before we're wet.*

Claire asked, "When will we know if it's OK, if Mack convinced them?"

"Soon."

I gently bumped the throttles and turned the wheel, pointing our bow back to southwest on a course running parallel to the shore. I glanced to my right and saw the bright sun reflecting off the windows of the large beachfront homes on Sea Island. On the beach, someone had already set up a big red umbrella. It was a beautiful Sunday morning. And somewhere ahead there was a curved line, lying invisibly across the blue water. The three-mile radius from the Barrier Island Club. And the President of the United States. If we stayed outside that line, we'd probably live. And the president may not. If we crossed that line, she may live. And we may not.

We were at the mercy of whoever controlled C-WIZ. I prayed Mack was doing a good job of making our case. And I wondered when we'd know.

Claire said, "Are you sure about this?"

I ignored the question and eased the three throttles forward, hoping to make us look less threatening. *Jock's Trap* moved forward as the hungry intakes sucked in seawater. I cut my eyes from the water ahead to the *Sullivan*, and back again, wondering where in the hell that line in the water was.

I eased our speed up to about 35 miles an hour when the radio crackled. "This is Coast Guard Cutter *Sullivan* calling the red go-fast off Sea Island, come in."

Claire stared at me while I pulled the mic off its rest. "This is *Jock's Trap*, go ahead," I shook my head at the dumbass name of our boat.

"*Jock's Trap*, hold your current position. We are sending a boat to your location."

I grabbed the binoculars and saw a smaller boat pulling away from the cutter, coming this way.

"*Sullivan*," I called, "did Admiral McCallan reach you?"

"*Jock's Trap*, please cut your power at once and hold your position."

Shit, answer the damn question. "Did Admiral McCallan call you?!"

"*Jock's Trap*, you are in restricted waters and approaching a no-go line. Please stop at once, or we will have to take action."

My sweating hands felt loose on the wheel. Claire was staring at me. I couldn't think of anything to say.

Then the radio voice changed. "*Jock's Trap*, this is Captain Tyler onboard the *Sullivan*. I spoke with Admiral McCallan. That does not—I repeat, does not—change the order to you. Stop your vessel at once."

"Captain, I'm Carson Hood. Admiral McCallan knows me! If we don't do something to warn the president in the next few minutes, she could be killed!"

"We'll talk about that when your vessel is stopped. You are crossing the no-go line now. Kill your engines or we will open fire."

The scramble phone rang. Claire grabbed it, listening. She looked up at me and said, "Mack says he just heard on his scanner something has happened on the bridge!"

I keyed the mic, "Captain, there are two of us onboard this boat. The passenger is a woman, a contract employee of the federal government. Do not fire on us. We are trying to help!"

I turned to Claire. "Tell Mack we have to go, tell him to keep trying with the *Sullivan*!" I rammed the throttles all the way, and *Jock's Trap* took off like a missile, knocking us both hard against the seatbacks.

Chapter 46

President in the Crosshairs

In the armored vehicle's driver's seat, Kilgore was on the radio. Lomax, riding shotgun, waited nervously.

In the back, Taggart had just confirmed the GPS coordinates of the armored vehicle, and was watching his monitor as the system's satellite-quality lens zoomed in. He waited for the image of the president, and the tiny red light indicating the infrared radar had locked on to her body heat.

Neither appeared.

The red light blinked, indicating the infrared radar was still looking for a body heat image. The main monitor showed only blurry shades of gray. "Shit, something's wrong," Taggart said. He wheeled to look at Strom, but the doctor was busy with the teracapacitor and ignored him.

Taggart spun back to his monitor to recheck GPS values. The vehicle's coordinates were right. The target's coordinates were right. He tried to manually zoom out a few feet to confirm where the weapon was aimed, but in his panic he hit Auto Zoom-Out, and before he could stop it, the image on his monitor withdrew to a wide-angle shot showing the whole clubhouse.

"Shit!" he cursed his mistake, and held down the Manual Zoom-In button, watching as the image on his monitor raced toward him. With the clarity of continuous autofocus, he saw the image come forward until he recognized the scene.

He tapped the button twice more, zooming in. That told him what he needed to know. The target wasn't there.

He stopped the zoom, looked more closely at the image, then continued slowly zooming-in. Each touch of the button brought the image closer, while autofocus and autoexposure made it clearer and brighter.

"Shit!" he said again louder, determined to get Strom's attention. "Nobody's there!"

"Check your time," Strom said without looking up. "It's too soon."

Taggart checked his watch and monitor. Both verified Strom was right. And both were linked by radio control to the U. S. Naval Observatory atomic clock broadcast signal—the same time used by the White House and Secret Service.

It was 9:00. The target—like most VIPs—was late. No big deal. Yet.

Meanwhile, in the cab of the armored car, Kilgore watched his left rearview mirror nervously as a Glynn County patrol car with lights flashing rapidly approached from the rear. As the car drew near, the officer stopped 15 yards back, straddling the white line that separated the right traffic lane from the shoulder. As he got out of his cruiser and walked toward the armored car, Kilgore saw the flashing blue lights of another fast-moving Glynn County patrol car coming the other way on the other side of the bridge, followed immediately by a blue-and-silver Georgia Highway Patrol Dodge Charger. Kilgore guessed the two would do a U-turn at the bridge's southern end and be there soon.

"Uh-oh," Lomax said quietly as the two cop cars flew by.

Kilgore, still watching the outside mirror, growled, "Shut up, Lomax."

Seconds later the first Glynn County patrolman was standing outside Kilgore's window. He was waving cars by and saying something, but Kilgore had forgotten to turn on the outside mic and couldn't hear him.

Kilgore faked a smile, motioned just-a-second to the cop, then flipped two switches turning on the external microphone and speakers. He grabbed the hand-held mic and looked back at the patrolman. "Sorry. I had the outside mic off. Couldn't hear you."

Still watching and waving cars by, the patrolman said, "You guys alright in there?" It was hard to hear him over the roar of armored vehicle's 900-horsepower engine and cars speeding by.

Kilgore nodded and said, "Yeah. We're OK," hoping that was the end of it.

Outside, the patrolman was responding to someone on his lapel mic.

The second Glynn County patrol car, followed by the GSP Dodge Charger, approached from behind, slowed, and pulled just ahead of the armored vehicle. Both officers left their lights flashing, but stayed in the car, an act that both relieved and confused Kilgore.

When the Glynn County patrolman Kilgore had been speaking with finished talking into his lapel mic, he looked back at Kilgore and said, "What's the problem?"

Remembering his practiced answer, Kilgore replied into the mic, "I felt the transmission slipping coming up the bridge. We're heavier than most 18-wheelers, and the transmission's usually the first thing to go." He waited a second to let that sink in, then added, "I figured better to stop here instead of gaining speed on the downslope and not be able to downshift. Sorry I had to do it on the bridge."

"S'okay," the patrolman said. He checked for cars that needed waving by, then leaned back, scanning the armored vehicle. "This rig looks new. You shouldn't be having transmission trouble."

Kilgore nodded and smiled as if to say he understood, then lied, "This thing's got 400,000 miles on it. Company likes to keep 'em looking new."

When the patrolman didn't say anything, Kilgore added, smiling, "Not good business for customers to see their millions being hauled around in a beat-up truck."

The cop nodded and said something else into his lapel mic.

Ahead, the Georgia State trooper had gotten out of his blue-and-silver Dodge Charger, put on his wide-brimmed hat, and started toward the armored vehicle. He was still too far away, but Kilgore had the distinct feeling that, under that wide brim, the officer was staring straight at him. Lomax shifted uncomfortably in his seat.

"Easy," Kilgore whispered to Lomax, being sure the mic was not keyed, "*Easy*."

Lomax didn't reply.

In the Champion's Suite on the third floor of the Barrier Island Club, the president checked her Rolex, straightened her notes and stood up. She brushed the wrinkles from the front of her blue suit, gave herself a quick glance in the large mirror, ending the self-appraisal with a smile.

Satisfied, she picked up the Signal Phone installed by the White House Communication Agency and heard the immediate, "Yes, Madame President."

"I'm ready."

A moment later, there was a knock on her door. Lead Secret Service Agent Jeb Howton and three members of her Presidential Protection Detail stood waiting. Howton said, "Madame President, the Press Secretary and Chief of Staff will meet us on the first floor."

She smiled, nodded and took her place in the center of the group as they walked to the elevator.

No one spoke during the short ride to the ground floor, and when the elevator doors opened, Chambers smiled at her two waiting senior staffers, and walked past them toward the rear door of the Barrier Island Club and the outside patio.

Thirty seconds later, in the bright morning sun, she strode proudly away from her parade of followers, stepped up to her podium, and stood there basking in the respect due the President of the United States. Howton took his position slightly behind her, near the Press Secretary and Chief-of-Staff. As the standing ovation from the most powerful media owners in the world continued, she nodded to guests she recognized in the front row of tables.

This is going to work, she told herself, *I will make history today by apologizing and admitting I was wrong, and then start on the road to making things right. I can save it all, starting right here.*

When the applause finally subsided, and her guests sat down, she began with a warm welcome, calling a few guests by name, and then thanking everyone for coming to what she called, "this historic occasion, to start the healing process in America."

As much as she wanted to get straight to the point, she knew better. She remembered what worked on the campaign trail—keep 'em smiling.

She opened with a couple of practiced witty lines appropriate to the occasion and was rewarded with another long round of applause. She smiled. She felt great. This was so easy. *Why didn't I think of this sooner?*

As she segued into her reason for inviting them here—the crippling Hispanic Civil Rights Crisis in America—she felt she had her audience in the palm of her hand. She was excited, anxious to pull each of them in with her carefully planned reasoning—and why there were no other options that could be implemented so quickly and easily and have such a profound and immediate positive impact on the country.

Then she would deliver the heart of her message—the apology from the President of the United States—and the appeal that would imbue each person in the audience with the feeling of personal involvement. A personal empowerment, to step forward and help change the world. To make a difference, with immediate and direct benefits that would last long after each of them has gone on.

She couldn't wait to see the look in their eyes as they heard her personal apology and stood ready to accept the burden of responsibility she was asking them to take upon their shoulders.

She never made it that far.

Outside the armored vehicle, the Georgia State Patrol trooper had now reached the first Glynn County patrolman, and they were talking. Kilgore turned up the volume, trying to hear, but the armored car's engine and passing traffic drowned them out.

After a moment, the trooper said something to the county patrolman, who nodded and stepped away to focus on the traffic. The trooper stepped closer to Kilgore's door and stared up at him. Kilgore nervously turned down the internal speaker volume and waited.

"Can I see some identification, please?"

Kilgore struggled to remain cool. That wasn't supposed to happen. "I'm sorry, officer," he replied into his mic, heart pounding in his chest. "All I can do is refer you to my dispatcher. She made the 911 call."

The trooper didn't react. Kilgore could tell he didn't like being told no.

After a nervous pause, Kilgore said, "We're not allowed to open anything to the outside. Company rules."

When the trooper still didn't say anything, Kilgore added nervously, "We're even on a closed-loop ventilation system. No outside air." Then laughingly added, "And I don't think my partner took a shower this week."

Kilgore chuckled and looked at Lomax. The smaller man tried to smile, but was paralyzed with fear.

The trooper stared at Kilgore.

In the rear of the armored vehicle, Strom checked his final numbers. The teracapacitor was fully charged, ready to supply the massive short-term bursts needed to power the device's main components—particle accelerator, focusing magnets, laser chamber and beam nozzle. He still didn't know who the target was. Quinterro had told him several days ago not to ask again.

When Strom was sure of his numbers, without looking up, he said a quiet "Ready."

Taggart stared at his monitor. He had been assured that the weapon would fire without any flash or sound at either end, but just in case, he wanted to fire as soon as possible. When the president first stepped up to the podium, there would be the sounds of applause and a few motor-driven cameras, accompanied by the blurring brightness of camera flashes. If the device *did* make a slight flash or sound, it would be lost in all that. But the cameras would only be there for a few moments. The president had agreed to that, but had insisted the reporters and photographers leave before she began her address to the media owners.

Taggart's monitor began to flicker, and the IR reading fluctuated wildly. He realized the camera flashes had begun. The president must have walked through the rear door of the Barrier Island Club and would be approaching the podium any second. Soon his monitor was filled with the image of the head and shoulders of the most powerful person on earth.

While the president smiled and waved, Taggart watched a series of blinking icons on the right side of his monitor, confirming that all automatic pre-firing functions had been initiated. The infrared radar had auto-locked on the warmth emanating from the president's head and neck. The IR's auto-lock simultaneously triggered the eye-safe ranging laser which fired 120 microbursts a second, measuring the exact distance to the target.

The display showed 7,045.71 meters. Just over 4.3 miles.

That data, instantly converted to millimeters, was passed to the firing computer where it was used to set the Bragg Peak for the proton beam—the area of maximum tissue damage. Knowing the exact distance ensured the near-light-speed particles would do their greatest atomic shredding approximately 114.3 millimeters beneath the skin covering the president's head. About 4.5 inches behind the president's eyeballs.

Taggart watched the changing numbers flicker on his screen. All the target-lock functions were continuous. Every one-hundredth of a second, the IR relocked, the range was re-measured, and the new distance was sent to the firing computer.

Suddenly he realized Strom was out of his seat and standing behind him.

"No!" Strom screamed when he saw the president's face on the monitor.

Taggart spun his chair around at Strom, and said, "Shut up and sit down you old fool, or you'll get us all killed."

"This can't be," Strom said, still staring disbelievingly at the monitor. "Quinterro said we were going to kill drug dealers. This is insane!"

The horror of the moment seized him, and again he saw his life rise and fall in fast-forward—*Childhood genius. Brilliant physicist. Respected physician.*

Murderer. And now, Assassin! My God, how could this happen?

Dazed from the shock, Strom's only answer was that it must not happen.

Taggart stared at the shocked doctor, and gently moved his left bicep closer to his chest, verifying the handgun was still there. He cut his eyes back toward the monitor and saw what he needed to see. All three icons—teracapacitor, particle accelerator and laser chamber—flashed green. The weapon was still ready, waiting for him.

Visually, he could see system had locked on the president, and no one else was in danger. He needed to hit Fire now—before Strom could cause a problem. But the firing computer required all three levels of target ID verification before the firing key was armed. The verifications would only take a few millionths of a second, but it required him to hit the ID key to record the verifications first. That meant taking his eyes off Strom for a split second.

He stared at Strom. The man seemed in shock, weak with fear. As fast as he could, Taggart turned back toward his keyboard to hit the ID key.

But he had underestimated the old man. Before Taggart could hit the ID key, Strom went for his own keyboard. Taggart heard him move and wheeled around, pulling out the pistol as he did. Strom froze when he saw the black gun aimed at his chest.

"Sit down, Doctor," Taggart said, looking across the gun's front sight, "on the floor in the corner."

Strom backed into the corner and slowly slid to the floor. "Mr. Taggart, please," he said, "this is insane."

Convinced that he had made his point and subdued Strom, Taggart turned slowly back to his keyboard. He kept the gun in his right hand, aimed toward Strom's position in the corner while his left hand hovered over the keyboard until finding the ID key.

In less than 30 millionths of a second, Facial Recognition, IR Heat Signature, and Iris Scan all verified the identity of Ann Roberts Chambers. The weapon icon on Taggart's monitor flashed green. The firing key was armed. Taggart moved his finger to the firing key.

In the monitor, the president, still smiling and waving, turned slightly to her right, and paused. She seemed to be staring straight at Taggart. His logical mind was saying that was, of course, impossible. The armored vehicle was over four miles away. He was almost through with that thought, gently applying pressure to the firing key when Strom's right arm locked hard around his neck and jerked him backward out of his chair.

Chapter 47

Seventy-five Rounds a Second

Inside Candlestick, the Secret Service's second-floor Command Center in the Barrier Island Club, the Communications Agent suddenly pressed his headset tighter and turned to the Ops Chief, Ron Wallace. "The *Sullivan* has a new sonar contact near the Hampton River."

"What the hell? Where's it coming from?" Wallace demanded.

"They think it was with the gambling boat. Wait a minute . . . they got a visual. It's a red go-fast. It's being ordered to stand down now."

"Is it?" Wallace asked as he spun around to the wall-size aerial photograph.

"I can't tell," the Comm Agent replied, concentrating. "Lot of radio traffic all of a sudden."

Wallace quickly found the Hampton River on the huge aerial photograph. It was north of Sea Island. He pulled the measuring tape pinned to the Barrier Island Club to the river's mouth. The straight-line distance over land and water was almost eight miles, a mile or two farther by water. "Find out, dammit," he said, demanding to know if the go-fast had stopped.

He checked the *Sullivan's* position, five miles offshore from the St. Simons lighthouse. If the go-fast made a run for the channel, it would be in plain view of the cutter for over seven miles. The cutter's C-WIZ could stop him in two seconds anywhere along that path.

"Dammit," Wallace added, "I said we didn't need that gambling boat out there, and nobody would listen."

A second Command Center Agent said, "The guy was the deputy commandant of the Coast Guard."

"*If,* that's him on the boat!" Wallace shot back. "Find out, now!"

The Comm Agent started to say something, then stopped and

listened again. "Shit. We've got the *Sullivan* talking to the go-fast *and* the gambling boat, and now there's somebody else telling the *Sullivan* not to shoot."

"The go-fast must be with the gambling boat," the other Command Center Agent suggested.

"He's got no authorization for that!" Wallace snapped back.

"Is the go-fast stopping?" Wallace demanded again. He looked at the map. From the president's location at the Barrier Island Club to the go-fast's position at mouth of the Hampton River—eight miles. Then from president's location to the armored car on the Sidney Lanier Bridge—five miles, in the opposite direction.

"I want to know now!" Wallace snapped, then added impatiently, "Have we heard from Bouncer One? He should be on the bridge by now. Where in hell is he?"

"Driving up now."

"Anything else going on, anywhere?" Wallace demanded.

"Negative. Everything else is quiet."

"The go-fast is still way out," Wallace said, thinking, "and Phoenix is on dry land—over 150 yards from the shoreline. Plus the go-fast would have to get past the *Sullivan*, and that'll never happen." Wallace had been in the navy and had seen what a C-WIZ could do. If that gun can shoot down a missile coming right at it at 2,000 miles an hour, he thought, it could certainly handle a fiberglass speedboat poking along at 100.

"Coast Guard has a chopper with 50 calibers moving in," the Comm Agent said, still pressing his headset to his ear.

"Tell the *Sullivan*," Wallace said, "to keep that go-fast way-the-hell out there."

On the *Sullivan*, Captain Tyler ordered C-WIZ to fire a burst 100 yards ahead of the speedboat. A second later he felt the vibration beneath his feet as a short whir of the C-WIZ's rotating barrels spat 500 large armor-piercing rounds in the speedboat's path. He watched with high-power binoculars as the blue sea in front of *Jock's Trap* erupted into a white wall of water.

Focusing on the speedboat, the Captain didn't see beyond the white spray where bullets ricocheting off the water shredded the tops out of palm trees on the undeveloped south end of Sea Island.

———————

"Jesus Christ!" I screamed, while Claire just screamed.

The water directly ahead of us turned into hundreds of geysers shooting white water to the sky. I slammed the throttles forward and *Jock Trap's* lunged through the spray and back into open air.

"What was that?" Claire screamed.

"A warning," I shouted back.

I stole a quick glance at her. She was scared. "They killed Taz, and they're going to kill us too!"

Looking toward the *Sullivan*, I saw two smaller Coast Guard boats angling at us, closing fast. I wanted to pick a course that would put the closest one between us and the *Sullivan*, but the driver was too smart for that and chose his course to intercept us without getting in the way of the *Sullivan's* C-WIZ.

I hit the throttles hard to be sure they were at max. The speedometer said 115. Keeping one hand on the wheel, I reached for Claire with the other, trying to tell her we were OK.

Without warning the water at our bow exploded from another burst from C-WIZ. Only this time the bow took some hits. The bow spotlight and a port rail disappeared in a splintering blast of fiberglass.

That did it. I yanked the throttles back and cut the wheel hard to starboard. Our speed fell off and *Jock's Trap* stood on its starboard gunwale as we spun in a tight circle and lost all forward momentum. The closest chase boat altered course to close on us.

I grabbed Claire by her shoulders and pulled her close. She stared past me at the chase boat closing on our position.

"Look at me, dammit!" I said. "I love you. I'll be back in a few minutes."

She was staring at me crazily, trying to understand when I picked her up by her upper arms and lifted her over the side of the boat. She screamed, "No!" as I let her fall. I waited a second to see her bob back to the surface, then snatched the marker flare I had been hiding, popped it on and tossed it into the water beyond her. I straightened the wheel and rammed the throttles to the stops.

I glanced over my shoulder. The closest chase boat did what I had hoped. It went for Claire.

Captain Tyler's nerves were about to snap. He heard one of the 25-foot Defenders was picking up a woman from the water.

Meanwhile Mack was back on the horn pleading with him not to fire.

"Dammit, Admiral, I can't sit here and do nothing while that son of a bitch races toward the president!"

"Yes, you can, Captain, trust me!"

"C-WIZ!" Tyler demanded. "Give me another burst right off the bow."

"Captain," the voice sounded tentative, "the target is almost out of the prescribed field of fire…."

"Now, dammit!" the Captain screamed.

"Aye, aye, sir." C-WIZ chose a point barely ahead of the speedboat's bow and released a one second burst. The target continued on its speed and course as the Executive Officer standing beside Captain Tyler shouted, "Cease fire! Cease Fire! Cease fire!"

The XO, watching through binoculars, had seen rounds ricochet off the water, shredding the roof of a beachfront home.

"Captain!" he said, talking fast, "Homes on the beach! Ricochets!"

"Shit!" Captain Tyler said, realizing his career was over.

"Captain," Mack said. He had heard what happened. "I'll help you with this. Don't give up."

Tyler ignored the former Coast Guard Commandant and asked C-WIZ how long before the speedboat makes the turn into the channel and has no land behind him.

"Few seconds, sir. He's moving fast."

Tyler said, "Let me know when he makes the turn."

———————————

After I passed the bend on East Beach, I moved closer to the shore, racing toward the channel where I would turn east, away from the *Sullivan* and that mean-ass gun.

If I made it that far.

The first chase boat stopped to pick up Claire—my reason for begging the *Sullivan* not to shoot.

Also, with one chase boat no longer after me, and me outrunning the second one, the *Sullivan* had only one last option—75 armor-piercing rounds a second from C-WIZ.

I was wondering why I wasn't dead yet when, to my right, I saw some morning beach walkers. They stopped and stared as I tore across the water at over 100 miles an hour only feet from shore.

I assumed they must be the reason C-WIZ hadn't opened fire on me again. That gave me an idea.

The curve of the southern end of the island has some shallow water. Plus, a half-mile into the channel, the St. Simons Pier extends nearly 100 yards out from the Village. At its end, it has lateral extensions 50 yards each way, making it a giant concrete T. Between lovers, vacationers, drunks and fishermen, someone's on the pier twenty-four hours a day.

After turning into the channel, with my shallow draft, I could stay so close to the shore that the *Sullivan* wouldn't dare fire because the pier would be right beyond me. It might work.

I stole a quick look at my watch and saw it was after nine. Maybe I was already too late. Maybe I should stop now. I was weighing that as I reached the channel and began following the shoreline's curve to the west.

I stayed close to shore, feeling OK about my plan to keep

C-WIZ from turning me into fish food, when suddenly both sides of the speedboat erupted into walls of white water. I was trying to figure out how the C-WIZ missed when a dark shadow passed over me and raced across the water ahead of the boat. *What the hell!*

A small, gray helicopter gunship had appeared out of the blinding white of the sun and raced over my head directly in front of me. Bullets fired into the water from above don't ricochet as well. That meant the chopper's guns could chew me to pieces without having to worry about ricocheting bullets killing innocent people. I had a new problem.

And only one not-so-good idea.

———————

On the rear patio of the Barrier Island Club, President Chambers was recounting the importance of FDR's relationship with the media in the days before World War II, when Jeb Howton heard a helicopter somewhere in the distance. He was whispering into his wrist mic when another faint vibrating sound echoed across the manicured grounds. "Candlestick, what the hell is going on?"

On the lawn, European Union's RadioPlex chairman looked over his shoulder, thinking a portable phone was vibrating nearby. To his left, the CEO of American News Corporation suffered no illusion about the sound. The retired navy commander recognized the sound of a helicopter gunship and 50-caliber machine guns when he heard it. His mind raced, trying to reconcile the deadly faraway noise with the perfect calm of the immediate surroundings. Despite the fact the president was looking straight toward him, he turned in his seat and scanned the water behind him.

Behind the president, Howton pressed his earpiece, then stepped forward. Nearby agents began to move in, but he signaled *not yet*. He approached the president, gently touched her right arm, and interrupted her, saying, "Madame President, I need you to come with me please."

Embarrassed at the interruption, she turned to him and began to say something when a red and white Coast Guard helicopter gunship shrieking at full speed cleared the top of the Barrier Island Club by inches. The president hadn't time to duck before she was completely covered with Secret Service agents, who huddled her between them, running her back toward the building through an alley of other agents who had instantly appeared with guns drawn.

The outdoor dining room erupted into pandemonium as guests and waiters fell to the ground amid screams and profanity. Shouted orders and the crackle of radios filled the air as black-clad Counter Assault Team members appeared everywhere, all aiming automatic weapons away from the building.

On the other side of the clubhouse, two identical presidential limousines screeched to a stop under the porte-cochere, surrounded by black SUVs and more men with automatic weapons. Some stood in the open, weapons raised, aiming away from the limos. Others crouched beside vehicles or behind nearby trees.

At the small island airport less than a mile away, Marines burst out of the double doors of an unmarked hangar office and spread out in an arc making a hundred-yard dash toward the three white-top presidential helicopters.

Inside one of the hangars, a fire engine roared to life and started across the tarmac behind the three aircrews.

At the Barrier Island Club, the protective shell of Secret Service agents rushed the president through the main lobby of the club building, out the front entrance and under the porte-cochere. There, they unceremoniously shoved her into the waiting back door of the first of the two identical limousines. Two agents—one on each side—joined her in the rear, as Jeb Howton threw himself into his front passenger seat screaming, "Go, go, go, go, go!"

Agents were still piling into the second limo as both started rolling. In a deafening wail of sirens, motorcycle outriders led the way, followed by lead cars, SUVs, the two limos, and more vehicles and wailing motorcycles close behind. Screeching away from the porte-cochere, the emergency motorcade accelerated down the driveway, past the gatehouse and streaked down the oak-lined quarter-mile drive leading to the public world beyond.

The intersection of the club's driveway and Kings Way is a single-lane traffic circle that physically forces vehicles to reduce speed. Fortunately, the Secret Service had a plan eliminating that in an emergency. As decided several days before, two columns of law enforcement vehicles immediately formed a wide temporary lane across the manicured lawn, allowing the motorcade to bypass the roundabout. The speeding vehicles angled over the driveway curb and tore a wide and ragged black path across the perfect grass before hammering over Kings Way, bouncing hard on the other side, and racing over the just-flattened airport fence.

Less than a mile away, the powerful jet turbines and huge blades of the three white-top presidential helicopters were already spinning up, while the aircrews inside each chopper shouted through emergency pre-flight checklists. No one except the pilots, limo drivers and motorcade agents knew which green-and-white helicopter the president would board, thus making it Marine One.

The crews of the three helicopters heard the Secret Service Airport Site Agent in their headsets. "Phoenix is onsite. Thirty seconds!"

The copilot of the number three chopper looked up and saw in the distance the black vehicles barreling his way at take-off speed down the center of the main runway.

The motorcade vehicles, initially single file, had now fanned out forming a protective pocket around the two identical black limos as they all raced through 150 miles an hour toward the three green-and-white presidential helicopters spinning up at the far end of the field.

As the formation reached the choppers, the SUVs split into two streams, forming a protective band encircling all three aircraft. As agents and black-clad Counter Assault Team members poured from the vehicles, filling in the gaps between the cars, the agents in the second limo raced out and formed a protective corridor from the right rear door of the first limo to the stairs of the center helicopter.

Howton waited another beat to be sure all were in place, then said, "Let's go!" He grabbed his pistol and threw open his door, turning immediately to the door behind him, where another agent was helping the president out of the car. Immediately, the President of the United States was surrounded by agents and rushed across the short distance and up the narrow stairs of the middle helicopter. As the heavy door slammed, the pilot radioed, "Marine One lifting off!"

The pilot quickly raised the big bird off the pavement and held it there briefly while agents and Counter Assault Team members rushed into the two remaining helicopters. Those two were airborne seconds later and in unison the three aircraft turned toward the northwest, accelerated furiously and disappeared over the tree line.

Ten miles away at the Brunswick-Golden Isles Airport, Air Force One had already spooled up her four monster turbines and was taxiing toward the take-off runway.

The two Air Force F-22 Raptors, high overhead whenever when the president is traveling, initiated immediate return-to-low-altitude maneuvers to escort an emergency Air Force One take-off. The Four additional F-22s that had accompanied Air Force One from Washington had already been scrambled from Hunter Army Airfield outside of Savannah, and were streaking toward St. Simons, rattling Sunday morning breakfast dishes in every waterfront home in their path.

———————————

The small gray chopper overran me, pivoted in the sky and headed back. A thousand yards in the distance, where the Barrier Island Club met the channel, another helicopter—this one a larger, red-and-white Coast Guard chopper—streaked across the shoreline and out over the water. I wondered if I was too late.

Ahead, the pier's concrete pilings rushed at me like dragon's teeth. Beyond the pier, there was nothing but open water where I'd be a perfect target for the smaller chopper's machine guns.

I needed cover now.

The smaller chopper was coming too fast. Any second, I'd be in his gunsights. I aimed the bow for the narrow gap between the concrete pilings on the far end of the pier and prayed.

Out of the corner of my eye, I saw people on the pier running for the Village parking lot.

Closing on the pier at 50 miles an hour scared hell out of me, but it kept the few slow runners on the pier between the chopper and me.

He passed overhead going the other way as I reached the pilings. I yanked the throttles all the way into reverse and held on. The jet boat's reversing scoops did their job well. *Jock's Trap* flew through the narrow slit of the first two pilings, then stood on her nose as I tried to stop her in the dark concrete forest. I didn't hit anything head-on, but *Jock's Trap* bounced off concrete pilings like a pinball until she lost all forward momentum.

The first impact was a good one, and the sickening sound of breaking fiberglass and twisting metal rattled in my brain. Something sharp stabbed me in my right side and I went down hard. I rolled over to sit up, but a stabbing pain stopped me cold. I lay still for a second, staring up at the dark bottom of the pier while sloshing waves banged the red boat against the pilings. I could hear the roar of the chopper, waiting.

When I reached for the pain, my hand hit something. I slowly raised my head and saw something shiny sticking out of my right side. I dropped my head back down and tried to breathe. When I looked again, I realized it was part of the shattered windshield frame. I eased it out, with the help of some colorful words, and looked at the bloody end. It hadn't gone in too deep. I didn't feel like I was dying.

I did however seem to be making quite a pool of red.

I pulled myself to a sitting position and found the onboard first aid kit in a bin below the helm. Getting to my knees, I steadied myself against the forward bulkhead and found gauze and wide tape. The rhythmic banging and rocking—and the fact the outgoing tide hadn't pulled me back into the sunshine—told me the waves had wedged the boat between the pilings. And the helicopter was still hovering just outside. He hailed me on his loudspeaker, but he was going to have to wait. I'll be damned if I was going to bleed to death just to surrender.

Using all the gauze and most of the tape, I made an ugly, thick bandage on my right side that stuck out like a growth. It would either slow the bleeding or soak up all my blood.

Regaining my feet, I could see cracks in the fiberglass, but they appeared to be above the waterline. I raised the hatch cover in the floor and saw the storage area was damp, but not flooding.

Putting the boat in gear to get me off the pilings, I tried for just enough RPMs to keep the outgoing tide from pulling me back out into the open channel. The chopper had dropped down to four feet above the water and was hovering in a whirling mist right off the end of the pier. Between the pilings, I stared directly into his twin 50-calibers.

I was wondering what was next, when an upside-down, scraggly bearded face appeared overhead and a drugged-out voice said, "Duuude, I don't know what you're smugglin' but there's a million cops up here."

So far everything I had done had driven me closer to the president. And had just about gotten me killed. The Barrier Island Club was only 1,000 yards away, but it was obvious I wasn't going to make it. And thanks to the news from my new spaced-out friend above, it was also obvious I was about to have lot of company.

––––––––––––––––––

On the rear patio of the Barrier Island Club, one of the agents remaining to keep the site secure, found the high heels left behind by the Commander-in-Chief as she was rushed from her podium. He was wondering what to do with them when he heard a familiar roar from high above. He looked up and saw Air Force One heading for the shortest possible straight-line distance to Washington, D.C. and the safety of the White House.

"Shit," he said to no one, looking around at the mayhem, "that must have been close."

Chapter 48

Blood on the Bridge

The Glynn County patrolman and the Georgia State Trooper were still directing traffic around the large, armored vehicle when Taggart's nine-millimeter handgun went off twice. Outside of the thick armored walls of the vehicle, the sound was barely audible, especially over the roar of the vehicle's huge engine and the noise of the passing traffic. If Kilgore hadn't jumped and spun around to look through the cab's rear window, the officers on the scene might not have known something was wrong.

Kilgore knew right away he fucked up.

The trooper and patrolman had both turned away from the traffic and were looking right at him. Kilgore tried to appear calm, but sensed he wasn't doing a very good job of it. All he had seen in his quick glance to the rear was Strom splayed out in the corner with blood all over the side of his head. Taggart, below the window, was rushing back to his computer. Something had gone horribly wrong.

And now the trooper was moving toward Kilgore's door.

A moment ago, Kilgore had been nervous, but was still thinking everything was going according to plan. He had tried to calm himself by thinking of the hundreds of thousands in cash he would have as soon as this thing was over.

Now, suddenly, he had problems tearing him a new one. The trooper, now right outside his window staring at him, was not happy. Worse, Lomax was squirming like a girl, trying to sneak a look in the back. Kilgore snatched his pistol off the seat beside him and rammed it low into Lomax's ribs. He checked to be sure the mic was off and said through tight lips, "Sit still you stupid shit."

In the rear, Taggart got back to his computer, but he couldn't tell what had happened. He thought he hit the firing button before Strom jerked him out of his chair, but he wasn't sure. And he couldn't tell by what he was seeing.

He looked at the screen and saw the president was still there talking, but none of the pre-firing indicators were illuminated. What did that mean? Did the weapon fire or not? All his training had been about the minutes and seconds before the firing, not after. He didn't know what anything was supposed to look like after the shot!

He hit the firing button. Nothing happened. He hit it again. And again. Nothing. *Shit! What's happening?*

He eased up to the window into the cab and softly said, "Kilgore. What's going on?"

Kilgore ignored him. He looked busy talking on the mic to someone outside.

"Lomax!" he whispered, "What the hell is going on?"

Lomax started to turn to answer him, but Kilgore shoved the gun barrel deeper into his ribs and he froze.

Taggart wheeled back around, looked at the computer screen, the weapon and the teracapacitor. And Strom's lifeless body in the corner. "I got to get the fuck out of here."

He grabbed his uniform cap, checked to be sure the handgun was safely back in his shoulder holster under the blue uniform blazer, and headed for the rear door. He glanced at the small TV monitor showing the scene behind the armored vehicle. When he didn't see any cops, he unlocked the door, set it so it would lock behind him, and stepped out into the bright morning sun. He did one quick glance around, then eased the heavy door closed. He heard it lock hard. There were several cars backed up behind the armored car waiting to change lanes and go around. Taggart lowered the bill of his cap and started waving the cars around as if he were helping the cops. Gradually, looking official, he made his way away from the vehicle.

––––––––––––––––––

I stood there, staring into the helicopter's twin 50-caliber machine guns, and felt failure seep into my bones. I wanted to feel lucky to be alive, but knowing I had owned the chance to save the life of the most powerful person on earth, and was failing, was overpowering. Suddenly, I was exhausted. All I wanted to do was lie down. I leaned back against the seat bolster and felt my shoulders drop.

I slowly pulled *Jock's Trap*'s throttles back to neutral, felt the change in the engines, and let the outgoing tide pull me slowly toward the ocean.

My hippy-dude friend had been right. There were enough cops on the pier to start a war. I turned toward them, figuring it would be easier to surrender to them than a helicopter. I made a slow wave with my hand to show I was through, and wanted to put the injured boat in gear, drive around the pier, and pull up on the beach.

As I slowly turned back to the helm to cut the wheel, the chopper jerked straight up, spun away and headed down the channel toward the bridge at light speed. *What the . . . ?*

Confused, I turned around, and saw a hundred cops running for the parking lot. In one second, I had gone from Public Enemy Number One to nobody.

The sudden ringing of the scramble phone nearly made me jump overboard. "You were right," Mack said almost screaming. "It's on the bridge!"

"I'll call you back!" I said, dropping the phone.

I cut the wheel toward the bridge five miles away and jammed the throttles to the stops. The speedboat's hull was wounded but not her engines. The intakes sucked water and I blasted away from the pier like a rocket. As I accelerated through 90, I prayed that in this smoother water in the channel, none of the cracks in the hull would burst open and send me cartwheeling to a certain death.

Flying across the flat water, I remembered the strange warning on the farewell note Captain Jack left on *Rivianna's* helm months ago: "Remember, bridges are not your friend." I tried to push that thought away as I got closer and closer to the biggest bridge in Georgia.

Soon I saw the armored car on the crest of the bridge, surrounded by blue flashing lights. The only way I could get up from here was from the bridge's southern end which was over marsh. So I aimed *Jock's Trap* bow for the grassy area just before the steep stone and grass incline that led up to the bridge's southern end.

I kept the speed up as long as I dared, cut it 30 yards out and braced myself. The long, narrow boat sailed far into the tall grass and black mud before sliding to a jerk-stop. I killed the power and climbed over the side, dropping into the muck and started slogging toward the long incline up to the roadway.

It was steeper and higher than it looked. I climbed more than ran up the near-vertical grade, bracing my feet and pulling myself up with handfuls of tall grass. I fell, slid downhill, got up, then fell again harder, grabbing grass to stop the slide. Holding on with one hand, I rolled over on my back, and tried to breathe through the shooting pain in my side. I stared, panting at a blue sky and wondered where the president was.

My logical mind said the Secret Service had already rushed her away, I hoped in time. But in my spinning delirium, I could see her still standing at the presidential podium, narrow black crosshairs centered on her forehead.

I struggled to roll back over and push up on my knees. As I tried to stand, the pain stabbed my side again, and my face dropped into the muddy grass. I felt for the bandage, but couldn't find it. The rest of the climb was a blur of falling, star-spangled pain, getting up, and falling again.

At the top of the grassy slope, I felt more than saw the low concrete sidewall, and fell over it onto the roadway. I lay there panting, hurting, trying to make sense out of a world turned on its side. The warm concrete felt good on my face, and I wanted to close my eyes. I heard sirens and shouts, but it all sounded far away.

When tires screeching to a stop brought me back, I braced myself for the pain, rolled over, tried to push up. I looked at the steep roadway toward the crest of the bridge.

A car door opened nearby. I turned and through blurry eyes saw the familiar blue and gray of a Georgia State Patrol SUV. "Freeze!" the trooper shouted, aiming a shotgun at me across the hood. I couldn't speak or lift my arms, so I held up my bloody hands. He kept the shotgun on me and moved closer, staring as if I were a wounded animal he was about to finish off. In a deep voice, he demanded, "Stand up and turn around."

Kneeling in a spreading pool of my own blood, I looked up at the man and tried to say something, but my voice sounded far away.

"Stand up and turn around," he repeated, now screaming.

Again, I tried to speak, but couldn't make words. When the officer stepped so close I could smell the oil on his shotgun, I looked away from the dark barrel, wiped my face with a bloody hand, shook my head and finally rasped, "I can't."

When I looked back to see his reaction, he was staring toward the crest of the bridge. I looked too.

I felt time change. The world dropped into slow motion. From up the roadway, a blurry figure was walking toward us. There was something familiar about the man, and I tried to stand, but couldn't. I came back down on one knee and felt the handle of the Admiral's Glock in my right pocket press painfully against the tear in my side. Still crouched over, my right shoulder leaning against the low concrete sidewall, I reached for the bloody Glock, eased it out, and held it hidden between my right leg and the concrete.

The trooper said something to the mirage-man walking towards us but got no reply. The blurry figure kept coming. As he got closer, I saw he was wearing a blue-blazer-style uniform and cap. But it wasn't his clothes that made my blood run cold. It was his face.

I blinked and tried to make sense out of the impossible. I was shaking—from the long climb up the hill, from losing blood, and from fear at what I was seeing. I wanted to say something, but couldn't. I wanted to think straight, but couldn't. I tried to wipe the sweat from my eyes with my left hand, but only smeared blood.

When I looked back up the bridge, the stranger walking toward us was pulling a pistol from under his blazer and firing. I flinched, and the trooper beside me fell hard. When I looked back, the uniformed man was staring at me. I needed to get the Glock up, but couldn't. The man in the blue blazer kept walking, staring.

Suddenly, from behind him, there were shouts. "Drop it! Police!" He spun around, fired twice in their direction, then turned back aiming at me. I was ready. I fired three shots. The mirage man dropped his gun and staggered sideways, red spreading across his chest. He fell, leaning on the top of the low concrete sidewall, then slowly rolled over it, falling out of sight. In the fog of my slow-motion world, I watched him disappear, and I wondered what just happened.

As the cops rushed in screaming, I dropped the Glock and fell back against the bridge sidewall.

Amid shouts of "Hold your fire!" I saw more uniforms just before my vision narrowed to a pinpoint and the world went black.

When I came to, I was on my back, and someone was pressing hard on my side. "Relax," a voice said, "you're going to be OK."

I tried to say something, but my mouth wouldn't work.

"We gave you something for pain," the man said. "And you've lost a lot of blood. You'll feel pretty woozy."

"Woosy," I tried to say.

I lay there on the warm concrete, trying to remember what had happened. I wanted to sleep, but then heard something that scared me back to reality. It was a woman's voice. She was crying, screaming. She was nearby, but I couldn't see her. Gradually I realized it was Claire! She was hysterical.

"Claire," I said, trying to sit up. "Claire . . ."

I rolled over, felt the vertical concrete and pulled myself up. I made it to my knees where I could see over the bridge's low concrete sidewall. There, on the slope below was Claire, on her knees, bending over someone sprawled on the grass hill. The person lying there was covered in blood. It was the man from the bridge. The one I just shot.

Claire was rocking back and forth, crying hysterically. Every time she rocked forward, her head and hair hid the man's face. Every time she rocked back, I saw it again. I watched her, unable to speak. Unable to understand what was happening.

The face Claire was crying over was mine.

Chapter 49

The Man in the Uniform

The gentle hiss of air conditioning. A white ceiling. Antiseptic smells.

"He's waking up." The voice sounded far away.

Two blurry figures came into view.

"Am I dead?"

"No," Mack said, using his Admiral's voice, "but you damn near used up all the hospital's A-positive blood."

I was wondering about that when the figure on my left moved closer, softly kissing my cheek.

I tried to focus. "I don't . . ." I turned my head as I spoke and felt pain shoot through my right side.

"Easy," Mack said. Faces were finally taking shape.

"How do you feel?" Claire asked.

"Like I lost a javelin-catching contest?"

Half-smiles only. And the seriousness of what had happened began returning. "What?" I tried to sit up, but pain stopped me again. "What happened? Did the . . . ?"

"Easy," Mack said again, as Claire gently held my shoulder down. "There'll be time for all of that later."

"You need to rest," Claire said without smiling.

"I gotta know," I said.

"OK. He's right," Mack said to Claire. Then turning back to me, he said, "you've earned that much." Then he hesitated so long, I thought he'd changed his mind. Finally, "First, you've been out for a couple of days. You had metal and fiberglass fragments lodged in your right side. They had to operate, and you lost a lot of blood, before the operation, and during. So they've kept you sedated."

"The president . . . ?"

Mack finally smiled. "President Chambers is fine. Another few seconds and it might have gone the other way."

"So, what happened?"

"There's a lot nobody knows, and may never know, like exactly what happened in the armored car. And what I'm about to tell you, I'm not even supposed to know, so this has to stay between the three of us. Got it?"

Claire and I agreed.

"OK, after the president was safely evacuated, the Feds immediately closed the bridge and all other nearby roads, and rerouted Highway 17 traffic through Blythe Island. Then they brought in a heavy-duty low-boy trailer and quickly hauled the armored car to an old hangar at FLETC. A preliminary inspection turned up what appears to be a particle beam weapon, complete with a portable power source and military targeting system. There was also a notebook with instructions, which will come in handy because the only other thing in the back of the armored car was a dead Hector Strom. It looks like the driver and right-seat man in the cab got away, but there's still a big search going on. Somebody might find them, but I doubt it."

While Claire and I were digesting that, Mack continued. "In the old FLETC hangar, with the armored car still on the lowboy, they wrapped it so no one could tell what it was, and drove it at 2:00 a.m. to a dark corner of the Brunswick airport, where it was hurriedly loaded onto a waiting C-17 Globemaster and flown to points unknown.

"The only other thing I've heard is that the information in the notebook indicates the damn thing works. From several miles away, it apparently could silently fire an invisible particle beam that painlessly shreds enough brain cells to initiate a slow bleed. A day or two later the victim collapses and ultimately dies of what appears to be a stroke."

As that sank in, I said, "So, that's what happened to Ryan."

"It looks like it," Mack nodded.

"And . . . ?" I turned toward Claire as she squeezed my hand.

"Ryan's gone, Honey."

I felt my chest fall, "Yeah. I guess I knew that."

"If their plans had worked," Mack continued, "the men in the armored vehicle could have fired the weapon, secretly injuring the president, and then, in keeping with their mechanical-problem story, been towed away by an accomplice in a heavy-duty wrecker. They all would have disappeared, and no one would have had a clue anything happened. A couple of days later the president would have suffered what appeared to be a stroke and died soon after that. By then the men and the armored car and weapon could have been out of the country."

"But," I said, "something did go wrong . . ."

"Yes," Mack continued, "because of you and Claire."

As that sank in, I knew there was more. "What else? The world must be a little crazy . . . a U.S. president nearly assassinated by a secret weapon. Now what? What's going to keep somebody—maybe the same people—from trying again?"

"First," Mack said, "now that the Feds know that kind of weapon is possible, they're working on a way to stop it."

"How do you stop an invisible beam?"

"With an invisible shield, is what I hear. Apparently, to get the exact targeting and range, the weapon uses a clear targeting laser, and the Feds think they can create an invisible sensor in front of the president. And the millisecond it detects a targeting beam, the sensor switches to maximum power, creating an invisible shield strong enough to scatter the weapon's beam into a cloud of particles that harmlessly dissipates. The good guys monitoring the sensor would know something happened, but no one else would."

"What about the attempted assassination? Isn't the media having a fit?

"Nope. Except for us and damn few Feds—mainly Secret Service—no one knows about the weapon, or that the president was ever in danger. The Feds with all their smoke and mirrors are saying one of the Coast Guard helicopters had a failure in its communication and ID electronics and was unable to send or receive any messages. So the radar guys assumed the worst, reported it as a threat, and that's when the Secret Service reacted."

"In other words," I interrupted, "nothing about an assassination?"

"No," Mack shook his head, "of course not."

"What about what happened on the bridge?" I asked. "They can't ignore that."

"A botched armored car robbery."

"Yeah, right."

"The truth is," Mack continued, "you and Claire—and her friend Taz—were correct."

"Taz . . ." I said, remembering.

"She's OK," Claire said, "it looked worse than it was. The police are saying she was shot when she surprised burglars at the foundation that morning."

"That's bullshit!"

"Yes. But where's our proof?"

"This is insane! They can't do that!"

"What are their options?" Mack added.

"The truth!"

"The truth is already hidden deeper than who killed Kennedy. It could be years, maybe decades, before anyone finds out."

"That's ridiculous!"

"What do you expect them to do? If they said a weapon was discovered, the evidence would ultimately lead back to the CIA's Janus Project.

"And," he continued, "then we have the President of the United States nearly assassinated by a secret weapon created by the CIA.

"And," he added, "no one has a clue who tried it. Do you know the kind of fear that would create? Ann Chambers pissed off half the people in the world and scared the other half to death. Anyone could have wanted her dead."

He let that sink in. Then Claire touched my arm. I looked at her and knew there was more. I waited.

"It's about Ryan," she finally said.

I took a deep breath and felt bone-tired. "If I hadn't gone to him, he'd still be alive."

"We're not sure." She waited before continuing. "We think maybe they used Ryan . . . maybe for some kind of help."

"No way." I snapped, "Never."

"No," she said, quickly explaining, "I don't mean with the assassination. It looks like somebody may have offered him money to look the other way, for what they may have said was a small smuggling operation. Something harmless."

"He was a good man."

"Yes, I know," she said, "But they could have sworn no one would be hurt and dangled a fortune in front of him. You said he was worried about the election. Maybe he needed cash for his campaign. Or retirement in case he lost."

I wanted to close my eyes, forget all of this, but I couldn't quit now. "I still don't see what any of this has to do with me."

Mack spoke up. "Son, the Feds think the bad guys used your grave to hide the targeting equipment."

"But why me? Why my grave?"

When neither of them answered, I knew something else was wrong. I tried for a deep breath and couldn't get it. It was hard to believe there was something worse than what I had already heard. But their eyes said there was.

I waited, and before either of them spoke, my own mind opened a door to something I hadn't remembered. Something my unconscious had filed away as a bad dream, hallucination.

Abruptly I remembered the face! The man in the uniform on the bridge! I shot him before he could shoot me . . . My blood ran cold.

"What?" I whispered.

Claire lowered her head.

"Son . . ." Mack said. His eyes tore through me.

"Tell me . . ."

"The man in the uniform," he began, "was part of the assassination plot."

"I know . . ." I said, waiting. "I need to know who he was . . ."

Mack stared at me before answering. "I think you already know," he said quietly. "I think maybe you've always known . . ."

In that instant, as if a portal had opened onto another world, I saw the answer to the question that had defined my existence. A lifetime of searching. A lifetime of not knowing why. The feeling—the knowing—something was missing.

I had spent my whole life searching for something that I didn't even know existed. And abruptly, I knew. At the instant of death, a life was revealed.

I was right all along. It wasn't just my father missing from my life. It was someone more a part of me than even him. Someone with whom I had never known separation. Whose every movement, every heartbeat I had known. Someone who I thought was a part of me. And would always be. Someone I had only known in our mother's womb.

I once had a brother.

A twin.

I knew because I just killed him.

Chapter 50

A Doctor Plays Solomon

Forty Years Ago

The old doctor was tired beyond his years. He had been at the hospital for 30 hours, completing his shift, and starting another. He had slept when he could, but not enough.

There was only one patient left he was concerned about. Susan Taggart in Labor and Delivery. She and her husband Davis had been at the hospital all day. She had miscarried twice before, and something was wrong with this labor, but the doctor didn't know what. He had given her something for pain, and was going to lie down for a few minutes.

Tell Mr. Taggart in the waiting room his wife is sleeping, he told the L&D nurse. Keep an eye on her and let me know if anything changes.

He found an empty room and lay down.

Five minutes later, another nurse—this one from the ER—woke him and said another pregnant woman had just walked into the Emergency Room alone, doubled over, tears streaming down her face. Her water had broken, and the baby's head was crowning. The ER nurse said the woman's name is Elsie Raney.

The tired doctor listened, rose, and wondered if it was a full moon.

While he was scrubbing up, the L&D nurse watching the Taggart woman rushed in. Doctor, she said, Mrs. Taggart's started rapid contractions. The nurse smiled and added kindly, "Can you do two at once?"

Both women were sedated, and forty minutes later, it was over.

One delivery had been an extraordinary surprise.

The other, a disaster.

The young woman named Elsie Raney who had stumbled into the ER alone had unexpectedly delivered twins. Boys.

Susan Taggart's baby was stillborn.

Afterwards, standing in the hall with the two nurses, the old doctor took a deep breath and said, "I have made a decision. It is my decision, and mine alone. But it is something the three of us must take to our graves. Is that understood?"

The nurses nodded, scared.

He breathed heavily, then said, "Outside in the waiting room, there is a young man. He has a good job and a beautiful wife," he said pointing to where Susan Taggart lay sedated. They have been trying unsuccessfully to have a baby for years. They want a family."

"The other woman, Elsie Raney," he said, "walked in here tonight alone. She is single—widowed, I think—and works as a waitress."
He stopped.

The nurses waited, wide-eyed.

Motioning to the delivery room where twins were just born, he said, "I'm going in there and tell that young woman she has a beautiful baby boy."

One of the nurses gasped.

"And then," he continued, "I'm going into the waiting room, and tell Davis Taggart the same thing."

Silence held the three people in place until the old doctor spoke again. "It is the right thing to do."

As he turned and trudged away, he added, "No one will ever know."

Chapter 51

The Hardest Goodbye

The Present

Claire took a month off from the foundation and moved in with me on *Rivianna*. To be my nurse, she said. I needed her help more than I had expected.

As I began to recover, however, a strange thing happened. *Rivianna* began to feel smaller. Little things like turning sideways to pass each other went from being cute to awkward. Claire knew it too.

We shouldn't have been surprised. We'd been through a lot. She had to deal with knowing her work at the foundation had indirectly helped someone nearly assassinate the president. And almost led to the death of her trusted friend and assistant Taz.

And I had buried my best friend Ryan—but not the question of his involvement.

But most importantly, I had learned the truth about my own life, about the *missing* feelings that others said were due to never having known my father. I had always known it was more than that. In those final seconds on the Sidney Lanier Bridge, I had come face to face with a man who shared my blood, my birth and my face.

And I had buried him as well.

With all of that, how could Claire and I not have foreseen what we were putting ourselves into? How could we not have known *Rivianna* would become a pressure cooker of grief and guilt and questions without answers?

One evening in the third week during a silent dinner, Claire calmly announced that she was leaving early and going home. Her boss had called, she said, they needed her back at work.

I didn't question her story or ask her to stay. I knew we both needed time and space—the two things that bedeviled us at the beginning. We needed them now.

Mom always said things are darkest just before dawn. Ryan said things are darkest just before the light disappears forever. This time Ryan was right.

I was on the fantail and Claire was below packing when I got the call. My mom, hospitalized a few days ago with chest pains, had just suffered a major heart attack. My mom, Elsie Hood, was gone. Moments before, after all I had been through—and now with the woman I love packing to leave—I would have said my heart was too exhausted to feel much more. I would have been wrong. The news that my mother had just died hit me in the gut like nothing I had ever experienced. As the shock settled in and the words became real, my head spun and I reached for *Rivianna's* rail.

I had been at the hospital with her the day before. And thank God I hadn't told her anything. I let her die the way someone let me live . . . never knowing the strange truth.

As all of that swirled in my head, I considered not telling Claire. To let her go back to Atlanta like we decided. But I couldn't. In an imperfect world, we had made that perfect promise. No lies. Nothing held back. Ever.

I made my way back inside and was standing at *Rivianna's* helm when Claire showed up in the doorway with her suitcase.

I stalled, wondering how to say it. Then finally, just, "Mom died."

Nothing. From either of us. As if time and space and emotion didn't exist. Were we a billion light-years apart? Or was that Claire I felt in my soul?

She lowered her head and her face disappeared behind her beautiful dark hair.

I waited until my chest hurt, and then said, "Don't go. Stay with me, please."

A long pause. Then the suitcase hit the floor, and still not looking up, Claire came to me, burying her face in my chest. She cried into my shirt while my tears wet her hair.

Two days later in the darkness before dawn, Claire and I sat in *Biscayne's* cockpit as Mack gently backed his beautiful, blue-hull sailboat out of her slip. We motored slowly south, away from the lights of the marina, then turned east into the channel toward the Atlantic. Several minutes after passing the pier, now easing through the low, dark rollers of an incoming tide, Mack began a slow turn to port and we headed north, well offshore to accommodate *Biscayne's* deep keel. Twenty minutes later, when the shore lights ended at Gould's Inlet, I nodded and Mack eased back on the throttle, then turned off the engine. More friend than Admiral now, he said, "We can stay as long as you like."

The gentle rocking and sound of waves against the hull sounded both familiar and strange. In low clouds far out over the ocean, lightning flashed and we never heard a sound. When dawn drew a line on the horizon, I nodded at Claire, and she eased the small, bronze urn into my hands. She helped me walk to the stern, kissed my cheek, and returned to stand with Mack beside *Biscayne's* big wheel.

I stood there with the cool morning breeze on my face, shifting with the gentle rocking of the big sailboat. The heavy bronze cap unscrewed easily. When it was free, I faced the glow on the horizon, and I wondered what life would be like without the one who gave life to me.

I waited, not wanting to do what I had come here for. When I knew there would be no answers to my questions, I thanked God for her life, and that I had been loved so much, for so long. Then facing the coming day, I poured my mother's remains into the slow, low waves. When the sound of sandy ashes hitting water ended, I let the urn fall. And I said goodbye to the only family I had ever known.

The days that followed were slow and quiet. Claire knew when to sit with me and when to let me sit alone.

One rainy afternoon sitting under the fantail canopy, I opened a small box stowed away years ago—things of mine Mom had saved since I was a child. And things of hers I had saved, just because. It was an unordered, decades-long collection of cards, letters, photographs, report cards, yellowed news clippings, some old jewelry of hers and more. I sifted slowly, carefully, through the little treasures, once. Then again. When I finished, I closed the lid, looked across the rain-splashed water and felt the loss becoming permanent. It was almost as if I could see a line across time, separating all that came before from all that would follow. I closed my eyes, listened to the cold rain and saw my mom sitting in the sun, smiling like she always did when she told me everything would be OK.

Sure enough, in the days that followed, time began to do what nothing else could. It slowly eased my understanding of my mother's death, from shock, to sadness, and finally to the reluctant acceptance we all know, or will one day. I missed my mom, and always would. But, like she always said, there is only one doorway from this world to the next. And we shouldn't be so scared of it. Or feel so far away from those who have already passed through.

With time my outlook gradually improved, and one afternoon days later, Claire and I were on the fantail preparing to enjoy a quiet, brassy sunset with a cool glass of Chenin Blanc. As a soft breeze rippled the water around us, I took a deep breath, let it go and thought how lucky I was to be with this beautiful woman on a beautiful boat in this beautiful place. I was so content in that moment, when from nowhere, a different thought arose.

When I was sure, I pulled my chair closer, hesitating while she watched me, then said it. "You and I should take a trip."

"On *Rivianna?*" she asked, without enthusiasm.

"No," I assured her. "We need a change of scenery."

"Where do you want to go?" she asked, now more comfortable.

"Anywhere you do."

"Anywhere?" she asked, as if I were kidding.

"Maybe somewhere you've always wanted to go."

She looked away a moment, then turned back, smiled softly and said,

"Paris would be nice." I nodded agreement, while she waited and let Paris sink in. Then, "But that wouldn't be my first choice."

I waited. She was enjoying this.

"Did I ever tell you about my roommate Lexi at Auburn?

"I don't think so."

"Brilliant girl, beautiful, and crazy sense of humor. Her family lived on a big ranch, with horses and cattle and stuff. The day we graduated, she gave me a huge hug and said she wasn't letting go until I promised we'd see each other again. I promised."

Claire hesitated, took a sip of wine, then casually asked, "What are your thoughts on going to see Lexi . . . letting that be our trip?"

"Sure," I answered. "Where does Lexi live?"

Claire smiled. I told you she was enjoying this. "Guess."

I didn't see that coming, so I thought about the horses and cattle. "Texas."

"No."

"Arizona."

"Nope."

"New Mexico?"

"No again."

"Rhode Island."

"*Rhode Island?*" she said, exasperated.

"OK, I give up."

"Lexi lives in Rio de Janeiro," Claire said definitively.

"You want to go to *Cuba*?"

"You're impossible."

"Just kidding. I know the capital of Portugal."

She tossed the last of her wine in my lap. "It's Brazil, Bozo."

"Oh yeah, I knew that," I said, staring at the white wine soaking into my pants. "Brazil it is, then. Damn, that wine was cold."

"That's what you get for failing geography."

"Thanks. You gonna keep me after school too?"

"Maybe," she said, grinning. Then more seriously, "Now, back to this trip. This is important to me. I should have done it before now . . ." She stopped.

I didn't say anything—I was busy drying my lap—and my silence apparently concerned her. "Wait a minute," she said, now suspicious. "Are you pulling my leg?"

I paused the lap-drying and looked right at her. "I might pull both of your legs later, but right now, I'm telling you, we're going to Brazil."

Her eyebrows rose a bit on the leg comment. Then she slowly broke into the most beautiful smile I ever saw. I looked into those gorgeous brown eyes and knew, she could have said Lexi lived in Turkmenistan, and I'd have said *let's go*.

"You touch base with Lexi," I said, using my serious voice, "and extend your leave-of-absence at work. I'll start checking flights."

Now reassured, and taking a sexy sip from *my* wine glass, she looked at me and said, "You really *are* going to take me to Brazil, aren't you?"

"Yes," I said with conviction, "but right now, I really am going to take you somewhere a lot closer."

She smiled.

I smiled.

We missed the sunset.

Epilogue

At midnight, the pilot of a Gulfstream 550 gently reduces power to the plane's two Rolls-Royce turbofan engines as the aircraft softly touches down on the long runway. After braking and rollout, the sleek jet taxies to the private terminal where it rolls to a stop and the big engines begin winding down. As the plane's cabin door opens and the stairway descends, a black Mercedes limousine appears from the dark hangar and comes to a stop at the bottom of the jet's stairway. Seconds later, the only passenger, a big man with copper skin, descends the stairs and climbs into the limo's spacious back seat. The driver hands the man a small envelope. As the limo heads for the airport exit, the passenger opens it and reads:

> Welcome my friend. My driver will take you to a penthouse on
> the edge of the city where you can relax, sleep if you like, and
> get ready for tomorrow. Everything you requested is waiting for
> you there.
>
> Benicio

Quinterro slips the note into his inside coat pocket, rests his head against the seat back and feels the surge of power as the big limo accelerates out of the airport. Seconds later the long, black vehicle disappears into the night traffic.

Ahead, a large overpass sign says . . . Welcome to Rio de Janeiro.

Acknowledgements

Even in fiction, modifying an existing medical device to assassinate the president ended up being very controversial. Experts in health care, the federal government and the Department of Defense refused to answer any questions or discuss it with me in any way. There were however a few independent researchers, physicians, engineers and nuclear scientists who did. To protect their privacy, I have omitted their names from this list. They know who they are, and they know this book would not have been possible without their help.

On the less controversial, editorial side, Laura Jones and Arlene Robinson were amazing. Any flaws in the book are mine, not theirs.

And, as you can see, Rick Turylo's cover art and Clark Kenyon's inside design provide a level of exceptional talent and professionalism.

The late Taylor Schoettle, an amazing local naturalist, provided great help, both in person and through his books, still on sale in the Golden Isles. Don't let their casual binding fool you. They are very well written and cover a lot more than plants, animals and seashells—like why the climate, weather, tides and waves keep moving our islands around.

Other friends and family who provided valuable assistance include, in no particular order, Anne McKay Garris, David Boland, Bruce Fendig, Chris Hanner, Jill Smith, John and Rhonda Howton, Keenan Carter, Dale Tushman, Jack Kilgore, Rich and Renée Hensler, Bill and Judy Merritt, Clive and Brooke Oatley, Bill Gowen, Jock Hart, Sam Peabody, Ron Watson, Jay Grantham, Carmen Talarico, Bob Thompson, Dixie McGurn, Lea Maye Smith and Arthur Long.

And of course my beautiful wife Deborah, who when things got tough encouraged me by saying, "You're never gonna finish that damn book."☺

I also want to thank my parents, Bud and Peggy Carter, who provided unwavering support for, well, forever. After my dad read the manuscript (maybe the only fiction he ever read), I asked what he thought. He said, "It does make you wonder WTF's going to happen." I took it as a compliment.

And finally I owe so much to the late Sharon Smith-Henderson, my first writing coach and editor, who encouraged me at every turn, especially when my writing life got trampled by the real world. I have on the wall in my office her marvelous, timeless quote:

Your problem is you think you can write a book and have a life too.

About the author

Chuck Carter is a former business writer, editor, publisher and PR agent whose clients and subjects include Microsoft, Compaq, Dominion Semiconductor, Honda, E-Z-GO Textron, Bridgestone/Firestone, Sony of Latin America, the Chicago Bears, Mitsubishi Polysilicon, Imagyn International, 7-Eleven Corporation, NGK Ceramics, *The Japanese-American Economic Review* and National Science Center. U.S. Government clients include the Atomic Energy Commission, Transportation Security Administration, Federal Law Enforcement Training Center and Department of Homeland Security. For PR clients, he earned free placements in *The New York Times, Newsweek, The Philadelphia Enquirer, Better Homes and Gardens, Consumers Digest, American Health, Modern Medicine* and Reuters-Global. His News Releases have been translated into foreign languages in Europe, South America, Africa, the Middle East, and the Pacific Rim. While he was editor and publisher of a west coast Florida newspaper, voter participation in covered precincts was exactly twice that of the rest of the city. And a New York television special he promoted generated such a response, the outsourced call center's phone system crashed. This is his first novel.